From Stardust

Book 1 in the Aarilyan Seas Series

Meagan Kaye

Bound In Ink, LLC

Book Cover by art_by_adesilets and Meagan Kaye

Editor Rooted In Writing

Map by Cartography Bird

Art by @art_by_adesilets

To anyone who needs a little more adventure in their lives

THE ISLANDS
MAPPED
IN THE PRESENT AGE
TALAYAN
ARBOR
URIBA
SENPLIS

SOUTHERN
NELINA
THE
HURRICANE
PALNEY
THE
DOCKS
ATWOOD
AARILYA
THE
CAVE
LARAMOSE
THE ISLE
OF KINSLET

Prologue

"Let this emergency meeting of the Aarilyan noble families begin," Mr. Kindelan announced. He and thirteen others surrounded an enormous wooden table which took up the majority of the room they occupied. "First order of business?" he asked.

"The Family Marsh, m'lord," a young boy said from the corner of the room. He held a tablet of paper and pencil, writing as each person spoke.

"Only order of business. Isn't that the only reason we are here?" Mrs. Santel said, her golden curls bobbing as she shook her head with impatience. A few murmurs spread through the room.

"Anyhow." Mr. Kindelan cleared his throat. "Tragic, what happened. But quite a predicament it has put our families in."

"Tragic? Treasonous, more like. They brought it on themselves," Mr. Tandin said. His sleek black suit complemented his greased mustache.

"Quite," Mrs. Santel agreed.

Mrs. Reese pinned Mr. Kindelan with a pointed stare. "And with only a daughter left, how will the name carry on?"

"Hush now." Her husband patted her freckled shoulder.

"It won't carry on. She would marry, and the new family name will take on the title," Mr. Tandin countered. He circled the room as he spoke.

"We haven't added a new family since the noble families came over from Nelina to found Atwood Place!" Mrs. Santel exclaimed.

"It just doesn't sit well," Mrs. Reese said.

"What if ... we revoked the Marsh family's status?" Mr. Pierce adjusted his glasses as he stood. "The family has always been a small one. They rarely agree with everyone here and haven't had much of an impact on our Aarilyan history as it is. It would be remarkably easy to just ... erase them from the Aarilyan nobility altogether." He chuckled as he paced.

"What about Lilly?" Mrs. De Sansol asked plainly.

"The Marsh girl?" Mr. Garmet scoffed. "We'll just say she died with her parents. We can sell her to a ship's captain. She'd make a fine cabin girl, eventually. Perhaps she'd even meet the same end her parents did."

Mrs. Tandin huffed. "That's far too much trouble. Why not just drop her on the streets somewhere and let her fend for herself?"

"A fine idea," Mr. Santel said cheerily. The others murmured agreement.

"We will take her in," Mrs. De Sansol said. The room fell quiet. They exchanged glances, each waiting for another to contradict her.

"Dear ..." Mr. De Sansol whispered.

"I will take her in," Mrs. De Sansol repeated. "She will be a playmate for Maria, and when she comes of working age she will be employed as our maid. In any case, it's our best chance of making her forget her family's noble origins." She stood and exited the room, taking care not to meet anyone's eyes on the way.

"All those in favor of revoking the Marsh family's nobility?" Mr. Kindelan asked.

"Aye," the men said in unison.

"So be it. The De Sansols will take in the child, and the Marsh family's deaths will be marked, the Marsh name removed from current standing."

Chapter One

Lillian stood still as Mrs. De Sansol, her employer and the noble lady of the household, berated the line of maids next to her. Her red curls, dulled slightly with age, bounced as she spoke animatedly. The young, mousy girl next to Lillian flinched every time Mrs. De Sansol raised a hand. It wasn't uncommon for the De Sansol's to strike a servant if the offense was large enough, and dropping a full tea platter on the tile in the middle of a room full of noble guests was certainly a large enough offense.

"You are all trained better than this," Mrs. De Sansol continued, "and being new to the household is no excuse." She pinned the mousy girl with a hard stare as she took the long wooden spatula from its spot on the kitchen wall. Lillian closed her eyes as Mrs. De Sansol deliberately walked slowly along the line of girls, the wooden spatula made a whooshing sound as she swung it back in forth which each step. "Who put the new one on tea serving duty in her first week?" she asked icily.

"Ma'am, we are so very short handed with the illness going through the staff—"

"I do not care how many maids are available, I care that one dropped my good porcelain dishes in front of the Tandin's," she hissed at Eileen, the housekeeper, and the one in charge of assigning the maid's shifts.

Lillian wished she was back upstairs where she would normally be this time of day, being a ladies maid and companion to the De Sansol's daughter, Maria. But half the staff were sick, and Eileen had asked if she could help with the afternoon tea. She was regretting her decision at the moment. She hated being anywhere near Mrs. De Sansol when she went on a tangent.

"Were you the one who gave the tea platter to that girl?" Mrs. De Sansol asked Eileen. Eileen's lip quivered but she stood tall and nodded. "Step forward and hold your hands up, you also." She pointed the spatula towards the mousy girl. They both did as instructed. Lillian looked away as the first smack resounded through the room. Eileen didn't let a sound out as Mrs. De Sansol eyed her over.

"Don't make a sound, or she'll repeat the punishment," Lillian whispered quickly as Mrs. De Sansol turned their way. The mousy girl visibly shook as Mrs. De Sansol came to stand in front of her.

"Let this be a lesson to you girl. I don't accept less than perfection in my household," she said as she raised the spatula and brought it down on top of the mousy girl's knuckles with another smack. Despite her warning, the girl let out a surprised yelp. Lillian sighed as another smack quickly filled the room. "You may get back to your duties."

No one dared to move until Mrs. De Sansol had left the room, then everyone scurried back to their positions. Lillian wrapped her arms around the girl's shoulders and pulled her into an embrace as a sob escaped her.

"I didn'a mean to," the girl wailed.

"I know," Lillian soothed as the girl's tears soaked the brown fabric of her uniform. She rubbed her back a few rounds more before she prompted the girl to stand up. "Now, go dry your eyes and get back to work. Don't let them see you cry." The girl nodded and scampered off towards the bathing room. Lillian sighed as she took in the flurry of activity now filling the large kitchen. Thankfully, as Maria's ladies maid she wasn't exposed to the De Sansol's cruelness often. It made her stomach churn. Most of the nobles in the community of Atwood were the same, with a few exceptions. Lillian had almost become accustomed to it. If it were her choice she would have left long ago and sought a position elsewhere. As much as Maria had become a friend after the years they spent together, Lillian yearned for freedom. The kind of freedom she often read about in her novels. But she couldn't leave Atwood.

She sighed as she took the newly set tea tray from Eileen and told her to go ice her hand. The smell of the lavender chamomile was soothing as she carried it out of the kitchen. It had been seventeen years since the De Sansol's had taken her in, after her parents had died. The only thing she had left of them was a ring she wore, she didn't even have a last name. She had been six years old at the time, the same age as Maria, and so the De Sansol's had taken her in as a playmate.

When she had come of age she transitioned to a ladies maid, but in recompense for their kind act of caring for her over the years the De Sansols only paid her a few coins per month. Hardly enough for any personal items needed, let alone enough to save. And so, she was stuck in Atwood until she could afford to leave and find another position, one with more freedom. Perhaps one involving books. She smiled at the thought as she walked down the long hallway to the morning room. She nodded at the steward, Curt, as he opened the opulent double doors, and she swept in.

"Oh, Lilly!" Maria blustered as she entered and gently set to tea tray on the middle table. Lillian had to hold back a glare. Maria knew better than to address her so directly, and informally, in front of guests. She could only hope Mrs. De Sansol didn't reprimand Lillian for the slip up. A quick glance her way told Lillian Mrs. De Sansol was more upset with Maria than herself. She let out a little sigh of relief as she set to filling cups for everyone and Maria continued. "We just got a letter from Aunt Jaqueline in Southern Nelina! She's set to have her baby soon and asked mama to come help. And mama said you could come along!" Lillian froze as she handed a steaming cup to Mrs. Tandin, but quickly righted herself. Southern Nelina was across the Aarilyan sea. They would have to sail there. Across the ocean. The thought sent another shiver down her spine that she suppressed.

"That is wonderful, Miss De Sansol. I'm sure your guest does not wish to hear about your aunt or the trip. I do hope you are taking care to keep him entertained," Lillian gently reminded. Maria turned back to the young man sitting next to her, her bouncy red curls swishing as she did so, and Lillian handed each of them a cup of tea. Her eyes wide, she blinked a few times at him. He was a year her superior and had sandy brown hair and brown eyes nearly the same color.

"Oh! Mr. Tandin, I am not boring you, am I?" she asked. He chuckled softly as he placed an arm along the back of the shell-colored chaise, leaning back into a languid pose that exuded arrogance.

"My dear Miss De Sansol, I hardly doubt anyone could be bored in your presence." Maria smiled triumphantly as she took a sip of her tea and Lillian moved to stand against the wall until she was needed.

"Are you sure you should go?" Mrs. Tandin whispered loudly to Mrs. De Sansol. "Nobles do not have the best experiences crossing the sea." She flicked her gaze to Lillian a moment before she looked back towards Mrs. De Sansol, worry coloring her eyes as she fidgeted with her golden ringlets. The family her parents had served had been crossing the Aarilyan sea when their ship sank. It was part of the reason the ocean scared her so. She silently pleaded Mrs. De Sansol would consider Mrs. Tandin's words.

"Oh Emily, you don't believe in that nonsense, do you?" Mrs. De Sansol chuckled, and she patted her hand as if she were a small child. She turned to Lillian then. "You are dismissed, send Eileen in to gather the tray after the Tandin's have left. Lillian nodded and headed towards the door as Mrs. De Sansol considered in a lower tone, but Lillian was still able to hear before she pushed through the double doors. "Not every noble meets an end to the sea. The Marsh family was merely unlucky. The whole of Atwood cannot be cursed." Lillian shook her head at the notion and scurried off towards the kitchens.

*L*illian *stood surrounded by faceless pirates—all wearing buckled coats, curved swords, and worn hats. They formed a perfect circle around her as she faced a large stone wall that stretched up into forever. In front of the wall was a stone circle with strange markings. As the pirates each raised a hand, the stone glowed and the markings swirled before her eyes. She felt drawn to them, compelled to place her fingers upon them. She extended her hand, her delicate fingers reaching but getting no closer. Suddenly the circle became a bowl and filled with a dark liquid. The liquid overflowed. Blood. The bowl tipped over, and Lillian stepped back quickly. But the circle of pirates was closing in on her. She stumbled as she tried to get away.*

And then she was falling. Falling, falling into darkness. No ... Water. It surrounded her, enveloped her. Suffocated her. Tears filled her eyes, mixing with the weightless water around her as they spilled. She reached a hand into the dark abyss around her, but there was no one to take hold of it.

The carriage jolted to a stop. Lillian blinked once, twice, a third time before she remembered where she was. She set the book she had been reading before she had fallen asleep to the side, and smoothed her simple brown housedress. Perhaps a pirate-themed novel was not the best choice to read while sleepy. Or perhaps it was their upcoming journey that caused her unease. It had only been two short days since the De Sansol's had received the letter from Aunt Jaqueline and they were officially headed to Southern Nelina.

"Oh, goodness. We can't be here already," Maria muttered, smoothing nonexistent wrinkles from her dress—something she always did when agitated.

Though the trip from the noble community of Atwood to the harbor was hardly an hour long, the two women were tired from packing the last few days, and Lillian was anxious about the trip.

Lillian had never left Aarilya, had hardly ventured outside of Atwood other than to run errands or visit the harbor festival once a year. The elite community of Atwood consisted of a single lane, lined on both sides by eight opulent mansions, though the one at the end on the left had been empty for as long as Lillian could remember. It had belonged to the Marsh family, where her parents had worked. That was all she saw every day. She was nervous to cross the sea, but as she had considered it over the past few days she realized she was excited to visit somewhere new.

A chance for a proper adventure. Like one of her novels. She had considered what one of the characters in her books would do and had decided they would take on the adventure, and so shall she. Truly, it was the journey that she wasn't sure she could handle. Her fear of the depths below had been easy enough to manage, since Atwood was nowhere near the harbor, but on a boat right on the ocean? That was another situation entirely. Besides, she would have to keep it hidden from the De Sansols. Her employers were not an empathetic sort, and they would not abide weakness.

But it would be worth it, she reminded herself, to get out of Atwood for a bit. Perhaps she would even meet someone who could sweep her off her feet and take her away from her life as a maid.

"Lillian?" Mrs. De Sansol called from the other carriage. "Oh, where is that girl?"

Maria gave her an empathetic smile as Lillian stepped out of the carriage. She patted her soft chestnut bun as she looked around. They had stopped in the middle of the cobblestone road just before the harbor. The day was lovely, the temperature mild and the smell of salt in the air. The port buzzed with people loading and unloading cargo. Lillian was stunned by how many people were walking around. Navy men rushed one way while porters carried crates and boxes and baubles another. The items themselves were as unique as the men carrying them. Mechanists from Telayan carried crates made of steel and gears while the Astrians carried many boxes labeled "wild animals." They hoisted containers of purple, blue, green, and every color you could imagine, onto ship after ship.

And the ships! They were quite large. Their wood and steel bodies rose taller than any of the buildings in town. They were just like Lillian had imagined they looked in her novels. She felt as if she was one of the heroines in one now as she thought of the journey they had ahead of them. As she turned, a box across the harbor caught her eye. Was it shimmering? Almost as if it was trying to disappear and glow at the same time. But when she looked again, it looked like a normal crate. The men carrying it turned away before she could see it better.

"Oh, Lillian, there you are! Fetch my luggage, will you? And no dawdling, girl. We don't have all morning."

"Yes, Mrs. De Sansol," Lillian muttered, as she wandered over to the back of the carriage. She let out another sigh and looked out over the harbor once more. Even with the short notice, Mr. De Sansol had been able to use his connections to secure passage on a navy boat headed out today.

"What's the matter, hun? Never been to port?" A man met her glare from atop the carriage, startling her. He was average size, not too muscular, but with a nice tan. His short brown hair was combed back sleekly. Though he wore an officer's uniform, he seemed to have been sent to help with the luggage.

"Only for the festival. It is a lot busier than I imagined," Lillian said.

"This? This ain't nothin'. There's only two ships leaving port today. Some days there are five or six on the same day." He hefted a suitcase down and handed it to Lillian.

She set it aside, and he handed her another. "Oh, my. I can't even imagine how busy it must get on those days."

"Oh, sure. The docks get so crowded you can barely move. Don't even think about carrying anything. That's why we come in the middle of the night to load things on. We've been here for hours. But seems others have the same idea, so it's not always as productive as we hope." He went to hand her the last suitcase but lost his grip. It fell in front of Lillian, right into a mud puddle that splashed up onto her uniform. Lillian frowned. Mrs. De Sansol was not going to be pleased. The young man swiftly hopped down from the top of the carriage and scooped up the suitcase.

"I'm sorry, miss." He frantically brushed the mud from the suitcase. "I'll be in somethin' deep if Captain Davis hears about this."

"Is he that frightening?"

"Oh, uh, not really. Just wants to keep your family happy, is all," he muttered as he continued to wipe the case.

"Here, this should help." Lillian pulled her muddied apron from her dress. It couldn't get much dirtier anyway. The young man grinned as he took it from her and cleaned the last of the stubborn mud off.

"Thank you, miss." She offered a small smile as he handed the apron back to her. "Anyhow, I best be getting this luggage away. My name's Jeremy, by the way. I hope to see you again." He tipped his head in a brief farewell just as two more military men showed up and scooped up the last of the luggage.

"Lillian! Oh, where is that girl?"

Lillian hurried over to where Mr. and Mrs. De Sansol were waiting with Maria near their carriage.

"Finally! Where on earth have you been?" Mrs. De Sansol screeched.

"Finishing with the luggage, ma'am."

"Come, we are supposed to be boarding by now. Take my handbag, girl. We must be going." She looked her up and down and tutted at the muddy hem. "For heaven sakes, your appearance is reflection on this family. Take Maria and fetch a clean dress before we board. Quickly," she stressed before marching off towards the boat.

Maria grinned as she took in Lillian's uniform.

"Maria ..." Lillian warned. With the luggage already boarded, the only option was for Maria to do what Maria did best: shop.

"I'll only be a moment," she said, already eyeing the shops near them.

"Something sensible. I don't need your mother upset with me."

"Of course," she mumbled as she headed to a small boutique near the docks. Lillian followed behind.

"Nothing too expensive. It will surely end up coming out of my pay."

"Mhmm," Maria muttered, clearly no longer paying attention. Just as they reached the door she stopped, and turned to Lillian. "You stay out here, Lilly."

"Maria, we don't have time—"

"Exactly. We don't have time for you to nitpick as I choose something."

"Fine. But be quick or I'm coming in after you," Lillian conceded in an effort to hurry her along.

Maria's eyes lit up as she hurried into the small shop.

Lillian leaned against wooden boards of the outside of the shop, glad for the opportunity to take in the harbor once more. Small quaint shops with peeling paint on the exteriors lined the stone walkway and people wandered about and peered into each window as they passed. A couple of older boys grinned as they talked amongst themselves. Lillian could hear their conversation as they neared.

"There is so a blood moon comin'," the shorter one, a blond, said as he shoved the taller, brunette boy on the shoulder playfully.

"Maybe so, but ain't no Pirate King," the taller shook his head, clearly exasperated with the blond boy.

"You think we'll see his ghost if we stay out all night?" the blond asked, ignoring the taller boy's comments.

"Ain't no such thing as Pirate Kings or ghosts or curses. You're getting too old to believe them nursery stories." The taller boy ruffled the blond boy's head before he took off running in the other direction. The blond yelled after him as he followed. Lillian smiled at their playfulness.

True to her word, only a few minutes had passed before Maria popped out the door with a dress hanging over her arm.

"You can change here." Maria shoved the dress at her, pushing her toward a lavatory. "Hurry, while Mother and Father are confirming the accommodations. I'll wait by the dock." She practically skipped away.

Lillian rolled her eyes and slipped into the small lavatory, swiftly stepping into the new dress. It was cream-colored with small yellow flowers painted across the fabric. It stopped about a foot from the bottom, revealing a pale-yellow underskirt that formed an elegant train. The square neckline and short sleeves were lined in yellow satin that bunched, and a large ribbon wrapped around the waist. Maria had provided a cover up as well. Lillian twisted her ring absently as she admired herself in the small, dirty mirror. Her favorite part was the bow that wrapped around her slim waist and tied at the back. She was thankful the dress was long enough to cover her old brown boots. Even without the mud, they looked terrible. It has long been past time for a new pair. She quickly tightened her bun, tucking a curl behind her ear, and exited the lavatory.

Her thick waves never wanted to stay put, no matter how many pins she stabbed it with. She had just secured her final pin when she misplaced her foot on a stone and slipped. She let out a loud gasp. She was headed right into another puddle. Before she could react, a large hand closed around her arm, deftly pulling her to the side and out of the path of the mud. She steadied her breath as she took a proper step away from the stranger.

"Well, aren't you a right fine-looking lady, miss? Good thing you didn't end up in that mud. Although, it seems it wouldn't have been the first time this morning." The stranger smirked, looking at the muddy dress she held in her hands. "Johnny McEntire at your service." He made a mock bow at her. He was tall, at least six feet, bronzed and fit. He must work at the docks, she surmised. His physique suggested he spent all his days outside lifting things. Although his short blond hair must have been just cut to the current style with a slight curl at the nape of his neck, his attire was definitely not Aarilyan. He wore a simple dark blue button-up shirt, covered by a matching overcoat with gold trim. He was still smiling at her, and it reached all the way up to his bright blue eyes. Those deep eyes took her in, head to toe, as if he were measuring her worth.

"Well, thank you, Mr. McEntire, for your help. But I am running rather late. My party is waiting for me on the dock." She gestured to the boat.

"Ah, the good ship *Rossut*. The only passengers on that are the De Sansols. Looks like they're about ready to leave without you. Doesn't seem the kind of family you'd be part of." He gave her a curious look, which she returned with a frown.

"Well, I am. Now, if you will excuse me." She pushed past him rather rudely, which caused her a twinge of guilt. He had saved her from an unfortunate puddle. And she couldn't deny he was quite handsome.

"Well, you just be careful now, Ms. De Sansol. You never know what danger lurks on a military boat," he called after her, but she didn't bother turning around. She was already rather late.

Chapter Two

Lillian yawned as she sat up in her cot, which was not nearly as soft as the one she had at home. There was limited cabin space for civilians on the boat, as big as it was, so she and Maria had to share one—a fact she was sure Maria was not happy about, though she hadn't said anything. At least they had separate beds, small as they were. Maria was not shy in pointing that out.

Lillian threw on one of her regular uniforms. Her newly acquired cream-and-yellow dress hung neatly with Maria's clothes. She fought her hair up into a bun. This was day two of their week-long journey across the ocean. They had spent all of yesterday unpacking and with what little time they had left in the evening, Mrs. De Sansol had insisted on sitting Lillian down and making sure she'd memorized everyone's routine and the rules she was to follow. As if they hadn't been the same rules and routines she had followed for the last seventeen years. She shook her head at the thought.

Lillian searched her things for a thick cover-up. She slipped it on as she quietly exited the cabin. Though it was so early, the ship's departure was in full swing. In the halls, men were rushing everywhere. Lillian scurried between them, trying to stay out of the way and remember how to get to the kitchen.

"Oh!" She gasped as she turned a corner a bit too sharply and came face to chest with one of the men. He was quite tall, and from his uniform seemed to be of higher standing than an officer, perhaps a lieutenant. She would have to refresh her knowledge of the naval hierarchy. She expected an apology as she met his glare but was met with a sneer as the man pushed past.

"I believe you owe me an apology." Lillian frowned.

He spun to face her. "You should watch where you're going." She stepped back as he approached her. "You shouldn't even be on this ship. It's too dangerous for *civilians*. If you know what's good for you, you'll stick to your quarters." He turned on his heel and continued down the hall. Lillian let out a breath as she patted down her skirts. What had he meant by "It's too dangerous for civilians"? She couldn't imagine this ship was any more dangerous than a passenger one. Mr. McEntire had said something similar on the docks. She was beginning to feel a bit uneasy about this trip. Lillian sighed. She needed to find the kitchen and get back before the De Sansols woke.

Luckily it wasn't too much further, and she soon found herself at a swinging door with a circle of glass in the middle, underneath which read GALLEY. She pushed it open and slipped inside.

It wasn't elegant at all, just two long, crude tables that resembled benches more than a table, which were bolted to the floor. To the right was a cooking area with two large stoves, a sink, and an icebox. Between the cooking area and the tables was a long counter. Presumably where the food was set when it was ready. The stove had a few pans on it and the smell of eggs and salted meats filled the air around her.

"What you lookin' for there, ma'am?"

Lillian jumped, startled by the sudden voice. A man emerged from a door along the back wall, he looked to be the cook. He was a large man who wore a white shirt covered by a stained white apron. He was older, gray already covering most of his dark hair and wrinkles graced the creases of his dark skin. He was smiling a genuine smile. One which Lillian returned.

"I, um, I was just looking for some tea."

"I'll do that for you, miss." He turned and went into the room he had come from, a back room marked STORAGE. A minute later, he emerged with a bag of tea. He set to boiling water and stirring the coffee. "Have a seat, will ye? Ye're up earlier than I expected. Thought I'd be sittin' round here til midday waiting to make yer breakfast."

Lillian pulled up a chair next to the counter and sat down. "Well, I'm only the maid, Mr. ..."

"No Mister. Chuck'll be fine," he said.

"Mr. Chuck—"

"Just Chuck."

"Well, I'm the maid the De Sansols. My name is Lillian. They like an early breakfast, I hope that will not be a problem." She liked this man, she decided. He would be good company for the rest of the voyage. And if she stayed to their cabin and the galley then she could avoid the deck and looking over the ocean.

"That will be just fine, miss." He poured the tea and coffee into the mugs she indicated and put little tops on them to keep warm. "D'ya need cream or sugar?" He set them on a tray for her.

"No, thank you. This will be just perfect." She took the tray out of his hand and thanked him again. "I'll be back down shortly for the food." He smiled again and began pulling out plates and cutlery as she left.

After serving Mr. and Mrs. De Sansol, she set up the small table for her and Maria.

"I thought you promised me a hot breakfast if I rolled my lazy arse out of my warm bed," Maria said. Thankfully, she was already dressed.

"It's coming, Maria. Have some patience. And finish your tea before it gets cold." Lillian bustled around and made Maria's bed before she sat down to join her for breakfast.

"It's awfully chilly this morning. I really didn't expect it to be this cold." Maria warmed her hands on the tea cup before taking a sip.

"If you think it's cold now, just wait until we get farther out to sea. Then the temperature will really drop." Lillian served up their plates.

"Well, if it gets much colder than this, I might just have to commandeer a few more blankets. Funny word isn't that, 'commandeer'? I learned it from one of the military men yesterday. It means to take something. The military commandeers things all the time." Maria looked proud of herself as she stuck a forkful in her mouth.

"Maria, you know your mother would be exasperated if she found out you were spending time around the men of this ship. It's not *ladylike*." She stressed the last word jokingly. Mrs. De Sansol thought everything was unladylike, but it was still Lillian's duty to warn Maria when she was doing something her parents would not approve of.

"Yes, *Mother*," Maria teased in return. "Besides, there's nothing else to do on this boring boat. I need a little excitement every now and then."

"You've only been here a day. Besides, your mother brought plenty for you to entertain yourself with, such as sewing, knitting, crochet. And there are always your studies." The girls giggled.

Maria was not one to sit still for things that required either patience or concentration.

Lillian stood as Maria shoved her last forkful rather unceremoniously into her mouth. Manners didn't matter when her parents weren't in the immediate vicinity. Lillian took one last bite herself. As she was gathering up the dishes, there were two short, precise raps on the door. Lillian looked at Maria quizzically. Mrs. De Sansol never knocked, and they weren't expecting anyone. She opened the door just a sliver to peer out. It was the young man from yesterday. His hair was slicked back again, and if he wore a different uniform, she couldn't tell.

"Hey, uh, I mean hello. Jeremy. We met yesterday when I helped with the luggage." He looked at a loss for words, as if he hadn't planned this far ahead and wasn't sure she would even remember him.

"I remember." She didn't elaborate, mostly because she wasn't sure exactly why he was there. She opened the door wider. They stood there for a few moments awkwardly.

"I, uh, am not on duty right now. Do you wanna do something? I could show you around the ship." It seemed difficult for him to get the words out, but he stood confidently as he waited for her to reply. She smiled. She was technically dismissed until the midday meal, and Maria was already busying herself. Although the fact that there was a military man at the door specifically for Lillian was not lost on her.

"I have to clear the dishes and take them to the kitchen. We can start there," she suggested as she went back to the table and picked up the rest of the stacked dishes.

He laughed. "If by kitchen you mean galley." Lillian returned his laughter with a pointed stare. She remembered what it was called; she just felt silly saying it aloud.

"Lilly, don't be too long." Maria pouted. "There isn't anything to do by myself in here."

Lillian sighed. "You are welcome to join us."

Maria looked as if she had been slapped. "I will not sit in the kitchen with the help."

"You and I sit in the kitchens at home all the time." Lillian pointed out as she shuffled the breakfast dishes into a neat stack and picked them up.

"That's different. You're ... you." Her gaze flicked to Jeremy and back to Lillian. "Just don't take too long."

"Very well, Maria," Lillian said in a placating tone. Jeremy moved aside, allowing her to maneuver out of the door with the dishes, and followed her down the hall toward the galley.

As promised, Chuck was still there, sifting through the pantry. The smell of fresh food was replaced with that of soap as she noticed the tables and grills had been cleaned. He looked up as they entered. "Hello there, miss. See ya got yerself a new friend. Jeremy boy, how are ya?" He pronounced Jeremy's name in an odd way. With his offhand accent, it sounded more like "Jermy." But Jeremy seemed used to it.

"Jeremy, ya let this lady carry them dishes here herself? Where's yer manners?" Chuck gave him a disapproving stare as he took the dishes from Lillian's hands and nearly tossed them in the sink. Jeremy looked mortified that the thought hadn't crossed his mind to help.

"It's all right, really. That's what I'm here for, after all. It is my job." She slipped into the chair that was still placed next to the counter. "Jeremy offered to show me around the ship a bit today. I thought we could start here, since I'm already somewhat familiar with it."

"Well, ain't that awful nice of him? There ain't nothing much here that ya ain't seein' right now." He gestured around the area. "The only other part is the storage room right there. Just got food and what have ya."

"Hey Chuck, why don't you show her one of your card games? I bet she would enjoy learning something new to do with her friend." Jeremy pulled a chair next to hers. His eyes were alight with excitement. "Chuck's got lots of downtime here between makin' food. He got real bored with the card games he knew, so he started makin' up his own. They're actually fun."

Chuck laughed and pulled a small deck of playing cards from the pocket in his apron, as if he'd known Jeremy would ask to play. They were stacked neatly and carefully but Lillian could tell they were used often, as they were worn and turning brown at the corners. Standing over the counter, he mixed the cards together in his hands. He explained the rules as slowly as he could for her and laughed when she scrunched up her face in confusion.

"It's okay, miss, I'll keep explainin' as we play."

"And we promise not to let you win too fast."

Chuck dealt the cards, his hands moving so fast Lillian could barely follow his movements.

"Go ahead, pick up yer hand." She straightened the small pile as she picked them up, doing her best not to let them show. "Now, look at yer cards there and choose yer best."

L illian laughed as she set her last card down, winning her third game in a row. Chuck smiled; Jeremy looked downright sore.

"I thought you said you would not let me win too easily?"

"I don't get it! I had both of you beat!" Jeremy stared at the cards in his hands sullenly, then aimed a pointed stare at Chuck. "Are you helpin' her cheat just to beat me?"

"No, boy, 'course not. She's just better than ya expected, that's all." Chuck smirked toward Lillian. "I have to be startin' the noon meal now."

"What time is it?" She had gotten too caught up in Chuck's made-up card game and Jeremy's humor.

Jeremy checked his pocked watch. "Quarter after eleven."

"Oh, goodness." She darted from her chair, her hands patting her bun to make sure it wasn't askew. Maria was going to be furious with her. "I must get back. Thank you, that was quite fun." She hurried toward the hall but turned back just before the door. "May I come back? This afternoon?"

Chuck had already begun pulling pots and pans out and setting the stove alight. He turned back at Lillian's question.

"Ye're welcome here any time." Chuck patted Jeremy's back harshly, nearly knocking him over.

"Uh, yeah. I don't go on shift til three." Jeremy replied, clasping his hands on his head and rocking back on his heels.

Lillian slowed as she neared their cabin, she could hear voices inside. The De Sansol's must have decided to visit with Maria. They may be cruel to their staff, but Maria was their pride and joy. They made a point to eat every supper together and one or both of them would often stop in throughout the day to visit with her. Maria found it suffocating at times, but Lillian thought it endearing. She often had a sense of melancholy when she watched them during their time together, the realization that Maria might be a friend, but she wasn't family hitting her more often as of late. She'd never had someone who only wanted to be in her presence or wonder how her day has been. She tried to explain that to Maria and remind her not to take it for granted, but Maria waved her off.

She waited outside the door until Mr. and Mrs. De Sansol decided to leave, which was only a few minutes more. She pointed her gaze down as the couple exited, but Mrs. De Sansol stopped in front of her. She looked up to catch her icy gaze.

"Make sure to keep Maria out of trouble. She isn't to be allowed out of her cabins alone. Is that understood?"

"Yes ma'am," Lillian says with a dip of a curtsy as Mrs. De Sansol walked on. Lillian huffed as soon as they were out of earshot. Maria must have told them she had wandered after some of the officers.

When she got back to the cabin, Maria was already huffing and puffing. "Why do I have to practice *every day*? Why should I have to practice at all? Isn't this supposed to be a holiday?" She sighed heavily.

"That's something you have to discuss with your mother, Maria." Lillian shut the door behind her.

"But she will just say I have to discuss it with Father. And I already know what he is going to say."

"*Proper young ladies are not truly proper unless they are well-rounded,*" the girls mimicked in unison.

This brought a smile to Maria's face. "You were gone forever. What were you doing?" She bit the corner of her lip.

Lillian collect the knitting needles from where they were lazily placed around the room. "Goodness, Maria. Your mind always turns to the scandalous. Why don't you tell me what you *think* I was doing, and then I will disappoint you."

"Oh, I can only imagine that cute little soldier boy swept you off to some secluded corner and whispered pretty things in your ear to make you giggle." She sighed with longing, her hand over her heart. "And then he would show his affection by planting a kiss on your cheek before he released you. At least, that's what he would do if he was in one of those novels you're always reading to me."

"But we aren't in a novel, Maria." Lillian laughed. "This is life. And although Jeremy is a sweetheart, and I'll admit he's quite nice to look at, I don't feel *connected* to him. When I meet the man of my future, I want to know. I want to feel that spark right away." Lillian handed the needles to Maria.

"Like in your books?"

"Yes."

"But we aren't in a book." Maria shot back at her, a glint of smugness in her bright eyes.

"No, we are not," Lillian said, her eyes narrowed just as Maria set the needles down on the wooden table in front of her. "Maria," she warned.

"I can't focus on knitting just now. I've been cooped up in this awful room all day."

"Your mother specifically instructed me to keep you out of trouble," Lillian said.

"Then come with me on deck, and you can keep me out of trouble." Maria grinned. Lillian's stomach churned at the thought of going up on deck. She had done quite well at convincing herself they were still on land as long as she was below, but up where she could actually see the ocean... she wasn't sure she could handle that. Maria, however, was unlikely to let up until she agreed.

"If I go on deck with you, will you do your knitting when we return?" she asked.

"Yes, I swear!" Maria brightened as she stood, already heading towards the door. Lillian sighed before she followed.

Chapter Three

"Lilly, I think we actually need to go *up* in order to get up the stairs," Maria pointed out as they passed the staircase.

"We are going to the galley first."

"Not to play cards, I hope."

Lillian laughed. "Perhaps another day. I want you to meet Chuck and Jeremy, and they might be able to show us around on deck. Perhaps teach us some new words aside from *commandeer*."

"I like *commandeer*." Maria pouted as Lillian pushed the galley door open. Chuck and Jeremy sat at the counter, the deck of cards splayed out in front of them.

"Ah, are you here to give us a chance to win back our dignity—oh." Jeremy stood up straight.

"It's okay, Jeremy. Maria will not bite. Unlike her mother." He didn't relax, his eyes shifting from her to Maria and back again.

"Maria and I are going to go up on deck. Would either of you like to join us?"

"Yeah, I could show you round a bit."

"I'll walk ya up, but can't dally. I got things to do." Chuck gathered all the cards into a pile and then back into his pocket. Maria stood quite still, looking every inch like her mother when addressing the help.

They walked down the hall, Chuck and Jeremy in front, Lillian and Maria behind. She could tell Maria was excited. She was too. Neither of them had been on deck since they first came onto the boat. The metal stairs groaned as they walked up them. The higher they got, the more Lillian could feel the boat rocking. Maria took hold of Lillian's arm. Lillian took a deep breath as her stomach churned with fear.

"We're coming up the starboard side of the ship. That's the right side." Jeremy seemed to enjoy knowing something they didn't. Lillian wasn't going to admit she knew that already from the novels she read.

The deck was relatively calm. Lillian had imagined the men would be rushing back and forth everywhere like they had the day before. There were a few men moving sails or washing the deck. Others sat on the floor or the railings and played cards or coins. Lillian saw a few of them tuck their pipes out of sight. Aside from that, they didn't even acknowledge the ladies' presence.

"Well, I'll be seein' ya at supper, miss. Ma'am."

"Goodbye, Chuck," Lillian said.

"It was nice to meet you," Maria responded automatically, but she wasn't looking at Chuck. She was staring out over the ship. She walked up to the railing in awe.

"Look, Lilly!" Maria gasped. "I cannot see anything but blue forever. How do they keep from getting lost?"

"They use a compass." Lillian stayed a few steps back. Maria hadn't been exaggerating. The deep blue of the ocean, nearly the same color as her own eyes, stretched out in every direction.

Though the sun had started to drift behind some dark clouds, there were enough rays shooting over the gentle rolling waves to brighten the scene. The beauty of it hit Lillian at the same time the light headedness did and she took another step back.

"I know that." Maria narrowed her eyes. "I only meant I feel so small out here, compared to everything."

"It does get scary out here sometimes, when we're on a long journey an' we don't see land for weeks." Jeremy leaned his back over the railing. "Some of the men get real nervous being trapped on a small boat for so long."

"They don't hurt anyone, do they?" Maria asked, genuinely concerned. Jeremy laughed.

"Nah, they just get annoyed real easy. Besides, this journey's only a few more days. You ain't got nothin' to worry about." He smiled. "So like I was saying, this is starboard, and that's port. And this ship's called a brigantine."

"I thought the boat was named *Rossut*," Lillian said.

"The name is *Rossut*, but the type of ship is called brigantine." He chuckled at her confusion.

"Aren't all ships the same?" Maria asked rigidly, crossing her arms at his glee.

"No," Jeremy said, straight-faced now.

Lillian decided it was best to change the subject, but before she could, two men came out from one of the doors on the other side of the ship. She couldn't hear what they were saying, but Lillian could tell that they were arguing. Jeremy's stance turned rigid as he turned back towards the women.

"We should go back down." He gestured toward the opening they had just come from.

"I don't want to," Maria protested. "It's beautiful up here." The two officers became louder. They were face to face, nearly yelling.

"Lillian, best not to be up here right now. We can come back later," Jeremy pleaded. Lillian followed him, but she continued to watch the men. Maria grunted, defeated; she wasn't going to stay on deck alone. The others that had been around either left or moved far from the men as well, who were shouting now.

"It's not safe! Not with them. This ain't what I signed on for. It ain't what the crew signed on for either!"

"Do you want to catch them or not? This is our *only* chance. Those damn pirates are sneaky bastards. And you signed on to follow your captain."

Maria gasped. Jeremy was very nearly shoving them down the stairs as the men continued yelling.

Maria could not stop pacing. At first Lillian thought it was out of worry or anxiety, but as she watched her now from the edge of her cot, she realized it was out of pure excitement. She paced from the door to the porthole window again and again as her smile grew with each outlandish, and possibly risqué, thought that crossed her mind. Lillian sighed. This was going to be a long afternoon of keeping Maria focused and away from the upper deck.

"Oh, Lilly. Can you imagine? Pirates!" Maria grinned.

"Maria, pirates are just a bedtime story I am sure your father regrets ever telling you." Lillian sighed. Although she wouldn't admit it, she was a bit nervous after the exchange. It must be the same thing the Lieutenant and Mr. McEntire had been wary about. But how would Mr. McEntire know there was something unsafe about the Rossut?

She felt she needed to find out what it was before it affected the De Sansol's. Heavens knew if something happened to Maria, Mrs. De Sansol would find a way to blame Lillian. And since she was treating this trip as an adventure, and she the heroine, that felt like exactly what the heroine should do.

"I'll bet they are handsome. Are any of the men in your stories pirates?" Maria continued. Whatever was going on, she was sure it didn't involve actual pirates. There were no such thing. They were part of stories for young children and adventure novels. She wondered briefly if the naval officers had been only trying to frighten them.

"Yes, and they are murderous thieves. They steal, rape, and kill. And none of them are good looking." She stood and collected Maria's clothes, which were strewn across the room. "Now remember that we have supper with the captain this evening. You'd best start dressing." Lillian stared at Maria, a grin spread across her face. She knew reminding her of the supper with the captain would turn her off the subject.

"Oh, Lilly, we are going to have supper with the captain, a navy captain! This day has been truly exciting," she said as she turned and allowed Lillian to unlace her dress.

She huffed as she let Lillian unlace her dress. "If pirates aren't real, then why were the navy men talking about them?"

"To scare us."

"Oh pish. Why would they want to scare us?" She stepped into a lavender dress.

"I'm sure I don't know, Maria. Perhaps they don't want us going up on deck." Lillian pulled the laces tight and tied them.

"Mother and Father went up for their walk before the noon meal. I don't see them talking about pirates."

"Maria," Lillian warned, "don't you go saying anything about any of this to your mother. You know how she feels about this sort of thing."

"You worry too much."

"I do, and it is for our own good. Now stand up straight. How does that feel?"

Maria twirled her skirts. "Perfect."

"Are you sure it's not too tight?" Lillian asked cautiously.

"It can never be too tight, Lilly."

"Remember the Kindelans' supper party? I don't need you fainting again."

"Oh Lilly, you—"

"Worry too much. I know. I have to worry to make up for your lack of it. Maria, you need to promise me you will be on your *best* behavior. And no mention of any pirates."

"Yes, yes, I know." Maria grabbed Lillian's arms and spun them both in a circle.

"Maria." At Lillian's stern tone, she stopped spinning. "Your best behavior. Do you promise?"

"Yes, all right. I promise. No speaking loudly. Only speak when spoken to. Always sit up straight. I know how to act."

"And?"

"And ... No mention of pirates." She sighed in obvious disappointment.

"Thank you. Now, would you like to do my hair?"

Maria smiled. "Yes, of course Lilly."

M aria stuck another pin in Lillian's curly brown hair, stabbing her scalp.

"Ouch! Maria, that's the third time you've stabbed me. I am starting to think it is on purpose."

"I am almost done, Lilly. Just hold still." She slid one last pin in and handed Lillian her small hand mirror.

"It is beautiful, Maria. But your mother did say to keep it simple." Lillian stood in her pale cream-and-yellow dress that Maria had bought for her on the docks. Being out at sea naturally enhanced her curls Maria had pinned up her hair in an elegant coronet. Back home they would dress up in Maria's best dresses and Maria had done up her hair many times for fun, but only in private. The De Sansols had insisted she dress her best for the captain, even if she was to only stand to the side. She felt more beautiful knowing that the dress was her own, not something of Maria's she had borrowed. She was glad to have a chance to wear it again.

"That is simple. I'll get you some shoes," Maria said, looking at her bare feet.

She came back a few minutes later and handed Lillian a pair of cream sandals.

"Those should be perfect." Maria took her mirror from Lillian and touched up her own face. "And don't say they aren't simple, because they are the only pair I own that doesn't have bows or glitter on them."

"They are fine, Maria. Thank you." Lillian slipped the sandals onto her feet. Just as she stood up, Mrs. De Sansol walked in.

"Are you girls ready? They should be here any minute to escort us. Maria darling, you look wonderful." She kissed her on both cheeks and adjusted the shawl hanging loosely over Maria's shoulders. "You must be at your best this evening. The captain is our host, and I expect both of you to act like ladies." She glanced at Lillian. "Your actions reflect upon our family."

"Yes, Mrs. De Sansol."

Mrs. De Sansol pursed her lips. "Maria, dear, you could have been a little more conservative with Lillian's hair."

"Yes, Mother," Maria said automatically, though the look on her face said she really wasn't paying attention.

Though the door was open when the dark-haired soldier arrived at exactly half past the hour, he still knocked to announce his presence. Maria nearly swooned. Luckily, Mrs. De Sansol was oblivious. Had she noticed Maria's "unladylike" actions, she would have been furious.

"Please follow me to the captain's quarters." Once again he swiftly turned on his heel and walked briskly down the corridor, not waiting for a response. Mr. and Mrs. De Sansol hurried after him, Maria and Lillian shortly behind them.

To reach the captain's quarters, they had to follow the same path they had earlier that day up on to the deck. Lillian had never seen the ocean at night, let alone been on a ship in the middle of it. It was absolutely gorgeous, if not a little nerve-racking. The sun was just beginning to set on the horizon. Orange, red, soft pink at the bottom where it met the horizon and dark grays, blues, and a little purple up in the clouds. Lillian sucked in a small breath at the sight and stepped near the railing—or as close as she dared go. Maria continued on but her arm was still linked through Lillian's. She tugged her forward and Lillian reluctantly allowed Maria to pull her away.

When they arrived at the captain's quarters, the officer opened the door without hesitation, as he did everything, and guided the De Sansols in. The room wasn't exactly lavish, but it was much nicer than any others on the ship. The bedroom was separated by a door, as was the lavatory. The room that they entered had two lounge chairs and a small table, barely big enough to fit the five of them, and it had its own small stove.

The captain greeted them with a large smile that didn't quite reach his eyes. Lillian was surprised he wasn't wearing a uniform, but his crisp white shirt and black trousers were elegant nonethe-less. He wore his salt and pepper hair parted just to the side and perfectly slicked back. Maria tightened her grip on Lillian's arm. Lillian sighed and decided her task when they returned to Aarilya was to get Maria married before her hormones led her to someone's bed. Being her ladies maid, that would most definitely fall on Lillian's head.

"Well, hello, Mr. and Mrs. De Sansol." The captain clasped his large hands around Mr. De Sansol's and gave a hearty shake. He also clasped Mrs. De Sansol's hand, but much more gently, and gave her a kiss that didn't quite touch her cheek. Turning his eyes toward the girls, his smile faded just a little before he plastered an even larger one on his lips. "And which one of these lovely ladies is your daughter?"

"Maria, dear, introduce yourself to the captain." Mrs. De Sansol placed her hand on Maria's waist and nudged her forward.

Maria stepped closer to the captain and held her hand out, a full debutante grin on her lips. "I am Maria De Sansol, sir. It is such a pleasure to have the opportunity to accompany you and your crew on this voyage." She curtsied as he kissed her hand, which he held a little too long, causing a blush to creep across Maria's cheeks. Finally, he turned to Lillian. His eyes held hers, but something flashed in them. Curiosity perhaps, but a bit more ... devilish.

"Then you must be Lillian."

"Yes, sir." Lillian curtsied but did not offer her hand. "I am a maid to the De Sansol family."

"Hmm. I see." He eyed Lillian from head to toe, a friendly smile on his lips. An unsettling shiver ran up her spine at his scrutiny, but she stood still. "I hear that you and Miss De Sansol were witness to a bit of excitement out on deck today."

"Oh! Are you talking about the pirates?" Maria perked up. Mrs. De Sansol gasped and stared at Maria in utter horror. Maria had the good grace to shrink the tiniest bit. Lillian groaned inwardly.

"Now, Miss De Sansol." The captain pouted nonchalantly. "We are all adults here. And we all know that there is no such thing as pirates. Mr. Grayson will explain the situation when he arrives. Please." He beckoned Mr. and Mrs. De Sansol. "If you will follow me." He pulled out a chair and flashed his wolf-like smile. "Miss De Sansol, I would be honored if you took this seat, next to mine."

Maria's face lit up as she sat down, hanging her shawl across the back of her chair and effectively exposing her shoulders.

"Well, thank you, Captain Davis." She giggled.

Lillian took her place against the wall behind Maria as Mr. and Mrs. De Sansol took a seat.

"Please, call me Dall." His eyes settled on each person around the table. "We still have a little while on this voyage, and I would like for everyone to feel comfortable." His eyes lingered on Maria before they flicked to her spot against the wall momentarily.

Lillian frowned. It was becoming apparent to her that Dall was no gentleman. Unfortunately, Lillian was the only one who could see it. Maria was so far over the moon the only thing she could see were stars in her eyes, and Mr. and Mrs. De Sansol were more polite and gracious than Lillian had ever seen them.

The captain raised his finger, and the officer began to pour the wine. "I don't know about you, but I like my wine cold and my food warm." Everyone but Lillian laughed. "Please, enjoy. My first mate should be here shortly with the food." He raised his glass, leveling his gaze right at Lillian, and took a hearty gulp.

Chapter Four

After the food had been served and some time had passed, a knock came at the door. The officer opened the door, and one of the men who had been arguing on the deck. He was older, his hair gray and his back slouched, but he still carried himself with an air of authority.

"Ah, Mr. Grayson," the captain said. "Impeccable timing."

Dall nodded towards the man and motioned for him to address the table. He cleared his throat before he began.

"I would like to formally apologize to the De Sansol family for my actions and the actions of the crew on deck this afternoon. It seems we may have mistakenly offended and frightened the women. The crew and I enjoy reading adventure novels in our free time, and we did not realize the ladies were on deck while we were acting out a scene from the novel. I would also like to apologize for our offensive language." He stared straight ahead through the entire apology, not making eye contact with any specific person. His delivery seemed scripted.

Mrs. De Sansol was quiet a moment. Then she aimed her stare at Maria.

"While I was unaware that any altercation had occurred, your apology is accepted, and I expect you and the crew to be more considerate in the coming days."

Mr. Grayson looked to the captain as he turned to leave. Although to Lillian there didn't seem to be any change in expression, there had been a definite message shared between the two.

"Dessert, anyone?" Captain Dall asked, his smile large as ever.

A strong breeze had begun to blow out on deck as they headed back toward their cabins. The remainder of supper had been quite boring. As they ate, they'd listened to Captain Dall talk, mostly to Maria. Lillian was surprised that Mr. and Mrs. De Sansol said nothing about the way he spoke to Maria. She thought his over-familiar manner would spark some sort of tangent from Mrs. De Sansol, but she laughed and engaged in small talk all evening. In fact, as Lillian walked behind them silently, Mrs. De Sansol seemed nearly as taken by the captain as Maria was.

"He was quite charming, wasn't he?" Mrs. De Sansol said.

Maria giggled. "He has an air of confidence and sophistication about him." Maria mimicked the captain's demeanor as she walked. Mrs. De Sansol laughed, something Lillian had not heard since she was a child. Perhaps it was the wine.

"What about you, Lilly? What did you like about Dall?" Maria attempted to drag her in into the conversation.

"Very little," Lillian said curtly. Maria and her mother stopped walking.

"What do you mean?" Maria tilted her head quizzically, as if she couldn't comprehend the idea of someone disliking the captain.

"I did not like the *captain*," she repeated. "Not at all."

"There wasn't even one thing about his company that you enjoyed? Not his laugh, or his jokes, or the way he spoke with such sophistication?"

"Maria," Mrs. De Sansol said, stepping in before Maria went on one of her rants. "Lillian dear, what about Captain Dall did you not like?" Even Mr. De Sansol had stopped walking. They stood outside, near the stairwell leading down to their quarters. The wine was definitely affecting Mrs. De Sansol. She hadn't called Lillian 'dear' since she was a young girl.

"He is suspicious," she blurted out. "There is just something about him. I feel unsafe in his company. And he is far too familiar with Maria. He leans in too closely to her when he speaks, and he touches her for too long." Lillian was surprised at how calm she remained as she spoke. "And frankly, Mrs. De Sansol, I'm alarmed that you haven't noticed."

The moment the words left her mouth, Lillian regretted them. Mrs. De Sansol might be deep in her cups but there was no way she would let outright insubordination go unpunished.

Mrs. De Sansol gasped. "Lillian—"

"She is right, dear." Mr. De Sansol interrupted the tongue-lashing his wife was about to unleash. Lillian let out a small sigh of relief. "He was a bit too forward with her. Maria, the captain may be charming, but you are a De Sansol, and you are not going to marry a ship's captain, no matter that he is of the navy. You may converse with him as you wish, but do not allow your schoolgirl crush to surface again."

Maria looked positively heartbroken as she watched her father retreat down the stairs. She reached up to adjust her shawl and gasped. It was not there.

"Oh! Mother, I left my shawl in Captain Dall's quarters." She smiled sweetly. "I'll run and fetch it."

"I'll get it for you," Lilly said.

"I can fetch my own things," she snapped.

"Maria, Lillian will get it. It is her job, and we need to dress for bed." Mrs. De Sansol continued down the stairs as her husband had, expecting Maria to follow without question. Maria huffed and shot another glare at Lillian before turning angrily and following her mother.

Lillian sighed and walked back to the captain's quarters, stopping just in front of the door. She raised her hand to knock but paused. Someone was speaking inside. It was Captain Dall and Mr. Grayson.

"They take issue, sir."

"And what do they take issue with, exactly, Grayson?"

A pause. Even Mr. Grayson must fear the captain.

"Civilians being on board, sir. The crew was not consulted before you allowed them passage."

"And what do you expect of me, Grayson? To ignore our mission because the crew does not agree with my orders? That sounds like the beginnings of mutiny to me," Dall said calmly.

Ice ran down Lillian's spine. If a naval mutiny was anything like the one's she had read about, it would most definitely be dangerous for them to be aboard.

"No, not at all Sir." Mr. Grayson said flatly. It was quiet a moment before he spoke again. "What about Stevenson?"

"No, we won't worry about him just yet. I only want K—"

"Excuse me, miss." Lillian was startled as an officer addressed her from behind. "Is the captain expecting you?"

"No, he's not, actually." She straightened. "Miss De Sansol left an item in the captain's cabin. I was sent back to fetch it and I was unsure whether to knock."

The lieutenant stared at her as he turned the handle and pushed, letting the door swing open on its own, exposing the two of them standing there. The captain and Mr. Grayson stopped talking immediately.

"Captain." He announced as he took her elbow and roughly guided her into the cabin. "This girl has been standing outside your door for quite some time."

"Ah, Miss Lillian." Captain Dall smiled as if he was expecting this meeting. "Thank you, Lieutenant Mitch. You are dismissed." He looked Lillian up and down. His demeanor had changed since supper. He still had a charming air about him, but it didn't quite cover his more primal side any longer. The side Lillian had seen bits of earlier, that no one else seemed to notice. A menacing aura seemed to radiate from him. "Well, I didn't think you would be the one to cause trouble around here. I believe you are here for this?" He ran the shawl through his fingers. "Pity. I had hoped Maria would be the one to come and take it from me."

She snatched it from his hands and turned for the door, but Mr. Grayson stepped in her way.

"Not just yet, Miss Lillian. Or shall I call you Lilly? I believe there are a few things we need to discuss," the captain continued. "You didn't say much during supper. I can tell you are an intelligent girl. I'm sure you've put a few of the pieces together. Please, have a seat." He gestured toward a chair. "Mr. Grayson, some wine please."

"No, thank you, Captain. I just came for the shawl, and I shall be on my way."

"Sit," he commanded. She contemplated the possibility of pushing through the two men, but ultimately decided against it, and sat. Satisfied, Dall continued. "You heard a rather heated discussion that was supposed to be private." The captain aimed his stare at Mr. Grayson. "Now, I am going to tell you the truth, and you are not going to repeat these words to anyone—ever. I trust you understand that if you were to disobey me, I could make life quite ... complicated for you." He bent down, his face inches from hers, his hand resting on her shoulder. "Or for Maria. Am I understood?"

She kept silent, her eyes never leaving his.

"You're a stubborn one, aren't you? Grayson, the wine." Mr. Grayson brought over two glasses. Captain Dall took one for himself and handed the other to Lillian.

"No, thank you," she said curtly.

"It's not a request, Lilly."

"Lillian," she corrected.

He smiled, one side of his mouth lifting higher than the other, and put the wine glass into her hand, forcing her to take it. He held her stare, daring her to defy him again. The devilish glint in his eyes had her thinking it was best to play along at the moment. She took a swallow.

"There, now. Was that so terrible?" He turned his back to her. "As I was explaining earlier." He swirled the wine in his glass. "You are aboard a navy ship. And as the navy, one of our primary tasks is to hunt down mercenaries. Specifically, those who travel the sea and attack other vessels, both navy and civilian. Some folks have come to refer to these mercenaries as pirates. Children's bedtime stories. But no matter their title, they are plaguing our seas. We received word that one of their ships is in the area, and we plan pursue it."

"With civilians on board?" Lillian asked.

"It's nothing personal. Our mission comes first, even before your safety. Fortunately for you, the weather is not with us. A hurricane is brewing, and even I am not crazy enough to steer us into a storm. So, you may rest easy. We will divert course around the weather and arrive in Southern Nelina in a few days, as planned. Until then, you will not speak of the pirates. Not even to Maria."

He downed the rest of his wine before handing his glass to Mr. Grayson. "You are dismissed. Mr. Grayson will see to it that you arrive at your room safely."

"I won't need your assistance, thank you," she said, seething.

He shrugged and shut the door behind her.

"She's going to be trouble," Captain Dall said.

"Aye, sir. You think she believed it?"

"For now."

Chapter Five

In the short time she had spent with Captain Dall, dark clouds had begun to roll in, and the wind was becoming fiercer by the minute. Though Lillian wasn't versed in ocean weather, this storm was rolling in a bit to quickly for her taste. The wind whipped her hair about her face as she hurried towards the stairs that led to their cabin. All she wanted to do was turn in for the night and pray tomorrow was a better day. She rushed down the stairs and the hall, and finally into her door. Maria was sitting in one of the chairs looking at her hand mirror. She did not greet Lillian.

"The weather outside is turning quite horrible. It is a little frightening." She hung the shawl in the closet. "The captain said it looks like a hurricane."

"You took an awfully long time to fetch a shawl," she said, still not looking at her. Lillian sighed. It was going to be one of those moods, then.

"We were discussing the weather, as I said. Look at me." Maria looked up, furious and hurt.

"Maria," Lillian said softly, sitting next to her, "I do not care about the captain. In fact, I detest him. And I think that we would both be better off if we stayed away from him."

"You were gone for half an hour, Lillian. It does not take that long to discuss the weather."

"I swear, that is all we spoke about." She laid her hand on Maria's arm, but Maria pulled away angrily.

"Don't you think I know when you are lying?" Tears formed as she stared at Lillian, daring her to lie again.

"Alright, you want the truth?" Lillian snapped. She was angry. At Maria for being so dramatic. At herself for lying. But mostly at the captain for putting her in this position. She had to make a decision. She couldn't tell Maria the truth, she didn't know what Dall was capable of doing if she were to disobey him. "The truth is, I wasn't with Dall the whole time."

"Then where were you?"

Thunder struck outside, as if fueled by Maria's anger. It sounded so much closer than Lillian had expected. A few heartbeats later, the room was alight with a flash of lightning.

"I went to Captain Dall's cabin, and I got your shawl, then I left." She hesitated, then moved to close the curtains over the porthole window.

"And where did you go?" Maria followed.

"I don't want to tell you." She sighed, already hating the taste of the lie that was about to leave her lips.

"Then I don't believe you. You're just trying to cover your tracks again. You said you would tell me the truth." Maria stood, furious once more. "You are a terrible person, Lillian."

Another clap of thunder, louder this time, caused both women to jump. Maria huffed and turned from Lillian.

"Wait, Maria." Lillian grasped Maria's arm. "I'll tell you, but you can't say anything." Maria faced her once more. Her eyes lit up, as

Lillian knew they would. Maria loved a secret, and Lillian never had them.

"I won't, I swear." Maria sat down again, smoothing the wrinkles from her nightdress. "Tell me, please. I won't tell anyone."

Lillian sat next to her. "Especially not your mother?"

"I promise."

"All right. After I left the captain's cabin ..." She paused. "I went to see Jeremy." She turned away, ashamed. She wasn't meant for this. She wasn't adept at lying and scheming. She was a follower, not a leader. Her position as a maid supported that. No matter her dream of freedom, this trip had an end and Atwood was the reality of her life.

"Lillian!" Maria gasped. "Did you really? Goodness, I knew you liked him. I told you he was cute. He really is your little soldier boy. Oh!" She gasped again. "Did you go to his cabin?"

"No! Maria, we met in the galley. We just talked. Nothing more."

"Oh." Maria sounded disappointed.

"Are you happy now? Are we done arguing?"

"Yes. Although I would hardly call that an argument. You should have just told me the truth in the first place."

Lillian shook her head in disbelief.

A squeak escaped Maria as the walls shuddered, a large gust of wind running along them. The weather was definitely getting worse. Hadn't captain Dall said they were going to sail around the storm? Perhaps they had been to far into it when he had made the decision.

"What was that you were saying about the weather?" Maria asked, suddenly remembering Lillian's mention of it when she had returned.

The rocking of the boat had increased significantly as they had fought and Lillian's stomach churned violently as it bobbed. She pressed a hand to it in an attempt to calm it. Maria stepped closer to Lillian as another clap of thunder rang through. It sounded like it was directly over the ship now. This was not the adventure she had wanted.

"It was growing worse, but captain Dall assured me we were headed away from the worst of it. Why don't we try and find something to distract us, hmm?" Lillian struggled to hide the shake in her hand as she patted Maria's calmingly. Images of the dark depths below flittered across her mind before she took a deep calming breath. "You never finished your knitting. Why don't we try that."

"Lillian," Maria shot her a look that said are you serious? "Knitting is not going to drown out the thunder, or calm the boat."

"Well, do you have a better idea?" Lillian raised a brow in question.

Maria opened her mouth to answer when the room suddenly jerked violently. Both girls screamed as Maria fell to the ground. Lillian quickly helped her up. The girls held on to each other as the room jerked once more.

""I think we should go upstairs, Maria."

"No! It is safer down here." She was nearly in tears.

"Something is wrong, Maria," Lillian said sternly. "We need to find your parents and go upstairs. I don't like it anymore than you do, but the captain will tell us what to do."

Maria hesitated but then nodded in agreement. Lillian knew mentioning the captain was the quickest way to get Maria to agree. The walls shook and the room groaned as it started to tilt. Maria clasped Lillian's arm even tighter. They opened the door and were met with Mr. and Mrs. De Sansol in the hallway looking just as panicked as Maria, still in their night clothes. Lillian was the only one who hadn't had a chance to change yet, and she was cursing the short sleeves of her cream and yellow as the bitter cold of the air caused goosepimples to coat her arms and neckline.

"We need to go upstairs," Lillian instructed. Mrs. De Sansol shook her head, just as Maria had.

"I think it would be best to stay down here where it's dry." Mr. De Sansol nodded in agreement.

"The ship is tilting. We need to head upstairs and find the captain." They hesitated, unsure of what to do. The walls continued to creak and groan as the ship rocked. Lillian nearly groaned at their stubbornness. "Let's find Captain Dall, if he says it's safer down here, we will come back down," she reassured them. Mrs. De Sansol looked to Mr. De Sansol and, after a moment, he nodded.

With Maria still wrapped around Lillian's arm, they hurried down the hall, her parents following closely behind. She had to use all her weight to push the door open against the weather. They all gasped at the sight out on the deck, it was the most terrifying thing Lillian had ever seen. Every man on the ship was out there. Most were trying to hold the sails; some were using buckets to toss water back over the rails. It was obvious just how slanted the boat had become, the waves were crashing high over the ledge as if Poseidon himself were trying to drag the ship to the bottom. Lillian shuddered at the thought.

The thunder shook and lightning struck so close that Lillian could feel the electricity run through the air. The brief flash lit up the sky and she was paralyzed at the site of the swirling vortex of water and clouds in the distance. They could feel the fierceness of the wind as it swirled around them. Maria's clawed grip tightened around her arm and brought her back to their situation.

She searched the deck but the captain was nowhere to be found, or his errand boy. Another bolt of lightning lit up the sky as it struck the main mast, catching fire. It cracked and hung for a moment before it toppled down into the ocean, dragging at least a dozen men down with it. Maria and her mother whimpered; Mr. De Sansol pulled them close.

On the far side of the ship, Lillian spotted Jeremy. He was with the men who were shoveling buckets over the side. He didn't look scared, but rather focused and determined. As soon as he spotted them, his eyes grew wide with terror. His bucket hit the ground and he started running toward them, the men around him yelled angrily as they continued to shovel the water out. Lillian started towards him, but Maria tightened her grip.

"Lillian, it's not safe. Don't leave us," Maria whimpered.

"It is okay, Maria. I need to find out where the captain is." She squeezed Maria's hand to reassure her. "I will be right back. I promise." She held her gaze a moment before Maria finally gave her a slight nod. She released Maria's hand and headed toward Jeremy.

Suddenly another crack of lightening lit up the sky and the ship shuddered with an ear-splitting crack as if a thousand cannons had exploded against the hull. The force sent everyone on deck flying. Lillian's eyes went wide as she tried to grab for Maria, but they were separated in an instant. Her head slammed against the railing before she hit the water. The sound of screams surrounded her, but wasn't sure who or where it was coming from.

Lillian tried to gasp for air but only water filled her lungs. There were dark figures all around her, whether they were people or segments of the ship she could not tell. She had lost Maria, and everyone else. She realized too late that she was underwater. Panic rose up from her stomach so blinding that she couldn't see straight. She shook her head to clear it, but nothing changed. What little strength she had wasn't enough to kick to the surface and her head throbbed from the impact it had taken. Her worst fears were coming true, and she was too weak to do anything about it.

She was drowning.

Lillian gasped again, but her lungs only burned as they filled with water. She reached out and flailed her arms in an attempt to get back to the surface, but her vision had begun to blur and her limbs were growing heavy.

Then someone was there in front of her. They grabbed her, and they both kicked as hard as they could, up through the freezing, heavy water, until finally they broke the surface. She coughed as the water fought to come up. The ocean spilled from her mouth and her nose. Finally, she was able to take in a long, ragged breath. Her eyes burned as she opened them. Slowly the person came into focus as rain still pelted them. It was Jeremy in front of her. She tried to look around her, take stock of what exactly had happened, but the pressure in her head was too intense. She squeezed her eyes shut against it. She needed to focus, needed to find Maria and the De Sansols. But all her focus was on fighting the waves as they threatened to pull her down.

She opened her eyes and tried to focus once more but could hardly see past Jeremy. He looked as horrible as she felt. He struggled against the rain as he grabbed a large plank that was floating nearby and pulled it closer so that she could hold on. He was breathing hard as he laid his head down on the wood. Her head pounded harder as she lay down as well, closing her eyes, but when she opened them again the storm had passed. Her dress clung to her and was no longer a barrier to the freezing temperatures of the ocean. She could hardly feel her legs past the cold. She searched the area She looked around frantically to spot Maria, Chuck, or anyone else. There was no one. Only Jeremy and some wreckage from the ship floated nearby.

"Are—" She coughed out water once more. "Are you okay?"

He laughed hoarsely as he turned to face her. He was bleeding from a deep gash on his face, his light hair matted to his forehead. "Am I okay? Are *you* okay?"

The pain pushed into her temple with the slight movement. They were still in the water. Panic rose again. They were in the water and there was nothing around them. No land. No other ships. The plank they clung to their only savior. She could feel her cheeks heat as her breaths came rapidly.

"Hey," Jeremy soothed. "We've got this sturdy driftwood to hold us." She took a shaky breath as she let his words calm her a bit.

She took him in once more. "You're bleeding."

He hissed in pain as she pressed her fingers to his cheek. "Well, it didn't hurt til you t-t-touched it." His teeth chattered as he spoke.

"Sorry." She started to smile but gasped when a sharp pain struck her head. She felt dizzy. Jeremy's face fell. "I need to find Maria." She tried to kick her feet to move them closer to the wreckage.

"I'm sorry, Lillian. There's no one left. No one but us. And you got quite a bump yourself." He motioned to her temple. His face was filled with sadness and regret.

"It is not your f-fault Jeremy." She laid her temple against her arm, and as she did so, she noticed something wrong with the water. It wasn't blue or green. It was red. Why was it red?

She looked at Jeremy's side. His shirt was soaked in blood. "Jeremy!"

He would no longer meet her eyes. "It might as well be my fault. I knew what the captain was doing. I knew he was leading us on a suicide mission. I should have fought back. I should have warned you. Perhaps it would have helped. I could have saved everyone." Tears filled his eyes. Or perhaps it was her eyes. It was becoming difficult to see.

"Jeremy ..." Her head spun, or was it the ocean spinning? She couldn't tell up from down anymore. Her eyes started drifting. She tried to keep her heavy lids open, tried to ask him if he had seen where anyone else had gone, but she couldn't.

"I'm sorry," he whispered once more. He brushed a lock from her face.

Then everything went black.

Chapter Six

Her head hurt, a dull ache but nothing compared to the stabbing pain earlier. She was warm, very warm, and the smell of sea salt and musty wood surrounded her. She tried to move her arms, but they would not budge. Her legs were the same. She was restrained. Panic set in. Opening her eyes, she tried to sit up. She achieved a small amount of leeway, enough to free her arms to support herself. She frowned when she saw what had restrained her. It was only a blanket that had been tightly tucked around her body. She sighed, shaking her head at her own anxiousness.

She could feel the gentle rocking of the ocean, nothing like it had been, but this wasn't the same boat. Everything around her was made of wood, not steel as the navy ship had been. Wood planks ran the length of the room, as well as the floor and ceiling, only broken up by the thick support beams. She ran her fingers across them, savoring the warmth. Then she remembered losing sight of

Maria. Then floating in the ocean with Jeremy—Jeremy's wound! She gasped and stood up quickly from the small cot. Her head protested and the dizziness returned, but she had to find out what happened and where she was.

The air was quite chilly in the room once she released the blankets. It was then that she noticed she was in her undergarments, or rather, Maria's undergarments. She frowned as she looked around the room for her dress. There was nothing to be seen aside from the small cot, table, and chair. Against the wall stood a small closet with three drawers, all of which were empty. She decided at that moment that finding Maria and the others was more important than decency. She wrapped the blanket around her shoulders, hugging it close as she opened the door.

The hallways were small and cramped. It was hardly ten feet in either direction before she came to a door or a staircase. It was quiet enough that she could hear the waves softly washing against the sides of the boat. She ran her hand along the damp wood of the walls as she made her way up the short staircase; her head had begun to pound slightly at the movement. Once at the top, she could see the sun was just beginning to rise in the east. Was it the same night, or had night fallen again?

The deck was half the size of the *Rossut*'s, and only one young man stood watch. Or sat watch, rather. He leaned against the main mast, one leg propped up and the other out straight. His arms were crossed against his chest and his head was down. A three-cornered hat hid his eyes. Lillian couldn't tell if he was sleeping or bored. His clothes were quite informal, dirty even. His plain blue long-sleeved shirt was half tucked into frayed black trousers.

"Excuse me?" she called quietly. If he was sleeping, she didn't want to startle him. She didn't know what he was capable of. His head lifted slowly, and as soon as he saw her he stood.

"Well, hello, lady. Yer awake." He smiled. His teeth were crooked, and at least one was missing, yet he couldn't be more than a year older than her. His hair was short and matched his soft brown eyes. "Am I the first person ye've come across? Well, all right then. Welcome aboard. Let's go see Mr. McEntire." He seemed friendly, but Lillian was cautious. He headed back across the deck to where she had come up, but she remained where she was.

"Excuse me, but can you tell me where the others are?" she asked.

"Mr. McEntire will want to explain everything to ya," he said without turning around. His words made her uneasy. There was a door on either side of the staircase she had come up, the man led her to the one on the left. He knocked twice and waited. The door opened almost immediately. Standing there was a tall, blond, blue-eyed man. The one she had seen on the docks in Aarilya, who had saved her from falling into the mud only a few days before. A lifetime ago already. He wore the same blue button-up, though his overcoat was gone, and black trousers. He smiled brightly when he saw her. Her unease increased as he laughed. She took a step back.

"Well, aren't you a sight? Still a fine-looking lady, though." He bowed as she pulled the blanket tighter. "Thanks, Kidd, I'll take it from here." He turned to her.

"Nice t'meet you lady." He nodded to Lillian before he departed.

"Well, don't just stand there. Come in where it's warm, Miss De Sansol." He purred the name she had given—a lie she could not blame on Captain Dall. She had no intention of correcting him now, not when she wasn't sure where she was or who these people were. Her suspicions that Mr. McEntire was involved with Dall arose once more. He stepped to the side so that she could walk past. She hesitated.

"I won't bite."

She took a small step forward. The room was warm. A small iron stove in the corner burned wood for heat. Next to the door stood two cushioned chairs and a small end table. Straight ahead, a wall of windows stretching from floor to ceiling framed in blue curtains overlooked the ocean, and directly in front of it was a large bed. A shiver ran down her at the vast emptiness outside the window. She jumped as he shut the door behind her, earning a chuckle.

"Nervous?"

"Am I to understand you are the captain on this boat?" she asked, standing a bit taller. He smiled, obviously aware that she'd ignored his question.

"I'll be whatever you want me to be. Please, sit down."

She did, but because her head was throbbing, not because he had told her to.

"Where's my dress?"

"Ahh, right to the point. I like it." He laughed. "It should be here fairly soon."

"How soon?" The softness of the blanket rubbed against her sensitive skin as she tightened her grip around it.

"Within the hour. I have a pair of long johns you can borrow if you're cold."

"No, thank you, Captain McEntire. I'm fine."

"You can call me Johnny," he said as he stood in front of the wood stove. She started to tell him she wouldn't. He was a captain and a stranger, and propriety demanded the more formal address. But she had the feeling that would put Captain McEntire on a whimsical tangent that she wasn't mentally equipped to deal with at the moment. And learning what had happened to Maria was more important.

"May I ask if you know what happened to the others?"

"Others?" He furrowed his brow.

"My family. The other people aboard the *Rossut*." She held his gaze.

His smile fell slowly as he sat up straight. "I am sorry, Miss De Sansol, but you were the only person we found. I assumed you knew you had been alone."

She processed his words, trying to control the emotions that were welling up in her chest, threatening to explode. They couldn't just be gone. Chuck and Jeremy. Maria. *Maria*. It had been her job to stay close to Maria, to keep her safe. And now she might be ... She might be dead? The tears unwittingly spilled down her face. She wiped them away, but it was no use. More just kept coming. She couldn't breathe. She was alone. She had no one. She felt like she was six years old all over again, standing in an empty foyer with nothing but a teddy bear to comfort her. She gasped in breath after breath, but it wasn't enough. She couldn't breathe. She could hardly see, her tears were so thick.

"What did you do to her?" a deep voice growled. She hadn't heard the door open, but now there was another man in the room, her dress draped across his arm. He was down on his knees in front of her in an instant. An unsettling electricity ran along her skin the moment he was there, which only proved to increase her unease. His dark hair hung over his forehead, gray eyes full of concern as he looked her over.

"Hey. Breathe. Just breathe, love. Deep breaths." He put his hand to her cheek and started breathing deeply with her. She was getting dizzy again. She tried to pull her face away from his hand, but he held her still with his other. She tried to slow her breaths as she stared into the depths of his silver eyes, to no avail. They were filled with worry as he held her gaze. "God, you're burning up." He moved his hand to her forehead and swore. That was the last thing she heard before the world went dark again.

"**W**hat the devil did you do?" Kale yelled as he watched Lillian slip into unconsciousness again, slumped within the chair.

"I didn't do nothing, Kale! She asked about her family, I assumed she knew they were dead."

"Johnny!"

"It's not my fault they died!"

"Dammit, Johnny. Do you have an ounce of delicacy in you? We need her alive. You're alone with her for five minutes, and she's unconscious." He shook his head angrily. "What am I going to do with you?"

"What was I supposed to tell her? 'Oh, they're alive. They are all dancing happily on an island somewhere'?"

Kale growled.

"Don't you growl at me. None of this is my fault."

"You better hope she wakes up from this fever." Kale bent down and scooped her up to lay her on the bed, her tangled curls fanning out below her. "Get me a damp cloth. A cold one."

"Yes sir," Johnny said sarcastically, but followed his command. Kale tucked the blanket around her shivering body and swept the caramel-colored strands from her face. When they had spotted the wreckage of the *Rossut* in the waters, they'd thought the De Sansol family gone. And their chance at the treasure of a lifetime gone with them. The entire crew had been distraught. Not an hour later, Kidd spotted the girl floating on a beam. Their luck had turned. They couldn't have gotten the chance to save her from certain drowning only to have her succumb to a fever.

Johnny returned with a cold cloth.

Kale laid it across her forehead. "You're going to pull through this, girl. For both of us."

The smell of food made her nauseous. She groaned and rolled over onto her side.

"You might want to get dressed before you come out from those blankets. Though I can't say I would mind." The dark-haired man chuckled as she sat up, clutching the blankets to her chest. He sat at the small table, facing her. His night-black hair was a bit longer than the current style in Aarilya, disheveled as it fell across his forehead, and those gray eyes watched her, a smirk on his lips. "How's your head?"

"Much better." There was hardly any pain left. It was still sore when she pressed her fingers to her temple. "Who are you?" She was sitting on the bed in Captain McEntire's room, but he was nowhere to be seen.

"If you need a label, I suppose I'm the captain, but you can just call me Kale. I was hoping the smell of food would bring you around. You've been out for nearly two days." He set the bowl of porridge on the bed next to her.

"Two days?"

She had been asleep for two whole days? That was nearly the same amount of time she had been aboard the Rossut. Were they back at port in Aarilya? By the gentle rocking of the boat she thought not. She hoped they weren't heading somewhere else. She had seen Captain McEntire, or rather Mr. McEntire she supposed, at the Aarilyan port, but that may not be their normal berth.

"Your dress is on the chair there. I'll let you change—if you don't need anything else?" She shook her head. "I'll be right outside the door. Just knock on it once you're finished." He stepped outside, shuting the door quietly behind him. She could question him when she was fully dressed.

She got out of bed to fetch her dress, the one Maria had chosen for her. Tears welled up in her eyes as she remembered what Captain McEntire had said—or rather, Mr. McEntire, she supposed. It was hard to accept that Maria was gone. That everyone was gone. They had died. Maria ... Maria was dead. Tears spilled down Lillian's cheeks. She'd let go of Maria's hand, and now she was dead. Lillian slipped to her knees and sobbed silently into the pale fabric of the dress. She stayed like that awhile, as the grief and guilt racked her body.

Finally, when her eyes were empty, she took a ragged breath and stood tall as she attempted to channel her inner book heroine. She had to face whoever had saved her. Had to find out where they were and when she could get back to Aarilya. She wasn't sure what she was going to do once she was there, but she would think about that later. She no longer had a position with the De Sansol's, she had the freedom she had always wanted. But she had very little funds to get by on until she found a new position, and no letter of reference from an employer. Perhaps she could sell a few of her novels. The thought made her a bit sad. She would figure something out.

Lillian pulled the dress up over her chemise and tried to lace it up. She got a few strings tightened but could reach no further on her own. She sighed; she would need help. Especially when her body was still sore from being thrown around the ocean. She knocked softly on the back of the door, and it opened immediately.

"I need some help," she said, her eyes down as embarrassment spread across her cheeks.

It wasn't proper for a man to assist a woman in dressing, but she was fairly certain there were no other women aboard the ship. She turned her back to him and pulled her chestnut waves out of the way. After all that had happened in the past days, she was surprised the bow had stayed secure. For a moment they stood there, neither moving. Then she felt the warmth of his fingers through the thin fabric of her chemise . Her cheeks flushed further at the thought of a man's fingers being so close to her bare skin. He laced up the dress quicker than she had expected, leading her to imagine he had a fair amount of previous experience, which deepened her blush.

"You should eat," he said. "It's been at least three days since your last meal."

As if her body had just come to the same conclusion, her stomach tightened with hunger. He turned to leave again, but she set her hand on his arm, stopping him. He turned, a brow raised.

"Please, can you stay with me? If you do not have other duties to attend to, I mean. Or ... send someone else in. I just ... I don't want to be alone right now. Perhaps not Mr. McEntire, though."

"I can stay. For a bit," he said. She dropped her hand. "But you'll answer my questions."

"Thank you." She sat on the bed. "I have some questions of my own." The smell of the food still nauseated her, but she was ravenous, so she forced herself to eat.

"You are a De Sansol?" He held her gaze as she took a small spoonful of the porridge.

"Why is that hard for anyone to believe?" she asked. The smell of the plain porridge wafted to her nose and caused her stomach to tighten again, but she took the bite anyways.

"Did Johnny ask you that already?"

"Not here. I met Mr. McEntire on the docks. He questioned my lineage then as well."

"You met Mr. McEntire on the docks?" His brows furrowed angrily, then shifted into bland curiosity.

"Yes." She hesitated. The memory of their encounter flashed in her mind. Mr. McEntire had known the family's name when she had mentioned which ship they were boarding. Kale nodded as he contemplated.

"Was I truly alone?" She turned her gaze back at him, tears threatening to spill over once again. It was hard to ask, but she had to know.

"Yes. You were floating on a piece of wood. You must have been floating for a while. There wasn't any other wreckage around you. Was your ship attacked?"

"I do not believe so. I think it was the weather. We ... we sailed right into the hurricane, and it sank the ship." She took another spoonful of porridge.

"Why would a ship with civilians on it sail directly into a hurricane?" His tone was tinged with alarm and ... suspicion? She hesitated. But Dall was dead; there was no longer any reason for her to lie.

"The captain. He was chasing a band of pirates."

He leaned forward. "And your family believed this?"

"Just me."

"Why you?"

"Because he told me. I had my suspicions. He knew this, so he told me it was true. Perhaps only a portion of his truth though, to keep me from questioning. He threatened me not to tell the others."

"How?"

"He was not specific. There was no need to be. He said he'd given up the search because of the weather, but I knew when the storm got worse that he'd lied. I was worried about what would happen if we caught up to the pirates, but I never considered ... I never thought the storm would sink the ship." She looked away, a tear slipping down.

"It's rare to find someone outside the military who believes in pirates." He leaned back once more, trying to lighten the mood.

"The captain called them mercenaries. But it does not matter what we call them. They're thieves and murderers," she said angrily.

Kale laughed so loudly it startled her. "You sound like you have a lot of experience with these thieves and murderers."

"I read," she snapped.

He continued to laugh. "Those are just stories. They aren't real. *This* is real. *We* are real. And if we were murderers, would we have pulled you from the ocean?" he asked.

He was teasing her. How could he be teasing her when the pirates were part of the reason their snip had sunk, part of the reason everyone she knew had drowned.

She stood up angrily. "I don't see what you find so funny."

"I'm not joking, Miss De Sansol." But he was still smiling. "We are in fact the very pirates your Captain Davis was hunting down. Have been for some time. And to think we were at the same port for days. But he's obviously not too sharp if he led his entire crew, including civilians, into a hurricane."

She raised her hand to strike him, but he caught it, his gray eyes turned stormy. She tried to wrench free. He held fast.

"I see you hold a lot of anger toward us, but you're going to have to let that go, girl. You are going to be here for a long while. And it's not us you should be angry at. It's not our fault the idiot sank the ship. In fact, do you recall seeing him before you knocked your pretty little head? Because I would bet my ship that, coward that he is, he wasn't even on board when the storm hit."

She remembered looking for Dall when they had first come on deck. She hadn't seen him. She'd assumed he was there, but there were too many men, and the weather was too harsh. It had never occurred to her that he might have abandoned them.

Kale released her arm, and she steadied herself on the chair. She never should have let Dall threaten her like that. Perhaps if she had said something, they could have saved the ship. She and Jeremy could have done something together.

"It's no use blaming yourself, either," Kale said, as if he could hear her thoughts. "Captain Davis is a vicious son of a bitch. You aren't the first person he's put in danger, and you won't be the last. I think you'll realize the navy isn't always the hero." He turned to leave.

"Wait," she called after him. He paused. "Why am I to stay on board a while? Surely we aren't that far from land? If it's been two days we should be near Aarilya, shouldn't we?" she asked, a pleading note in her voice. He grinned as he stood.

"I told you; we're pirates. And we do what pirates do best—hunt treasure. Now, this particular adventure requires a woman of noble birth, Miss De Sansol. And I suggest you do what you're told while you're here, or we won't be quite so ... accommodating. Finish your food. Someone will come and show you back to your cabin."

"What would you need a noble woman for on a treasure hunt?" she nearly shrieked. Panic was rising once more as her fears were coming true. They weren't headed back to Aarilya. She had no idea where they were headed, or where they were currently. She would be trapped aboard this ship until this man gave her permission to leave. The freedom she had thought she had gained was being ripped away from her. This ship was nothing more than another cage.

"That's none of your concern at the moment," he said.

"You can't be serious!" She gasped. "You must take me back to Aarilya!"

"Oh, must I?" He stepped back to face her, mere inches away.

"Y-yes!" She tried to take a step back, but her knees hit the frame of the bed. "A ship is no place for a lady. I need to return home." She straightened and stuck her chin out in an act of false bravado.

He chuckled. His eyes flicked to her cheeks, clearly reveling in her reaction, which only deepened her color. "I'm sure you'll make it home. Eventually. Think of this as a little adventure, m'lady." He made a mock bow as he stressed the last part, then turned on his heel and left.

"Wait!" she called, but he was already gone.

Chapter Seven

Lillian could never have imagined that she would end up a prisoner on a pirate ship. Just a few days ago, pirates had been something that only existed in her novels. She was not sure how many men were aboard, but there was no way to escape in the middle of the ocean. And so far, they did not seem the merciful type. If she revealed she was not of noble birth, they may maroon her. Or worse, throw her overboard, here and now. The things they might force her to do ... Her cheeks heated at the thought. No. For now she would keep up the ruse until she could plan her escape. That's what a heroine would do.

The door opened, and Mr. McEntire walked in, smiling as usual. She wiped her eyes and sat a bit straighter.

"Good afternoon. Are you going to finish that? I like my girls with some meat on their bones, you know." He twirled her hair playfully. She pulled away. "Aw, did Kale upset you? He can be rather good at that."

"I'm finished. Are you going to show me back to my room?"

"That's what the captain said." He said *captain* as if it hurt him to do so. "But I was thinking something different. You've slept enough. How about we take a tour of the ship? She may be quite a bit smaller than your previous vessel, but I can guarantee she has a lot more personality." He held out his hand in invitation.

She hesitated, but he was right. She didn't want to sleep, and she definitely didn't want to be stuck alone in that small cabin. If she truly was going to be here for a while, it wouldn't hurt to get to know the ship. Particularly if she wanted to escape.

"Fine." She stood, ignoring his hand.

He chuckled. "I like 'em feisty too." It only took him two steps before he was in front of her, opening the door. "M'lady. What's your name, anyhow?"

"Lillian."

"Lillian. Pretty. I like Lilly better, though. It makes me imagine a beautiful flower blossomi—"

She spun to face him. "It is Lillian. *Never* Lilly," she spat. She'd never liked that nickname, but Maria insisted on using it. Hearing it now only made her heart ache.

He put his hands up, retreating half a step. "Lillian it is." She waited for a snide comment. When none came, she turned back and they continued walking through the ship.

"So, this is the deck," he said blandly. "I'm sure you've seen one before. And you met Kidd already." The same young man leaned against the mast, this time standing, along with another man. He flashed his crooked smile as Mr. McEntire introduced him. "He's on watch this morning."

His skin and eyes were a dark contrast to his long, light-colored braids. He wore a shirt and trousers, same as Kidd, but they were both tan. There didn't seem to be any consistency between the crew's uniforms. So very unlike the crew of the *Rossut*.

"What is he on watch for?" Lillian asked. If she could get some information on the watch schedule, it could help her plan her escape.

"Anything and everything. Keeps an eye on the weather, lets Kale know if any other ships are coming near."

"Will he be out here all day?"

"I'm takin' over," Chase answered, his pointed chin dimpled with his smile.

"And you're out in the sun all day?" she asked.

"No one specific keeps watch during daylight, most of the men are out here anyways." Johnny said.

She filed that away.

On the far side of the ship, a wide staircase between two doors led up to another deck.

"That leads to the sleeping quarters." He motioned to the door on the right. "You don't want to wander down there unless you'd like to catch a bunch of men in their skivvies." He grinned. "This over here is the galley." He opened the door to the left. She could hear men laughing and yelling. "Most of the men are in there now. It's breakfast time."

She stepped inside, and almost immediately it became quiet, all except one man who continued to laugh until someone smacked his arm. They stared at her. A little more than ten men sat on benches around a large table. Each of them wore clothes similar to the Kidd's, most worse for the wear.

"Good morning, boys." Mr. McEntire walked in behind her. "I know you all aren't well-versed in manners, but is this any way to greet a lady?" The men laughed, but Mr. McEntire was serious. He glared at them, and all at once they scrambled to get over the benches and onto their feet. Each shouted over the next some variation of "Good morning, miss."

"That's better." Mr. McEntire smiled. "This is Lillian De Sansol. You are all aware that she will be on board for a while. Kale and

I expect everyone to treat her well. And if you have a problem with that, you can shove it." He smiled.

"Can she cook?" a thin man asked. "I can't bear another bite of Eddie's food." They all laughed.

"If you don't like it, you can starve!" the other man—Eddie, she assumed—yelled. He was the one that had continued to laugh when she walked in. His build was stocky, and his arms were thick with muscle. They were covered from shoulder to knuckle in various tattoos. If she had happened upon someone like him at the docks, she probably would have walked another path just to avoid eye contact. But his grin was disarming in its genuineness as he slapped one of the other men on the back.

"Now, now," Mr. McEntire called to settle the men. "This here is a genuine lady. I doubt she can do much of anything." The men roared with laughter again.

Lillian prickled. Having served a noble family for most of her life, she was anything but useless. In fact, she was quite proud of the skills she had picked up and curated under the De Sansol's employ.

"Excuse me!" she said loudly. It fell quiet once more. "I can do a great many things, thank you."

"I'm afraid drinking tea at a house party won't come in handy here. Although if you know how to stitch, that could be helpful," he joked. The men roared with laughter, including Mr. McEntire.

She huffed with frustration and turned to leave, expecting Mr. McEntire to follow, but it he was too busy laughing at his own jest. She groaned angrily once more. The sun was almost fully risen now, glistening off the ocean. It was almost blinding. She walked over to the rail, stopping a few feet from it as uneasiness filled her stomach. Thoughts of the storm and being flung overboard immediately filled her head and she took step back.

The wind in her hair was a nice relief after being cooped up below deck. She untied the ribbon and let her hair fall. Running the ribbon through her fingers reminded her of Maria. She thought of letting it go, so that it might get lost in the wind and the ocean.

"Going to jump?" The voice startled her. She looked around to find the source. Kale stood behind her, watching.

"It would be better than being around your crew," she said shortly.

His brows furrowed as he stepped closer. "My crew will not harm you," he said quietly.

"So you say. How am I to trust a pirate?" She pushed past him, heading back to the stairs.

He followed. "We've done nothing to show otherwise."

"You've kidnapped me!" She turned angrily to face him. They stood just at the top of the stairs. He held her eyes, his own stormy as they shifted and contemplated. The ship creaked as it rode the waves in the silence.

"Temporarily," he said icily.

She scoffed, crossing her arms. "There is no *temporary* in a kidnapping. Either you're holding me against my will or you're not. And in this case, you and your filthy crew are." She glared. His jaw tightened as he stepped closer, only a few inches from her. She wanted to step away, but she summoned all her courage and held fast. She was the heroine of her own story and she would not wither beneath a scoundrel of a pirate.

"What is it you need?" he asked.

"I want to go home!" she cried.

"That's not possible." His eyes were still stormy, but he sighed, and there was something else there. Guilt?

"I will not stay on this ship with a bunch of ... of mercenary rapists!"

He growled then and advanced a step, knowing she would retreat—right into the wall. "This is what you wanted isn't it? For one of us to live up to your fanatical expectations so you can cast us as the villains in your story?"

He planted his hands on either side of her, his face only a breath from hers. She flinched, putting her palms against his chest in an attempt to push him to arm's length. The warm muscles of his chest shifted beneath her palms as he moved to her ear. "Well, villains have stories too. They have families and friends and motivations, same as you girl." His eyes didn't leave hers. Didn't so much as blink. "The only difference is the villain is willing to risk everything to get what they need. Even themselves."

"Step back, sir," she said through gritted teeth.

He smirked, leaning in, easily pushing past the resistance of her hands, their faces only a breath apart. "Maybe if you took the time to act like a human, you'd realize we're not the villains."

Then, just like that, he left. Lillian stood there stunned as she watched him walk away. A tear dropped onto her arm. For someone who so vehemently claimed not to be a villain, he was terribly good at playing the part. Her chest heaved as she caught her breath and she slipped down the stairs to her cabin.

By early evening, there was a knock on her door.

"Go away." She lay beneath her blanket on the small cot as rays from the early evening sun slanted through the small porthole window. She had been watching as they lazily spread across her small cabin all afternoon. She had contemplated the different avenues for escape, but there was nothing she could do until they made port somewhere. She had even considered taking the small rowboat. But the truth of it was, she had no idea where she was or how far from land they were.

And a rowboat was too close to the water for her liking.

No, she was completely at the mercy of these pirates until she was closer to land.

"Supper's ready," a male voice called. She didn't recognize it as Johnny or Kale.

"No, thank you," she said.

There was a pause. "Kale would like you to join us in the galley." He sounded a bit nervous.

"No. Thank you," she said more firmly. Another pause, then he shuffled away. Staying in her room was a small rebellion, but the only one she had at the moment. A few minutes later there was another knock. She ignored it. Something was set on the floor, and the footsteps receded. She waited a few more minutes before cracking the door open. A bowl of rice and some bread sat on the floor just outside the door. She darted a look around before taking the food into her cabin.

At least she wouldn't starve while she isolated herself.

Lillian stood at the small mirror the next morning, attempting to lace up her dress on her own. She had been trying all morning and had almost gotten to the top after taking the dress off and lacing it most of the way up, then squeezing back into it. She decided it was laced high enough to be proper and tied a sloppy bow. Her arms ached as she lowered them and she sighed at the sight of her messy hair. She needed a brush. She had run her fingers through as much as she could without causing more frizz. Perhaps a braid would work best to prevent any further damage. She tied it off with her yellow ribbon, then sat on the edge of her bed.

She would have to go out eventually. She had been thinking about Captain Kale's words all morning. As much as she hated to admit it, he was right. None of them had done anything to harm her so far, aside from calling her useless. She pursed her lips. And though it had felt good to rebel a bit by hiding her in her cabin, if she stayed in her cabin every day, she would not find a chance to escape. No. Her best option was to try and get them on her side until she could find a way off this rocking piece of wood. She straightened her shoulders. That was it then. The only way to escape was to befriend the pirates. If she could hold her tongue during one of Maria's tantrums, then she could certainly be civil with a few bloodthirsty mercenaries. She sighed as she exited her small cabin and headed up to the deck.

This late in the morning, no one was standing watch. In fact, no one was on deck at all. She walked to the railing and looked out over the ocean. It was crisp and clear today, the sun shining and only a light breeze to ruffle her hair. She could never get tired of watching the sea. Despite the churning it caused in her stomach, she couldn't deny the beauty in the vastness.

She thought about heading to the galley to see if anyone was in there, or maybe to find some breakfast. Her stomach growled. Then something caught her eye on the upper deck. She shielded her eyes to see better and saw Kale standing at the helm, watching her. A hat shaded him from the sun. Not the person she wanted to start with. In fact, he was the last person she had hoped to be cordial with. But walking away now would seem a hostile move. She sighed as she approached the stairs. She stopped at the bottom, where the mast blocked the sun, so she could see him.

"Morning," he said softly. All traces of the anger from yesterday were gone. There was a shift in his demeanor. He was almost... soft today. She felt herself relax a bit, that same strange calmness she had felt that first day washing over her as their eyes met. As if she had known him before, but she couldn't recall ever seeing his face.

"Good morning," she said, equally as soft, leaning against the railing.

"Trying to get your bearings?"

"I was admiring the way the sun makes the ocean sparkle."

He blinked, taken aback by her answer. He had been expecting a smart retort, or outright anger as she had yesterday. But her anger had faded as well.

"It's good, that you can still appreciate the beauty out here after you've seen the destruction. Not many people can do that." He looked back toward the ocean. He seemed much more at ease out here, at the helm, the calculated steel replaced with concentrated ease as he watched the waters. The man in Mr. McEntire's quarters yesterday had been the pirate captain—this was just a man content to be where he was. Maybe she could befriend him after all. Maybe she could do it quickly enough to convince him to let her go at the next port.

She looked back out over the water. "I never knew the ocean could be that powerful. It was quite frightening. But it doesn't make it any less beautiful today."

Her stomach growled again.

"Did anyone bring you breakfast this morning? Everyone's in the galley now, if you're hungry." But she was hesitant, after yesterday.

"I am not sure I want to go there, alone."

"Did someone upset you yesterday?" His brows furrowed. Obviously forgetting he was the one who'd pinned her to the wall. She blushed at the memory.

"What happened?" That was almost a growl.

"Nothing. Only ... they were making fun of me."

"They do like a bit of teasing." His shoulders relaxed as he leaned against the rail and looked down at her. "Being on the ocean so long can get boring if you don't have a sense of humor. What were they saying?"

"It was Mr. McEntire, mostly. He said I was ... useless."

"Useless? That doesn't sound like Johnny."

"Well, he didn't use that exact word," she conceded.

"What did he use?" The corner of his mouth tipped up. It made him look much younger, boyish even.

"He said that because I was a lady I cannot do much of anything. And drinking tea at parties does not count."

It did sound silly repeating it now.

"Now, that does sound like Johnny. And I'm afraid he's right. Tea party etiquette won't help you here."

"I can do many things," she said again, but without the anger.

"What sort of things can you do, then?"

"I can sew. I can read, clean, garden. Cook a bit. I'm not afraid to get my hands dirty. I—"

"That's enough." He chuckled. "I'm sure you can do many more things. Unfortunately, your understanding of work may be quite different than ours, *Lady* Lillian."

"I can help with any task I am given." She pursed her lips again, making him laugh once more.

"You are very stubborn. It's cute. You will have plenty of chances to prove yourself." He stared at her, waiting for her to object.

"I fear I would become rather bored if I were not participating," she said. This playful banter was good, easy even. She would need trust on her side if she was to escape.

"Are you sure you're a lady?" He chuckled once more.

She thought about what Maria might do if she were asked to work. She would whine and pout until one of the men offered to do it for her. But Lillian was too strong-willed to act like a child, even in her charade as a lady. It was an exciting notion, actually, to join the crew in their duties. It would give her a chance to observe the men and find out just what type of people these pirates were. She could learn their routine, the watch shifts, and their destinations.

"Anyhow, enjoy your freedom today, because tomorrow you join the ranks." He turned to leave.

"Wait," she called after him.

"I've got matters to deal with up here, girl. If you want to keep talking, you best come up," he called over his shoulder. She hiked up her dress a bit and followed him up the stairs.

Chapter Eight

Kale stood at the helm. His dark hair blew with the wind, which was much fiercer up there than below. He wore clothes similar to Kidd's: a plain white shirt—the top few buttons were left unfastened, and the long sleeves rolled to his elbows—tucked into dark black trousers. But he also wore a set of matching suspenders, and a dusty black three-cornered hat. A black overcoat had been tossed to the side near the helm, similar to the blue one Johnny had worn when they had met ashore. His clothes didn't have any holes, but they were still quite worn.

"Well?" he asked. "Were you going to converse, or did you come up just to stare at me?" The corners of his lips tipped up.

"Your clothes need patching. So do the other men's, I'm assuming," she retorted, ignoring his flirtatious remarks.

"Yes." He chuckled. "An obvious result of the lack of a woman aboard the ship. We had a man who knew how to sew, taught from his mother, but he's no longer with us." He looked sad, almost resentful. "That will be one of your duties while aboard. As you can see, you'll have your work cut out for you." He ran a finger through a somewhat large hole along the back of his shirt sleeve she hadn't noticed.

She clicked her tongue in disapproval. "With all of you men here, no one bothered to even try and learn?"

"One. He sliced his finger on the needle, got gangrene, and died," he said, straight-faced.

"That's not possible." She laughed.

"It's nice to hear a woman's laugh. And it is possible, just highly unlikely," he said. "Truth is, we can patch a sail fine enough, but lack the skill, nor the patience, for the finer needlework. And going into a harbor town and having it done isn't the best use of our funds or our time. So long as we keep warm, these rags serve their purpose." It was quiet. Kale watched from the helm as she stood against the rail. She reveled in the comfortable silence as the wind blew the ocean mist through her hair. The longer she was at sea, the curlier her hair had become. The moisture in the air agreed with it.

"Why does Mr. McEntire call you Kale and not captain?" she asked.

"All the men do. You'll find we're rather informal. Sometimes the men will call me captain. Most times not. They follow my rules—that's what's important. You can refer to us however you please, of course, but everyone here will prefer their first name. Especially Johnny."

"And Kidd? Is that his real name?" She inclined her head. She assumed they called him Kidd because he was so young.

"Who knows? That's the name he gave when he joined, and that's what we've called him since. We don't ask questions. When someone joins the crew, we're only interested in who they are now, not their past."

"Kale! You up there?" Johnny yelled from below, a note of urgency in his voice.

"Yeah." Kale winked at her. "What'd you do now?"

She smiled at his playful demeanor. "I didn't do anything."

Johnny started up the stairs. "That girl ran off and now I can't find her—Oh. This isn't funny." He looked almost angry. "You weren't in your quarters. I thought you'd jumped ship or something. Then Kale might have *actually* killed me."

"Yeah, I probably would have," Kale joked, but the two passed a look that was quite serious. "Seems we have a new seamstress aboard. Lillian has graciously offered to spend her time patching our clothes."

"See, I told you your sewing skills would be handy." Johnny smiled. Lillian was not impressed; she was still sore from his earlier accusations.

"You know nothing of my skills Mr. McEntire, I may be completely horrid at sewing. And according to you, I have no other skills, so you may as well throw me overboard now."

"Aw. We wouldn't throw you over. We went through all that trouble of saving you, and we've much bigger plans for you." Kale chuckled as he played along.

"Well now, you heard her, Captain." Johnny smiled, but there was a devilish glint in his eye. "She wants to be thrown overboard."

"Johnny," Kale warned as Johnny started toward Lillian. She stiffened at the warning and looked toward Kale, fear rising, but Johnny had already closed the distance between them and scooped her up.

"What are you doing?" His smile grew as she started to struggle. "You're going to drop me. Put me *down*!"

Fear clamored through her body as he held her over the rails, ready to drop her into the churning ocean below. The knot in her stomach grew at an alarming rate. She couldn't get a breath in to tell him to stop, to beg him to put her down.

"Johnny!" Kale growled.

Johnny was watching her intently. The freezing black sea below thrashed against the boat. All the fear from the shipwreck, from being underneath that icy surface, water filling her lungs, welled up inside her. She screamed, clutching at his shirt, pressing herself into it.

His chuckle reverberated through his chest.

A moment later they were both jerked back. Kale grabbed hold of Lillian and set her on her feet next to him, his arm still around her waist. She hid her face against his shoulder, trying to control her tears. A gull screeched overhead as the waves below crashed against the side of the ship.

"What are you doing? Are you trying to kill her?" Kale pulled Lillian closer to him. She was shivering.

"I wasn't going to drop her, and even if I did, that water wouldn't kill her. You and I jump in all the time."

"She isn't us," Kale said.

"I was just having a little fun. It was a joke," Johnny huffed.

"No one else found it funny. Take the helm." Kale guided Lillian down the stairs to the deck below. He didn't even glance back to see if Johnny would follow his command. She was still shaking as they reached the bottom, but she was no longer crying. The last thing he needed was for Johnny to traumatize her.

"I'm sorry," she said quietly, looking toward the floor. Kale stopped walking. He pulled her face up so that she was looking at him. Her eyes, a soft blue that tugged at him the way the morning sky over the ocean did, were filled with sorrow and more than a little fear.

"Don't apologize. It wasn't your fault. Johnny has a sick sense of humor. He's lucky I didn't deck him right there. But I promise you, he won't do anything like that again. Not on my watch."

"I shouldn't have panicked like that." She looked away. The breeze dried the last of the tears from her cheeks.

"You nearly drowned just a few days ago. Even if that weren't the case, it's natural to be afraid when put in a situation such as that. You should feel no shame. Understand?" The smell of her wafted over him, of lilies and sunshine. He smiled at the irony.

Unable to resist with her so close, he ran a thumb along her jawline. The motion sent a shiver through her body. Their eyes locked for the slightest moment before she pulled her face from his grip, and took a step back. On instinct he reached for her, but the sound of the galley door opening had him stopping before he touched her. Most of the crew tumbled out of the galley then, having heard her scream. Kale looked to them.

"She's all right." He looked to her again. "You're safe now." His face shifted to a playful grin to try and soothe her. But the sight of her tearful, fear-stricken face would not leave him for a long while. "Let's get you to your quarters."

It had become quite cold as evening drew near and all Lillian wanted to do was sleep, though that's all she had done since she'd been rescued. If you can call it that. Her arms were bare as she no longer had any sort of cover up. She rubbed them beneath the covers to create a bit of warmth. She wished she had been wearing one of her uniforms, it would have been much warmer. Perhaps then she wouldn't have been pulled into this mess.

Kale—he had mentioned big plans for her before Johnny had assaulted her. She wondered what those plans were. What could she possibly offer in a treasure hunt? Or rather, what could a noble woman offer? Perhaps they assumed because a lady would be rich, she would be able to identify certain valuable items? Anyone from Southern Nelina could do that—they were known for their luxurious tastes. It had to have something to do with Atwood, but she couldn't imagine what.

She was lost in her own thoughts when there was a knock at the door. Not a knock really, but two precise raps. Her breath caught as she hurried to the door, but it was only Kale standing there. She had foolishly hoped it would have been someone else.

"Something wrong?" Kale asked, noting the change in her features. A dark wooden stove sat at his feet. She looked up at him questioningly, ignoring his concern. "It gets pretty cold around here. You need something to keep you warm. May I?" He raised a brow.

A pirate captain requesting to enter a cabin on his own ship? She nearly smirked as she stepped out of the way. He lifted the stove and brought it in. It looked to be quite heavy, but he carried it with ease, setting it down near her bed.

"I also brought these." He held out a light tan hat, a pair of brown pants, and a white shirt that was very nearly yellow, though thankfully long-sleeved. "They aren't pretty, but they are warm. You'll catch your death with your shoulders exposed like that in this sea air. And I can't imagine it's very comfortable. The hat'll keep the sun off your face."

"They'll do just fine, thank you. You didn't take them from someone, did you? I mean, no one is going to go cold for me, are they?"

"No." He chuckled, leaning against the wall. "They're extras. Been sitting in storage."

"Oh, good." She held each of the garments out in front of her and looked them over back and front. They weren't terrible looking. With a little stitching, she could even make them presentable.

"Are they of acceptable quality, my lady?"

"Well, I think they're from last season, but I guess they'll do." She folded them neatly and smoothed them out as she set them on the small table.

"Are you ready to meet the crew?"

"I thought I had." She turned to face him.

"Knowing Johnny, I'm sure it wasn't a proper introduction," Kale said with a chuckle as he pushed off the wall. His smell wafted through the room, sun and salt and . . . sandalwood.

"I suppose you're right."

"They're a little rough around the edges, but I think you'll get along just fine. Tonight, we celebrate. And tomorrow we'll see if you can keep up as well as you say."

"What are we celebrating?"

"That you're alive, of course. A lot of the crew didn't think you'd wake up from that fever. And out here, we'll take any chance to celebrate."

Lillian took a deep breath. The cacophony of male voices and smells assaulted her senses as she stood in the entryway of the galley. It was just as loud as it had been the day before, only growing louder as Kale entered. She had asked Kale to go in first so that she'd feel more comfortable. He'd laughed but agreed.

"Hey, Kale! Yer early!" A man with a very thick, red beard that matched the mop of curls on his head slapped him on the back as he walked past.

"Kale! Ya want me to deal you in? We're just about to start a new game." Another man, this one with hair on neither his face nor his head, held up a deck of cards. She recognized Kidd, and Eddie with his tattoos, and the other man with the light hair and dark skin ... Chase, she remembered. But the rest were a sea of faces. She didn't know how she was going to keep them all straight.

"No thanks, Rick, I've got other business first." He motioned to Lillian standing behind him. "Besides, it's about supper time."

"Aw, Eddie's cooking today. It won't be ready til the morn," The bald one, Rick, said. They laughed, including Kale. He had a nice laugh, deeper than she had imagined. She was surprised at how comforted she felt hearing others' joy. When teasing her wasn't the cause of it.

Lillian followed Kale through to the back of the room, past the table, until he stopped at a wooden counter. He picked up a small bell that hung from a post and rang it until everyone quieted down. She spotted Johnny sitting near the wall. Their eyes met; he didn't look the least bit apologetic. In fact, he still looked quite pleased with himself. She pursed her lips and looked away.

"All right now, everyone." Kale waited until it was completely quiet. "I would like to start this evening by pointing out the obvious fact that our lovely Miss Lillian De Sansol is alive." The room erupted with roars of approval. The commotion was so sudden she nearly jumped out of her skin. Kale waited for it to calm once more.

"She has survived a shipwreck!" Kale grabbed her hand and raised it in the air. The men yelled again joyously. "Floating around in the ocean for hours alone." Another roar, even louder than before. "A horrendous fever." Louder still, each of them stomping their feet on the ground and their drinks on the table.

Lillian discreetly covered her ears.

"And even our own Mr. McEntire's ill-found humor." Apparently only she noticed the sting in his voice. They all laughed. Johnny raised his glass as if toasting his own triumph.

"She isn't anything like we expected." Kale smiled at her, and something in her chest tightened beneath his gaze. "In fact, she has graciously appointed herself head seamstress. So, those on second shift tomorrow, if you need anything patched, fixed, taken in—or taken out—put your clothes in the empty cabin next to Lillian's. Once she's finished with those, the rest of you will bring yours. Understood?" The men cheered their approval. "Would you like to add anything, Lillian?"

It was odd to hear Kale say her name. Until now he had only addressed her as Miss or Miss De Sansol. Everyone stared at her expectantly.

"I, uh," she stuttered, taking in all the faces. She cleared her throat. "No, thank you." The men chuckled.

"All right, everyone's aware that this lady is part of our crew for now, so let's introduce ourselves. First names only—she has a bad habit of calling us Mister." He raised an eyebrow at her playfully as they laughed. They walked around the table as each of the men stood up, one by one.

"I'm Rick, miss," the bald man who had invited Kale to join their card game said. He was tall and had some bulk to him, but he wasn't large by any means. His face had some age to it, tanned from the sun and crinkled around his golden eyes. "And this here is my brother, Richard. But we call him Rich." He motioned to the man with the thick red beard. He was nearly identical to Rick, save for the beard. She wondered if they were twins. Both men clasped her hand in a tight shake.

"Nice to meet you." She smiled.

"Thomas," another man said. He bowed his head as he shook her hand. He was dark-skinned and had somewhat of an accent she didn't recognize. He wore a flatcap that covered his dark curls and jutted out a little over his eyes. It had a rather large tear in the front.

"Nice to meet you, Thomas. You bring me that hat with your clothes, and I can fix that tear."

"Oh, I don't know about that. I'd like to keep it with me." He bobbed his head in gratitude, nonetheless.

"Thomas and that stupid hat. He never takes it off—he damn near sleeps with it!" Rich yelled. His deep, hearty laugh resonated through the room. His red bear shook with each chuckle and Lillian had to suppress a laugh of her own at the site.

"Well, I tell you what," she offered. "You bring me that hat when you aren't busy, and I'll fix it right there in front of you."

His eyes lit up as he nodded his gratitude.

"Well, I guess I'm next." Kidd stood up. "You already know my name. And I know you are wondering, so I'll tell ya, I'm the youngest on board at nineteen." Lillian was surprised. She had assumed he was older than her own twenty-three years.

"Not for four more days!" The man next to him smacked Kidd across the back harshly.

"Close enough!"

"Close enough ain't done. A man don't pretend he's a man. He is or he ain't." The man laughed heartily at his own joke. He had short, thick black hair covered by a cap, and a black beard so full and curly you could hardly see his lips. "I'm Jack," he said without getting up, and went back to drinking.

"I'm Antoine. But everyone calls me Tony." Tony's dark hair was slicked back neatly. He took her hand and kissed the top. Her eyes widened at the intimate gesture. Then she remembered she was supposed to be a noble, and that was a customary greeting to a noble lady. She dipped her head slightly in return as she had seen Maria and the other nobles do. Only she wore a smile as she did, rather than the bored, flat expression they all had.

"All right, Tony." Kale patted him on the shoulder, but Tony held tight. "No need to scare her off on the first day."

"I apologize, I don't mean to scare her." His dark green eyes held hers. "In my hometown, this is a sign of respect when in the presence of a lady, especially a beautiful one such as yourself."

A blush crept across her cheeks. She had never been called beautiful before. Though she knew she was attractive by typical standards, her position warranted her more unnoticeable than anything. "Thank you, Tony. It is lovely to meet you."

"And I'm Dave," a large man said energetically. His curly blond hair covered his face and stuck out from beneath his cloth hat. He pumped her hand, a huge smile splayed across his round face.

"Nice to meet you, Dave," Lillian laughed.

"And these fellows are Chase and Landry." Kale introduced the last two men sitting at the table. They both stood and tipped their heads to her.

"It's nice to meet you."

"It's our pleasure," Landry, said. He was as tall as Chase, and thin, but had a bit of muscle on him. His hair was golden, with streaks of light brown woven down as it stopped at the base of his neck, his eyes were soft brown, flecked with a gold nearly the same color as his hair.

"Yes, our pleasure," Chase reiterated as they sat down.

"And last, is Eddie. Our chef for the evening." The whole room shouted their distaste at the tattooed man.

"If you don't like it, you don't gotta eat it!" Eddie sneered. "It's very nice to meet you, Miss Lillian." His sneer turned to a smile immediately. "If any'a these men give ya a hard time, ya let me know. I'll take care of 'em for ya." He handed her a bowl of what looked like a crude stew, and a hunk of bread.

"Thank you. This smells lovely."

"Thanks, Eddie." Kale took a bowl from the counter. "Let's eat!" He raised his bowl in the air signaling to the men. He guided Lillian to an open spot against the wall as the men surrounded the counter.

"It's not fancy cooking, but it keeps our bellies full."

She took her first bite. It was bland, but not terrible.

"Eddie refuses to use spices. Says they're a valuable commodity to trade if we're ever in a pinch. He's right." He smiled. "But I think I'd rather have the food with a bit of flavor."

"You don't have a cook on board?" she asked as she took another bite of the tasteless stew.

"No, we are a band of misfits. We have a routine, and it fits us well. We all share the workload," he said. She looked around at all the different men. They were quite the group of misfits. And most were in jolly spirits as they teased and wrestled. It was not what she had been expecting. Kale had seemed almost proud of them as he introduced each one. They were a far cry from the pillaging pirates she had read about.

But still, they had kidnapped her.

"What about you? What do you do?" Her eyes met his.

He held her stare a moment and she felt the electricity in the air caress her skin, as she had the first time she had seen him in Mr. McEntire's cabin. Abruptly, he went back to stirring his stew around before answering.

"What kind of duties?" She dipped her bread into her own stew and took a healthy bite.

"Duties such as kidnapping a noble-born lady, planning our next heist, and other matters that don't concern a lady such as yourself." He smiled as he said it, but there was a clear warning in his tone not to pry. It was clear he wasn't ready to reveal everything to her just yet.

She could dig a little deeper into that another time. She changed the subject. "Mr. McEn—Johnny doesn't seem to respect you like the others do." Johnny still sat on the other end of the table against the far wall. A few men had joined him, and they were playing a card game around their supper bowls.

"He has his reasons," Kale said curtly.

Perhaps it would be best to focus on eating for now. Their conversation was growing more bitter by moment. Or perhaps a change of subject.

"Does your ship have a name?" she asked.

"*Stardust*."

"*Stardust*? An odd name for a ship that sails the seas."

"It is a saying we have onboard: 'From stardust we came, to stardust we remain.' It has two meanings: When we die we return to stardust, but also, no matter where this life takes us, we will always remain a part of this crew."

"That is quite beautiful." It hit her how close they all were. They acted like a family, she realized. Not just a family who were obligated to care for each other either, but one they found and cultivated into this wonderful group. Something she no longer had. Never had, really. Not in the way these men did. The emptiness she had felt in her chest aboard the Rossut returned twofold.

This is what she'd been looking for. Longing for. What she had been missing since the day her parents had died. She twisted the gold band around her finger absently at the thought. This is what she needed to find for herself. But could she find it in Aarilya?

No. She had no ties to anyone there.

"See, there? If our own lady of the ship can stomach my stew, the rest'a ya can't complain," Eddie teased from his spot a few places down the bench. She smiled as the others groaned and shot back their own retorts.

Perhaps... she could find a place here. Kale had told them to treat her as one of their own, had said they would include her in their daily routine. As strange as the thought seemed, perhaps it could work. Excepting her fear of the waters.

Perhaps not.

She frowned as she finished the last bite of her supper and stood. "If you don't mind, I would like to retire for the evening."

Kale seemed surprised but nodded his assent.

Chapter Nine

Lillian rolled over grudgingly and pulled the blanket tight against the chill. She wasn't sure what had woken her, but she was not ready to leave the warm bed.

"Morning, sunshine." She sat up quickly, clutching the blanket to her chest. Johnny was sitting on the edge of the bed. "Rise and shine."

Though she was wearing the old pair of clothes that Kale had given her to keep warm in the night, they were a size too large and hung loosely on her. She wanted to adjust them a bit before she wore them in the presence of others.

"Aw. There's no need to cover yourself in front of me." His blue eyes twinkled.

"Why are you here?" she said with a great deal of irritation. It was far too early for his antics.

A mischievous grin spread across his lips as he stood. "You want to be part of this crew, don't you? We were all up a half hour ago. I am here to escort you to pick up the clothes you'll be patching."

"I thought Kale wanted them to put in the next cabin."

"Yes, that's where they are."

"Then why do I need an escort?" She frowned, her brows furrowing in confusion. They hadn't bothered keeping tabs on her so far. Certainly not when she wasn't even leaving the confines of the hall outside her cabin. Had she done something to cause suspicion?

"Because we've docked, and you're certain to run ashore at the first opportunity." He motioned grandly to the door, still smiling. *Oh.* She wondered where they were. She vaguely recalled the continents outside Aarilya from Maria's history lessons. Uriba shared the western border to Aarilya and the eastern border with Arbor and kept to themselves, rarely allowing visitors. Arbor was known for its forests and canopied harbor, only a few days from Aarilya by ship, Southern Nelina for its sandstone and pearl buildings. Or they could be at the various small islands in between, which seemed the most likely. With the days she had been unconscious, she couldn't be sure how far they had traveled.

"Where is Kale?" she asked cautiously.

"Busy."

"Are you going to watch me all day?"

"No, m'lady. I'm going ashore with everyone else."

"I don't understand."

"Well—"

"Johnny. Why does every task I give you take three times as long?" Kale's voice came from the hallway. He appeared in the doorway, wearing different clothes: slacks and something close to a gentleman's jacket. They were far nicer than his usual attire but still out of date. He cut a nice figure in them. He sighed when he saw Lillian still bundled in the blankets on the bed. "You have no tact, man." He pointed his stare at Johnny. "We are on a schedule,

Lillian. Do you want to be stuck in here with nothing to do all day, or would you like to fetch the clothing?"

"Am I to be locked in?" she said indignantly, earning another sigh from Kale.

"Yes."

"And what if I get hungry?" She didn't actually care. She was angry that she was going to be locked in a small room on an empty ship, and she knew asking questions would delay it, if only a little longer. Besides, if someone was tasked with bringing her food, perhaps she could sneak past him and escape. To where, she wasn't sure. Perhaps pushing Kale's buttons wasn't the best path to earning his trust, but right now she wasn't thinking about consequences.

"Breakfast's on its way, and we'll be back before lunch," he said impatiently. "In fact, here it is now." Dave walked in with a bowl and a big smile. Damn. No chance to slip out easily, then.

"Good morning, Lillian. How did you sleep?" he asked brightly as he set the bowl down next to her. His blond hair hung freely today with no cap on. She smiled brightly back.

"Dave," Kale said sternly. "Time."

"Oh. Yes. See you later, Lillian."

"Last chance," Johnny said. "Better hurry."

"What if I finish all the clothing and need to get more?" she pushed.

Kale's lips tightened. "Goodbye, Lillian. We will see you this afternoon."

They turned to leave.

"Wait!" She jumped up from the bed, no longer caring about her clothes being two sizes too big, and hurried into the next room. The room was sparce and had no furnishings. A few barrels lined the back wall and permeated the air with the smell of salt and moist wood, while the piles of clothing filled the center.

Both men watched—one impatient, the other seemingly amused—as she dug through the mounds of clothing to choose what she wanted to work on. The items had been separated according to whether they needed to be patched, hemmed, or taken in.

"I hope you aren't planning to attend anything formal while on shore," she said smugly.

"And why is that?"

"Your clothes." She scooped up the pile she had created and faced him. "They're much nicer than your previous ones, but they're still run down. And it wouldn't matter anyhow, if they weren't run down, because they are two seasons out of style. Anyone at a party would spot you immediately." They followed her back to her room.

"Well then, I guess it's a good thing I'm not going to any parties." Kale shut the door, locking it with a click. Her shoulders slumped, and she dropped the pile of clothes on the floor.

Locked in.

On the chair next to her bed, someone had left a small sewing kit. It wasn't in great condition, but it would do for now. Although she would likely need more thread. She wished she could have told Kale that before they went ashore.

She walked to door and jiggled the handle. If it was open, she could use the request for more thread as an excuse if she was caught. It didn't budge. Grabbing the small sewing kit, she surveyed the items. A needle would be too small to pick the lock, but the scissors may work. She pulled the small pair out of the kit and went back to the door. She slid one blade into the keyhole and wiggled it around haphazardly. After a few attempts she heard a small click. Her heart leaped. Hopeful, she pulled on the door handle. Nothing. Sliding the scissors out, she realized what the click was: She had bent the tip off. She sighed as she set the scissors back in the kit and picked up the first garment, trousers with a gaping hole in the leg, and set to it. There would be no getting out until someone unlocked the door.

A few hours had passed, and after first fitting the clothes Kale had given her to a more proper size, she was through nearly half of the pile of clothing, most of which should have been thrown out years ago. But from what she'd seen, they probably couldn't afford new clothes every season. She laid another torn shirt across her lap to be patched, but before she started, she heard footsteps coming down the stairway. Soon after, there was a knock on the door. They must have returned.

"I do not know why you're knocking. You know I can't open it." She scowled, assuming it was Johnny being puckish. The key rattled, and the door opened. Thomas walked in, his flatcap still sat on his head.

"Sorry, Lillian, I thought it wouldn't be polite just to open the door."

"Oh, no, Thomas, don't apologize. I thought it was Johnny teasing. I didn't expect anyone to be back so soon."

He shook his head. "Oh, they aren't. I stayed behind to watch the ship. We can't leave it completely empty, or someone might try and steal it."

"I see. Have you been here this whole time? What brings you down now?"

"Well, you said you could fix my cap for me." He took his flatcap off his head. "Kale said not to open the door, but I figured since we were the only ones here and all, now would be good time."

She stared past him at the open door, contemplating her odds against him should he grab hold of her as she tried to slip past.

Sweet Thomas. She had promised to fix his cap. Perhaps once she was finished she could distract him and make her escape.

"Of course." She sighed and took the cap. He shut the door behind him.

"May I?" He motioned to the empty cot.

She nodded. Giving the cap a once over, she only found two small tears. There was only a small amount of thread of the same color, and she hoped it would be enough.

"You take good care of this cap," she said, threading her needle. "Does it mean a lot to you?"

"Yes ma'am. My mama gave it to me when I was a boy. She was real sick, and she wanted me to have something to remember her by, even though it was actually my father's cap. After she passed"—he made the sign of a cross over his chest—"I kept it by my bedside. It didn't fit me right til I was a nearly grown."

"That's sweet. You were young when she passed?"

"Yes, barely six years."

"That's when I lost my parents as well. It's funny, the things you remember. Only bits and pieces here and there. I remember the way my mother smelled, and the tilt of my father's smile." She finished up the last patch with a small amount of thread left over. "I wish I had something to like that to remember them by. I have this ring, but no special memories are tied to it." She held out her hand and wriggled the finger that held the simple band.

"They'll always be in your heart."

She handed the mended cap back to him. "Yes, that's true."

There was a ruckus up on deck, loud and rushed. She could hear Kale yelling.

"Uh oh," Thomas muttered as he put his cap on, saying a quick thank you as he walked out. He didn't bother to close the door, let alone lock it.

She decided to follow.

Up on deck, it was certainly a scene. Men rushed about, trying to pull the sails down and secure the ropes.

Kale was yelling commands in every direction. "Stand by to make sail! Lay aloft and loose topgallants! Clear away the jib!"

"What happened, Kale?" Thomas asked as he came on deck.

"That damn Stevenson! He caught up to us somehow." Kale yelled, showing more fury than she'd ever seen. It was even more frightening than one of Mrs. De Sansol's fits. He was heading toward the helm. She was almost knocked off her feet as the ship lurched forward but was able to steady herself. Her heart sank as she watched whichever port they were at slip farther away as the ship returned to sea.

"Damn it, Thomas!" Kale swore when he saw her standing there in the middle of the deck as all hell broke loose. "Go back down below, Lillian, or so help me ..." He didn't bother to enforce his command, continuing to the helm. She stayed where she was as the men hurried all around her. Their work was quick, but focused. She wasn't sure why they were all still in a rush. They'd gained quite a distance from the shore. Whatever trouble they had run into wouldn't be able to follow them now.

"Hit the deck!" Kale yelled fiercely.

It was then that Lillian saw the other ship. Twice the size of the *Stardust*.

With a loud whistle, a cannonball flew through the air. Someone grabbed Lillian and pulled her to the ground just as it hit the side of the ship. The deck beneath them shook violently, and Lillian had a vision of it caving beneath them.

"It will be all right, Lilliana. Captain Stevenson is a coward. He will retreat once we fire back," Tony reassured her. His body still shielded her from the direction of the fight. She took a quivering breath as she confirmed everything around her was still intact and stable.

"Port-side cannons at the ready!" Kale yelled as the boat turned. The ship steadied, and for a moment everything was silent and still. "Fire!"

The deck beneath her shook as three cannons went off, one after another. She gasped and covered her ears against the deafening sound.

Lifting her head the slightest bit, she peered past Tony just enough to see two of the three cannonballs pierce the hull of the other ship. They left two gaping holes in its side, and she hoped the damage to their own ship was not as severe. The other ship did not retreat as Tony had said. It headed toward them.

"Reload!"

"Kale, there's no time. They're going to board," Thomas warned.

Kale stood for moment, contemplating his options before finally shouting, "All hands on deck!" The men rushed up the stairwells, Kale hopped over the railing, landing on his feet below. They all gathered around Kale on the main deck. Tony stood and joined them. Lillian stayed back in hopes that Kale wouldn't send her down below.

"Where's Kidd?" he yelled.

"Here, sir!"

"You take that damned stubborn girl down to the stores and you keep her there. And you." He pointed to Lillian. "You keep disobeying me, and I *will* lock you in the brig for the remainder of the journey." His eyes blazed with that quiet fury. "Kidd?"

"Yeah?"

"Make sure *nothing* happens to her. Do you understand?"

"Yes, sir!" Kidd promised, his young face face more solemn and serious than she thought it could get.

"Good." He dismissed Kidd, who apologized as he escorted Lillian across the deck. She faltered at the opening, watching Kale command the crew.

"The rest of you, do anything you can to keep them from boarding the ship. This is *our* ship, *our* home. We will not let a coward like Stevenson take it from us." The crew cheered. "He took us by surprise and has gained an advantage. He has strength in his numbers, but *only* in his numbers. We have strength in each other, and we won't let him defeat us! From stardust we came."

"To stardust we remain!" the crew finished.

Stevenson's ship was nearly upon them. Lillian watched as the men grabbed whatever weapons they could and lined up against the railing. Kidd tugged on Lillian's arm, but she stood fast.

"Kale, take this." Johnny handed Kale a small gun. "It's always good to have a backup."

"Thanks." Kale laid his arm across Johnny's. "Good luck, brother."

"I make my own luck."

Kale laughed as he stuck the small pistol in the waistband of his trousers. "Okay, men, this is it. Don't waste a shot if you don't have to. I'll see you on the other side."

Lillian finally followed Kidd down the stairs as Kale counted down the other ship coming into range. "Three ... two ... one!"

Chapter Ten

A storm of bullets hailed down on the men of Stevenson's ship as they tried to lower boards across the gap. They fell into the cold waters below, taking two of the boards with them as Kale and the crew reloaded. With three boards left, Stevenson's men wasted no time in taking up the job and pushing them over. Two had reached the rigging and used the extra rope to swing themselves over to the *Stardust*. Rick and Rich traded their guns for swords and met them as soon as they landed.

"Well, that one was weak," Rick said, adjusting the hat on his bald head as he shoved his sword through a man's gut and tossed him into the water. "If they're all like that one, we'll have them down in no time." He chuckled.

"Aye. We can only hope it will be that easy." Rich parried a slash toward his arm. "How about a hand here?"

"I'll get the next one." Rick smiled as another man swung on to the deck.

The rest of the crew fired once more, knocking two more men and another board down into the ocean. There were still at least thirty of Stevenson's crew to their twelve.

"Well, well. Look who it is. Fancy meeting you here, Captain Kale." Captain Stevenson appeared on the upper deck of his ship. He leaned over the rail casually, stroking his dark red beard, the hair beneath his hat braided down his back. He wore the same dark blue jacket and tan trousers as he had when Kale first crossed paths with him ten years prior. He was certainly a man set in his ways. Kale would be damned if he let Stevenson get his hands on the map.

The crew fired again, taking out three more men, but they still managed to get one of the boards fully across. Kale watched as Eddie shoved it back. Stevenson's men caught it just before it toppled down.

"Oh, I do apologize. You don't use that title, do you? Every ship needs a captain, Kale. Without a leader there is no order. No order leads to mutiny and betrayal. Mutiny and betrayal lead to the loss of your ship. Thus, here we are."

"Over my dead body." Kale growled as he let off another round into a man that was climbing the rigging. He fought the urge to take a shot at Stevenson. He'd never hit him at this range.

"That's what I was planning." Captain Stevenson smiled wickedly. His men changed tactics and shoved the last two boards over, knocking Eddie, Dave, and Jack down. Before they could act, four men ran across and jumped onto the ship. Kale shot at them, hitting one in the chest. But with the rest of the crew busy fighting the men already on board, more rushed across. Kale unsheathed his sword and joined the fight.

Below deck, Lillian was frightened, both from being down in a dark, unfamiliar place lit only by the small lantern Kidd held, and by the fight carrying on above her. Oddly enough, she also found herself worrying over the men. The sounds from above were quite ferocious, but she couldn't tell what side they were coming from. With every gunshot, she took a deep breath and tried to imagine it was the other ship's crewman that fell. She already felt close to these men. These pirates. She felt connected to them in a way she hadn't felt with anyone else, not even Maria.

Lillian counted down from ten as she listened to the clanging of metal against metal, pierced by the occasional gunshot. Kidd wasn't much of a distraction, as he eagerly listened through the door to see if any had made it down the stairwell. She could tell he would rather join the fight than sit in the bottom of the ship with her. She wished she could help as well. She could hear far more than twelve men on deck, so she knew they had boarded, and Kale's crew was most likely outnumbered.

She had an idea.

"Kidd?"

"Yeah?" He didn't bother to turn from the door.

"Are we near the cannons?"

"Yeah, they are right above us. But don't worry, no one is going to fire them. They're all busy fighting on deck."

"What if we did it? Fired the cannons. Perhaps as a distraction?"

He thought for a split second, then smiled a crooked smile.

Kidd stuck his head out the door and listened for any sign that someone had made it down. They hurried down the passageway and up the stairs to the cannon room. It spanned the whole ship. Four large cannons pointed out from each side. Kidd peered through one of the portholes to make sure there was no one manning the other ship's cannons. Satisfied that it was empty, he beckoned her over. She could see the ship through the gunports. It was nearly fifteen feet from theirs, and the cannons were higher up. Nevertheless, they would definitely do quite a lot of damage at this close range.

"We have to do this quickly because Captain Stevenson is going to be livid. He may send men down. So we're going to load all four of 'em, then fire 'em. Got it?"

"Got it," she replied. His soft brown eyes were so alight with mischief she couldn't help but return his smile. Coming up with a plan and actually implementing it were two very different things. It felt dangerous, and a bit exciting.

The cannonballs were much heavier than she anticipated, but she was still able to help Kidd load them. Once they had all four cannons loaded, packed, and primed, he rechecked each of them twice more.

"I guess they're as good as they're going to get." He looked as nervous as she felt. "You should stand back. And cover your ears," he added. "I'm going to fire each of the cannons, and then we run back to the stores."

"Right."

"Not walk. *Run,*" he emphasized, handing her the lantern. She held her hands over her ears as best she could. He counted down from three and then pulled the line on the first cannon.

Kale slashed and parried as more men attacked. His crew were fighting well, but they were soon being overrun.

Johnny fought beside him. "Aw, come on, Kale. This should be nothing compared to that bar fight in Uriba." He shoved a man over the rail.

Kale laughed. "Most of those men were so drunk they fell over on their own weapons." He sliced the back of a man who was about to run his sword through Tony. "What about the time all those women chased you through the streets of Laramose? Surely that took more cunning than this."

"Ah, that's the problem. Fighting doesn't require a whole lot of cunning. It takes brawn. And men. Which we seem to be quite short on."

Kale grunted in agreement as Johnny sprinted to the other side of the ship to help Dave.

"Oh, *Captain*," Stevenson sung out. Kale turned to find him standing at the helm. He growled and ran toward the upper deck, knocking over two men. How the hell did he slip past everyone? "I think I look quite regal on your little boat," he said as Kale reached him.

"That's enough, Stevenson. It's you and me now." Kale pointed his sword at him in challenge.

Stevenson chuckled as he pulled out his own sword. "You really think you could ever beat me?"

They circled each other, swords outstretched. Stevenson made the first move, swinging his weapon toward him. Kale dodged out of the way, slicing his sword down but only catching a button.

"This is my good coat, Kale. I won't have you ruining it!" Stevenson growled as he stabbed toward Kale's chest. Kale parried and caught the hilt of Stevenson's sword. But Stevenson twisted aside, and Kale's sword was flung down to the lower deck. Without hesitation, Kale pulled the gun from the back of his trousers and fired.

The butt exploded in Kale's hand, sending the bullet toward him instead of away. He hissed as it grazed his cheek.

"Oh, Kale," Stevenson chuckled. "It looks like your backup plan backfired." He pressed his sword into Kale's chest just hard enough to draw blood. Another hiss escaped him as the tip dug into his skin. "Looks like it's my show now. And the first thing I am going to do is tear your precious *Stardust* down board by board, pile it all up, take a *piss* on it"—he pushed the sword a tad deeper—"and light it aflame. After, of course, I take the map." His grin turned wicked as he stepped towards Kale, backing him against the railing, and dug the tip in a bit deeper.

The deck shook below them as there was a loud boom, then another. Cannon fire. Two more shots rang out. *Their* cannons. Stevenson soon came to the same conclusion.

"No! My ship!" Stevenson shrieked. He shoved Kale down and ran to the portside railing. Sure enough, Stevenson's ship had three gaping holes across the hull. Three of Stevenson's cannons had fallen to the deck below. Another hung precariously on the edge. "You'll pay for this!" He sounded the retreat.

Kale got to his feet, surveying the damage to Stevenson's ship as the *Stardust'* screw cheered victory below. It would take Stevenson a month at least to repair the massive damage. Kale's smile turned to a frown as he stomped down the stairs, realizing who would have been able to set and fire those cannons.

On deck, the crew rejoiced in their victory. They cheered as Kale came near. He was glad to see everyone standing, for the most part. A few had wounds, but none were fatal.

"We did it, Kale! We beat them." Landry gleamed as he patted Kale on the back.

"I wouldn't say we won." He still smiled. "But we certainly held our own until they did." The men cheered.

"Looks like you got a boo-boo there, Kale," Johnny smiled, but his eyes held a bit of concern. "Do you need a nurse?" He pushed his finger against Kale's chest wound.

Kale hissed, then grabbed Johnny's arm, twisting it behind his back. "You're going to need a nurse in a minute."

"Okay! Okay. I give." Johnny rubbed his arm.

"Great idea with the cannons though!" Dave smiled brightly. "Good thing Stevenson loves his ship more than he hates us."

"That wasn't my idea." Kale's lips tightened.

"Oh," Dave said. They grew quiet as Kidd and Lillian came on deck, only the cry of the gulls sounding above them. Even the sea was calm as it lapped the hull below now that Stevenson's ship was on the horizon.

Lillian gasped as she saw the men. Nearly everyone was bleeding in one spot or another. The only ones without any wounds were Johnny and Eddie, although she suspected they had some bruising, by the way Eddie held his stomach and Johnny his arm. Kale looked the worst. Blood covered the front of his shirt, but he didn't seem to be in pain. He turned toward them, and she noticed his cheek was grazed too. She would have expected them to be weary and nursing their wounds. Instead, the men were laughing and recounting how they got each of their new scars. She fought the urge to get a pail of water and a rag to disinfect them, standing fast as Kale headed toward them. She wanted to ask if his chest was okay, but his eyes held hers, filled with fury and a bit of fear. She felt all that progress she had made in befriending him slip away.

"What were you two thinking?" he roared.

Kidd stepped up. "It was my idea, Kale."

"No—" Lillian started to protest but Kidd cut her off.

"We could hear you were outnumbered. So I thought if we shot the cannons, it would be a good distraction to give you the upper hand." The crew circled around them.

"That's not true!" Lillian yelled, momentarily surprising both Kale and Kidd, and even herself a little. "It was *my* idea, and we both acted on it." Adrenaline still coursed through her.

Kale stepped in front of her, nearly in her face. "Do you not value your own life?"

She stood her ground. "My life would not matter if they killed all of you. They would have killed us too."

His gray eyes darkened when he was angry, and standing this close she could make out small flecks of amber in them. "What if he had sent men down to retaliate? He certainly had them to spare. What if—"

"We had a plan," Kidd interrupted.

Kale turned his rage toward him. "A plan? What plan, Kidd? To hide amongst the cargo? I gave you one job! To keep her safe!"

"She *is* safe."

"What you did was dangerous. It was an unnecessary risk. What if Stevenson had fired his cannons instead of fleeing?"

"But he didn't."

"What you did—"

"What *we* did," Lillian interrupted, "ended the fight before anyone was seriously harmed." She pinned Kale with her stare. He held it, his own eyes alight with fury, but she did not shrink.

"What you did could have gotten everyone on board killed," he said in a hushed tone far more frightening than his yelling. A shiver went down her spine, but she remained tall. "Kidd has never fired the cannons. Did you know that? One mistake and it would have blown us all to pieces." Kale didn't so much as blink.

"Kale." Johnny was standing next to him.

"What?" He whipped toward him.

"They saved your life." Amazingly, Johnny was the voice of reason. "You were unarmed."

"I had it handled," Kale growled.

"Stevenson had his sword to your chest when the cannons went off. It's done now. Yeah, a lot of things could have gone wrong. But they didn't, and everyone is alive and well, because of them." He put his hand on Kale's shoulder. An attempt to soothe his fury.

"It's not the first time we've improvised," Eddie said.

"And it won't be the last," Jack added with a huff, crossing his tanned arms. His hat had fallen off during the fight, leaving his tangled black hair exposed.

Kale took in the crew. All seemed to be in agreement, though none would meet his eyes. They were right, and he couldn't argue that. It wasn't any different from things they had done in the past to win a fight. The only difference was that she was there. And if she had been hurt, or if Stevenson had gotten a hold of her and the map ... everything would have been over. He shook his head and stalked toward his cabin, still seething. The rest of the crew crowded in towards Kidd and Lillian.

"That was dangerous," Johnny warned them. "But it was brave, and it stopped the fight. You have my seal of approval." He smiled. "Let's go celebrate."

"What about Kale?" Lillian asked quietly.

"He'll be fine. He just needs to stew in his anger awhile."

Chapter Eleven

Lillian sat among the men as they celebrated in the galley. The *Stardust* was back on course, and the waters were calm. She had received just as many apologies for Kale's behavior as she had congratulations on her and Kidd's actions. Each of the men took turns telling her their stories of the fight. She was sure more than a few were embellished. At least they agreed to let her clean them up with alcohol and a rag, although they hardly sat still long enough to do it properly.

She finished bandaging Thomas, who had a bright pink gash running down the top of his dark-skinned arm. He had reenacted how he had been swinging down the ropes to tackle an enemy when he bumped into Chase instead, causing him to fall and lose the element of surprise. The enemy, who was nearly seven feet tall in this version, had stood over Chase and sliced his sword toward him. Thomas deftly deflected it with his arm, then kicked the man to the ground and stabbed him. The wound should have been stitched up, but he refused. They all had. Battle scars were like trophies to them—the bigger and darker, the better.

She had already inspected Eddie's midsection for any sign of broken bones and found none. Johnny was the only one left.

"What about you?" she asked him.

"What about me?" He sat at a table with some of the other men, a mug of amber liquid in his hand. The candlelight illuminated his golden hair and crystal-colored eyes.

"Do you have any injuries aside from your arm?" The men laughed at that.

"None that you need to worry your pretty little head about."

The midday meal came and went and there was no sign of Kale. The men had slowly dispersed to finish their work until only a few remained, playing cards. Johnny was one of them. They had tried to convince her to join, but she wasn't familiar with their game, and they were betting. She was too fond of her few belongings to put them up as collateral.

"Johnny?" she asked, after watching them for a while.

"Well." He looked up from his hand. "I think that's the first time you've called me by my first name. Starting to take a liking to me, are you?"

"Not in the slightest." She pursed her lips. "Kale said I should call everyone by their first name."

"Since when does a pirate tell a lady how to act?" He raised a brow.

"Since I am apparently your prisoner."

"Oh, come now. You aren't a prisoner. We don't keep you locked in the brig now, do we?" He eyed his hand as Chase laid down a card.

"Being locked in my cabin isn't much better," she huffed.

"Spend a night in the brig, and you'll think differently. Did you have something to ask me? You're breaking my concentration." He frowned as Chase took the few coins from the middle of the table.

"Why does Kale care about my well-being so much?"

"Because you're going to bring us quite a bit of money," he said, without looking up. He winced as Thomas deftly kicked him under the table.

"How?" she asked, surprised at his honesty.

"We do what pirates do best. Search for treasure. And you'll play a big part in this search." He glared at Thomas as he adjusted his cap and laid a card down. "You'll have to ask Kale for anything more."

Kale had said as much that first day and had shot her questions down pretty quickly when she had asked. It wasn't something she felt like trying again anytime soon. Though it seemed the rest of the crew knew the answers as well, based on Thomas's reaction to Johnny's answer. Perhaps she could convince one of them to tell her.

Kale sat in one of the armchairs, his bloody shirt crumpled in the chair next to him, as he peered over a worn-out piece of paper at the small table. The edges had deteriorated a long while ago. He frowned as a soft knock came from the door.

"Enter ... Oh."

It was Lillian. He folded the map gently and slid it under another pile of papers, before he slipped a shirt on.

She wore the outfit he'd given her that morning, but ... She had taken it in, he realized. It hugged the curves of her body and fit tightly against her legs. She was thin, he had known, but seeing her in clothing that hugged rather than flowed lit something within him, as if they had always been made for a woman to wear. The yellow ribbon she'd worn in her hair yesterday was now laced in and out of her collar of the shirt as well as the hem of each pantleg, adding a feminine touch. He tore his eyes from her and focused on the table instead. No matter the pull he felt every time she was near, he had to keep his distance. He'd promised himself he'd keep his distance from the moment they pulled her from the icy waters. She was a lady, noble-born, and well educated. If spending a short time aboard a pirate ship didn't ruin her reputation, any attention from him certainly would. Aside from that, she would hate him by the end of this hunt.

"Do you need something?" he asked finally.

"I won't apologize for what I did," she said.

He sighed, running his hands over his face and up through his hair, that one unruly piece immediately falling back over his forehead. He had overreacted, and he knew it. Johnny was right. If she hadn't been aboard, that stunt would have been well within their repertoire. Which is why it was surprising that the idea had come from her. She was becoming a fine pirate after all, and after only a few days. But it wasn't just their lives on the line any longer, they had to be more careful.

"I'm not asking for an apology, Lillian. But I need you to understand that it was dangerous. And Kidd should have known better. I can't have you putting your life at risk like that."

"Why? You told the men to treat me like one of the crew, but you don't allow me to act as one."

He sighed once again, leaning his palms against the table. "I don't want to fight with you right now." She was quiet. He attempted to change the subject. "You turned out to be quite the seamstress. It's hard to believe those were ever men's clothes."

"I told you I wasn't useless," she said.

"I never doubted it. Ah yes, I have something for you," he said. He pulled out a canvas bag that had been sitting beneath the table.

From it, he took a small green bag, which he handed to her. She looked at him questioningly.

"Open it."

Carefully untying the drawstrings, she gasped as she peered inside. She dumped it out on his table. Ten spools of different colored thread spilled out. She smiled as she sorted through the colors. Most were variations of brown, black, and white, but there was also a dark green, a red, and a pale yellow that matched her dress perfectly.

"I noticed the kit didn't have much thread in it. Is that enough for now?"

"Oh, it's more than enough." She beamed. "Thank you." Her pale blue eyes met his, and her gratitude shone through.

He smiled. "I found this as well." He pulled out two pieces of fabric that were folded neatly. One was a light brown, the other a dark green. "Those are for you to do with as you like." Her eyes grew wide. "But I need to know something."

She was so enthralled with the fabric that she didn't respond. The pieces were small, perhaps twelve square feet each, but enough for her to make something of her own with.

"Lillian."

She jumped as he placed his hands under her chin, pulling her face so that their eyes met again.

He held her there, making sure he had her attention. "If you had the fabric, could you make me a formal suit? One that is in current style?"

"Well, it's been a while since I made anything larger than a handkerchief." She paused, then smiled. "But I am positive I can do it. I would need some time, though. And I need to take your measurements."

"That's fine. We have time, for now." He pulled out yards of black, grey, and white fabric. "Is this enough?"

"Oh my, yes. That is more than enough. I'll need buttons though. Nice ones. They should be round and about the size of your thumbnail." She ran her hands over the smooth fabric. "This is very fine fabric. It must have cost a fortune. Why not just buy a suit for that price?" she asked. He shook his head.

"It didn't cost me anything. I have a ... business partner who owns a fabric store."

"Oh. Well, there will be fabric left over. Do you need anything else made?"

"You can use the extra as you please. We will be docking at another port in a day or two to make repairs and pick up some of the supplies that we didn't have time to get today. I'll pick up buttons then. If you need anything else, let me know." He took a few odds and ends out of the bottom of the bag, then slid the fabric back in and handed it to her.

"Kale?"

"Yes?" he asked warily.

"May I look at your chest?"

He was surprised by her question, then remembered his wound. "It's fine. Just a cut."

"Please?" she pushed. "The others let me tend their wounds. I can see you've cleaned your cheek nicely." She lifted her hand to brush the scrape, then thought better of it. "I would just like to take a look. It will make me feel more comfortable."

He sighed as he gave in and lifted his shirt.

"It's deeper than I thought." She gasped quietly as she lifted her fingers again to touch but paused as he stiffened. It was unheard of for an unwed woman to touch a man with no shirt on. And the thought of her fingers on him stirred something in his chest. After a thought, she continued her reach forward, and he didn't stop her. He hissed as her fingers grazed the wound. She traced her fingers around the edges lightly. When she looked up at him, he knew what she saw in his eyes, whether she did or not. He willed it away. The pull he felt towards her was all consuming when they were this close. He needed to be the one who kept it in check. He wouldn't take advantage of her naivete. He pulled his shirt back down.

"It should be covered, but I'm sure you won't allow it. It will be fine," she said, pulling her hand away.

"No." He chuckled; his face playful once more. "Our scars define us. That's how we remember our battles."

"The others said as much." Her laugh was light and airy, and he loved hearing it. "Did Captain Stevenson slice your cheek also?"

"No. My gun misfired." His eyes went dark, and Captain Stevenson's words rang back to him. *Without a leader there is no order. No order leads to mutiny and betrayal.* Had someone betrayed them? "I'm very lucky to only have a grazed cheek."

She gasped. "That's ... from a bullet?" She reached up and ran her thumb parallel to it, this time not hesitating.

"Yes. You know, you aren't like any lady I have ever met, Lillian," he said, grasping her hand. He couldn't take any more of her touching. She stood still at his words. Did they make her nervous?

"How is that?" she asked cautiously.

"Most noblewomen can't stand the sight of blood. They would never even think to touch a cannon. And they would faint at the idea of eating in a galley full of loud, dirty men."

"Well, you've never met a lady like me," she said immediately, sitting down in one of the armchairs as if she belonged there.

"No, I guess I haven't." He took his chair once more, opposite her. They stared at each other, letting the comfortable silence fill the room.

"Johnny didn't have any injuries," she noted, breaking the tension.

"He's an excellent swordsman."

"I suppose. May I ask you a question?" she asked carefully.

"Certainly. But I can't guarantee an answer."

"You said that Johnny has his own reasons for disobeying you."

"I did." He frowned. Where was she going with this?

"May I ask what they are?" She held his gaze. He didn't respond right away, contemplating how much, if anything he should reveal to her.

"This whole crew," he said slowly. "We're more like brothers. That's why we don't use titles like 'captain' often. But Johnny and I grew up together. We started this together. When it became more than a game, when we needed funds the most, Johnny decided he didn't want the responsibility. And so, I became captain, so to speak. I became the decision-maker, and the one responsible if anything went awry. Sometimes he doesn't like my decisions, so he acts on his own. That's fine. He's here for the fun of it, and he isn't hurting anyone. But it's becoming more and more often that we disagree." His eyes turned stormy. "He is beginning to step over the line. Like that stunt he pulled with you on the deck yesterday. That was over the line."

"Do you trust him?" she asked.

"With my life."

"Do you trust everyone on the crew that much?"

"Yes. I wouldn't allow them on my ship if I didn't trust them to have my back in every situation." He smiled fondly. "You'll see, while you're here, we are a family. We take care of each other."

"Yes, I've seen that already." She sighed sadly. She must miss her own family. He wondered if she still grieved them in the night. Perhaps she was close to the family they were set to visit in Southern Nelina and they could take her there when their adventure was finished.

"You continue to use phrases like that. *After a while* or *get used to it*. Am I really going to be here that long?" she asked.

"I don't know, Lillian," he said. The first bit of truth he'd offered her on the subject. He could tell his secretiveness was starting to bother her, but she was just starting to calm down and open up to the crew. If he shared his plans ... He couldn't risk her trying to escape.

"I thought you were the master of making plans. Do you not have a plan for me?" Her expression begged the truth from him. She needed to know something, anything about the path that lay before her.

"Plans change. Sometimes you have to figure it out as you go along." He stood, ending the conversation. She sighed. "It's almost time for the evening meal, and I have things I need to finish." He held his hand out to help her up. She dismissed him and stood on her own. "You also may be the rudest lady I've ever met." He moved to open the door for her.

"And you are the politest pirate I've ever met."

Chapter Twelve

The air was already turning brisk outside as dusk loomed on the horizon. The chill raised goosebumps across her arms as Lillian ventured to the edge of the rail. The sun rippled with the waves as they met, creating unimaginable colors. It was a scene fit for one of the paintings in the De Sansol mansion, and Lillian was seeing it with her own eyes. She was experiencing it in person, in the middle of the vast and beautiful ocean. The rolling of the ship didn't bother her as much anymore, and the view of the horizon was enough to calm her fears of the ocean below. So long as it was calm.

She sighed as she leaned against the rail, propping her cheek on her palm. It frightened her that Kale wasn't sure of her future. It frightened her even more that she wasn't entirely sure she wanted to leave now, should the opportunity present itself. There was nothing left for her on land, any land. She had no family, no home to return to. Either the crew would drop her in some unfamiliar port, or they'd take her back to Aarilya. Either way, she would be homeless.

But this, being here on this ship with them, with **pirates**, it was like a story straight from her adventure novels. A real adventure, like she had always dreamed. One she hadn't realized she had wanted for herself. And she was growing braver each day, more confident in herself and the things she was capable of. She could do anything she put her mind to, now that she had the freedom to make her own choices. Perhaps even convince this misfit crew of pirates to take her in as one of their own. Permanently.

"Well, hello pretty lady. Why do you look so sad?" Johnny leaned against the rail next to her. She straightened.

"I'm not sad. I'm watching the sunset."

"Beautiful, isn't it?" he said, his gaze on her.

"Yes, it is." She did not take her eyes off the horizon.

"It's different every night out here. Different position, different size, different colors. I have never seen the same sunset twice." He turned to look out over the ocean as well. "Even the ocean is magnificent when it's the only thing around. It has always fascinated me how calm it can be, and then, with no warning at all, turn angry."

"That reminds me of Kale." She smiled. Johnny looked at her, then chuckled.

"Yeah, I guess it is kind of like Kale. Perhaps that's why he feels so at home out here."

"How do you feel about him?"

"About Kale?" He remained quiet, contemplating his words. "We're like brothers. We fight sometimes, as all family does."

"You all trust each other so much, so blindly. You all care so deeply. I find myself a bit envious." She sighed. When he didn't reply, she turned to find him staring at her. She had never seen him so serious for so long.

"You know you can trust us too, Lillian." He took a strand of her hair and ran it through his fingers, twirling the ends softly. She was caught by his momentary softness toward her.

"Yes," she said. She turned away, pulling her hair from his fingers. "I can trust you to sell me to the highest bidder."

"It's not like that, Lillian. I mean, yeah, we will probably hold you for ransom, but you still get to go home. We aren't cruel." He stroked her forearm. She spun toward him, anger and tears filling her eyes.

"You cannot ransom me, Johnny. My family is dead! I have no home to go back to. I have no one. Nothing." She didn't give him time to respond. As she ran across the deck, he called after her. She ignored him.

She slammed the door to her cabin behind her and threw herself onto her small cot. Was she overreacting? After all, he was being sweet for once, but she was filled with an overwhelming number of emotions. Longing for her parents, fear of the future, loneliness. She had never truly been alone. She had never even been given time to mourn the death of her parents. She mourned now. She mourned her parents, and she mourned Maria, Mr. and Mrs. De Sansol. Jeremy. Chuck. Her sobs racked with grief, she cried late into the night.

She lay on her cot, now empty of tears, listening to the waves brush up against the ship. She could not sleep. After a few minutes, she decided she would finish the sewing. She sat up and felt dizzy, her head pounding from crying so long. Her mouth was as dry as a desert. Her hands shook as she poured the water and drank deeply from the tin cup.

Walking to the small table, she picked up the bag Kale had given her with the fabric and spools of thread and began to organize it.

Once satisfied, she went to collect more items of clothing from the next room. She opened the door and gasped as Tony fell in.

"Excuse me, Lilliana." He got to his feet. "I apologize."

"How long have you been there?" she asked. His hair and clothes were mussed. Was he sleeping against the door?

"Um, well, Kale asked me to be here. To check on you."

"I see. Well, I am fine Tony, thank you. You may leave."

"All right." He turned to leave but hesitated. "Lilliana?"

"Yes?"

"You can always talk to us if you're sad. Or lonely. I find it to be easier to handle things when you are with family." He took her hand and kissed the back of it.

She was touched by his sympathy. "Thank you, Tony."

The crew was genuine, she was sure of that. Even Kale and Johnny liked her well enough. But a pocket full of coin would always be more important to them than a stranger. Despite that, she had decided amid her fits of tears that she would treat her time with them as an adventure, no matter how long or short it was. She would participate and learn as much as she could, and when the time came for her to leave, she would have a story to tell. She collected the last few articles of clothing, took them back to her cabin, and set to work.

The sunlight shone bright on Lillian's face, or rather, right in her eyes. She groaned, laying her hand across her forehead as a reprieve. She couldn't recall the last time the sun had woken her. She sat up fast, realizing no one had come to fetch her. Someone had obviously been in her cabin. There was a breakfast plate on the small table, and the pile of clothing she had fixed the night before was gone. But judging by the sun's position through her window, it was nearly midday. She pulled on her shoes, then hurried through the hall and up the stairs.

Almost everyone was on deck enjoying the fair weather, some working and others lounging around playing cards or other games. Kale was at the helm, his dark hair whipping around his face in the morning wind. He was laughing at something Rich was saying.

"Well, look who it is." Eddie crossed his inked arms.

"Good morning, sunshine." Chase chuckled, tossing a few light braids over his shoulder. They both stopped mopping, smiling at her as she passed.

"Is it still morning?"

"Just shy," Chase said.

"What should I expect up there? Will he be upset with me for sleeping late?"

"Nah, you'll be fine. We all have off days." Eddie laid a comforting hand on her shoulder. She patted it, then continued across the deck.

The stairs creaked with each footstep as Lillian ascended. The sun shone high in the sky and a few gulls cried from the rigging above, flapping their wings slightly with each gust of wind that shook the ropes.

"I was wondering if we would see you today."

"Why did no one wake me this morning?" She pulled her hair into a tight braid against the wind.

"Tony said you had a late night." Kale's smile faltered. The sound of her sobs had carried across the deck the night before. They had discussed whether someone should go in and attempt to comfort her but seeing as none of them had quite that delicate a personality, they'd decided to let her cry it out. "We thought it would be best to let you sleep this morning."

"Would you let any of the men sleep in?"

"If that's what they needed." He moved the helm a bit to the west.

"Well, then I guess I don't feel so bad. But you didn't have to ask Tony to stand outside my door."

"He was more than willing." Truth be told, they were all worried about her mental state. Having someone watch her door was the obvious choice, if only to grant them peace of mind that she wouldn't jump ship in the middle of the night.

"That is not the point. I know some of the things you do are because you view me as a commodity, something you need to keep safe until I perform whatever task you brought me on to do."

"It's not th—"

"Listen, please. I am not finished," she interrupted. "I am not upset, I understand. But I want you to understand that I will not hurt myself, and I will not leave this ship. I give you my word."

They stood there in silence, their eyes locked as he contemplated her words.

"I do not view you as an object Lillian, but you will play an important role in finding this treasure, to all of us. I need you to promise me one more thing, and in return I will not lock you in your cabin again."

"Anything." She breathed.

"Give me your word that you will follow my orders, even when you don't want to. I can't have you taking unnecessary risks."

"All right."

"All right what?" he prompted, a slow grin forming.

She chuckled at his need for complete confirmation. "All right, I give you my word. I will follow your orders, Captain."

He chuckled, shaking his head at her. He liked when she showed this playful side of her. "You sound like Johnny when you say that."

Her smile fell a little. "I need to apologize to him."

"He understands, Lillian. He said the two of you had an honest conversation last night, no sarcasm involved."

"I suppose that is as close to a real conversation as Johnny could get," she said. "He was like a completely different person without the rude quips."

"Don't expect it to last. Johnny will always be Johnny."

They stood in silence for a bit, both watching the ocean as Kale gently tilted the helm one way then the other. The air was brisk as it swirled around them, bringing with it the sound of the men laughing. Beneath them, the ocean was calm, only small ripples spreading out as the **Stardust** glided easily through it.

"How do you know where you're going without a compass?" Lillian asked after a while.

"I have one, here. I know our destination is northeast, so I adjust the ship as the compass moves. Would you like to try?"

"Absolutely."

He chuckled at her eagerness and moved aside, keeping one hand on the wheel, so that she could stand in front of him. His now familiar smell wafted around her as he took her hands and placed them on the spindles. Like salt and sandalwood.

"The ocean will always pull. Do you feel that?" He gently laid his hands over hers. All she felt was the way his deep voice resonated as his chest brushed against her back. She straightened at the contact. Then the wheel tugged, but Kale held it in place. "It's a constant battle of wills between you and the sea, each having to give a little to the other for the ship to stay on course." His hands still firmly pressed to hers as he let the wheel spin to the right a few inches, then gently pulled it back to center.

She gasped as his hands left hers. The cool breeze skittered across the tops of them at the loss of contact. She had full control of the helm now. She hadn't realized quite how much control Kale had had. The wheel pulled harder against her grip.

"Keep it so the needle on the compass stays toward the northeast," he reminded her. She allowed the force to slowly turn. Once it was stable, she pulled it back to the center as Kale had done.

"Good," he chuckled. "You are a quick learner."

"It helps to have a good teacher." She grinned. He reached up and tugged playfully on a loose strand of hair. Her smile softened as she looked to him, but she gasped as the wheel jerked to the left unexpectedly. Kale caught the spindles just as she lost her grip.

"Like I said, constant battle of wills. You can't let your guard down."

Her heart was beating, and a blush spread across her cheeks as he took his spot against her back once more. "I guess I'm not as quick a learner as I thought."

He placed her hands beneath his once more. "We learn more from our mistakes than from our successes." Her breath caught at the warmth of his breath against the sensitive shell of her ear. His voice had dropped, and she could hear the smile in it.

Was he ... flirting? She had noticed the way he had looked at her occasionally, but this ... this was different. Whenever they had come in close contact before, he had pulled away almost immediately. Now, he stood closer, his touch more intentional. It sparked a flutter in her chest, a feeling she had only gotten from her novels.

"I suppose that's true," she breathed.

She felt the moment he pulled away. He shifted back slightly and stood tall, his chin just above the top of her head. If she had felt brave, she could have leaned back and would have settled perfectly against his chest. She wasn't that brave.

"You seem to know quite a few sea terms. Did you learn them on the navy boat?"

"Some," she said, surprised at the change in topic. "Although most I've learned from reading adventure novels."

"You read quite a bit?" he said, amused.

"Oh yes." Her eyes shone brightly as she recalled the many books she had collected over the years. "I have read on my own since I was very young. Back home I had a large collection, but Mrs.—um, Mother would not allow me to bring any but one." She had been positively heartbroken. One book would not have lasted her the month they had intended to stay in Northern Nelina.

"Hmmm" was his only response.

"Do you like to read much?" she asked.

"I enjoyed it as a child. But I don't have much time now."

"Your family, they were well off?" she asked. The smell of brine surrounded them as the breeze picked up, blowing a few strands of her hair free from her braid.

His lips tightened in response. "We are going to be docking late this evening. I trust you will hold to your promise?" he said, an obvious end to that line of questioning.

"Yes," she said softly.

"Good. You should eat something."

"Thank you, but I am not hungry."

"Then perhaps you should let Johnny know you are doing okay. He was a little worried yesterday, which is a lot from him." He lifted an arm for her to duck under. She did so but remained by his side.

"Please do not do that. Do not dismiss me. It seems every conversation we have ends on bad terms. I will not ask about things you do not wish to talk about, if only you tell me you do not wish to talk about them."

"I don't want to talk about my past," he said bluntly, his lips still pressed together, eyes staying on the horizon ahead of them.

"Understood," she conceded. "Can you ... can you tell me where we are headed?"

He was quiet, contemplating. "Not yet."

She had the urge to brush the one strand of unruly hair back, but refrained as she nodded solemnly and tucked her own hair behind her ear.

"What about you?" he asked. "What was your grand life in Aarilya like? Before your trip across the sea?"

"It doesn't seem fair that you can hide your past but ask about mine."

"If you don't wish to talk about your family, you don't have to." He leaned against the wheel.

"No, I don't mind." She paused as she decided where to start. "My parents were the most wonderful people I have ever known.

They were sweet, even when others thought it was inappropriate and turned up their noses at them. They never cared what others thought or said about them. They always did what they believed was right."

"You loved them very much." His face was pensive, unreadable.

"And Maria," she said fondly. "She was my friend. She was puckish but she could be sweet at times. We kept each other company."

"Was?" he asked, puzzled. "Was she on the ship with you?"

"Yes. She was ... my maid," she covered.

"How long had she been your maid?"

"We've been friends ever since we were babies. We were born within two days of each other. We were playmates as children, and then when we became adults, she became my maid." The lie felt heavy on her tongue it and made her sick to her stomach to do it to Kale, but she was not ready to reveal the truth to them. Not yet. Not if she was considering asking them to allow her to stay.

"I see. Do you miss them? Your parents and your ... maid?"

"I do. Rather deeply. And the others as well."

"I am truly sorry for the circumstances you have been brought into. I hope that you can find it in your heart to forgive me ... someday." He stared out over the ocean, not making eye contact. He looked truly regretful. She should have felt sorry for him, but his words only made her uneasy. He was still hiding something from her.

"I don't blame you." She hesitated. "I blame Captain Davis most. Whether alive or dead, he purposely steered my family and all those men into that storm. He alone is the one responsible for their deaths. But that isn't what you are apologizing for, is it?" she asked sorrowfully. "You are truly sorry for whatever end our journey is headed to, aren't you?"

His eyes widened, shocked at her ability to read him. Whatever he had done so far had not merited such an apology, and from what she knew of him, of his personality, whatever was coming he felt he had to do. Felt he had no other choice. She could see it written across his features. If he felt such guilt over dragging an innocent stranger into this, then his motive had to be noble. And for that, she could forgive him.

"I forgive you, Kale." She laid her hand across his on the spindles. "I forgive you for what it is you feel you need to do in the future."

His lips tightened. "You cannot forgive me for what you do not know."

Chapter Thirteen

Lillian watched Kale at the helm. He was so at home there, as if he pulled his joy straight from the ship itself. She smiled a bit at the thought, but the change in his demeanor when she asked him about the future worried her. She had no luck pulling information of a plan from him or from the crew. She would have to figure it out herself. When she had been in his cabin, he had been cautious about hiding that map from her view. It had to have something to do with the treasure. Perhaps she could sneak into his quarters and take a look at it. It wasn't a solid plan, but it was a start. If she wanted to stay aboard then she needed to prove herself, but she couldn't do that if he didn't include her in the plan. No, she would have to find a way to get the information herself.

She looked back toward Kale. He was staring solemnly out over the ocean when his face split into a grin.

"Ah. There she is." He pointed out over the ocean. She looked to see another ship off in the distance. It was hard to judge from this far out, but it seemed even smaller than Kale's.

"What is it?" she asked.

"Told ya the tip was good." Chase grinned as he topped the stairs, his rich brown eyes alight with adventure.

"Aye. You did." Kale still smiled.

"You see her out there, Lillian?" Chase beamed as he pointed.

"I see a ship. Though I must admit I do not know its significance."

"That there's Crack Jack. He's on the run after a heist in Uriba. He's got a bounty on his head." Chase looked toward the small ship, excited.

"So we're going to capture him?" Lillian asked, surprised.

"Nah, he's too dangerous to have aboard with you. We'll attack and take his spoils. He runs a light crew, like us, but scuttlebutt says he lost a few during the heist," Chase said.

"And the wind is with us. We can catch them at a dead run. Ready the spinnaker!" Kale shouted. "Hold on, Lillian." His grin grew.

Jack and Rick pulled the ropes and unfurled a second sail, which the wind soon caught. The ship lurched. In no time they were upon it.

"All hands on deck!" Kale called. Johnny repeated the order below. All the men gathered on deck, weapons in hand.

"In position?" Kale called.

"Aye," Johnny replied.

"Raise the Jolly Roger!" Chase ran down to the lower deck and joined Landry, shifting and pulling on a rope attached to the main mast, and before long, a large black flag topped it. Kale grinned at the crew as he descended the stair, Lillian following closely behind.

"No prey!" he shouted.

"No pay!" the men finished.

Rick and Rich brought in the sails as they neared their destination. The rest of the men lined the railing, facing Crack Jack's ship.

"Well, see 'ere. If it ain't Kale." Crack Jack grinned from his helm, which was situated in the center of his ship. It was small enough that it only had one deck, unlike the *Stardust*.

"Give it up, Crack Jack. We heard you've got a pretty penny on that boat, and you lost some numbers getting it." Kale grinned back; a pistol aimed right at the other captain. Crack Jack eyed the crew lining the rails before turning his eyes on Kale again.

"Aye. Don't think I can take ya this time." He nodded. "Though I heard Stevenson's on yer tail. Don't think ye'll be keepin' me loot long."

"Oh, don't hold much stock in that. I've already sent Stevenson packing." Kale chuckled. "I'll be sending my own Jack over, then." Kale motioned to Jack, who boarded the small rowboat, Johnny and Eddie lowering him down.

"Damn ye, Kale. Ya know I be the only Jack aboard me own ship. Send someone else," Crack Jack practically whined.

Kale chuckled and shook his head. "I can't chance any of my lesser-skilled men to hold you. Take it as a compliment."

Crack Jack shook his head and called his men on deck as Jack climbed the rigging and boarded his boat.

"Have two of your men fetch the chest," Kale instructed. Jack took Crack Jack's weapon and held it to his back for insurance. Crack Jack nodded to two of the younger men aboard, who disappeared through a small door, emerging only a few minutes later with a large chest.

They loaded the heavy chest onto their own rowboat, then lowered it and transferred it to Jack's. Once they returned to the deck, Jack instructed them to stand against the opposite railing, facing away. He backed himself and Crack Jack up to the rigging he'd climbed aboard. Then he chucked Crack Jack's sword across the deck, gave him a little shove away, and quickly climbed back down the rigging to his waiting rowboat.

Once he'd made it across the small expanse between the two ships, Johnny and Eddie tossed down some rope and raised the boat back up, with Jack and the chest in it. It took Chase and Landry's help to heft the extra weight of the chest in the boat.

"I'll be payin' ya back for that, Kale." Crack Jack eyed him. His words were vicious, but he wore a wide grin. It seemed Kale and this captain played this game often.

"I would feel insulted if you didn't." Kale chuckled and tipped his head toward Crack Jack. Once Jack and the chest were loaded, he gave the orders to raise the sails once more and positioned the ship to turn away. Once they had put some distance between them and there were no signs that Crack Jack would follow, Lillian turned to Kale again.

"That seemed almost civil," she said.

"Aye, we've been at each other a long time. It's nothing personal," he said. He motioned for her to follow him to the chest.

"What does 'No Prey, No Pay' mean?" she asked.

"Simple, it's the way of life out here. If we don't track and loot other ships, we don't get paid. If we don't get paid, we don't eat." He smiled as Jack and Johnny hefted the chest to the middle of the deck and opened it. There were a few bags of coin, and a handful of gems.

"Nothing significant," Johnny said.

Kale shook his head as he sorted through the gems. "We'll send word at the next port."

"Send word?"

"The duke of Uriba's an acquaintance of ours. He's the one who said that Crack Jack had hit his port. He asked us to make sure nothing of value was taken. In exchange, we can keep what's left." He nodded to the chest.

"You've been to Uriba?" she asked. Uriba bordered Aarilya to West and was completely shut to outsiders. Only those who knew someone there and had permission from the duke were allowed to enter. The dark duke, they called him. And Kale knew him.

"What will you do with all of it?" she asked.

"We have a few more things to get for the hunt. The rest will go to food and supplies." Johnny picked out a small opaque lavender jewel. He looked to Kale as he held it up. Kale nodded softly, and Johnny slipped it into his pocket.

"Any catch your eye?" Kale asked as Lillian peered into the chest. He crossed his arms, grinning and raising a brow, his silver eyes dancing with mischief. She returned his smile as she shook her head. "You can take one, you know. Payment for putting up with all of our scheming."

"This one is pretty, Lillian." Kidd held up a light, dusty pink gem.

She shook her head slightly. "I am not sure that would be enough payment."

Kale blinked before he dropped his arms and walked towards her. A slow grin formed across his lips as he neared, that playful air from earlier returning. Her breath caught as he stood before her.

"Tell me then, what would be enough payment?" His grin broadened.

Her smile faltered. She had meant to play into his flirtation, but the fluttering in her chest held her words at bay. "I didn't mean ... it was only a jest. I don't need anything." She took a step away from him, closer to Kidd and the others who were now peering at the different gems and dutifully ignoring their encounter.

"Everyone wants something. Think on it. Once this is all over ... whatever you desire, I'll make it happen." His smile softened as he ran his thumb along her jaw before walking away.

She gently rubbed the spot his thumb had touched as the crew laughed behind her at some jest Kidd had made. It threw her off when Kale acted that way toward her. Most of the time, he was cordial. Some of the time he was angry or secretive. But he only seemed sincere when he looked at her the way he just had. Like he had bared his soul for her to take, if she wanted. Then he would turn and walk away.

Every time.

Was it deliberate, to throw her off, to keep her in line? She couldn't quite trust him so long as he still kept secrets from her. She needed to figure out his plan. For her and for the treasure hunt.

That evening Lillian took a bit longer to ready herself for the evening meal. She hoped if she waited long enough, Kale would head to the galley, and she could slip into his cabin and take a look at the map. She waited a few more minutes before she headed upstairs and across the deck.

She peered through the small porthole of Kale's door. He was sitting at his desk, peering intently over a letter. His shoulders sagged heavily, as if the very weight of the world pushed down on him. The map was nowhere to be seen. As she turned to leave, he caught sight of her in the small window and motioned for her to enter. A cool smile replaced the weariness and he set the letter down, leaning back casually in his chair.

"To what do I owe this pleasure?" He raised a brow.

"I just wanted to see if you were going to join us for supper."

He watched her a moment before smiling softly. "You go on ahead. I'll be there shortly."

She held his gaze, debating her next step. The curtains behind him were pulled shut but there was a gap left open where the moonlight shone off the water outside, illuminating the room far better than the candles that were lit. Finally, She nodded and slipped back out the door quietly.

After she had gone, Kale stood in his cabin and stared out of his porthole. He would have to join everyone in the galley soon for the evening meal, but for now he was enjoying the peace. He needed peace now, to think. He was letting his guard down around her. He couldn't help it. Her smile. The way she looked up at him with those soft blue eyes. They softened something in him, made him want to touch her. Protect her. Every time he was near her he felt pulled towards her. It filled him with regret for having brought her on board. Guilt for dragging her into this complicated treasure hunt. Guilt so deep it nearly made him want to call it off. Nearly. But there was too much at stake this time around.

"Hey, Kale. There you are!" Johnny swung the door open. It made a cracking sound as it hit the wall behind it. So much for peace. "Uh oh, I know that face." His demeanor changed to a more solemn one as he took a seat at the small table, stretching his legs out in front of him. "What happened?"

"Nothing." Kale sighed. "Nothing happened, but ..." He paced across the floor and back to the window in thought. "Something isn't right. With Lillian."

"The girl? Is she sick?" Johnny's brow furrowed in concern.

"No. Just ... something doesn't add up. I can't quite figure it out yet."

"Come on, Kale. You're probably just under too much stress. Don't look for problems that aren't there. We have enough already to deal with. There haven't been any signs of Stevenson yet, but I doubt he's given up on the map. That's enough worry for a lifetime."

"I know. I know ... It's just, she doesn't act like a lady. I've never met a noble who acted the way she does. And when she talks about her past, her parents ... Something is off."

"People would say the same about us. We don't act like 'normal' pirates. Not everyone is exactly the same just because we label them."

"Yeah, I guess you're right." Kale sighed, running his hands up his face and through his hair.

"The guys are wondering where you're at," Johnny said. "Food's been ready for a bit."

"Just keep an eye on her, will you, Johnny?"

Johnny nodded and followed Kale out to the galley.

Everyone was already seated around the large table when they arrived, halfway through the meal. Kale grabbed a plate and sat next to Johnny. Lillian smiled from her spot at the other end of the table. Chase and Landry sat on either side of her. The room was loud as usual, and he couldn't hear what they were talking about. She laughed as Chase waved his arms around frantically. Everyone seemed to enjoy her company well enough. Rather than making him happy, it made him uneasy. He turned back to his food. Perhaps Johnny was right—he was looking for problems where there were none.

The *Stardust* rocked gently as the waves crashed against the hull, and the men wandered around gathering things that looked random to her. They had reached the dock sometime during the night, as Kale had predicted, and they were preparing to go ashore.

"You are getting better at waking up earlier." He chuckled. The sun had just begun to rise.

"Tony will be staying aboard with you. I trust you won't give him any trouble?"

"Does my word mean nothing to you?"

"I trust actions more."

"Not very trusting, are you? Have you been spurned before?" she teased, a small smile playing on her lips.

"Too many times to count. Better to err on the side of caution." He looped rope around his arms.

"You had said that if I needed anything to let you know."

"I did," he said slowly.

"Well." She pulled out a small piece of paper. "I made a small list. Mostly sewing items. More thread, and the buttons, of course." She handed it to him. He swung the coiled rope over his shoulder.

"I didn't forget the buttons, and I'll keep an eye out for the rest."

"Thank you."

"Lovely to see you this morning, Lilliana." Tony bowed over her hand. His mustache tickled as he softly pressed a kiss to it.

"Tony, I told you there is no need for that," Kale reprimanded, his face growing pensive as he watched the encounter.

"I apologize, Kale, but Lilliana is just so lovely, I cannot help myself."

"I do not mind," she said.

Kale shook his head. "I'm going to send a ship surveyor to take a look at the damage. He should be alone. If he has to bring someone with him, I'll send one of our men along as well. If he shows up here with more men and one of us is not with him, do not let him board this ship," Kale warned.

"Understood," Tony said.

"Lillian, I need you to stay out of sight while he is here. Having a woman on board is suspicious, and we don't need him asking questions. After he is gone, you can wander as you please."

"Understood," she mimicked.

"This is important. I need to know you will stay below deck."

"I will stay out of sight. You need not worry."

Kale watched her, looking for any sign of an untruth. "We will be back in a few hours." He called for the men to follow him ashore. They waved to her and Tony as they descended the ramp.

"I don't know what it's going to take for him to trust me," she said to Tony once everyone had gone.

"Keep being yourself, Lilliana. He will come around." His dark emerald eyes softened with kindness.

"It doesn't seem difficult for any of you," she said.

"We have it easier than Kale. We do what he tells us, free of the burden of decision-making. We were told to treat you as one of the crew while you are with us. This includes trusting you. One day we will have to let you go. Though it may be heartbreaking, it will be much harder on Kale. He will be the one that makes that decision."

They were silent for a moment.

"You keep saying I will leave, but not when," she said.

"You should know by now, Lilliana, we can't discuss anything of that sort with you. If you want answers, you will have to speak with Kale."

She sighed softly.

"Sweet girl, I don't like seeing your face drawn down like this. What can we do that will make you smile?" He touched his fingers to her chin.

"Do you play cards?"

Chapter Fourteen

Lillian and Tony flipped their last card over simultaneously, revealing a five and a knight.

"I believe that means you've won this round, no?" Tony chuckled. "Were we playing for coin, you would have cleaned me out."

"Well, it helps to play against a novice." She collected the cards. "Again? Or shall we play something different?"

Before he could answer, there was a rap against the railing.

"Hullo?" a man called out. He sounded older.

"Excuse me, Lilliana." Tony left her in the galley, closing the door behind him. She peered out of the small porthole, taking care not to be in a position easily seen, as Tony greeted the man.

"I'm the ship surveyor. Name's Stelan." He leaned against a heavy cane as he shook Tony's hand. "Your captain—Kale, think it was—sent me to survey your vessel."

"Of course, good sir. Follow me. You can see the damage is limited here on deck. A few splintered railings." Tony showed him where the damage was. "And split floorboards."

Stelan pulled a scrap of paper from his coat and scribbled a few things as he inspected the broken areas.

"The major damage is down below. If you will follow me, please." Tony led him down to the second storage level, where the cannonball had pierced the hull.

Lillian returned to the bench and began shuffling the cards and piling them back together. Tony had said it wouldn't take long for the man to look at the ship. She sat quietly, contemplating what game they should play.

Both men were below deck and couldn't see or hear her. She was alone. This could be her chance to escape. She hurried to the porthole and peered out cautiously. There was no one in sight. In the distance she could see a bit of the harbor, covered in trees. People walking around. Civilization.

She opened the door some, but hesitated. She had given her word to Kale. And if she tried to leave now and the surveyor saw her, it could mean a lot of trouble for everyone. But she may not get another opportunity like this one. Her hand rested against the door, keeping it propped open as she weighed her decision.

"You will be docked a few days more?" he asked.

"As long as it takes to make repairs," Tony replied.

The man nodded as he looked around some more.

"It would be wise not to sail as she is. You've been lucky thus far, but the wrong wave in the wrong spot could cause fatal damage." He scribbled a few more notes as Tony nodded. "Tell your captain I will be back this evening with my full report and estimate of repairs," he said curtly. Tony shook the man's hand and returned to the galley.

Lillian sat at the bench, shuffling the cards.

"That wasn't terribly time-consuming," she quipped.

"He was very efficient," Tony replied. "Thank you for staying out of sight. Kale will be pleased." He took his seat across from her as she shuffled the cards once more.

"Of course. I gave my word; I do not break it lightly."

"You are a noble woman, Lilliana. I will be sad when the day comes when you have to leave us. And I will not be the only one."

She smiled softly.

"I have a few things to take care of," he said. "Do you have something to keep you occupied?"

She thought of the small pile of clothes left for her to patch, and of the new fabric Kale had bought her, but she was growing weary of being only a seamstress. "Is there something I can help with? I'd like to be useful."

He thought for a moment. "You can help me with the mopping. And then, if you like, you can start the midday meal. They should return within a few hours and would enjoy not having to wait for Rich to prepare it."

"Perfect."

"C'mon, Dave. You act like you've never carried a barrel." Kale grunted and adjusted his grip on the heavy box as they approached the gangway.

"Who thought we should put all the heavy items in one chest anyhow?" he retorted. Kale exhaled in relief as they set down their load at the bottom of the ramp to the ship. The crew followed suit with their own crates of varying sizes.

"Is this really the time for a break, men? We're nearly home," Jack said sternly as he pushed past them, carrying a crate over his shoulder. Kale and Dave heaved a sigh as they hefted their box up once more and continued up the ramp behind him.

"Tony," Kale called as they stacked the supplies in the middle of the deck to be sorted.

After a moment Tony appeared from below. "Looks like a good haul, Kale."

"Aye. Did the surveyor meet you?"

"He did. He looked around and scribbled some notes. Said he'd be back around sunset to speak with you about the cost. Also mentioned the damage is severe enough we shouldn't leave port until the repairs are complete."

"I was worried about that. Help us get these crates taken care of." Kale wiped the sweat from his brow. "Where's Lillian?"

"She's in the galley making the meal. She wanted to be useful."

"I see." He sifted through one of the crates, lifting out a small box, and took it to the galley.

"Aye, so Kale gets to carry the smallest crates?" Rich called jokingly as he walked away. Kale chuckled and waved him off.

Kale was immediately assaulted with the smell of burning meat wafting through the air as he entered. Lillian sighed heavily as he entered. She scowled at something boiling on the stovetop. He watched her as she set her hands on her hips in frustration, her usual gentleness temporarily replaced by determination. She wiped the sweat from her temple as she turned. He smiled, leaning casually against the doorway.

"Trouble?" he asked.

"These are not the conditions I am used to cooking in," she defended as she turned to look at him.

"From the looks of it, there are no conditions in which you are familiar with cooking." He sat the box down on the table edge and walked toward her. "But I guess that's to be expected of a lady." He took over stirring the boiling pot.

She stepped to the side. "So I haven't had much experience in the kitchen. I am good at plenty of other things. And I'll learn." Her scowl deepened.

"Well, you can't be good at everything." He added a few spices to the pot, and a bit more water, then stirred it again.

"I can certainly try." She crossed her arms. "Enough practice and I can master anything. Or at least learn enough to be passable."

"That explains a lot." He chuckled.

"What is that supposed to mean?"

"It means, I love your determination. Anything you put your mind to, you do. And if you can't, you keep trying until you can."

Her arms dropped to her side and a small smile spread across her lips. "I could say the same thing about you."

He held her gaze a moment before returning to the stew, taking the pot off the stove. "Why don't you go and let the crew know the food is ready?"

"Is it salvageable?"

"Barely." He raised a playful eyebrow toward her. Rick and Chase pushed through the galley door then, carrying a few large boxes.

"You pick up one box, mate, and you make it the smallest one?" Rick heaved as he set a large box on the ground.

"Be thankful I saved your meal."

"Did the lovely lass try her hand at cooking?" Rick laughed, deep and hearty.

"That she did."

"Is it edible?" Chase joked as the rest of the crew clamored through the doorway.

"Smells like food!" Jack yelled over the other men, sitting down in the first chair he came upon. "I'm famished. Get me a bowl over here, girlie."

"I'll get the hard tack," Dave offered, pulling his hat from his blond curls. The other men surrounded her in the kitchen, offering up their bowls to be filled first. Kale smiled and set his hand on her back.

"Better get to filling these men's stomachs before they turn on you," he said into her ear as he served himself and took a seat at the table. The room grew loud as each of the crew entered and took a place at the table. They laughed and jeered at each other between mouthfuls of stew and tack.

Kidd was last in line. "Wish ya could have gone ashore with us today, Lillian. Lots of neat fabrics and buttons. Kale picked out some dreary gray ones. Even though I showed him all the bright ones you'd'a liked."

"That's because the buttons aren't for me. They're for his coat." She filled his bowl, then her own.

"You would have liked the shop anyhow. Maybe next time we stop at port."

"Ha! I doubt I will ever leave this drab boat."

They joined the men at the table.

Kale cleared his throat to get everyone's attention. When no one responded he rapped his cup against the table until it was quiet. "I would just like to remind everyone that tomorrow is a very special day." He grinned, lifting his cup in Kidd's direction. Kidd groaned next to her as the men laughed. "It's Kidd's nineteenth birthday tomorrow." The room erupted in cheers and whistles. Those close enough clapped Kidd on the back. "As such," Kale continued, "we will start the day with our birthday ritual." The men laughed and some cheered once more. "And end the night with supper and festivities." Kidd smiled sheepishly.

"What is this birthday ritual?" Lillian asked. The men erupted in laughter. Kidd opened his mouth to tell her, but Kale interrupted him.

"You'll find out in the morning," he said, grinning mischievously. Everyone toasted Kidd.

Later that evening, Lillian wandered up on deck just as the sun was setting. She had found she really enjoyed watching the sunset over the ocean. It had become her evening ritual. Her fear of the ocean was nearly gone. As she walked across the deck, she noticed Kale already leaning against the rail.

"Well, hello there." He returned her smile, straightening and watching her before looking back over the ocean.

"What are you thinking about?" She leaned over the railing. The water slowly lapped against the hull of the boat, the soft sound soothing her.

"I'm thinking … It's nice to be ahead of schedule for once."

"So there's a timeline to this treasure hunt." She smirked. He was in an unusually good mood, and her plan to take a look at the map hadn't panned out so well. Perhaps she could get him to reveal a bit more if she kept the conversation light.

"There's always a timeline," he teased back. "But this particular adventure has a strict deadline."

"Which would be?" She raised her brows playfully. He held her eyes a moment, then shook his head. "Why can't you tell me more?"

"Because if I told you everything, you would run, and I need you." He looked back over the ocean, his frown deepening. "You don't know what this means to me."

"Tell me, then."

He looked down at the hull. "My family, they're far away. I had a sister …" Anger flashed in his eyes. He paused and took a breath. "But she died. She left my niece behind. She's wonderful. So smart, just like her mother."

"How old is she?" Lillian asked quietly.

"Nearly twelve. Seems like only yesterday she was just a bit of a thing."

"You have not seen her in a while," Lillian said. The slight sag in his features confirmed it. Her chest twinged for him.

"It's been … a few years. I send them money from time to time, and now … Kylah, she's fallen ill. Something they can't figure out. They need funds for a special doctor —more than I have to give right now." He didn't turn toward her as she laid a hand on his shoulder. The heaviness of his burden weighed his very body down. She had seen it in his cabin. That letter must have been from his family. He considered himself responsible for everyone around him—not just his niece, but the crew, and her as well.

"So this treasure hunt ..." It was for Kylah. That's why he had been so conflicted. Why he felt he had no choice in kidnapping her, no matter how guilty he had looked about it. No doubt felt guilty for even posing it to the crew. A small nod was his only answer. She squeezed.

He turned to her then, reaching for her face, but paused and chose a strand of hair instead. He twirled it between his fingers. She stepped closer, needing to feel near him, to comfort him. His hand slipped up the back of her neck and into her hair as his eyes watched hers. She smiled softly, and he bent down slowly and placed a soft kiss on her forehead. It was hardly a kiss. She'd barely felt his lips touch her skin before it was gone, but her chest tightened, and her breath caught at the small connection.

"You should get some rest," he murmured, turning to leave.

She contemplated going after him, but she was rooted to the spot, still paralyzed from his small display of affection.

Exactly what did he need from a noblewoman? If it wasn't something she could provide ... if something happened to his niece because of her lie ... She couldn't bear it.

Chapter Fifteen

"Shh," someone whispered. "He's a light sleeper."

"Well, then stop talking," another spat. They crept silently between the bunks until they reached Kidd's. The only person not present was Jack, as it was his day to make the morning meal. Lillian watched from the edge of the group as Kale moved toward Kidd's head and Rick took his place at his feet.

"Dammit!" Kidd shouted awake, struggling when they grabbed him. As they lifted him from the bed and carried him outside, they sang.

Ooooooh,
The Captain found you in bed today,
Oh no, you're going to pa-ay!
The Captain found you in bed today,
Ho! Hay! It's your birthday today!

You came to us with not much to say,
'Tis the day of your birth today!
We accepted you within the day,
Ho! Hay! It's your birthday today!
It dinna take'ya long to learn our ways,
Ho! Hay! It's your birthday today!
It's a great day for a swim today,
Ho! Hay! It's your birthday today!
Today is the day we throw you o'the way,
Ho! Hay! It's your birthday today!

As they sang the last verse, they threw Kidd over the rails of the ship. He shrieked as he hit the ice-cold water. The men laughed heartily, throwing a rope to him.

"I th-think we n-need a new b-b-birthday ritual." Kidd shivered as Kale and Dave pulled him up the side. Dave clapped him on the shoulder with a hearty laugh, and Lillian handed him a blanket to warm up, a sympathetic smile on her lips. The sun was just coming up over the horizon, painting the sky fierce colors.

"Go get dry boy. After breakfast we are going ashore to pick up some cargo to carry to Laramose." Kale patted Kidd on the back with a smile.

"I'm afraid you won't be carrying any cargo today. Or any other day." They turned to find a tall, blond navy man standing on the ramp, surrounded by at least thirty other men in uniform. He held the ship surveyor from yesterday by the collar, tossing him a small bag of coin as he released him. "Arrest them if they'll come quietly. Kill them if they don't." They rushed across, swords already drawn, leaving Kale and the crew to scramble.

"Weigh the anchor! Ready the sails!" Kale yelled, grabbing Lillian's hand. Rich and Chase stepped between them and the oncoming band, giving them time to get away.

"What about the damage?" She held tight to his hand as they sprinted across the deck.

"We have no choice. That scumbag sold us out." He led her into his cabin. "Damnit!" Kale ran his hands through his hair. "Stay in here. There's a dagger under the table. Keep it near you." His eyes scanned hers, assessing. Gently, he put his palm on her cheek. "Be careful." He turned toward the door.

"But I've never used a dagger!" she said.

"You learn best on your feet, right?" He flashed her a smile before he shut the door behind him.

She watched through the small porthole for a moment as he made his way back to where the crew was huddled, fighting with their backs to each other. As soon as he reached them, Eddie and Tony fought their way back to guard the door. Lillian searched the room for something to blockade the door, but all the furniture was bolted down.

She slid her hand underneath the table, feeling for some type of drawer, and felt the cool metal of the dagger. She tugged it loose. It was larger than she had imagined, and heavier. The blade itself was longer than her outstretched hand. She hurried back over to the porthole on the door. She was not going to be caught off guard if someone made their way through to her.

"We're outnumbered." Thomas shoved one uniformed man away and slashed at another.

"As usual." Dave chuckled as he grabbed the man Thomas had shoved and threw him over the side. "There. One less man."

"Thanks." Thomas rolled his eyes. "Only about six and twenty more to go." He ran his blade through the man he had been fighting.

"Five and twenty." Dave grinned.

"Less counting. More fighting." Jack huffed as he grabbed a man's head and twisted.

"Four and twenty." Thomas chuckled, earning a hearty growl from Jack. The ship lurched as they moved into open sea.

"I sure hope Kale's got a plan. It's not going to matter how many men we kill if we all drown," Kidd said. He kicked a man who had run at him and grabbed his sword.

"No choice, Kidd. We stay here, they'll just call reinforcements," Eddie said, swearing under his breath. The fighting had led him and Tony away from the door to Kale's cabin just enough for one of the navy men to slip behind them. Tony moved to grab him, but another uniform stepped in front of him.

Lillian forced all her weight against the door as one of the navy men tried to force it open. She wouldn't be able to hold it shut for long. She thrust herself against it one last time, twisting to the side, and the soldier tumbled in. He dropped his sword. She was quick to kick it away from him. Backing herself into a corner, she held the dagger up threateningly.

She swallowed, steadying her voice. "Get out. I do not want to kill an unarmed man."

A wicked grin spread across his face as he got to his feet. "You think you can kill me? A simple lady's maid? Dagger or no, you don't stand a chance against me." She froze. "You're lucky Captain Davis wants special care taken with you."

"Dall? But he's dead. They're all dead," she whispered. But she knew as she said it that Kale had been right. Dall had escaped before the storm had torn the *Rossut* to pieces. The navy man laughed as he advanced toward her, a hollow, wicked sound. She stepped to the side and held the dagger up once more.

"You pathetic girl. You really think Captain Davis would die in a storm? No. You were supposed to die, alongside the pathetic family you worked for." She cried out as she stabbed the dagger toward him. He easily pushed her to the side and disarmed her, sending the dagger flying.

"No!" She screamed as he grabbed her arms, holding them against her. She couldn't move.

"You're nothing but a slip of a girl. What can you do against me?"

"Call for help." Dave sliced his sword down on the man's arm. He yelled, dropping Lillian to her knees. She reached for the dagger, but the man kicked out. She cried out in pain as his foot connected with her midsection, and she fell to the floor. Dave brought his sword down again but only nicked the man's shirt as he shoved his body backward and into Dave. Dave hit the chair and lost his balance. The man shoved him to the ground and grabbed Dave's sword.

"This is for my uniform." He smiled wickedly as he stabbed Dave in the arm, pinning it to the floor. Lillian stood unsteadily and ran toward him. "And this ... is for my arm." He reached for his own sword, which lay nearby. Lillian screamed as she threw herself on the man's back. But it was already too late. He had plunged it down through Dave's chest. Dave cried out in pain, his free arm flailing wildly, trying to push the man off him, to no avail. His movement slowed, then his arm dropped to the floor. He looked at Lillian one last time. His head fell to the side.

"No!" she screamed. In a fit of grief and rage, she bit down on the man's ear.

"You bitch!" He tossed Lillian across the room. She landed hard on her shoulder. He walked toward her. She tried to stand, but her legs buckled, and she slipped to the floor, just long enough for the man to reach her.

"My fucking ear!" he screamed. The back of his hand connected with the side of her face. She shielded her head as she crumbled the rest of the way to the floor. "Screw Dall. As long as you're alive, he'll be satisfied." He swung his leg back and connected with her stomach again, in the same spot. She screamed in pain. Again, and again, he kicked her. Finally, when she thought she might pass out from the agony, he reached down and scooped her off the ground.

"No," she sobbed. She pushed against his tight grip. Tears streamed down her face. But she had no strength left.

T hey were well away from the coast now, down to six or seven navy men aboard. Most of the crew had realized it took far less effort to just toss them overboard than to fight. Kale fought on the upper deck. He parried, pushing a man over the edge. He'd just spun around to defend himself from another when he spotted someone carrying Lillian across the deck, his arms wrapped around her arms and chest. She kicked violently but it was no use. Kale jumped the rail and ran to them. Johnny beat him there.

"Let the lady go, and you might leave with all your limbs," Johnny growled, his sword pointed at the man.

"She's no lady," the man cackled. "Get out of my way before I run my sword through you too."

"Looks to me like you're surrounded," Kale said. Jack and Tony were pushing the last two navy men toward the rails, while the rest of the crew had surrounded the man.

"You think Dall is going to let you get away?" the man said. "He's got ships ready to sail after you. Perhaps the little lady will live if you surrender quietly."

Johnny swept his arms toward the open sea. "I don't see any ships. Do you, Kale?"

"No, Johnny, I sure don't. What do you think? Should we call his bluff?"

"I tell you what." Johnny circled the man to stand behind him. "I'll give you one last chance to surrender the girl before I rip your arms off."

"Sounds fair to me. How about you guys?" Kale looked to the crew. They all nodded solemnly, weapons at the ready.

"Dave ..." Lillian whispered.

"Shut your mouth, girl!" The man growled, squeezing tighter. She gasped at the pressure.

"Let her speak," Kale demanded.

"He killed ... Dave," she said between sobs. "In your cabin."

"Tony." He motioned to his cabin, not breaking eye contact with the navy man. Tony nodded and ran inside. "You better hope that boy is still alive," Kale growled as he put his sword to the man's throat. He tightened his grip on Lillian. She cried out.

"You don't want to do that, *Captain*," the man spat the word at Kale as if it was an insult.

A moment later Tony emerged from the cabin. Blood covered his hands. He shook his head sadly. Kale's face tightened. He shot Johnny a look. In one swift motion, Johnny slashed the back of the man's legs. He yelled in pain, releasing Lillian from his hold as he fell to his knees. Kale pulled her to him before she could fall to the ground.

"You—" Before the man could finish, Johnny drew his blade across the man's throat. His blood spilled across the deck. Lillian gasped, hiding her face against Kale's chest. His arms tightened around her.

Jack and Eddie dragged the man's body to the railings and tossed it over the side. Kale held Lillian while the others went to his cabin.

"I tried—" She took a deep breath. Her tears had run dry, and she felt empty inside. "I tried to stop him. But I was too late."

"There was no way you could have stopped a man that large."

"I could. I could have. If I knew how to fight," she said.

"Looks like you have your own fighting style." He chuckled. "Was that your work on his ear?" Kale wiped the smear of blood from her chin.

She nodded. "Will you teach me? To fight?"

"Perhaps. But not today. Today we find refuge to repair the damage. And then we celebrate."

"Celebrate?"

"It's still Kidd's birthday. We won an unwinnable battle. And we celebrate the life Dave spent with us."

The crew carried Dave's body toward the rails. His shirt was bloodied, but they had closed his eyes. Kale set her down gently and led her by the hand to join them.

"Is there no better way than to toss him over? Some family to bury him?" she asked.

"If we had families that cared, we wouldn't spend our lives at sea," Chase said quietly.

"This is our family." Eddie put his hand on her back to comfort her.

"Dave was our family," Kidd whispered.

Jack huffed. "You were too happy all the time, Dave. It was annoying."

"But you made a good breakfast." Rich chuckled.

"And you had the funniest stories," Chase added.

Kidd wiped a tear. "Even when it wasn't appropriate."

"*Especially* then." They all laughed.

"Goodbye, old friend." Kale bowed his head.

The crew repeated his words in unison.

"Goodbye," Lillian whispered. They hoisted his body over the rails.

"From stardust we came," Kale said softly.

"To stardust we remain."

Chapter Sixteen

There were no docks as they approached a little lump of earth Kale had called Palney Island. They dropped the anchor and took a rowboat to shore. It took most of the day to patch the holes enough that no more water would leak in. Even with Lillian's help, they were still down a few men whose injuries were harsh enough to earn them a day's rest.

"Here, Lilliana. No need to dehydrate yourself." Tony offered her water. His arm hung in a sling across his chest.

"Thank you."

"Hey! Bring some of that over here!" Landry shouted, waving Tony over.

"Get your own." Tony smiled.

"Seems we're almost finished here," Lillian said.

"Aye. Kale is already preparing for everyone to go ashore."

"Who will be my guard dog this time?" she mused.

"No, sweet Lilliana, you will come with us. We are going to shore to celebrate. We wouldn't dare leave you behind."

"Unless you want to stay," Johnny said, sauntering over to them. "You must be sick of us by now. I know I am."

"Sick of your own crewmates?" Lillian asked.

"Sure. You get sick of anyone if you spend too much time with them. Except perhaps you. I could never get sick of you." Johnny twirled a curl that had slipped her tie.

"I wish I could say the same," she retorted.

"You will." He smiled as a few of the other crew emerged from below, carrying boxes.

Kale was not far behind. "Are we ready to row to shore?" The crew cheered in response. "Are you prepared to go with us?" he asked Lillian.

"I—I think so."

"Good. I trust you won't ruin Kidd's birthday by trying to escape. Everyone, grab a box. Kidd, Rich, Chase, and I will take the first boat over. Lillian you will ride along in the last one."

"Why can't she come with us?" Kidd asked.

"It's safer this way." Kale hefted a larger box and loaded it onto the small rowboat. Johnny and Jack lowered the boat down until it hit the water. As they rowed to shore, Lillian and the rest of the crew busied themselves stacking and organizing the remaining crates. The injuries to her stomach hurt so much that she had to stop and rest every few minutes. When Rich came back for the last trip, they only had two small boxes left. Lillian's breaths were heavy as she handed the boxes to Rich before she headed to the ledge above the rowboat.

The water below sloshed lazily against the small boat and the hull of the *Stardust*. Her stomach tightened at the memory of being beneath those freezing waves. Of wreckage floating around her as the air in her lungs screamed for release. She closed her eyes a moment and took a steadying breath. This was different. There was no storm. She was not in the water. She would not drown. She repeated the thoughts once more, climbing over the railing.

"Need help there, m'lady?" Johnny teased, his hand outstretched to steady Lillian as she situated herself on the rope ladder leading down to the small boat.

"Thank you," she muttered.

"What was that? I couldn't hear you. Did you say something that wasn't a snide comment?" He laughed.

She was too focused on climbing down the ladder to fix him with the pointed stare he deserved. Once she reached the bottom, Tony helped her across the short gap between the hull and the boat. She gasped as the small boat rocked with the newly added weight.

"Have a seat, Lilliana." Tony chuckled. "You'll get less seasick."

"Aww, is the poor lady not used to small boats?" Johnny mocked as he climbed down the ladder, the last of the boxes held over one shoulder.

"No, she isn't," Lillian retorted, gripping the side of the boat as Johnny hopped down.

"You'll be all right. It's a short way." Tony smiled reassuringly as he and Johnny began rowing.

They reached the shore within a few minutes. Lillian was happy to step off the rocking boat. Even on the sand, her legs felt as if she was still over the ocean.

"You okay there?" Chase took the small box she was holding.

"It's just, this is the first time I've set foot on land since leaving home." She reached down and ran the sand through her fingers. It felt amazing to have a change of scenery.

"Aw, it's nothing special."

"Don't get too attached. We are only here for a few hours." Kale extended a hand to Lillian. She took it, returning his grin with a soft smile of her own.

The sun had just begun to set as they finished setting up "camp." A large fire burned on the beach, far enough up that the tide wouldn't bother it. Lillian helped Kidd drag a large tree stump close to the fire to sit on.

"Happy birthday, Kidd." She kissed him on the cheek. He blushed, too stunned to respond.

Jack set a box down heavily and pulled a large jug out. "Your birthday, son. You get the first swig." He handed it to Kidd, who uncorked it and took a deep drink. The men laughed as he made a sour face. He passed the jug to Lillian, who passed it on to Eddie standing next to her.

"What's the matter, Lillian? Ya don't want to try it?" Eddie held the jug out for her.

"Not after the face Kidd made." She laughed.

"The first swallow's always the worst. It'll give your belly some warmth, though." He pushed the jug back into her hands. She held it to her lips for a moment. It smelled sweet but musky. She took a small drink and swallowed quickly—too quickly. A cough erupted from her. The men laughed. It wasn't too bad once it stopped burning, and it did make the pit of her stomach warm, dulling the ache from her bruises. Chase pulled a small guitar from one of the crates and played a soothing melody. The men passed the jug back and forth as the sun sank behind them.

"How about a story, Rich?" Kale said as he and Rich set up a spit.

"Okay. How about the time we were searching for the time-piece?" he said. The men nodded and muttered in agreement. "You'll like this one, Lillian. Have you ever been to Telayan?"

"I've never left Aarilya before this." She laughed as she took a seat on the log next to Kidd. The rest of the crew found spots either on tree trunks or the sand itself.

"It's an amazing mechanist city off the coast of Uriba, full of shiny metal buildings and machines that do everything from fixing things to fetching food for you!" Kidd brightened.

"Anyhow," Rich continued, "we had just sailed for three weeks straight over open seas. We were weary from our travels and wished to rest. That's when we stopped in Telayan. Needing some extra coin for supplies, we stopped by Johnny's lady-friend's business to see if she had a job for us. Tamela accepted us graciously and asked if we could find her missing timepiece. She offered us five hundred silver to bring it back in one piece. Now, normally a missing watch would be close to impossible to find in a mechanist city. Luckily Tamela knew exactly where it was. She instructed us on its hiding place and even provided a map. We thought it was going to be the easiest silver we ever made. But boy were we wrong.

"Our first obstacle was the towering jungle, where the cave was. The towering jungle is a mountain with nearly vertical sides, all covered in thick vegetation sticking straight out of the sides. We bested the mountain by using rope and hopping along the sideways trees." The fire crackled between them as night set in, and Rich continued his story.

"Next was the cave itself. Even at high noon, this cave was pitch black. Luckily Kidd here had brought some flint, but finding branches dry enough to catch fire was proving more difficult. We decided to use a regular branch and wrap a piece of cloth tight around it. This worked well enough, though we had to keep replacing the cloth as we ventured deeper and deeper into the cave."

"Rick ended up with no shirt at all!" Kidd interrupted.

Rich glanced at him. "Once we reached the spot where Tamlea had said the watch would be, we found a man. 'Give us the watch,' Kale said. The man looked even more confused than we were. 'I have no watch,' he said. 'Leave here. I be alone or she find me.' This man didn't speak well—he didn't even have a Telayanian accent. 'The watch, and we will leave,' Kale said.

"Johnny cut in, being his usual charming self. 'We seek a silver timepiece,' he said with a smile. 'Have you seen it?' The man grew very afraid at this. 'No!' he starts screaming. 'No, she can't have me!' He was yelling. Johnny tried to calm him, saying, 'We don't want you, we only want the watch,' but he only screamed louder. 'No. No. I am Timepiece. She cannot have me.' It began to make sense at this point. You see, Tamela is a witch skilled in many things, one of which is transforming objects into people for short periods of time. She had neglected to tell us that the watch we were searching for was in the form of a man." Rich paused for dramatic effect.

"Well, what did you do?" Lillian asked, intrigued.

"Jack knocked him unconscious and carried him back to town, where Kale demanded double what she had offered."

"That's not a very interesting ending." She leaned back on the log.

"It's the truth."

"That can't be the truth."

"Why not?" he asked.

"A mountain with sideways trees? And there's no such thing as a witch."

"Like there was no such thing as a pirate?" Johnny retorted.

"This is different. Pirates are people, not magic,"

"So you don't believe in magic at all?" Kale asked.

"I'm not a child."

"What a sad and boring way to live." Chase picked up his guitar once more.

"Lilliana, you should live with your eyes wide open," Tony said with a smile. "You will see so much more that way."

"Well, if Lillian wants to keep herself shut off from the wonders of the world, who are we to stop her." Johnny got to his feet and extended his hand to her. "How about a dance?"

But Kidd stepped in front of him, emboldened by the drink and the festivities. "Birthday boy first." He pulled her to her feet. She laughed as he spun her around the fire, and the men clapped and stomped along. There didn't seem to be any pattern to his steps. He moved with the music, and she happily followed along. After a few turns around the campfire, Johnny stepped in, sweeping her away from Kidd seamlessly as he spun her. His steps were surer, coordinated, but still didn't resemble any type of formal dance.

As the night wore on, Chase never missed a beat, and they all danced and drank until the fire started to lose its flame.

Later, Lillian sat on a log, catching her breath from the headiness of dancing and from the wine. She'd thought she would feel dizzy, but she mostly was tired. And sore. She pressed a hand to her stomach.

"You dance beautifully." Kale took a seat next to her. He offered her a cup of wine, but she shook her head.

"My mother taught me. She used to dance every day. It was one of her passions. One of many." She smiled.

"And you? What is your passion?" he asked. She looked to the stars as she thought for a moment.

"I guess I don't really have one. At least, I never really thought about it. Which is odd, because both of my parents were so passionate about so many things. I suppose I just put all my focus on Maria, so I didn't have time for a passion. Oh! Except perhaps novels. Does reading count as a passion?" She was rambling. "Do you have any passions besides sailing and brooding?" She leaned her shoulder against his.

"I didn't realize brooding could be a passion." He ran a thumb along her lower arm.

"Well, you do it so spectacularly." She looked up to find his eyes on her. He looked back to the sea. The waves slowly lapped against the shore, the calmer parts reflecting the starlight as an unending pool of night. The water rippled softly with the breeze. She could stare at the ocean all night.

"I never used to." He sagged.

She leaned closer, realizing that heaviness of his had started to set in. "Your need to take responsibility, for everyone around you." She laced her fingers through his, and he looked at her then. "It's a darkness that you carry around. You let it consume you, and you don't let any light in. You don't let anyone help carry that burden. But we're here for you." Lillian squeezed his fingers. "I am here for you. You can talk to me. I ... can be the light." She whispered the last sentence.

He leaned down and placed a small, lingering kiss on her her forehead before he unlaced his fingers and stood. She felt the emptiness where the warmth of his body had been.

"I can't ... I'm not ready," he said without looking at her.

She nodded. Tears pricked the back of her eyelids. But he didn't walk away.

"I never realized Mr. and Mrs. De Sansol were passionate people," Kale said, unpacking her earlier words. She stayed quiet for a moment, not knowing how to answer. "Lillian?"

"Hmm?"

"You were very talkative a moment ago. You don't want to talk about your parents?"

"I'm just tired is all. The wine." She waved her hand dismissively, not meeting his eyes.

"What's bothering you?" he pushed.

"I don't want to talk about it right now."

"Because you're keeping secrets from me?"

"You're one to talk about secrets." She traced a finger in the sand. "You didn't know my parents, so don't pretend what I say about them surprises you."

"I know enough."

"And why is that, Kale?" she spat, anger bubbling up. "Why do you know anything about them? You and Johnny both. How do you know Captain Davis? Why were you even in the same part of the ocean as we were?" Once she started throwing questions at him, she couldn't stop. It was as if she were possessed. The wine had made her careless, and she had held her tongue too long. She was tired of playing this game.

"Lillian," he warned as she stood.

"No! Don't *Lillian* me. You pester me for answers but won't give any in return. I am tired of getting the brush-off. I want to know. I want to know everything. I can handle it. And if you don't tell me, I swear I will lose myself on this strange island, and you won't have to be cryptic anymore, because I won't be here." She swayed for a moment, setting her hand on the log to right herself.

"You really want to know the truth?" he demanded.

"Yes!" she yelled, louder than she meant. The men were still celebrating by the fire. They had pulled a box out and were emptying the contents, which looked like fireworks, onto the sand.

"Fine, here's the truth. We were there, in that ocean, for a reason. You."

"Me?" she asked, stunned.

"Yes, you. Specifically, you. You and your mother, or one or the other. We planned to attack Dall's ship and kidnap you. But then the hurricane hit, and we had to change course, as any respectable crew would. Apparently Dall had other plans and instead lost the lives of your family and most of his crew—after saving his own ass, of course. Luckily you survived and happened to drift far enough that we came across you. Fate, I guess." He ran his hands through his hair.

"Why me?" she whispered.

"Because you're a De Sansol. A noble. An Aarilyan noble."

She was silent for a moment. The truth was on the tip of her wine-soaked tongue. If she told him now, would he leave her here? On an unfamiliar island in the middle of the ocean, with no family to return to? She didn't know which was worse; holding this secret in for so long, or the fear of letting it out.

"Why do you need an Aarilyan noble?" she asked finally.

"It doesn't matter."

"Yes it does."

"No, Lillian, it doesn't. I'm done arguing for the night." He turned from her.

"It does, Kale …" She paused a moment. She couldn't tell him now. She couldn't. Even after everything she'd been through with them, they would leave her here. Tears streamed down her cheeks at the thought of being abandoned. But if she didn't tell them, and it ruined their quest, she would lose them anyway. So she blurted it out. "Because I am *not* a noble."

Kale went deathly still, and she immediately regretted saying it. But she couldn't lie any longer. It had been bubbling up inside her, and the wine had loosened the cork.

"What do you mean? You're a De Sansol."

"But I'm not. I'm sorry, but I've been lying to you. To everyone. I was only a maid to the De Sansols. Maria was the daughter. I was a maid ... only the maid," she repeated softly. Tears flowed freely down her cheeks.

"That's not possible," he said. "You had noblewoman's clothes on. And Johnny met you on the docks—you said then that you were a De Sansol." But she could see in his eyes, he knew the truth. All his suspicions had been right.

"I lied," she said again.

He began to pace, his eyes darting back and forth, trying to piece things together. When he stopped to face her, his eyes were frantic. She knew the stakes he had in this. Not just the crew, but his niece. Regret filled her heart.

"Why?"

"Well, Johnny was so rude on the docks, I just ... And then when I woke up here, I was in shock and ... it just sort of happened," she said. He growled, running his fingers through his hair.

"Why do you need a noblewoman?" she asked again. He said nothing, but shook his head and stormed away from her. "Kale!" she called after him, but he didn't stop. The crew were setting off the fireworks, oblivious to the scene that had just unfolded.

The night sky lit up as two more exploded overhead. The slight breeze blew the embers into the water where they fizzled into nothing.

Kale pulled Johnny from the festivities until they were out of earshot.

"I told you something was wrong with her," he said, barely controlling his anger.

"What? What happened?" Johnny asked, looking across the beach where Lillian was sitting on the log.

"She's not noble, that's what."

"That can't be. Where did you hear that? I met her on the docks, remember? She has to be noble," Johnny assured him with one of his lighthearted grins.

"She lied." Kale grabbed Johnny's arm. "She's a goddamn maid." He growled as he let go and paced the beach, his hands in his hair.

"A maid? Well, that explains a lot." Johnny laughed.

"This isn't funny. What are we going to do now?"

"With Lillian?"

"With everything! We can't use her now. We won't be able to get another noble in time. And where are we supposed to take her?"

"Well, she could always stay with us," Johnny suggested.

"Yeah, I just confessed our plot to kidnap her. I don't think she's going to want to stay with us." Kale shot Johnny a look.

"Where else is she going to go? She has no family," Johnny mused.

"We don't know that. We don't know anything about her. All we know is that she isn't a De Sansol, and she isn't a damn noble!" Kale yelled. He rubbed his hands over his face. He could feel his panic building, the hopelessness. His darkness, Lillian had called it. She was spot on—he nearly smirked at the thought. He shook his head. She always seemed to see right through him. But he hadn't seen through her. She had lied to him, had kept the most important piece of herself a secret. The one thing he had required of her—and it had all been a lie. He bent down, holding his head between his thighs as he fought to catch his breath.

"All right, calm down," Johnny said quietly. "We will figure out another way. We always do."

"Not this time, Johnny. I can't see a way out. We're out of time."

"If we go direct to Aarilya, skip Laramose, we could make it. You still have your invite to that ball. Show up and work your magic.

We could be back on the seas with a new noble the next morning. Then it's only a few days to Telayan and on to the isle."

"Dall is bound to be patrolling Aarilya. And Stevenson will be on the outskirts keeping a lookout for us. If he gets the map, we're done for."

"He won't get the map. Even if he did, he'd still need a noble." Johnny kicked at the sand as Kale came to a stop, considering.

He nodded. "It might work."

"It *will* work. And you can sell that trinket, send the money to Kylah. That should be enough to get them through for a while yet." Johnny clapped a hand on Kale's shoulder.

He nodded once more. "And Lillian?"

"If you don't want her on board, then we leave her back in Aarilya, like you said."

"Even if she doesn't have any family?" Kale held Johnny's gaze.

"She's a capable girl. She'll figure something out. She's safer there than here with this motley crew." Johnny laughed as he clapped Kale on the back.

Chapter Seventeen

Lillian sat in silence as Tony and Eddie rowed back to the ship. Rick sat next to her, laughing.

"What about when my dolt brother dropped one and it shot right between his legs and straight into the fire?" He laughed again.

"Better in the fire than the box of firecrackers, like when we were in Arbor." Tony chuckled.

"Yeah, that party was over fast. Kale almost banned fireworks completely!"

"Wish you were feeling better so you could have joined us." Tony gently touched Lillian's shoulder.

"Too much wine for you?" Eddie asked, concerned. She stayed silent as she stared over the ocean. After it was clear she wasn't going to respond, they quietly continued their own conversation.

Once they reached the boat, she went straight to her cabin. She was frustrated and tired and wanted this night to be done with.

And sore, so damn sore. She had always assumed it wasn't a coincidence the pirates were in the same waters as the *Rossut*, but hearing the truth of it was still a shock. They had been there to kidnap her. No—to kidnap Maria. The thought of Maria being on this boat, interacting with the crew, was beyond her. It was so hilarious she began giggling. Her giggles turned to a laugh, which soon turned to sobs. She lay like that awhile, sobbing into her bedding, until she fell asleep.

She awoke the next morning before the sun was up. Her head was buzzing, and her body ached. For the first time, she missed her old room and bed in Aarilya. She flinched as she slowly pulled her pants up, and groaned as she tugged her shirt over her head. Her abdomen hurt even more this morning. She tied her hair and headed upstairs. Only Rich was on deck. Since they were still at anchor, there wasn't much for anyone to do.

"Good morning, Lillian," he said. He had a small knife in his hand and was carving something into a branch. "Feelin' better this morning, I see."

"A bit, thank you. Have you been on all night?"

"Aye. Rick should be relievin' me soon." He scratched his burly red beard and stifling a yawn.

"Is Kale around?"

"Still in his cabin, but he's awake."

"Thank you."

"Lillian," he called as she started to leave. "Did I ever tell you the story about the cat Kidd brought aboard?"

She turned back toward him.

"We were lookin' for work in Arbor when Kidd came across this stray tabby. Must have been eight years or so, scrawny as hell. Kidd decides he's gonna rescue it. 'A ship ain't no place for a pussy-cat,' I told him. 'Cats fear water, and they like steady ground, not rocking boats. Ya gotta bring 'em on when their kits.' But he swore up and down he would train this poor old cat. Anyways, once we got back to the boat, this cat went daft, just like I says. He ran like crazy. I ain't never seen a cat run that fast. He ran all around until he finally darted over the rails and into the water. Kidd already loved that cat so much he dove in after him. Got scratched all to hell, but he saved it from drowning. After that, the cat loved Kidd. He followed him around everywhere, even learned to follow commands like a pup would. He traveled on the ship with us for two years before he passed. Anyhow, he showed me that sometimes even if you don't think something belongs, you can make it work."

"What was the cat's name?" she asked.

"Ol' Taffy, Kidd called him." He laughed, and Lillian laughed with him.

"You're a good storyteller."

"It's the truth," he said, still whittling. She touched his shoulder briefly.

Reaching Kale's cabin, she raised a hand to knock just as the door swung open.

"Lillian," he said curtly. His brows were furrowed, and he refused to meet her gaze as he stepped out, forcing her to step back.

"I wanted to talk about last night," she started slowly.

"Ah, yes. Turns out we have no use for you anymore. So we will be taking you back to Aarilya. Unless you'd prefer to stay here." He pushed past her.

"That's it?" she asked, astounded. She moved in front of him once more, forcing him to look at her. "You're just going to dump me somewhere?"

"Like I said, we're on a schedule. The only reason we are taking you that far is because we're going there anyway."

"There is nothing for me in Aarilya."

"Not my problem," he muttered. And walked away.

She stood there on the deck as the sun rose behind her. She had thought Kale genuinely liked her, at least more than just as a piece in whatever game he was playing, to be dropped whenever she wasn't useful anymore. Apparently, she had thought wrong. What would she do in Aarilya? She had no family there. Perhaps she could get another position with one of the noble families. But did she really want to go back to cleaning someone else's mess? Planning their supper parties and tutoring their children? That was a lifetime ago. It was no longer a part of who she was. Perhaps she could open a store on the docks—perhaps a bookstore. She had a week, at least, to think about her future. It wasn't worth worrying over now.

The few men who had still been in their sleeping quarters emerged and headed toward the galley, where Kale had gone. Her stomach growled.

"Come on, Lillian," Rich said. "Let's eat." She followed him.

Rich and Lillian were the last to get their bowls and sit. Everyone was still laughing and telling stories about the night before. Each one got more fantastic, like when Eddie told of how he'd wrestled a monkey for the wine jug. Kale stood and cleared his throat as everyone finished their breakfast.

"Lillian has chosen to continue with us back to Aarilya. I'll be bringing a smith to repair the ship today so that we can set sail this evening. We have already lost time because of the attack and will be pushing as fast as we can. We should reach Aarilya in the next four days or so. Pray that the weather holds." Kale nodded at Johnny and they both left the galley.

"Glad to have you with us for a few more days." Rich patted her shoulder.

"Thank you," she murmured.

Kale went ashore shortly after, taking only Jack and Rich with him. Thomas, Chase and Landry played cards in the galley with Kidd. Tony, Eddie, and Johnny kept Rick company on deck.

"Hey, Johnny?" Lillian approached the group. They all sat around the mast, talking.

"Yeah, sweetheart?" He knew she would hate the nickname.

"Can I ask a favor?"

"You can ask. I may not agree." He laughed.

"Will you teach me to fight?" she continued.

They all burst into laughter. "What do you need to know how to fight for? Maids don't need to fight."

"Perhaps I don't want to be a maid anymore. What does it matter? Will you teach me or not?" Her anger sparked as they continued to laugh.

"All right, all right," Johnny said. "No need to get your knickers in a twist. I've got nothing better to do anyhow. What do you say boys? Want to help a damsel in distress?"

She scowled, perhaps Johnny hadn't been the best choice to ask.

"Good, you're going to need that attitude." He stood. "You're small, and weak. But you can use that to your advantage. Tony, let her use your sword." She turned to take Tony's sword, but Johnny swung his fist at her. She jumped back just in time but fell on her back. She groaned as she rubbed her abdomen. She was sure a nasty bruise had begun to form where she had been kicked.

"Johnny!" Thomas exclaimed. "Be careful."

"She wants to learn how to keep up with us big boys. I'm not going to go easy on her. You're fast," he said to Lillian. "Like I thought, but you need to work on your dexterity. Dodging isn't enough if you end up on the ground. Then I have the advantage." He held his hand out to her, she took it. He pulled her up, but as soon as she was on her feet, he pushed her backward and she fell again. She cried out as she landed hard.

"Balance, Lillian. Learn it." He laughed. This time she didn't accept his hand. "Tony, put your sword away. She can't handle that yet."

She glared. "Then what are we going to do all day? Keep pushing me to the ground?"

"If that's what it takes. If you don't have balance and can't dodge without a sword, then you can't do it with one." He lunged at her again. This time she moved to the side instead of back and kept her balance.

"Good!" Rick exclaimed. "Here, always protect yerself." He positioned her arms in front of her chest. "Even if you don't have a weapon, you need to watch your stance. Lock yer feet." She planted herself where she stood and kept her arms in front of her chest.

"Make fists. Be ready to punch." Eddie curled his tattooed fists to show her. She copied him and readied herself for Johnny's next attack. But it wasn't Johnny who attacked—this time Rick ran at her from the left, knocking her down. She rubbed her shoulder as she got to her feet.

"One and only rule in a fight: Stay aware of your surroundings," Rick said. "Focus on staying alive rather than defeating the enemy. If you only focus on your enemy—Johnny—then you don't see me." She nodded.

Johnny charged again. She stepped to the side and swung her fist at his back.

"Ouch!" she yelled as it connected.

"Not bad." He laughed, rubbing his back.

"That hurt!" She rubbed her fingers gingerly.

"Yeah, it's going to. There's some bags of rice in storage. Use those to toughen up your hands. And most importantly," he said, "never stop fighting just because you got a boo-boo."

Eddie grabbed her from behind, both of the men laughing. She squirmed, but he had a firm hold on her.

"Well, what are you waiting for? Try and get loose," Johnny said.

"I am!" she yelled. Fire burned in her eyes as she bucked against Eddie. He had a tight grip on her, same as the navy man had. Tears welled at the memory, at her uselessness. Her scowl deepened as she blinked them back.

"Squirming your body around isn't going to do anything. Think. What can you use?"

"There's nothing around! We're in the middle of the deck."

"True, but you have your body. What can you do?" Johnny prompted, surprisingly calm. Her frustration was rising. Eddie held tight, and she couldn't move her arms or hands enough to do anything. But her legs were free. She brought her foot up and stomped it down on Eddie's toes. He yelped, but his grip didn't loosen.

"That's good," Johnny said. "If you have enough room and enough force, sometimes that's good enough to get your attacker to loosen his grip—obviously not in this case. Eddie is much larger and stronger than you. Tony, any input?"

"Use your head, Lilliana," he said.

"Well, we've already established she's not the brightest." Johnny laughed at himself. "But Tony is right. If you use your head to bash Eddie's face, you will most likely break his nose. It will be painful to you too, but your attacker will let go. Go ahead, try it." She hesitated, and Eddie let go of her.

"No thanks. I don't need a broken nose today," he said.

"Wimp." Johnny laughed. "Practice your balance. And there's a barrel in storage that's full of sand. You can move on to that after the rice bags."

"That's it?" she asked.

"For now. I can't do everything for you. Think about what we taught you today, and I expect you to be better when we try again later."

"Later when?" She rubbed her arms where Eddie had held her.

"I guess you'll just have to keep aware of your surroundings." He returned to his spot by the mast.

She needed to test her balance. She had already gotten used to the rocking boat, but she wasn't ready to climb any of the ropes just yet. There wasn't much around to stand on. She put her hands on her hips as she eyed the deck slowly. This was going to take more time than she had expected. But she had nothing but time until they reached Aarilya. She wasn't sure what good it would do her once she was back on land. Ladies weren't meant to fight. But she wouldn't feel useless again. And if she ever saw Dall again—she would break his nose.

Then she saw the perfect spot.

Jack huffed as they walked the cobblestone streets toward the smith's shop. He, Rich, and Kale had been walking in silence since they had reached the docks, and it had become deafening.

"Look, I knows ye're upset about the girl, but are ya gonna stay mad forever?"

"I don't have to," Kale said. "Seeing as how we're dropping her in Aarilya in a few days."

Jack grunted. They walked past the small fish shops Palney was known for. Women stood outside some of them, showing off their wares and trying to lure customers in.

"Is that really what you want?" Rich asked.

"It's not about what I want. It's about what's best for everyone. And the mission."

"Droppin' Lillian in Aarilya cuz ye're mad at her is what's best for us?"

"I'm not ... mad at her." Kale rubbed his hands over his face.

"Could've fooled her," Rich said.

"And us," Jack added.

"She's pretty hurt with how upset ya were."

"The situation is not ideal. She lied to us, and now we are running out of time. And leaving her in Aarilya is what's best for her. She's nearly died twice already."

"The solstice ain't for another week," Jack said.

"We still have to travel to Telayan to see Tamela. Not to mention the time it will take in Aarilya to woo another noblewoman. We have no idea how long it's going to take to convince one to come to the harbor, let alone get close enough to drug her and drag her aboard without anyone seeing." He shook his head, frustrated.

"You still have that invitation to the party, don't ya? Turn on your charm and I'm sure you'll get a girl to follow ya no problem." Rich chuckled.

They stopped a moment, standing outside the smith shop.

"I do. But I haven't been in a proper social circle in a very long time. And it's a dance."

"Well, where's the problem? You're a fine dancer," Jack huffed.

"I can hold my own, sure. But I'm not up to date on the latest trend. Especially for Atwood. If I dance, they'll spot me for an outsider in an instant." He sighed.

"Well, you know who would know the trend, don't ya?"

"There's no way she'd agree. Not after I yelled at her." He'd seen the anger in her eyes when he told her she'd be going back to Aarilya. He planned on avoiding her the rest of the way. He couldn't ask her for help, not now. But if he was made, there would be no wooing anyone, and they would never get another chance before the solstice. He'd let everyone down. And he'd never get enough funds for Kylah.

He sighed once more. There was no way around it.

Rich patted his back as they went into the shop. "Lillian ain't the type to hold a grudge."

Lillian's breath shook as she tried not to look down. Her arms were straight out at her sides. She stared at her feet intensely, and inched one slowly forward, trying not to slip off the railing as a gust blew by. The waves crashed against the boat below her. She'd never realized quite how much the boat rocked until she stood on the rail. She lifted her foot once more, but felt uneasy, and jumped to the deck before she could fall.

"Damn!" she exclaimed, frustrated. When she had asked them tot each her to fight, she had imagined learning to hold a sword and place her feet correctly, not walking a rail and punching barrels. She pulled herself back up and stood a moment until she wasn't swaying any longer. She took one slow step, and then another.

"What are you doing?"

She gasped at the voice and jumped to the deck again. Kale and Rich had returned from the shore with the smith.

"Balancing," she replied.

He stood, watching her for a moment. "Take your shoes off" was all he said as he escorted the smith below.

Rich chuckled as he approached.

"Why take my shoes off?" she asked him.

"Yer feet can't feel the movement in shoes. It'll be easier to learn without 'em. Then add 'em later."

"Oh." She sat and removed her shoes.

"Also, you can't be afraid to fall," he said.

"I'm not."

"Sure ya are. You jump before you can fall. That conditions your body to fall every time you lose balance. You have to try and keep your balance, even when you feel uneasy, until you do fall. Practice on the other side, by the rope, so if you fall in the water you can pull yourself out."

"But the water is cold!"

"It'll help ya learn faster."

She peered over the railing at the crashing waves below and shuddered. Sure enough, a thin rope ladder hung down the side, nearly to the water's edge. She pulled herself up onto the railing and steadied her feet.

"Don't look down. Yer focusing on the water and not yer balance," Rich said. She looked straight ahead and stepped, one foot over the other. She felt uneasy but stayed until she gained her balance back. "Good," he said.

Step after slow step, she continued. She took two more steps.

Then two more.

Then slipped.

The water was even colder than she had thought. She screamed as she hit it. As her head slipped under, memories of the shipwreck, of water filling her lungs, blocked her vision. This was different, she reminded herself. She wasn't being pulled under, she wasn't drowning. Lillian shook her head to block them out, kept shaking until her vision cleared, and focused on the surface above. She kicked until she broke through, gasping at the cold air. She shivered as she grasped for the rope. It was just out of her reach. Some of the men had gathered on the deck and were looking down on her. Johnny and Rick laughed as she reached for the rope a second time. Her fingertips grazed the bottom, but she wasn't able to grab it.

"Someone throw her the life preserver," Kidd said.

"No," Johnny said. "She can do it."

Her teeth chattered, and her fingers were going numb. She reached for the rope again, but it remained inches above her frozen fingertips.

"Come on, you can do it!" Kidd cheered. Some of the others repeated the sentiment. She took a breath and surveyed the rope ladder, teeth still chattering. After a moment, she grabbed onto a small lip above one of the boards and pulled herself up higher, reaching once more, just enough to grab the ladder. Everyone on deck cheered as she reached the top.

"I'm n-not doing th-that again."

"Learn to balance better, and you won't end up in the water." Johnny laughed, handing her a blanket. She glared as she took it. She wasn't going to get any warmer if her clothes were still wet. She could go down and change into her yellow dress, but she would have to take off her chemise, or the dress would just get wet. She decided it would be best to allow the chemise to dry on her.

"What are you doing?" Kidd asked as she unbuttoned her blouse and pulled it from her wet skin.

"Getting dry." She slipped her trousers down, cringing a little from her belly as she bent over.

"But you're not decent!"

"You men walk around in your skivvies, no shirts, when you're hot or wet. Why can't I do the same, just because I'm a lady? Can you see my breasts?"

"N-no."

"Or my lady parts? Can you even see my stomach? No. This isn't any less decent than the trousers." She wrapped the blanket around herself and laid her clothes out to dry.

"I guess. It just doesn't seem normal is all."

"It's not normal. None of this is normal. I'm on a pirate ship, for heaven's sake!" She laughed.

Chapter Eighteen

Lillian practiced balancing the rest of the afternoon, only falling into the water twice more. She was dressed and dry by the time Kale and the smith emerged from below. She watched as he thanked the man and passed him a handful of silver.

"Was that all? Is he finished?" She was nearly breathless from strain of balancing, and having to climb up the rope ladder, and her body ached. But aching was a good thing. It meant she was making progress.

"Be ready to dock in Aarilya within a few days' time," he said. She sighed. As she turned to walk toward the galley, Johnny jumped at her from the corner. She tried to plant her feet, but it was too late, and she let out a yelp as her bottom hit the hard wood of the deck.

"Johnny, what the hell was that?" Kale yelled, surprised, as Johnny laughed.

"She wants to learn to defend herself. I'm teaching her how to keep her balance during a surprise attack." He offered her a hand. She knew better than to take it. Rubbing her sore bottom, she stood. Kale only grunted. "You're not getting much better at the surprise part. Let's see if you've improved when you're expecting it."

Johnny circled her slowly. She stayed still but kept a close eye on his movements. The second he lunged, she sidestepped and pushed him the opposite way.

"Good. Keep it up. And always keep an eye on your surroundings. You never know who might attack you."

She nodded but felt dizzy. She reached out to steady herself on Johnny.

"Lillian?" Johnny asked.

"Yeah?"

He and Kale took a step closer. "Are you okay?"

"I just ... just feel dizzy all of a sudden." Everything began to blur.

"Lillian!" Kale exclaimed. He and Johnny rushing toward her was the last thing she saw. She collapsed into Johnny's arms just as he reached her.

"What happened?" Kale growled.

"I don't know! She's been fine all day!"

Kale took Lillian from him.

"Lillian? What happened?" Rich ran over to the trio.

"She fainted. Johnny, you and Rich go ashore. Find a doctor."

"You think that's necessary? She probably just needs some rest. She's been 'training' pretty hard today." Johnny joked. But his brow was furrowed with concern.

"Damnit John, this is serious! Go!" Kale yelled. Johnny's mouth tightened, but he nodded and headed for the rowboat, Rich close behind him. Kale sighed as he hefted Lillian in his arms.

"I t's about time you came round," Thomas said. "We were worried."

"What happened?" She tried to sit up and gritted her teeth in pain.

"No, you need to lie down for a bit. Apparently you were hurt and didn't tell anyone," he scolded her, adjusting his cap.

"Just some bruising." She took in her surroundings. She realized she was in Kale's cabin, not her own. His table was clear, for once, no papers or maps covering it. The curtains over the back windows were closed, but she could see a bit of light peeking through. Enough to tell her it was early morning.

"Have you seen your stomach lately Lillian? It's more than a little bruise, and it's not just on your stomach, it's *in* your stomach. You were bleeding internally. Lucky it stopped on its own, and you didn't need to go ashore for surgery. What happened?" Thomas asked, his chocolate eyes concerned.

"The navy man, the one that—that killed Dave. He kicked me." She sighed. "Is Kale mad? Did we lose a lot of time?"

"Thankfully no. The doctor wrapped you up and gave us the okay to set sail. You only fainted last night. We're already on our way to Aarilya."

"Good."

"But you'll have to stay in bed until at least tomorrow morning. Lying down." He stressed the last part. She groaned. "I'm going to let Kale know you're awake."

"No. Not yet. Please?" She held his stare. She wasn't ready for a lecture from Kale, not yet. She was still quite sore. And tired, she realized.

"A few more minutes." He sighed. "And then I'm getting Kale."

Before she knew it, she was asleep again.

Thomas was leaning back in one of the chairs, but he sat up as Kale entered his cabin. Kale looked to Lillian, still sleeping on his bed, as he removed his hat and ran his fingers through his hair.

"How's she doing?" he asked quietly.

Thomas nodded. "She woke for a bit. She seems okay,"

Kale leaned back against the wooden table, arms crossed. "Do you think it's worth it Thomas?" he asked quietly.

Thomas looked to him, brows raised. "Is what worth it?"

"This treasure hunt. We already lost Dave ... disrupted Lillian's life, nearly lost her. On multiple occasions. Now we have to kidnap another, who—I guarantee—will not be so accommodating." He chuckled. "Stevenson's on our tail and will be until after the eclipse. Is it worth the risk of losing another of us?"

"This is the life, isn't it? To chase one score after another, until we die or grow old and retire. And how many pirates truly retire?" Thomas smiled. "And this is a big score. We need a big one. You most of all." Kale nodded, thinking over his words. "And Dall disrupted Lillian's life before we had a chance. Honestly, I think we offered her salvation. I think she'd be happy to stay on, if we asked."

"Good morning. Or should I say, good evening," a familiar voice said softly. She opened her eyes to see Kale sitting next to her.

"I'm sorry," she said.

"Why didn't you tell anyone you were hurt?"

"It really didn't bother me. No more than any other bruise."

"You must have a high tolerance for pain. That was certainly not any other bruise. And I'm sure Johnny pushing you around didn't help matters."

"Probably not." She tried to sit up, but he stopped her.

"You need to rest, or it won't heal properly. And I don't have time to find another doctor for you."

"I just need to sit up," she pleaded.

"No," he said firmly. "Not until morning."

"How am I supposed to get to my cabin, then?"

"You aren't. You'll sleep here tonight."

"Where will you sleep?"

"Don't worry about it. Here, drink some water." He held a cup to her lips. She hadn't realized how thirsty she was until the water touched her tongue. She drank deeply until the cup was empty. "We will be switching off, keeping an eye on you until tomorrow morning. There's no use in protesting either. It's an order," he said when she opened her mouth to argue.

"I don't want to be treated like an invalid. This is no way to spend the last few days of this adventure." She groaned as she leaned back against the soft bed.

"After everything that has happened, you still think this is an adventure?" He stood and set the empty tin cup on the table.

"Of course. I've never even left Atwood. Everything is an adventure compared to that."

"That's an amazing outlook on life. You'd make a pretty good pirate after all." He chuckled.

"Is that an invitation to join your crew?"

His playfulness was surprising, given his recent temperament. But she was learning his mood could change at the any moment.

"Not quite. Someone will be in shortly. You should get some rest."

"Kale?"

"Yeah?"

"I am sorry. That I'm not a noble," she said.

He stood silent for a moment. "I just wish you'd told me sooner."

Once he had left, she thumped the pillow in frustration. If only she knew how to appease him.

What was she going to do while she lay here all day? She looked around the room. Kale kept everything tidy.

A piece of paper caught her eye on the small table. It was the map she had seen before. He must have taken it out while he was on watch. She tried to shift herself up to see it better from the bed, but groaned as pain stabbed her abdomen. She had seen maps of Aarilya and the surrounding waters from Maria's geography books. On this map she could make out the bottom portion of Aarilya in the upper left-hand corner. She could also see the island of Laramose off to the east, and a few smaller islands south of that. Even further south, and to the west a bit, a small island was circled. It looked more like a hill, actually. And next to it was a symbol. She couldn't quite make it out from the bed. She tried to shift a bit closer but lay back down as she heard a sound outside the door, hissing in pain at the movement.

"Hey, pretty lady. I heard you're stuck on bed duty for the next few days." Johnny winked as he walked through the door. "I thought you might be lonely, and a bit hungry. Don't worry. It's broth, so it'll go down easy without you having to sit up." He laughed as he set a bowl down next to her.

"One day," she corrected. "I can get up in the morning."

"Really? Hmm. Perhaps we ought to get a second opinion. You were bleeding internally, after all. I think that merits at least two days of bed rest." He sat down next to the bed.

"No, thank you. I don't even want to sit still this long."

"Honestly, Lillian," Johnny looked down, turning pensive. "You should have mentioned you were hurt. All those times I pushed you, it could have caused some serious injury." He looked genuinely concerned.

"Were you worried?" she teased.

"Of course. We all were." He reached out and brushed her cheek.

"I doubt that."

"Why do you say that?"

"Well, I doubt Kale was very worried. Worried we would lose time, perhaps." She looked away, her chest constricted at the thought of him.

"You think Kale is that heartless?"

"Not heartless," she said. "He just has different priorities, I suppose. And I'm no longer a priority."

"I guess you don't know us as well as you think you do."

"What do you mean?"

"Oh, nothing." He stood and picked up the small bowl. "Here, have some broth." He held the bowl to her lips before she could protest. "You should get some rest. You'll need it if you want to be able to walk around tomorrow." He set the bowl on the small end table.

"Johnny?"

"Yeah?"

"You're not ... upset with me? For lying?"

A grin formed at the corners of his lips. "I'm not upset. Kale will figure out another way. He always does."

It was morning. Or was it afternoon? She couldn't tell, but there was sunshine coming through the small windows. She rolled over to find Kidd manning the chair next to the bed. She clutched the thin bed sheet to her chest.

"How long have I slept?" she asked.

"Only since last night. It's nearly midday," he said cheerily.

"Good." She started to sit up.

"Not yet!" Kidd said, jumping up. "Kale needs to examine you."

"Needs to what?" she asked, but he was already rushing out the door. He hollered for Kale, and Kale called back from the upper deck. A few moments later his footsteps approached.

"Thanks, Kidd. Off ye go."

"I thought I was allowed to sit, now that it's morning?" Lillian asked as he came in.

"Most likely, but I have to check the area to make sure you haven't injured yourself any further."

"You?" She gripped the blankets tighter.

"The doctor showed me how to do it. Now pull the sheets away."

She sat there a moment, stunned.

"Come on now, the bedsheets," he said again. When she didn't move, he reached over her, and with one hard yank, he pulled the bedsheet away from her chest. She blushed, embarrassed.

"What's the matter with you? Yesterday you wore this same chemise on deck in front of everyone, soaking wet. Why the embarrassment?" He was right, of course. There was no reason for her to be embarrassed now. But she couldn't seem to control it. It was different on deck, in front of the crew, than in his private cabin, with him. When she didn't respond, he shook his head and moved to stand over her. "Now stay on your back and lie still. Let me know if it hurts." He lifted her chemise to reveal her black and purple stomach. His face was intensely concentrated as he placed two fingers just above her belly button and pushed. She winced.

"Does that hurt?" His eyes held hers.

"A little," she said truthfully. He moved his fingers to the right a few inches and pushed again.

"Here?" he asked. She shook her head no. He slowly moved his fingers to the left side and pushed once more.

"No," she said softly, out of breath.

"Are you sure?" he asked, the corner of his lips raised.

"Y-yes," she stuttered. They sat like that a moment his hand still on her abdomen, their eyes locked. He brushed a thumb gently over her hip and all the blood in her body rushed to her face as she felt her cheeks flush bright red. He opened the mouth as if to say something, when the door swung open and Kidd walked in, finally breaking their gaze.

"You're fine to sit up." Kale ran his hands through his hair. "I'd like you to wait until afternoon shift change to get out of bed. If you start to feel any pain, let me know immediately." He stood and headed toward the door.

"You must be starving," Kidd said as he set the plate down.

"I guess I am." She collected herself as she pulled her chemise down and sat up slowly. She winced at the movement, her muscles taut.

"Guess you won't be able to practice your balance and whatnot for a while." Kidd watched her struggle to get comfortable.

"I didn't think so," she said softly.

"Too bad. You were gettin' pretty good."

"I was, wasn't I?" They both chuckled as she settled in, the pillows now bunched behind her and the sheet placed neatly back across her lap.

Chapter Nineteen

Lillian stretched lightly as she stepped out of Kale's cabin. She was still quite sore but much better. Twilight had nearly fallen. There were only two days until they reached Aarilya, and she intended on making the best of her time.

Surprisingly, Kale was the only one on deck. He really was quite attractive as he leaned against the railing, staring down at the water splashing against the hull. His gray eyes always contemplating and his dark hair blowing across his face. She watched as he ran his fingers through it, pulling it out of his face. She could feel the gentle brush of his thumb across her hip that morning. It sent a fluttering in her chest.

"What are you looking at?" she asked.

He seemed surprised to see her for a moment. Then he looked back to the waves crashing against them.

"Tell me, what do you see?" he asked.

She looked out over the ocean for a moment, watching the moonlight ripple across as it rose and fell.

"Water," she said. "And moonlight."

"That's all?"

"There's nothing else for miles and miles out here." She sighed and he chuckled lightly. Perhaps he was starting to warm to her again.

"Do you remember when I told you if you believed in magic, you would find it?" he asked.

"You were poking fun at me." She pursed her lips.

"I wasn't. Come closer." He motioned for her to stand in front of him. She moved closer, hesitantly.

"You'd better not push me in," she said. "I don't think I can handle the swim just now."

"I won't." Kale chuckled again. "Just humor me for a moment. Close your eyes." His hands rested on the rails encasing her. She did as he said, holding onto the rail for balance. "Now imagine a world where magic really did exist. Perhaps not in the way you would expect, but in small things all around you every day. Like when you find an item you thought you lost when you need it most. Or when the wind picks up just as you were about to give up on any breeze at all … Are you imagining?" His breath caressed her ear, and the warmth of his chest seeping through her back.

"It seems a silly notion," she said, her eyes still closed.

"It doesn't surprise me you'd think that. Most landlubbers don't believe in it. But when you're out on the sea as long as we've been, you see things. Things you couldn't dare to dream are in this world. You read novels, don't you? Try and open your mind to any possibility. Can you do that?"

She nodded. "I think so."

"Good. Open your eyes," he said finally. "What do you see now?"

She opened her eyes and looked out over the ocean once more. The moonlight still rippled across the water, the waves a little less calm than earlier. She started to tell Kale nothing had changed, but something caught her eye. She leaned over the rail and looked more closely at the water. She gasped as what she had thought was moonlight rippling now started to take a different shape.

"Strange and beautiful things happen in these waters, if you only let yourself see," he whispered. At first she saw only some unsettling of the water, like when you feed the fish at the pond and they all splash under the surface. Then all around, it began to glow, brighter and brighter, until they jumped gracefully out of the water, over and under themselves as if they were performing a dance. There were at least two dozen, small, perhaps the size of a shoe. They looked like fish but were long and perfectly oval with glowing circles of light decorating their bodies. As they jumped, sparks of light danced between them. All at once, they stopped jumping. They spread out what had to be some sort of fin from under their bodies, and their glow dimmed. From afar, someone might mistake them for mantas.

"They're called lightning fish," Kale said. "They come out just before a storm."

"But there isn't a cloud in the sky," she said.

"Perhaps not now, but I'm sure there will be one by morning. Lightning fish are never wrong."

"You'd put your faith in some fish?"

"I put my faith in the mysteries of the sea. I've sailed these waters a long time. Lightning fish are never wrong." He moved to lean over the rail next to her.

"Hmm," she said sarcastically as she looked up toward the clear skies.

"All clear below, Captain." Johnny approached them, brushing a piece of blond hair from his brow. "Beautiful, aren't they?" He motioned to the lightning fish. "Wow, there's even more now. Must be some storm coming. A big one, I'd say. Perhaps even a hurricane." He patted her on the shoulder.

"You believe in this too?" she asked, surprised.

"You don't doubt the fish, Lillian." Johnny laughed.

"There's not even a cloud in the sky!"

"It'll come. Don't you worry. Best prepare yourself for a rough night," he said.

"Let us hope it doesn't deter our course," Kale mused.

"Mmm," Johnny muttered in agreement. Lillian turned back toward the ocean and the empty sky above, smiling as she shook her head softly. Seeing fish that weren't there before was one thing. Using those fish to predict the weather was quite another.

That night Lillian dreamed she was aboard the *Rossut* again. She walked the halls and found them eerily empty. Such a large boat, and not a soul on board. She quickened her step, becoming frightened at being alone. A presence loomed behind her, following her. Pushing her forward. The walls were leaking, dripping at first. Then, as she hurried, the water rushed down them until she finally reached the stairs that lead to the deck. She climbed but got no closer to the top. The hall below her filled with the dark water that gained on her in no time, reaching her ankles, her hips, then her chest and finally her head. She gasped as it swallowed her whole.

Suddenly she was at the door. She pushed it open, and the water rushed out, dropping her on the deck. The sky was clear here, and the sun shone bright. Her breath shook as she stood. She wasn't alone anymore. She was surrounded by the crew of the *Rossut*. Maria, the De Sansols, Jeremy, and Chuck were standing right in front of her. She could reach out and touch them ... but something was off. Their eyes were blank, their skin pale, and they were dripping wet.

"You abandoned us, Lillian," they said in unison as they slowly advanced.

"No," she gasped in horror. The sky grew dark as thick clouds rolled overhead.

"You left us to die." Thunder clapped.

"No, I—"

"You left me alone." Jeremy took a step closer.

"No!"

"You stole my name." Maria stepped forward. Lightning struck behind her as the deck tilted.

"You abandoned us," they said again, surrounding her, pushing her toward the edge of the ship.

"I didn't mean to!" Lillian yelled. Maria reached out and pushed her over the rail. As Lillian fell into the cold water below, she screamed.

"No!" Lillian sprang up in bed. Her breath was ragged, and her hands shook. That was the first time she had thought of them in a while. It was fitting, she guessed, that it was a bad dream. Her hands still shook as she picked up her cup from her bedside table, taking a sip of water to calm herself. Though she had grown accustomed to the rocking of the ship and the rolling waves below, storms still stirred that forgotten panic in her.

Thunder shook the boat and a shiver went down her spine. She pulled her shirt and trousers on and rushed up on deck. What she saw was almost identical to the night the hurricane hit the *Rossut*. Right back in her nightmare. The familiar knot filled her stomach as she took in the scene. The whole crew was out there. The wind whipped violently around her. Eddie, Rich, and Jack were trying to lower the sails while the rest of the crew were bailing water back over the rails. Kale was up on the mast trying to secure the sails from the top, and Johnny was rushing around, lending a hand and barking orders.

"We told you not to doubt the fish," Johnny yelled over the thunder and crashing waves. Lillian's stomach roiled at the motion of the pitching ship. She should be helping. Or at the very least, get out of the way. But her feet were rooted to the spot.

"Lillian, you should stay below decks. It's just a storm, not a hurricane, and should blow over soon!" Kale shouted from the top of the mast, pulling her from her stupor.

There was a loud crack. The beam Kale was standing on snapped in half and came toppling down, bringing Kale with it. Jack, Rich, and Eddie jumped out of the way just as Kale hit the deck with a groan.

"Kale!" Lillian took a few steps forward, but the broken pieces of mast that were caught in the ropes swung toward her. She had no time to move. It knocked her over the rail and into the freezing waters below, just as Maria had in her dream.

"Lillian!" Johnny yelled. He ran to the edge and watched as she was pulled beneath the surface. The waves crashed violently against the hull as the *Stardust* rocked.

"Johnny! Help her!" Kale shouted. He limped around the broken mast, holding his bleeding leg. Johnny stood frozen. "What are you waiting for?" Kale screamed at him, but he didn't move. Kale cursed, moving as quickly as his injury allowed.

I t was happening again. Panic rose as Lillian sank down. The knot filled her stomach and throat. Black specks filled her vision as she tried to think, to do anything besides panic. She shook her head, clearing it just enough to let a few thoughts in. She couldn't let this happen again. Steeling herself, she tried to swim to the surface, but she felt heavy, like something was pulling her down. The ropes—they had twisted around her leg. She flailed and struggled but she didn't seem to get any closer.

Lillian reached down and tugged at the ropes. They were nearly as thick as her calves. Her fingers stung as she scraped and pulled and twisted. Finally they loosened and slipped down into the darkness below her. Her chest burned from holding her breath as the dark water consumed her too, just like it had in her dream. Her chest was about to burst. She gasped for air, but only water filled her lungs. She couldn't drown at sea, not like this. She reached out once more, grasping for the surface, for safety, for anything to tell her she could survive this. At last something reached back. She grabbed hold and was pulled up. The few moments felt like forever as they rose to the top.

As her head finally broke the surface, she coughed and sputtered, forcing sea water from her lungs again and again.

"You okay?" Kale shouted over the rain.

She nodded and he tugged on a rope wrapped securely around his waist. He pulled her close and held her tight as the crew pulled the rope, and them, back through the tumultuous waters towards the *Stardust*.

"Are you okay?" Kidd and the others helped them over the rail.

"I think so," she said, still coughing. She shivered as the thunder struck. The storm was moving away now. "Just a l-little cold." The chill settled deep in her bones. Thomas wrapped her in a blanket, then handed one to Kale. He groaned as he took it.

"Kale, you're hurt." Blood dripped down his calf.

"He'll be fine. Just a little splinter." Johnny's smile faded when he looked at Kale. "You both just need some rest."

There was a jumble of talking as everyone surrounded them, making sure they were okay. Kale excused himself and limped off to his quarters. The storm had moved on, leaving only a drizzle of rain and a broken mast to prove it was ever really there. Lillian assured everyone she was perfectly fine and tried to excuse herself as well.

"You should at least go lie down. Your stomach is still healing, and now you've nearly drowned!" Thomas exclaimed. The men mumbled an agreement. She nodded and wandered away as they went back to fixing the damage.

Once she was in the hall, away from everyone, she slid down the wall and let out a sob. Even as the rough wood pushed into her back, she could still feel the burn of the sea water in her throat, feel the pressure of the ocean pushing in on her. She wanted nothing more than to be back home, on land, with Maria and her parents. Everything she thought had been hard in her life was nothing compared to being in the middle of the ocean for days, weeks even. Nothing came close to almost drowning—twice. She wasn't made for this. She was a lady's maid, not some harbor wench who kept company with rough men.

Not that the crew had ever been rough toward her. She rather enjoyed their company. They always made her feel welcome, like she was one of them. They hadn't teased her when she wanted them to teach her to fight. Well, not very much anyway. And she was proud of herself for keeping up with them and learning a bit of self-defense. She really enjoyed being on the ship—when they weren't being attacked. And when she wasn't drowning.

Without Maria, there was nothing for her on land. She wasn't sure she would even find a position as a lady's maid right away. Being in the middle of the ocean sounded far better than spending the night on the streets. But would Kale allow her to stay on after they reach Aarilya?

"You okay?" Johnny asked, startling her out of her thoughts. She hadn't heard him come down.

"I'm fine."

"You sure?" He sat down next to her, his expression somber. "You've been through quite a lot recently."

"I am, actually." She laughed as she wiped the nearly dried tears from her cheeks. "Though I would prefer not to nearly drown every time I'm in the water."

"I'm sorry, Lillian." Johnny said, looking away from her.

"It's not your fault, Johnny. It was an accident."

He didn't seem convinced. "Well, you must be excited to get to Aarilya now. Be on dry land, huh?"

"I thought that I was. But I'm actually a little sad. I feel like I'm finally starting to find a place here."

"You want to stay, after everything?"

"I think I do. Do you think Kale would let me?"

"Who knows with him? But Lillian, you don't want to stay. Trust me. You'll be stuck with a bunch of smelly, arguing men for months at a time. Getting attacked all the time. Chasing down ludicrous treasure maps and other boring piratey things." He waved his hand dismissively. "That's not for you."

"But what if it is? I was so bored with my life when I was with Maria, and I didn't even realize it until I got stuck here. There's so much more to see and do in this world. More people, more fish, and who knows what else? I feel ... free here."

"You can feel free on land. You can travel and adventure there too. And it'd be much safer for you." He flashed his charming grin, but she saw right through it.

"What's the matter with you, Johnny? You were so supportive before, telling me I'd make a great pirate and teaching me to defend myself."

"Nothing," he grumbled. "Nothing's changed. You were a lady before, with a home and an inheritance waiting for you. There was no way you'd really stay." He ran a hand through his light hair. "There's a lot going on here that you don't know about."

He stood and started to walk away, saying over his shoulder as he went, "You should seriously consider staying shoreside when we reach Aarilya."

"Ugh!" She couldn't understand why he was being so contradictory. Now, more than anything, she wanted to stay on the ship. They had made her a part of their lives. They were the closest thing to family she had. The thought of leaving both saddened and scared her. She had to convince Kale to let her stay, no matter what.

Chapter Twenty

That evening Lillian sat in her quarters, contemplating how to ask Kale to allow her to stay on board. When it came down to it, she had nothing to offer. She wasn't as strong as the others, and she couldn't lift half the crates they had on board. She had no fighting skills, no knowledge of the world outside of the small Aarilyan nobility. The only things she was good at were cooking and cleaning, and cleaning wasn't going to help her much here.

There was no way he was going to let her stay on as part of the crew, as useless as she was. She had to find something she was good at that she could leverage with Kale to allow her to stay.

She jumped as someone knocked on the door. Cracking it open, she found Kale standing there, as if he had heard her thoughts and had come to personally accept her resignation.

"Hello," he said.

"Hello."

"May I?" he asked when she didn't extend an invitation to enter.

"Oh, of course. Sorry." A blush crept across her cheeks as she stepped to the side and opened the door wider for him to enter.

"How are you doing? Are you okay?" he asked.

"I'm fine. How is your leg?"

"Just a little scrape." An awkward silence fell for a few moments. If she was going to ask him, she supposed this was as good a moment as any.

"Lillia—"

"Kale—" They both started.

"Ladies first." Kale nodded to her.

"No, no. You go ahead," Lillian insisted.

"Well." Kale paused. "I need your help with something. It's a bit embarrassing, actually."

"What is it?"

"When we dock in Aarilya, I have a party I have to attend. Sort of a fundraiser. It's been a while since I've been to anything this upscale, and I was wondering if you would be able to, well ... if you could teach me to dance," he finished quickly.

A laugh bubbled out of her. "Teach you? To dance?"

"Well, obviously I know how to dance. And I'm fairly decent, if I do say so myself," he said defensively. "But I know these high-class folk do things a little differently, and you've spent a lot of time in their service. So I thought you might be able to bring me up to date."

"I see." She chuckled. "I suppose I do know a thing or two about dancing."

"You'll help me out then?"

"Perhaps."

"Perhaps?" He raised a brow.

"Well, if I'm going to help you out, I want something in return." She tapped her chin with her finger. This opportunity had presented itself, and she was going to take it. She circled him once, as if sizing up the task, then stopped in front of him, hands on her hips.

"Really?" he asked skeptically. "What did you have in mind?" She stared at him a moment, unsure. Afraid to voice her request aloud and be denied. Once she asked, there was no going back. She took a breath. She was the one in control. He needed something from her, badly enough to come and ask her himself, even when he was still angry with her for lying. That alone bolstered her into action.

"I want to stay," she said, the slightest quiver in her voice giving away her fear.

Kale turned away. "I don't think that's a good idea."

She stepped in front of him. She wasn't going to let him tell her no with his back to her. She let her smoky blue eyes burn into him. "Why not? You said yourself I would make a decent pirate. I'm learning to defend myself, so I won't be a liability. And I can help with the cooking and the sewing and help you with your little missions in the 'upscale' towns. I swear, I will make myself useful any way that I can."

"It's not safe for a woman here. You're a perfect example. You've only been with us a little while, and you've almost died a handful of times already."

"That's an exaggeration. And I think we can both agree that I've handled all my near-death experiences very well. I'm learning to be better and more reliable. I'm only asking for a chance. Please."

"Lillian," Kale pleaded.

"Kale." She stood her ground.

"Fine. I can't promise anything right now. But if you help me with this, I will give your request some serious thought," he finally replied. Her face lit up. It wasn't a no. Not yet, anyway.

She beamed, touching his hand gently. "That's all I ask."

Later that evening, Lillian sat in the galley between Landry and Chase, eating her food. Or at least, trying to.

"We have to admit, for being so fair-skinned, you've got a pretty thick hide," Chase said.

"Thick skin perhaps, but her insides are just as mushy as the rest of us. Perhaps even more mushy after losing so much blood." Landry slammed down his cup. They were both obviously quite deep in their cups as they laughed at their own jokes and poked fun at her. She didn't mind. It made her feel like she was a part of something, like she was one of them.

"Or is it less mushy, since she has less blood?" Chase countered. They both let out a roar that nearly made her jump out of her seat.

"Well, mushy or not, it doesn't seem to be affecting me much. I think I'm healing just fine." She took another bite of bread. The galley was full, and noisy as always. She had come to enjoy the time there. It was one of the few times everyone was together in one spot. They didn't have to worry about chores, or treasure hunts—they could just be. And the louder they were, the happier they were. It made Lillian grin to watch them tease and laugh at each other, but it also made her ache.

"We'll see if you're any better at fighting Johnny. Perhaps your injury was what made you so terrible," Chase teased.

"Fighting? You mean flirting?" Landry shot back. "Perhaps you was just pretending to be weak to get Johnny-boy's attention, huh?"

"I would do no such thing!" she said, but they couldn't hear her over their own boisterous laughter.

"Now, Lillian, there's no reason to lie." Johnny chuckled as he took a seat across from her. "Everyone here can see our chemistry. We might as well give them something to talk about."

"Johnny! You're going to start rumors!" Lillian said, aghast. The boys laughed.

"Sweetie, the rumors have been going around since day one. It's one of our few sources of entertainment around here. Best just to let go and laugh at yourself." Johnny gave her one of his mischievous smiles. "Or you can always give in and let the rumors become truths."

She took a sip from her cup to cover her grin. "As charming as you are, Johnny, I think I'll pass."

The table erupted again, and this time Lillian couldn't help but join in.

Once supper was finished, most of the crew wandered back to their quarters to get some extra rest before they docked in Aarilya the following day. Only Johnny and Eddie stayed to finish their card game.

"See you in the morning, Lillian." Kidd patted her shoulder on his way out. As he left, Kale came in looking for her.

"You ready?" he asked quietly, almost hesitantly.

"Are you?"

"As ready as I'm going to be, I guess." He held his hand out, and she took it.

"Such a gentleman."

"Well, I have to get in some practice before tomorrow evening."

The cool night air caressed their skin, the sea calm. The night sky looked like a diamond-encrusted cloth. The deck creaked below their feet as they approached the center.

Still holding her hand, he pulled her in a sweeping circle until she came to face him and rested his other hand on her lower back.

"Not bad." She chuckled, trying to keep from blushing. The heat of his hand on her back was already becoming a distraction. "Show me what else you know."

He pulled her closer, their bodies only a few centimeters from each other. His face was completely blank, focused, while she struggled to control the heat rising up her neck. She had never danced with a man; she had only stood in as a partner for Maria during her lessons. His salt and sandalwood smell was intoxicating as he swept her along the deck, stepping to the back, left, forward, right, again and again. He was sure on his feet, guiding her along as easily as he breathed, and she followed as if she were an extension of him. He looked down into her eyes as they began to circle the deck for a second time. His gray eyes were intimidating as they held hers, and she had the urge to kiss him. She stopped as they completed a turn, overwhelmed.

"Is everything okay?" Kale asked.

"I just need a moment." She cleared her throat as she turned away from him, hiding her blush. "Just a little dizzy."

"Were we spinning to fast?"

"No, no. You were perfect. It's just been a while since I've danced with anyone." She turned back to him. "You did well. But the popular dances right now are just a bit more ... flamboyant. Larger strides when stepping, more sweeping movements. And twirl your partner more often. Almost every pass, she should be twirled, ending with a dip before starting the next sequence."

He held his hand out toward her once more. "May I have this dance?"

His demeanor had shifted, suddenly more playful. He had a gleam in his eye as his hand waited for hers. She laughed as she took it. They twirled around the deck in large, graceful strides, as if it were their own private dance floor. He mimicked the movements she had described to him perfectly, as if he had danced them his entire life. This time, his face was not blank and focused, it was playful and graceful at the same time. His eyes never left hers, that gleam glowing brighter. She had never seen this expression on him before. He was letting his guard down, completely being himself.

She laughed as he spun her out and then quickly pulled her back into his arms, ending with a slow dip. Her breath caught as he held her there, their bodies pressed so closely together she could feel his chest rise and fall rapidly against hers.

His gray eyes held hers almost forcefully. His expression had shifted again, no longer light and playful but now intense. Her breath caught as he leaned in toward her slowly, and his eyes flicked to her lips and back again. Did he want to kiss her as much as she wanted him to, or was she imagining it?

Then his lips lowered to meet hers, though hesitantly, as if giving her the opportunity to pull away. Her eyelids fluttered closed. She allowed her lips to answer his, slow at first as she learned the rhythm he set, then becoming more fervent. The heat from earlier raced up her neck and into her cheeks. Her whole body was on fire as his soft lips guided hers. Her hand clutched his shirt, trying to pull him closer as his hand slipped from her back to her hip, gripping it in a tight embrace. Her mouth parted, beckoning more from him.

A gasp escaped her as he straightened, his lips no longer on hers, their bodies no longer touching as he stepped back. She felt empty at the loss of his touch, his warmth. Their eyes met, the fierceness in his turning to something different. Confusion? And regret, she realized. Her heart sank.

"I apologize. I shouldn't have done that." He turned away, striding off toward his quarters.

"Kale!" She called after him, but he didn't stop. She was still in shock. Had he really kissed her? Her cheeks still burned; her lips could almost feel his touch. She wanted to follow him, but she was afraid. What would he say if she did? Would he ask her to leave the ship for good tomorrow? Or would he invite her in? She wasn't ready to find out, either way.

Rather than be alone with her thoughts, she decided to return to the galley, where Johnny and Eddie were playing cards. She pushed through the door as casually as she could, her heart still beating through her chest, and made her way toward their table.

"Hey, girly. Thought you were headed to bed."

"Not just yet."

They still sat around the table, cards laid out in front of them. She took them in, the playful teasing and happy banter. This was better than stewing.

"You all right? You look a little red there."

"Just a little flushed," she said casually.

Johnny looked her over with concern, then shrugged. "Want me to deal you in?"

"**I**diot!" Kale yelled to himself. "Why would you do that to her?"

He stalked to the small mirror sitting on his bureau, leaned over, and stared at his own reflection. He could still feel where her body had pushed against his. His shirt wrinkled where she had grasped it, pulling him to her. He shook his head trying to shake free of the memory, of his thoughts of her. This was exactly the type of situation he had wanted to avoid. "Were you always this much of an idiot, or is it only when she's around?"

He had noticed her change in body language as he held her, could tell she was nervous to have him hold her. He had made sure to watch himself that first few rounds, that he wasn't holding her too close or inappropriately. But hearing her laugh and dancing with him across the deck had made his chest flutter unexpectedly. When he had dipped her and her eyes sparkled as she held his, he couldn't stop himself from feeling her lips, pulling her to him. And when she returned his kiss ... he lost every scrap of sense he possessed.

He knew having a woman on board was a bad idea, especially a young, beautiful one. And Lillian ... It didn't matter whether she was a lady or a maid. Becoming entangled with a pirate—with him? Nothing good would come of it. This time around he would lure one of the married noble ladies aboard instead.

"She has to go," he muttered. Before he did something they'd both regret.

Chapter Twenty-One

Lillian took a deep breath as she looked out over Aarilya. They had arrived early this morning. The harbor was a bustle of movement. There were three other ships docked, and more people rushed about than she thought would have fit. She was surprised at how hard it had hit her that she was back. It even had its own smell, she realized. The smell of something familiar, but past. The smell of a childhood, of a phase of her life that was truly over. It had only been a few weeks, yet it felt like a lifetime ago. She was a completely different person than she had been when she boarded the *Rossut* that day, only a few hundred feet from where she stood now. She had seen things she never imagined she would, done things she never thought she would be capable of doing. She had grown in every way possible. And she was determined now, more than ever, to do what it took to stay with Kale and the crew.

She couldn't go back to the life of a lady's maid, living only to please others. She had become her own person. She wanted to make her own decisions and live her own life. She became aware of the rough wood of the railing under her palms, the unsteadiness of the deck beneath her feet, the sound of the waves as they lazily lapped at the hull. Of the *Stardust*. They had all become familiar—comforting.

"How's it feel to be home again?" Kidd put his arm around her shoulders.

"Surreal. It doesn't feel like home anymore. I don't know that it ever, did now that I think about it."

"Nah, it wouldn't now, would it? You're a wandering soul, like me." He grinned. "You gotta be out amongst your own kind, spreading your light."

"And do I? Spread light?" She looked at Kidd.

"Of course! We may seem like a jolly lot, but most of that is because you're around. You remind us we aren't a bunch of pigs; we need to be considerate. We laugh more and joke more since you come aboard. And you knocked Johnny and Kale out of their funk. They was too serious before you, always bickerin' and spendin' too much time plannin' the hunt for the legendary treasure. What's the point of being a pirate if ya don't have a little fun?"

"Well, some would say the point is to pillage and loot," Landry said, knocking Kidd off balance with a punch to the shoulder. Lillian chuckled as she swayed with the movement.

"Well, sure, as long as they find some fun in it." Kidd laughed.

"What makes it legendary?" Lillian asked.

"What? What legend?" Landry repeated.

"You said Johnny and Kale were after a legendary treasure? What makes it legendary? Does it have something to do with tonight?" she asked.

"The one to get the pirat—"

Landry smacked Kidd across the back of the head. "The jewel heist Kale is attempting tonight. It's a solo job. In and out." Landry crossed his arms. Kidd glared at him as he rubbed his head.

There was something they weren't telling her.

"Does it have to do with the map in Kale's room?"

Both men's eyes went wide. Since they were caught off guard, perhaps she could press for more.

"How d'ya know about that?" Kidd asked. Landry smacked him on the head again. "Ow! That one hurt."

Finally, she was getting some answers, albeit accidentally. But they left her with more questions. Rubbing his head, Kidd shot a glare at Landry, who shot one right back, his gold-flecked eyes shifting to Lillian and back again.

"Whatever ya saw, Lillian, forget it," Landry warned.

"Is it a treasure map?" she asked eagerly.

"Why? Cause we're pirates, all the maps gotta be treasure maps?" Landry laughed.

"No, because it was very old, and it had a strange symbol on it," Lillian said smugly.

"We don't know what ye're talking about."

"What don't ya know?" Eddie asked Kidd as he walked over to the group.

"About the treasure map."

"How do you know about that?"

"Eddie!" Landry smacked the back of his bald head.

"What? She said she knew already!" He smacked Landry's head in return.

"Well, she didn't for sure. She was testin' for information." Landry glared.

Kale and Johnny waved as they returned to the boat. As they came up the gangway, Kale took in the men's faces. His smile faltered.

"What's all this about?" Johnny asked, grinning. "A lovers' quarrel going on over here?" He clapped Landry's back.

"Lillian knows about the treasure map. Thanks to these two." Kidd shook his head. Johnny's and Kale's faces fell. They both looked at her.

"Is it an actual treasure map? A real one?" Her smile grew, eyes alight with excitement.

"Some say so," Kale said cautiously.

"Forget about it, Lillian. You're home now. You don't have to pretend to be interested in us anymore." Johnny chuckled half-heartedly.

"You know I'm not pretending, Johnny. Where does it lead? Are you headed there after Aarilya? How does a noble woman fit in?" Lillian peppered them with questions. She felt like she was in one of her novels. Kale had mentioned a treasure hunt, but she'd assumed he meant looting another ship or something.

"It's none of your business, Lillian," Johnny snapped.

She turned to Kale, ignoring him completely. "Have you made a decision yet?"

"About what?" Johnny and Landry asked in unison.

"I haven't." Kale watched her.

"I can help," she said.

"With what?"

"Anything! Everything! I can help you find another noble. I can get you into the noble community!" she pleaded.

"No," Johnny said.

"How are you going to get us in without being seen? Once they recognize you it's all over."

"Kale!" Johnny yelled in disbelief.

"I'll figure it out. Please! Let me stay. I can sew more formal clothes for you, and for the crew as well. I can help you get into some of the higher social circles. I'll learn to do anything you ask."

"It's dangerous for a girl out on the seas," Kale countered as he leaned against the rail, crossing his arms.

"Exactly," Johnny said. "You don't want to risk your life just so you can have a story to tell."

"I don't care," Lillian said.

They stood there a few moments in tense silence, everyone's eyes on Lillian and Kale. She watched as he contemplated, clearly torn. She would do anything to stay. She let the desperation show.

The one unruly lock of hair peaked out from beneath his hat as Kale straightened. "You really want to do this?"

"With everything I am." Hope sprang in her chest.

"You'll keep up with the crew?"

"You can't be serious, Kale!" Johnny exclaimed.

"I promise," Lillian said.

"You won't put yourself into any more deadly situations?"

"Not if I can help it."

"You are stubborn as a mule." He chuckled. "We'll have to put it to the crew, but if they agree, then you can stay on—temporarily—while we finish this quest." He fixed her with a pointed stare. Kidd, Landry, and Eddie cheered, clapping her on the back. Kale smiled, shaking his head as Kidd wrapped his arms around Lillian and hugged her. The others soon joined in.

"Kale." Johnny followed as Kale stalked toward his cabin. As soon as they were inside, he pulled Kale back by the shoulder. "What are you thinking?"

"I'm thinking that was an awful lot of protesting back there. Is there something you know that I don't?"

"I thought it was pretty obvious. She's almost died three times already. Is that a liability you're willing to take on?"

"She's taking it on herself. I've never turned away a new crew member that wanted to be here." He pulled a bottle of amber liquid and two glasses from a cabinet near the table, filling one and handing it to Johnny, who gulped it down and set it back before Kale had a chance to finish pouring his own.

"She's different. She's a girl." Johnny leaned both hands on the table as he forced Kale to look him in the eye.

Kale held his gaze as he downed his own glass and set it next to Johnny's. "She says she'll work as hard as any of us."

"And you believe that? Or is the problem that she clouds your judgment?" Rage danced like electricity in his bright blue eyes.

Kale's turned stormy. "Watch it, John. My judgment is as sound as ever. Perhaps I should be questioning yours."

They stood there, eyes locked, until Chase walked out of the crew's quarters across the deck, carrying a mop and bucket.

Kale turned away first. "Get some rest, Johnny. You're not acting like yourself."

Kidd held Lillian's hand, dragging her behind him as he sprinted to the storage deck where the rest of the crew were tracking inventory. Everyone stilled as he burst through the door.

"Lillian is staying aboard!" he huffed between breaths.

"Huzzah!" they cheered.

Tony set a cloth bag back into the box he had been sifting through. "This is serious?"

"Kale actually agreed?" Rick rubbed his bald head in astonishment.

"I seen it. Says he'll put it to a vote," Eddie said. "Just for this mission, he says."

"That is surprising," Tony said. "But a good surprise."

"It sure is!" Rich agreed heartily. "We will have to celebrate tonight, after Kale goes ashore. We'll have us a party of our own to welcome you to the crew."

"When is he planning to go?" Lillian asked. "Ashore, I mean."

"After the midday meal, I think. And Thomas should be just 'bout finished preparin' it," Eddie said.

"If you'll excuse me, then, there are a few things I have to tell him about the nobles."

"Lillian?" Tony called after her. "We're awful glad you're stayin' on. Truly. Even if only for a bit longer." The rest grunted their agreement.

Once she reached Kale's cabin, she took a breath and knocked.

"Yeah," he called from within. She opened the door a bit and peered in. He nodded for her to enter. He stood in front of the table, looking himself over in a small mirror situated on it, along with two empty glasses and a bottle.

"Well?" he asked, holding his arms out for her to see. He wore the suit she had made. It fit exquisitely. Much better than she had expected, considering it was the first pieces of clothing she had sewn from scratch in a few years. The cream shirt contrasted well with the dark jacket and trousers. But something was missing.

He watched her take it in. "That terrible, is it?"

"It's wonderful. Do you have a scrap of the cream cloth lying around?"

"I gave everything to you."

"That's all right, I think I have some in my quarters. I can bring it out after the midday meal. Everything else looks wonderful." She smoothed his lapel as he straightened. He caught her hand in his. They stood there like that for a short moment before he removed her hand from his chest and turned away.

"Lillian, about the other night. When we ... When I kissed you. I—"

"It's all right, I understand. It did not mean anything. We don't have to discuss it any further," she said, looking down. She had thought of nothing else since. Her lips still warmed at the thought. But this tentative truce of theirs ... She knew he could change his mind at any moment while they were at port, and she wouldn't risk it. They were quiet for a moment.

"Right." Kale sighed. "Being part of the crew now. I wanted to make it clear—I won't take advantage of you like that again."

She nodded, and changed the subject. "Is that how you're going to wear your hair?"

"No. I was going to part it to the side, just here." He ran a finger across his head. "Is that still an acceptable style? I didn't think hairstyles for men change quite as often."

"They don't, you're right. That will look just fine. May I?"

"Lillian, you don't have to ask to sit. You should know that by now."

"Old habits. I actually came to give you a little insight on some of the families you will interact with tonight. Is now a good time?"

"Of course." He sat in the chair opposite her. The suit cut along his body perfectly as he crossed his ankles, leaning against the table. The dark black fabric brought out the blue shine of his dark hair. "What do you know?"

"Let's start with who is hosting," she asked, focusing on the task once more. There were a few parties being planned during the time they were to be Nelina, and she had lost track of the days.

"My intel says it's the Santels," he said. She wrinkled her nose in disgust.

"Not your favorite people, I take it." He chuckled.

"There aren't many good ones amongst the nobles, but they are one of my least favorites. In fact, the only decent people, aside from the De Sansols, would be the Tandin family." She sighed. "Anyhow, the Santels are very particular. The party will no doubt be the most extravagant event of the year. Mr. and Mrs. Santel, as well as their son Kellen, will be greeting everyone at the door, and if you wish to go unnoticed then make sure you are on time. Mrs. Santel makes a point to gossip about any late arrivals."

"How very catty of her." He chuckled.

"Rather so." She grinned. "And make sure to kiss Mrs. Santel on the right cheek when you greet her. Once you get past their welcoming party, you should be able to melt away into the crowd. Assuming that's what you want to do."

"It is, for the most part," he said. "Are there any other young ladies of the noble families?"

"If by 'young lady,' you mean around my age, then no. There is Emily Reese, but she is barely twelve years."

"Damn," he muttered.

"Are you going to tell me why you need a noblewoman?"

"No. Tell me about the other women then, the older ones," he asked.

She pursed her lips. "The only other noblewomen now are Mrs. Reese, Mrs. Santel, and Mrs. Tandin."

"And you said Tandin was decent enough, Santel is a terror. What about Reese? What's she like?"

"She's not a great person either, but she likes to pretend she is. She'll act charming to your face and talk about you behind your back."

"Wasn't there another family? I thought there were eight," he said.

"No. Just the seven if you include the De Sansols. Six left now."

"Hmm."

"Was there anything specific you want to know about the area, or the people?"

"No. I think you've provided more than enough information." He smiled. "Food should be ready by now." He stood, dismissing her.

"Well, if you think of anything else, you know where to find me."

"Lillian," he called, as she turned to leave. "Of course, you're free to do as you wish. But I would advise you to stay aboard the ship while here in Aarilya. If someone were to recognize you, it would complicate things for all of us."

Chapter Twenty-Two

Kale stood outside the gates leading to an obscenely large mansion. He took a breath, his invitation in hand. This was it. He looked over his suit one last time. It seemed to hold up against the other men he had seen walking in. Lillian had even brought a small square of cream cloth and tucked it into his breast pocket, which pulled the whole look together. She really had done an amazing job. He would have to get her something nice to repay her. Before she would leave them for good. But he couldn't think about that just now. He needed to focus.

He unfolded his invitation and approached the gate. The gentleman at the entrance looked over his invitation briefly as he handed it over, then let him through. He had two goals tonight, the first being to find a noblewoman he could easily woo or incapacitate momentarily to take back to the ship. The second was to meet with a contact of his and sell the gem he had been holding onto.

It should be easy enough. He needed the coin from the gem to send home. It would be enough to get them by for now, even with Kylah's medical expenses. The struggle was going to be in juggling both these tasks throughout the night without being made.

He had been to many parties, quite a few of them upper class, but he'd never been near Atwood. Lillian hadn't been kidding when she said this one was going to be extravagant. There was a long line of people waiting to meet the welcoming party at the door, and even more wandering around the front grounds, gossiping with one another. The men's coats resembled his own. A few were lighter, and even fewer had color to them. But the ladies' gowns were quite fantastic. They wore bright colors and intricate patterns, and the necklines and hems were adorned with ribbons, bows and even some gems.

The dress Lillian had been wearing when they found her seemed more of a nightgown compared to these. He could imagine her there, on his arm, wearing a gown as intricate as theirs. She would fit in nicely. He shook the image from his head. Focus.

Finally it was Kale's turn to be greeted. Mrs. Santel was at the head of the welcoming party. She had an air of absolute smugness about her. She stood tall, her chin and nose pointed to the air. Her golden curls were bound in tight ringlets, half of which were pulled atop her head. The rest hung down past her shoulders. Her dress was white with large smatterings of blue and purple, and a matching shawl hung across her shoulders. It was one of the more elegant dresses in the room. Beyond her stood Mr. Santel and their son, who wore matching white suits, each with a purple cloth peeking out from their breast pocket.

Kale flashed a charming grin as she presented her hand for a kiss.

"Now, Mrs. Santel, what kind of greeting is a kiss on the hand? Surely you're deserving of more respect than that." His grin widened. "May I have the pleasure of your cheek?"

"Quite right, young man. I would be flattered."

He leaned forward and placed the briefest of kisses on her right cheek, pausing a moment before leaning back.

"You've done a marvelous job with this benefit, my lady. I'll move on now, and let you tend to your other guests."

She giggled and waved him forward. A few handshakes later, and he was in the main ballroom.

It could have held the whole ocean. The walls were marble and gold, and the ceilings were vaulted as high as he'd ever seen. All the doorways were constructed of overly large, rounded arches, with gold doorframes and glass doors. He spied a clock along the wall nearest him. Half past six. He still had an hour until he was due to meet his contact.

He circled the room, sampling a canapé from a tray as one of the servers walked past, and watched as some of the older men mingled—discussing business, most likely, and how it would affect this or that. A few of the younger generation were focused on using their charm and wits to woo young ladies. And the young ladies were no less focused on being wooed or attempting to sway the attention of another.

He caught the eye of a woman across the room. She had been watching him. Her dark eyes held his as she started to make her way toward him.

"Well, hello, tall, dark, and handsome." Her deep ebony hair, a shade darker than her eyes, bounced atop her head. "I don't think we've met."

Back on the ship, everyone was preparing for the celebration. Rich and Rick continued up the gangway carrying a couple of crates. Lillian, Kidd, and Jack sat against the mast, playing cards.

"Come on, Lillian! Let's see what they brought!" Kidd jumped up, pulling Lillian's arm.

"All right, all right!" Lillian laughed as she followed him across the deck.

"What'd ya find?" he asked excitedly.

"Hold your horses, Kidd!" Rich set the box down. He pulled a few bottles of wine out. Lillian scrunched her nose, remembering the bitter taste.

Rick chuckled. "Don't worry, this stuff's smoother than the island swill."

"We'll see about that."

He dug deeper through the box and pulled out two cartons of crackers, a rind of cheese, and a bushel of grapes. "We thought you might like something fresh after only having dried food for so long." He handed Lillian the crackers and cheese.

Her face lit up. "Oh my goodness, this is amazing. But you didn't have to do that for me."

"Don't you worry, Lilliana, it's for all of us. We all like a treat when we go ashore, and this is a celebration!" Tony said, patting her back.

"You think that's great, take a look at these!" Rich grinned as he pulled a few small packages out. He unraveled the twine and pulled back the brown paper to reveal small pastries.

"Yes!" Kidd exclaimed.

"Where did you find these?" Thomas asked.

"A new specialty shop just off the docks. Sells all kinds of things. Couldn't say no after we saw these in the window." Rich wrapped the treats back up.

"Wine, cheese, and pastries? We are going to have our own fancy party right here." Kidd laughed.

"We certainly are. Nothing less would do to welcome Lillian aboard."

"You really didn't have to do all of this."

"Nonsense! We look for any reason to celebrate around here. Haven't you noticed?" Tony opened one of the cracker boxes.

"Should we wait for Kale?" she asked.

"Nah. He probably won't be back tonight. I'm sure he'll find a warm bed to stay in." Eddie smiled. Tony elbowed him. "Ow! What'd you go and do that for?" he asked, rubbing his ribs.

"Lillian might be part of the crew now, but she's still a woman. Have some respect." Tony glared.

A deep blush spread across her cheeks.

"I'll get a knife for the cheese." Kidd excused himself as the others set up barrels to put the food and drink on.

Kale swung the dark beauty around the room, just as Lillian had shown him. It was the common dance of the evening. And thanks to her, Kale was able to perform it effortlessly. He paused to dip his partner.

"I'm only saying, whatever family you do come from, you are definitely the black sheep." The woman giggled as he pulled her back up toward him.

"And why, exactly, would you think that?"

"Oh, I have a gift for these things. I've always seemed to be attracted to the scandalous men, the disinherited. The black sheep." She sighed dramatically. "And since I am most definitely attracted to you, it follows that you should fall into one of those categories."

"And what if I happen to fall into all three?" They paused as the music ended.

"Well," she laughed. "Then you might as well propose right this instant."

"Without even knowing your name? That *would* be scandalous."

"Can't say it hasn't happened before. Emilia Vantelisa." She bobbed a curtsy as she introduced herself.

"Kale ... Smith." He bowed, one arm behind his back.

"Is that really your family name?" she asked. His only response was a grin as the music began again. "May I have another dance?" she asked.

"I wish that I could. Unfortunately, I have a prior commitment." He bowed again. "Should you find me later, I would be happy to oblige."

"All right." She put on a pout as she extended her hand. He placed a kiss on it, lingering there for a moment.

Once he released Emilia, he made his way to the south door of the ballroom. He looked around for a moment to make sure no one was watching him, then snuck through the partial opening. He walked quietly down the darkened corridor. It was decorated in much the same style as the ballroom had been—whites and golds and some ornate fixtures to break up the monotony of the empty walls. He passed two doors on the left until he reached the third. He opened it and stepped inside.

"Well, you certainly are punctual, I'll give you that," the older gentleman said as Kale closed the door behind him. His pompous suit was hardly able to button, his gray hair was slicked back, and a pipe hung from the side of his mouth.

"Of course."

"Well, let's see it then."

Kale pulled a small black kerchief out of his inside jacket pocket, unfolding it slowly to reveal the gem. It was small, no larger than a fingernail, and it had an opaque purple color. When it turned and the light caught it just right, it shot beams of different colors across the room. The older man gasped.

"Well, I'll be damned," he said under his breath. "You actually got it." The man reached for it, but Kale pulled it back.

"My money, Mr. Candelt." Kale raised a brow.

"Oh, of course." Mr. Candelt dug through his pockets and revealed a bag of coin. He promptly handed it to Kale. Kale sized it, weighed it in his palm. Satisfied, he handed the gem over to Mr. Candelt.

"Nice doing business with you." Kale turned toward the door. "You know how to get a hold of me if you need anything else."

"Oh, Mr. Smith. I thought you ought to know. A gentleman at the party was asking questions about you."

"What sort of gentleman?" Kale stopped short.

"Don't know. Short hair, military cut. Perhaps a navy man?" Mr. Candelt said. "Anyhow, thought you should know."

Kale thanked him as he slipped out of the corridor, heading back into the ballroom, and scanning the crowd as he went. Mrs. Santel stepped into his path.

"Mr. Smith! Oh, how glad I am that our paths crossed."

Another woman stood next to her. She was tall and thin, with sharp cheekbones and a pointed nose.

"Ah. Mrs. Santel. How lovely to see you." He kissed her hand as she extended it. "And who is this lovely lady?"

"This is Mrs. Reese. My very best friend in the whole world."

"I can't believe I'm in the presence of *two* noblewomen. I am truly honored." He bowed deeply. "And it is so very lovely to meet you, Mrs. Reese." He took her hand and kissed it. As he stood, he scanned the room again.

"Thank you, Mr. Smith. You are quite charming." She giggled.

"Didn't I say?" Mrs. Santel giggled as well. "Mr. Smith, are you looking for someone?"

"Well, I had heard that someone I used to know was here at your gala. Has anyone approached you young ladies and asked about me?"

"Heavens no. And I should think they wouldn't. It's rather rude to approach someone asking about their guests."

"I would imagine it would be. Anyhow, I don't suppose I could interest either of you in joining me for an early morning breakfast tomorrow in town? My treat, of course. I found this beautiful little pastry shop I really think you ought to try."

"Ah, well, I do doubt we will be up any time that would be considered early. The night should run long." Mrs. Santel pouted.

"Perhaps we can do a nice supper, here on the terrace?" Mrs. Reese suggested.

"Unfortunately, I set sail tomorrow, mid-morning. Urgent business in Nelina, I'm afraid." He looked distraught. "You're sure you couldn't do breakfast? These pastries are definitely worth the missed sleep."

It took a little convincing, but in the end they settled on a little pastry shop near the docks, at nine.

Something caught his eye in the crowd as he looked up. A man stood across the room, watching him. He stood tall and his suit was neatly pressed, his salt and pepper hair parted just to the side and slicked back perfectly.

Dall.

He quickly took his leave of the noblewomen and was nearly to the foyer when Emilia stepped into his path.

"Why, Mr. Smith! You're not cutting out early, are you? You promised me another dance if I caught you. And I have." She tilted her chin, presenting her trademark pout.

"Miss Emilia. Unfortunately, I have to dash out. An unexpected emergency." He kissed her hand softly. "You'll forgive me, won't you?"

"I will. The next time I see you. When do you imagine that would be?" she asked.

"I couldn't say for sure. I travel quite a bit. But next time I'm in port, I'll be sure to say hello." He turned them both around so that he was closest to the door. "Good evening, Emilia."

"You don't even know my address!" she called after him.

"I'll find you."

Chapter Twenty-Three

He had been right about Dall slipping off the *Rossut* before it sank. Coward that Dall was, Kale shouldn't have been surprised. The captain must have caught sight of him while he was on the dance floor. They'd have to move the ship before he had a chance to make a report and call in reinforcements. As long as they could get the ship somewhere discreet tonight, he should be fine to meet the noblewomen in the morning. Dall would think they had run and wouldn't suspect they were still in the area.

Did Dall know Lillian was aboard? She had mentioned that he had threatened her on the *Rossut*. If he tried to hurt her for being near them … Kale nearly growled at the thought. Treasure be damned, he would hunt Dall down and tear him limb from limb.

Laughter carried down the gangway as he ascended the *Stardust*. Everyone was gathered around the main mast. Jack and Chase had even pulled crates over to sit on, and they had a barrel in the center as a makeshift table where they had set some wine, cheese and crackers, and pastries. Or what was left of them. Lillian sat next to Kidd. Kale watched her for a moment as he stood at the top of the gangway, unnoticed. He held his jacket across his arm. His cuffs and the top of his dress shirt were unbuttoned.

They laughed at whatever story Rich was telling. Lillian's loose brown curls hung down her back, her cobalt eyes shining with laughter, cheeks pink from the wine. She looked as though she had been a part of their crew forever, like she just … belonged.

His smile faltered. She may not be of noble birth, but she was a lady nonetheless, and a ship was no place for a lady. He had decided to allow her to stay for the duration of their adventure on a whim, because the thought of her leaving left an ache in his chest. But she had to leave once they were finished. He would just have to come to terms with it—and not make any stupid decisions. This run-in with Dall was proof of the dangers she would face if she stayed with them.

As soon as he stepped onto the deck, Lillian saw him. She smiled and waved. It was obvious she was a bit heavy on the wine.

"Kale!" she called.

The men turned to see him.

"Come join us!" Rich called. He grabbed a bottle of wine and took a long drink from it. "How did it go?"

"As planned." Kale took out the coinpurse and dangled it in the air. Everyone cheered.

"You surprised us. We expected you to stay out all night," Kidd said.

"They said you would—what was the phrase? Find a warm bed." Lillian giggled.

Kale's jaw dropped, then he smiled and shook his head. They were definitely a bad influence on her.

"What are these filthy men teaching you?" He laughed. "You've had enough wine for tonight. You should head to bed. You all should. I have a meeting in the morning, and we need to grab some more supplies from shore. Jack, we need to redock on the east side immediately." Everyone murmured their agreement as they began packing up. Lillian started piling the pastries off the barrel. Woozy, she set her hand on the barrel to steady herself.

"I told you that you had too much wine," Kale said.

The flush in her cheeks deepened. "I may not be a wine drinker. I only had a few drinks. Large drinks, but only a few." She giggled again.

"Here, take my arm." He chuckled as he extended it to her. She took it happily. "It will hit you quick if you haven't had much before. You'll have to build up a tolerance, if you want to drink with these men." She started to tilt, tipping him with her. "Here. Come here." He pulled her toward him. His breath caught at her pure, unfiltered smile.

"You really are very kind. And charming. For a pirate. I'm sure you charmed all the girls at that party. Even the maids. Why didn't you sleep in someone's bed? Warm bed? Did I say that right?" she babbled. So she was a talker when she was deep in her cups.

He bent down and scooped her up, one arm behind her back and the other below her knees. "And if I had, where would you have ended up? Passed out on the deck with the rest of the crew?"

"Mmm," she murmured, laying her head against his chest as he carried her. His warmth seeped into her body.

"Let's get you to bed."

"Will you kiss me goodnight?" she mumbled.

"No. But I will tuck you in."

As she looked around at the surroundings, familiar but not her own, she was reminded of when she had awoken that first morning aboard their ship. The wall of windows behind her allowed the room to fill with the morning light. She groaned as she sat up, putting a hand to her throbbing head, the cool, soft bed a small reprieve to her aching body.

"Ah, you're awake." Kale shut the lavatory door behind him. "You must have a terrible headache from the wine."

"Is that what's causing it? I thought perhaps I hit my head and couldn't remember." She rubbed her temples.

"It'll pass. Here, drink some water." He handed her a cup as he sat at the small table, buttoning up his shirt.

She took a sip, relishing the coolness of the water flowing down her throat. "You didn't have to put me to bed last night, you know. I am not a child."

"I didn't want you to freeze to death on the deck. Besides, you could hardly stand."

"I feel terrible when I take your bed. Where do you sleep?"

"Well, last night, I slept here. The other times, I took an extra cot in the sleeping quarters." He pulled a vest on over his shirt.

"Here? Here where?"

"On the bed. Where else does one sleep?"

"With ... me?" Her face turned bright red.

"I'll admit it was ... difficult." He smirked. "But I was far too tired to be bothered trekking across the ship. It's done now. I'm a gentleman, in that regard anyway, and I would never lay a hand on you."

"Of—of course not. I trust you," she whispered.

He looked up sharply. "You should learn to be more wary."

"I am wary. Just not of you."

Their eyes met and she blushed again. He pulled on his boots.

"Do I recall you saying you had a meeting this morning?" she asked. "What for?"

"It's better you don't know." He slipped on his jacket and smoothed his hair to the side. The one unruly piece still hung over his forehead.

"Kale, I do wish you would stop coddling me. You would tell one of the men, wouldn't you?"

He sighed heavily. "Lillian, I am not coddling you. I haven't told you because you wouldn't approve, and I don't have it in me to argue with you this morning."

"I won't argue."

"Really? I find that hard to believe."

She stood firm. "I promise. I will not."

"All right then. I am meeting with Mrs. Santel and Mrs. Reese this morning. I hope to lure one or both of them onto the boat."

"Because you need a noblewoman? For what?" She held his stare. He stayed silent. "Kale," she pushed.

"I am not ready to tell you that part." He looked away.

"Well, is there any other way? Do you need an actual noble-woman, or something from one?"

He hesitated. "Something from one, I suppose. But I don't think I could get it from either of them without bringing them on board."

"There must be some way. You think about it. I'm sure you'll come up with something before you meet with them." She set her empty cup on the table.

"Perhaps if I had more time." He leaned his forearms across his knees. He looked ... tired. Defeated, almost, at the thought of the task he had ahead of him. She pulled her hair over one shoulder and tried to smooth out the stray curls, but gave up, tossing it back and stretching lazily out of the bed. His bed.

"I had better get out there and help." She patted his shoulder before walking out the door, leaving him to stew in his thoughts.

Was she right? Was there another way to get what he needed? All he really needed was—his breath caught as he realized exactly what he was going to do. He pulled the strings tight on his boots, scribbled something on a piece of parchment, grabbed a bag of coin, and headed out on deck.

"Are Eddie and Rich ashore already to purchase the supplies?"

"They headed out about half past the hour," Thomas replied.

"Perfect. Johnny! Does Jameson still live on Edison Street?" Kale yelled as Johnny meandered up the ramp, obviously coming back from a long night ashore.

"A warning would have been nice before you redocked."

"And what, were we supposed to guess which bed you were in?" Kale asked.

A wide grin crossed Johnny's lips.

"About Jameson?" Kale said again.

"The medic?"

"That's the one."

"I haven't heard any different."

"Good, go and fetch him. Ask him about his phlebotomy skills."

"Fleba—what?" Johnny squinted. His hair was a mess, and his clothes were wrinkled. He looked as if he wasn't quite awake. "I'm not trekking all the way over there first thing. I need some food in me, at least."

"Fine. Kidd, you up to the task? You're familiar with Edison Street, aren't you?"

Kidd leaned on his mop. "Yes sir! Very familiar."

"Dr. Jameson lives at 894. Fetch him, give him this note, and meet me at the bakery in an hour."

"Aye, sir."

Kale had one stop to make before he headed to *Patisserie*.

Kidd had rung the bell and was waiting. No one stirred inside. He hoped Dr. Jameson hadn't gone for the day. Whatever Kale's plan, the doctor was a key part of it. Kidd rang the bell again and knocked on the door for good measure. Finally, he heard footsteps from inside, faint but getting closer, and a mumbled "I'm coming, I'm coming."

A man opened the door. He looked a bit older than Kale, but younger than Kidd was expecting for a doctor. "How can I help you, young man?"

"You're Dr. Jameson?" Kidd lifted a brow.

"I am. Are you in need of medicine?" He looked Kidd up and down. "Because I only give out prescriptions once I've looked a man over, and I'm sure it's needed." He stared Kidd in the eye.

"No, sir. I'm a friend of Kale." He handed him Kale's note. "He said to fetch you."

Dr. Jameson read it. "Well, you've caught me on a good day, as it seems I'm not terribly busy at the moment. I can aid in Kale's *scheme*." He winked as he said the last word. "If you'll wait here, I'll grab a few supplies."

It only took them a quarter hour to walk to the bakery, so they arrived a bit early.

"Should we head in?" Kidd asked. They watched Kale, who was speaking with two older ladies inside.

"He'll give the signal when he's ready," Dr. Jameson said. "Let's take a look at a few of the street carts while we're waiting."

"Is that a good idea? We don't want to miss the signal."

"Don't worry, we won't." Dr. Jameson laughed. Kidd's brows rose in confusion.

They strolled along, browsing the various wares. Kidd kept an eye on the bakery at all times. After a few minutes, Kale and the two ladies stood.

"They're leaving!" Kidd exclaimed.

"I'm sure it's all part of Kale's plan." Dr. Jameson assured him. One of the ladies leaned against Kale as they exited the shop. They exchanged a few words. Kale asked them a question, and both ladies shook their heads. The one leaning on Kale stood straight and extended her hand to Kale. He took it, but before he could kiss it in farewell, she lost her balance. She wobbled a few steps before collapsing into Kale's arms. He fanned her face and asked the other lady a few more questions. She shook her head vigorously. Kale looked around, seemingly frantic, until he spotted them.

"Help! Is there a doctor around?" he shouted.

"That's the signal."

Chapter Twenty-Four

Dr. Jameson came out of the grand bedroom with his medical bag and a drawn expression. Kale, Kidd, and a few of the staff stood in the hall, awaiting the news of Mrs. Reese.

"Well?" the butler asked. "Is it serious?"

"Hardly." Dr. Jameson adjusted his coat. "I'd be willing to bet its only exhaustion. There was a party here late last night, is that correct?"

"Yessir."

"Indeed. I'll run a few tests, but I stand by my diagnosis."

"Very good. Thank you, doctor. Should we expect a follow-up?"

"Within the week."

"I've a ship to catch. If you don't mind, I'll follow you out," Kale said.

"Not at all." Dr. Jameson said.

"Good day, Mrs. Santel. I do apologize for Mrs. Reese's mishap. It was far too early to ask of you. You should head home and rest yourself." He bowed and kissed Mrs. Santel's hand.

"Oh, think nothing of it." She blushed. "Safe journeys. You will come visit when next you are in the area?"

"Of course." He released her palm and followed Jameson down the stairs. Kidd waited in the foyer, following them out.

"Were you able to get it?" Kidd asked once they were far enough away from prying ears.

"I was. Two, in fact. I'll hand it off once we are at the docks. No use risking being seen." Kale and Kidd nodded their agreement.

"You are spectacular, Jameson. I've a bag of coin for your commitment."

"No need. I'll be paid well enough by the Santels for my services. And it was all good fun. Never a dull moment with you, Kale." They chuckled.

"If you've got another moment this morning, I'd like you to take a look at one of the crew. They had some internal bleeding a few days ago, and I'd like to have it checked before we set sail again."

Lillian swept the mop back and forth, spreading the soapy water over the deck while the men lugged all the crates of new supplies down the stairway. She stopped and looked up as Kale and Kidd made their way across the beach, a man following behind. Sometime in the night they'd moved the ship to the eastern side of Aarilya. Lillian hadn't asked why. There was no port here, but a small, almost hidden dock jutted out. It wasn't even quite a dock really, but rather some wooden planks someone had nailed together out over the water. Lillian was thankful she didn't have to cross it, but it was large enough to rest their gangplank on.

"Well? I don't see any kidnapped noblewomen," she said. "Did you find another way to get what you need?" The gangway bobbed with the ship as the sea rolled in and out.

"I did. Thanks to you." He was in fine spirits this morning, that playful gleam back in his eye.

She couldn't help but return his grin. "And, what was it?"

"I'll tell you tonight. This is Dr. Jameson Lee, but he goes by Dr. Jameson. He's going to take another look at your stomach."

"Another doctor?"

"I trust this one. Besides, the last one said it *would* be fine after rest. I don't want any surprises once we set sail. We can't afford any more mishaps."

"Very well, then. I'm Lillian." She extended her hand to Dr. Jameson.

He clasped it gently as a charming grin spread across his face. "Well, Kale didn't mention you were a woman. And a gorgeous one, at that."

"Why, thank you." Lillian blushed.

"Aren't you supposed to be a professional?" Kale asked.

Dr. Jameson winked. "I can admire the female form no matter my profession."

"You can see to her in my cabin." Kale gestured toward the door to his cabin.

Lillian followed Dr. Jameson through. "Would you prefer to see me on the chair or the bed?"

"The bed will be fine. I'll need you to lie back. A woman aboard a ship, and wearing trousers, no less! I can't say I've ever seen such a thing."

"Well, you can say it now." She laughed as she leaned back against the pillows. She liked this man. It was quite easy to fall into conversation with him. She pulled up her shirt to reveal the bruised area. It had lightened considerably but was still a bit black, blue, and green.

"My, it must have been quite a fall you took."

"I was kicked, actually. Repeatedly."

"Not by anyone here, I hope?" An edge had crept into his voice.

"No, of course not. Kale would never let someone like that on his crew."

He smiled softly and nodded. "Kale is one of the good ones, that much is true. I'm going to put my hands on you now. They may be a bit cold from the morning air. Does this hurt?" She hissed at his crisp touch of his hand against her abdomen, but she shook her head. "And now?" He pushed a little harder. She shook her head again.

"All right. I'm going to push against a few different areas. You let me know if anything hurts, and how bad."

"Yes, I understand." She shifted down into the soft bed, the cold sheets soon warming against her bare back.

"Your speech is very elegant. Did you grow up well?" He pushed here and there, sometimes with one hand, other times with both.

"I was a maid for a wealthy family. I was a playmate for the daughter, and as such I sat in on her studies and learned quite a bit." She hissed again as he pushed just above her belly button. "Ah, a bit there," she said.

He nodded. "Beautiful and well educated. What are you doing on this piece of cardboard? You could have suitors lined up around the corner."

"I'll admit, it's a strange situation. But it's the opportunity I've been offered in life, and I'm quite happy with it."

"Well, that's all you can ask for, I suppose. To be happy. Your abdomen seems to be healing on track. Continue to take it easy as best you can for a few days, and don't lift anything heavy for, oh, I'd say a week." He stood.

"I'll do my best." She sat up, tucking her shirt back into her trousers. He held the door open, and she walked out ahead of him.

"If you need anything at all, anytime you're in Aarilya, I'm at 894 Edison. They know how to find me."

"That's very kind, Dr. Jameson. Thank you." Kale stood off to the side, watching the exchange with what appeared to be bored disinterest. But she could see his jaw was tight, a bit uneasy.

"James is fine. Or Jameson, if you prefer. No need for the 'Dr.' amongst friends."

"It was wonderful to meet you."

Rather than shake her hand, he turned it over and kissed it. Kale lifted himself away from the railing he had been leaning on and headed their way.

"I mean it, anything you need. You know where to find me."

Yes, she liked this man very much.

"Everything shipshape?" Kale asked.

"Quite. She should take it easy a few days more. Otherwise, she looks incredible."

"We are good to set sail, then. Jameson." He shook Jameson's hand and pulled him into a quick hug. "Thank you again for your help. Until next time." Jameson nodded. He waved his goodbyes to the rest of the crew.

Kale turned to Lillian, that sparkle still in his gray eyes. "Last chance to change your mind," he said. "Are you ready to set sail, or jump ship?"

Lillian grinned. "I think you know what my answer is going to be."

"So we're stuck with you, then. All right, everyone! Weigh anchor and make sail. We are headed for Telayan!"

The crew cheered and set to work.

"You are part of this adventure now," he told her. "You deserve to know what we are doing, same as the rest. Tonight, we'll tell you everything." He tucked a stray strand of hair behind her ear.

"How can I help?"

"Finish swabbing the deck."

That night after supper, the crew settled around the main mast. Kale and Johnny were the last to join. Johnny's face was drawn. Lillian realized he had been quite sour the last few days. She had hardly seen him since their conversation in the hallway.

"Since Lillian has joined our small band for now," Kale started, "it seems only right that we finally fill her in on our big plans. Rich, you're our master storyteller. As such, I leave this to you." He motioned grandly to Rich, who stood and cleared his throat.

"To understand our epic adventure, we 'ave to go back to the beginning. Our tale begins three hundred years ago, with a young man named Samuel. Young Samuel grew up in Aarilya. Some say he was a fisherman's son, and he had a love for the sea. One day, his father injured his leg quite badly and asked him to fill in on some of his deliveries, one of 'em being to the Aarilyan noble community. Young Samuel was warned by his father not to speak to anyone at the noble's house—"

"Which family was it?" Lillian asked.

"The name has been long forgotten. As I was sayin', Samuel was warned not to speak with anyone on the grounds, and to keep his head down. He was to drop the barrel of fish at the rear servant's entrance and be done with it. But when Samuel was leaving, he bumped into the lady of the house. Most say her name was Catherine, but I have heard other versions with different names. She demanded that, as an apology, he join her on her picnic. Now, Samuel wasn't a confrontational sort anyways. And Lady Catherine's beauty had him tongue-tied right from the start. Her beauty, and her bold personality.

"Samuel continued to make deliveries while his father healed, and even after. He would make the noble house his last stop, to allow him more time with Lady Catherine. Each week she'd be waitin' with a picnic basket and demand that he join her. This went on for half a year before Catherine decided she wanted more. She told Samuel she was ready to marry, and that they were goin' to tell their parents. Lady Catherine may have been used to always getting' what she wanted, but Samuel was more realistic. He begged her to reconsider. While he loved her deeply, he knew tellin' their families would tear them apart. Catherine's stubbornness won out, of course, and they went to Samuel's father first.

"He was furious with the young couple, calling them mad and forbiddin' them to go to her family. He said if they told her parents, it would ruin him and his business, and he would make sure Samuel had no further part in it. Hearing this cut Samuel deeply. He loved his father and being a fisherman. He tried again to reason with Catherine, asking to keep their relationship a secret a little while longer so's he could establish himself as someone her parents could be proud of. She was sure her parents would be more acceptin' than his father, and convinced Samuel as much."

"I'm guessing a noble family was not as accepting of a fisherman tainting the bloodline as Catherine imagined," Lillian said.

"Far from it." Rich chuckled. "Her father was outraged. He ordered Samuel thrown from the premises immediately. Catherine threatened to leave with him. She was stubborn, but she got that trait from her father. And he knew she couldn't survive without the luxuries she had been spoiled with her entire life. He said that if she left with Samuel, today or any day, she'd be cut off completely. No money, no home, no family. He asked her to consider if she really loved this boy, or if she only found excitement in a secret relationship. Could she see herself a year from now, not having seen her family or friends, livin' in a shack by the sea? Smelling of fish?

"Samuel saw in her eyes the moment she changed. Her father had gotten through to her. Without so much as a goodbye, she allowed the servants to escort him out. He begged her to reconsider as they dragged him out. He tried to remind her of the fun they had on their picnics and how much he loved her. She never even turned round."

Rich shook his head.

Lillian frowned. "Poor young Samuel. To be brokenhearted, discarded so easily, after all the promises she made." The others nodded in agreement. "What did he do next? Did he try and win her back?"

"Well, he couldn't go home. He'd turned his back on his father. It's said he lived without a home, stayin' near the docks for close to a year. Then the War for Uriba broke out and the navy was formed. Being paid to live on a ship at sea was Samuel's idea of a miracle. He joined as a cabin boy but quickly worked his way up to captain. After only a year and a half, the war was over. Now, anyone who'd been part of the war effort was quite revered at this time. And a ship's captain was as far up as you could get in the navy, outside those coordinating the efforts on land. Samuel'd made something of himself. And each time he advanced rank, he let himself believe a little bit more that he could actually win the approval of Catherine's parents."

"Now that the war was finally over, it was all or nothing. He came knockin' on the noble family's door one dark night. An especially dark and gloomy night, as there was a blood eclipse. He expected some gratitude, even a bit of humility, but when the family entered the drawing room they had nothin' but disgust written on their faces. Even Catherine, who had a new beau on her arm and a rock on her finger the size of a small child. Her father screamed at him that he should never step foot in their home, and threatened to call the authorities. Samuel ignored 'im and went straight to Catherine. He told her he still loved her, all these years later, and that he was a highly respected navy captain now and could provide anything she desired. Catherine's new beau scoffed and accused him of stealing the uniform. All his hard work, his reason for bein', circled the drain. The new beau shoved Samuel's arm, and he went into a rage, knockin' the beau to the ground. Catherine screamed as Samuel punched the man over and over and over. Even after he stopped movin', Samuel kept punchin' him.

Catherine tried to pull Samuel off, but he pushed her away hard enough that she fell to the ground.

"As he stood, her father started toward him. Samuel pulled out his pistol and fired off a shot. Catherine's father fell to the ground. He fired another shot at her father's chest for good measure. The mother turned to run, and Samuel shot her in the back, then turned the barrel on Catherine. He stood there a moment, the gun pointed at her while Catherine sobbed in the corner. Finally, he turned, leaving her there like that. No one knows if it was because he still had enough love for her that he couldn't bring himself to pull the trigger, or because he wanted her to feel what it was like to have lost everythin', as he just had."

"How terrible. I would think I'd have heard of an entire noble family being murdered. Wouldn't that be something for the history books, at the very least?"

"This was three hundred years ago, and 'sides, the nobles are good at coverin' things up." Kidd laughed.

"That they are," Kale chuckled. "Just think about that family whose ship went missing nearly two decades ago."

"A noble family? I haven't heard of anything like that. I would have been a child." Lillian shook her head.

"It's true," Rich said. "A small family, two parents and a child."

"No, just the parents. The child wasn't onboard, but was never seen again just the same. They can't discard a noble name if the heir's still around."

"That's a terrible thing to do. I still hold that I would have heard about something like that if it had happened," Lillian said.

"Believe what you like, princess." Johnny chuckled as he crossed his arms and leaned against the mast.

"So, did they catch Samuel? The servants must have heard something."

"If they had, we wouldn't have a story," Rich said. "No, Samuel escaped somehow. He ran blindly, but his legs took him to the docks where he'd grown up. He couldn't very well go back to the navy—he'd be caught for sure. By this time, it was night and everythin' was quiet. A few ships were tied nearby. One had a few sailors on deck. The other looked empty. He quietly boarded the empty one. He was preparing it to set sail when a man came out. Samuel pulled his gun on him. He gave the man an ultimatum: He could stay aboard and help Samuel sail the ship, or he'd be shot and thrown overboard. The man agreed to stay. Legend says this man was Samuel's first mate, Nathaniel."

"Samuel and Nathaniel created a new life for themselves, robbin' small ships and using the gold to buy themselves anythin' they wanted. They added new thieves to their crew and pillaged larger ships. Samuel got the idea to use their small fortune to buy himself a fancy wardrobe and work his way into the many social circles across the seas, only to steal high value items from them. He was never caught.

"They say he grew old aboard his ship and—here's where our part comes in—when he knew death was comin', he ordered his crew to sail him to his favorite hidden island. He had an old acquaintance from his travels, a witch,who he brought along. He hid his amassed fortune in a deep cavern in the center of the island. He placed a large boulder over the opening and had the witch seal it. The only way to open it is to finish Captain Samuel's revenge plot that started so many years before, by drippin' the blood of a female Aarilyan noble onto the hidden crest at the entrance to the cavern, during a blood eclipse," he finished.

Chapter Twenty-Five

They sat around the mast, quiet for a moment as Lillian took it all in. The story sounded fantastical, like something she would have read back home by the fire. But they believed it. The excitement gleaming in their eyes told her that much. Even after all she'd seen, she found it hard to believe there was some massive treasure hiding in the seas near Aarilya.

"So you're after this supposed treasure?" she asked carefully.

"It's not supposed. It's real. Every pirate knows about it. But no one knows where it is," Kidd said.

"Except you guys? And the time limit ... Am I correct in assuming there is a blood eclipse coming up?" She recalled the two young boys at the Aarilyan harbor joking about the blood moon and the pirate king.

"In just a few days' time," Kale said. "One only occurs every hundred years or so, so this is our only chance."

"To open the passage to the treasure?" Lillian asked.

"The only decent treasure we've set our hat toward," Johnny snorted, taking a deep drink from his cup.

"Not just the treasure." Kale shot Johnny a look. "But also Captain Samuel's famed pirate sword. *Kingsword*, it's called."

"There's an unwritten law among the pirates that if someone should claim Captain Samuel's sword and present it to the council, they shall become the new pirate king," Johnny said.

"And what you needed from the nobles ..." She looked toward Kale. "What you had wanted from me ... was blood?" He nodded. "How on earth did you get blood from someone without bringing them aboard?"

"My good friend the doctor helped. Don't you worry, no one was hurt. I think you should know by now, that's not how we work."

Lillian nodded slowly. Everything was coming together in her head. Why they had needed her—or Maria, actually—and why Kale had felt so guilty about it. But one thing still wasn't clicking.

"What about Dall? Is he after the treasure too?" It didn't make sense for a navy man to seek out treasure when his sole purpose was to hunt down others who did.

"Dall has a ... vendetta against me. In fact, we will set sail this evening because of it. He spotted me at the party last night. He knows we're in the area and will be looking."

Jack cursed from his spot on the deck, calling Dall a few no-good names as well.

"Not to mention Stevenson will most likely be prowling the waters as well," Kale continued. "With the eclipse approaching, he is going to be frantic to steal the map and the blood. And he's like a dog. When cornered, he bites. But now is the time to celebrate. We've got everything we need to open the cavern, and we should have just enough time to get there before the blood eclipse."

"Except Tamela," Johnny said. "We'll pick her up in Telayan tomorrow."

"Who's Tamela?" Lillian asked.

"She's a witch." Kidd said excitedly.

"She's a friend," Kale corrected. "We'll need her to counter the seal when we put the blood on it."

"She'll cast a spell?"

"You don't have to worry. She won't harm anyone." Kale chuckled. "She's quite friendly. I think the two of you should get along great."

"Well, I think witchcraft is a little too farfetched for my beliefs, but you've proven me wrong before. I suppose we shall see how it goes. You seem to have this all planned out."

"A lifetime of planning," Johnny said. "I should hope we have accounted for most everything."

"Alas, the best laid plans often go awry," Thomas said. "We can only do the best we can."

"Too true." Jack nodded.

A sweet melody filled the air as Chase began playing his guitar.

"Would you like to dance, Lillian?" Rich's dark red hair peeked out from beneath his bandanna as he extended a calloused hand. Lillian took it.

"Are you nervous about the treasure?" he asked as he guided her across the deck in sloppy motions.

"No. I'm worried how devastated you all will be when we find there's nothing there," she said.

He only chuckled. "You have little faith yet, but you will see. It's there. And you'll learn to accept the things in this life that are less than ordinary once you see what we see out here on the ocean."

She couldn't help but smile at him.

"May I cut in?" Johnny grinned.

"Well, I guess I can't take all your time." Rich squeezed her shoulder as he conceded her to Johnny.

"I thought you didn't want me here," she said as he took her hand.

"I don't. I think this adventure is too dangerous for you. But since you are here anyways, I may as well enjoy you." He slid his hand dangerously low.

She adjusted it to a more appropriate height. "So you'll stop telling me to leave?"

"I care for you, Lillian. I don't want you to get hurt. That's the only reason I push you away. And why I will continue to do so." He swung her out into a circle and back again in one fluid movement. His steps were as sure as Kale's had been, if a little less elegant.

"The others don't seem to think it's that dangerous. Is there something you know that they don't?"

They stepped together along the wooden deck.

"I'm just more realistic. They're used to the danger; they've been on many treasure hunts and gone through many battles before this. They just assume you'll acclimate. But you've no background in anything physical and can't even defend yourself. The one small battle you fought nearly killed you."

"But it didn't, and I'm better now. You can teach me more, everyone can. And—"

"In three days, Lillian? How much can you really learn in three days? Stevenson's after the treasure too, and he's after us for the map. He's a ruthless pig who takes advantage of every weakness. I'm not sure we can protect you from him." His words were a whisper, but his face was angry stone. With every word his eyes pleaded with her.

"I think it's time you give someone else a turn." Kale took her hand from Johnny's. Johnny blinked away the anger and sorrow, the only true emotion she had ever seen him show. "If you don't mind, that is?"

He turned to Lillian. She shook her head slowly, watching as Johnny walked away. She couldn't understand him. She knew he was hiding something, but she couldn't put her finger on what. It didn't seem to bother Kale or any of the rest of the crew.

"Are you sure this is a good idea?" she teased, turning back to Kale. He pulled her close as Chase's melody turned slow. "Last time didn't end well, if I recall."

"I promised I wouldn't take advantage. Besides, it looked like you needed to be saved. What was Johnny getting so heated about?" His stray hair was down over his forehead again, but he didn't bother to brush it back. So he *had* noticed.

"He still doesn't want me to stay aboard. He says it's too dangerous for me."

Dancing with Kale was dangerous for her. She could feel her skin heating, pressing against his, as a blush rose once more. Since they had shared that kiss, her body seemed to react far quicker to his.

"He's not wrong. This treasure hunt, it isn't a game. We don't know what perils we will face once we find the isle. We'll face even worse if Stevenson finds us before we do. But I like to believe I've warned you enough times that you understand the hazard. And this is truly what you want," he said.

"It is," she said.

His eyes searched hers as they spun around the deck. Not the formal, fancy dance she had taught him the other night, under the stars, when he had kissed her, but a lazy, comfortable waltz.

"You weren't taking advantage, you know. The other night." Her blush reached her cheeks. "I think it was fairly obvious it was mutual."

Kale looked away. "I was, Lillian. You are a beautiful young woman in a strange situation. An inexperienced one at that. We aren't on land. There aren't chaperones to stop ... unruly behavior."

"I think we have more than enough chaperones." She laughed, looking at the crew. An attempt to rouse him from his seriousness.

"None that would care if I kissed you." He turned to look at her once more. His eyes burned as they held her gaze, their feet stilled as the music continued. The crew erupted in laughter, breaking the spell. Kale turned away first, letting go of her waist. "I shouldn't monopolize your time either."

"Kale."

"No. I promised, Lillian. Not only you, but I promised myself. There can be nothing more than friendship between us." He smiled softly. Sadly. "We should get back to the others."

Friendship? What she felt, what she knew he felt—no matter how he tried to hide it—was more than friendship.

Chapter Twenty-Six

The wind whipped through Lillian's hair as the ship pulled into the harbor on Telayan. They practically shone as the light reflected off the metal shops and buildings. She'd expected it to be symmetrical, each shop in line with the one before, but rather each building was unique. One rose tall and thin, while another was hardly tall enough for a person to enter, and wide across with many doors. One even had a curved roof. People bustled about the docks, which were also metal and showed signs of rust where the sea scraped the legs jutting out. Behind the bright city rose the towering jungle Rich had mentioned in his story. Quite the contrast to the shining city, as if they were two completely different islands. Even from the boat, she could see it rose straight up into the sky, and the trees grew out of the sides, just as they had claimed. She let out a small chuckle as she took it all in.

Jack came to stand next to her. "Quite a sight, ain't it?" She nodded. "I'd got used to it for a while, but now I don't see it as often. It's quite a sight."

"Did you live here? Before?" she asked.

"Aye, when I was a lad, near an adult." His dark eyes held a hint of sadness. They stood there quietly, taking in the sound of the waves and the busy murmur of those on the docks. "You ready to go ashore?" he asked.

"Me?"

"Ain't no one else around." Jack chuckled. "Ye're comin' with us to fetch the witch."

Johnny approached them, rolling his eyes. "She has a name."

"And she's a witch. We're both correct."

"The question still stands, Lillian. Are you ready? You're going to love Tamela."

"I ... I suppose so."

"Great!" Johnny clapped her on the back. "You'll be with me." Jack grunted from her side. "Oh, and Jack and Chase will be there too. Here." He handed her a small pistol. It was barely the size of her hand. "It's compact enough to tuck into a bag or pocket, somewhere easy to reach."

"I've never fired a pistol before." She looked up at him. "I'm not sure ..."

"It's just for emergencies. Anyone you don't like gets close to you, just point it at them and pull this trigger." He pointed to the small, curved trigger below the barrel. She nodded and tucked it into the pocket of her trousers. Thank goodness for men's pants—were she wearing a dress, there'd have been no place for it. "But you've only got one bullet, so as I said, emergencies only."

"Hell, one bullet ain't gone do much if there's trouble. Take this too." Jack handed her a blade, small but larger than the gun. Its leather sheath was well worn and on its way to falling apart.

"I can't take your blade, Jack." She shook her head, stepping back as he presented it to her.

"It ain't nothin'. I got more." He lifted his vest with a crooked grin, showing off four more blades of varying lengths. "You can return it once we're back on the boat."

"If you insist." She slipped it gently into her other pocket.

Johnny grinned. "Now, let's get off this rocking piece of driftwood."

It was a short trek past the docks and through the small harbor city to Tamela's shop, which was an anomaly in the shining city. If you weren't looking for it, you could have easily passed not knowing it was there. The plain sandstone walls blended with those around it. The door, the same shade of beige, was narrow and windowless. No sign hung above. Nothing but tendrils of ivy hung from the edges of the roof, down to Lillian eyeline, and running the length of the avenue. Johnny didn't bother knocking as he pushed the ivy aside and opened the door.

The smell hit Lillian before she followed Johnny in, Jack and Chase behind her. It smelled of jasmine and soil and rain, thick and heavy. It was near to black as they moved from the sunny morning to the dark interior, and Lillian's eyes took a moment to adjust. She reached out and grasped the back of Johnny's coat to guide her through. She felt the chuckle reverberate through him.

"Careful, princess. You might give Tamela the wrong idea about us. She'd be devastated if she thought I'd settled down."

Lillian scoffed. As her eyes adjusted she took in the space. Shelves lined every wall, top to bottom. Perfectly organized shelves, she realized, not the hodgepodge clutter she would have expected. To her left, all the bottles were arranged by color and size. Below were a collection of herbs. First the dry ones, hanging from the underside of the shelf above, then the live ones in small pots, all lined up just so. In front of the group was a small counter space with a few rags folded and set level with the corner of its wooden top, behind which narrower bookshelves framed a doorway. Not a space open between them, most of the books looked worn and well read. They seemed to be sorted by category. Lillian could just make out a group of books on herbology. The rest were in another language entirely, or too high on a shelf for Lillian to read in the dim light. To the right were larger shelves covered with potted plants of all sorts.

"Damn you!" Johnny hissed, Jack let out a few choice curses, and Lillian gasped as the room came to light, the brightness of it stinging their eyes. Had she seen candles anywhere? When she opened them again, a woman was walking through the doorway behind the counter. She looked remarkably average, just as the room did, to be called a witch. She stood just under Lillian's height, her skin tan and dark. Her silver hair was sleek, with a single braid lain atop the right side, hanging down over her chest—over her breasts, Lillian realized, which were bare save for the hair covering them. Her eyes were dark, but they shimmered as she took in her guests. And though her chest was bare, she wore a skirt wrapped a few times haphazardly around her waist, tied with a length of rope.

"Apologies," she crooned. "I was not expecting company."

"The hell you weren't," Johnny said, a bit of anger still in his voice. Jack and Chase remained quiet at Lillian's back, content to let Johnny handle the calculating woman.

"Now, John, darling, there's no reason to get upset." She came around the counter and strolled up to Johnny, placing her hand on his chest and sliding it down just the slightest bit. Johnny covered her hand with his own. They were perfect for each other. Where he was playful and brash, she was languid and watchful, but they had the same cunning wit.

"I could never be upset with you," he crooned back. "Are you ready?"

Her smile deepened, her eyes sliding lazily over to Lillian. "And who do we have here?" She shifted past Johnny to get a better look. She was the source of the jasmine, Lillian realized. "A beautiful female." She cocked her head to the side, and her smile shifted to a grimace. "Wearing these god-awful pirate clothes. But they suit you, and the path you have ahead. You've grown stronger. You'll thrive as a pirate, given the chance. But you'll have to make a choice first. A choice between your companions."

Lillian made no reaction, save for a slight widening of her eyes. She was a witch, not a fortune teller. How could she know these things? Perhaps this was a test, to get a rise out of Lillian.

Tamela held her gaze a moment before replacing her seriousness with a flippant mask. "John, darling, tell me your new friend's name."

"My name is Lillian. And you must be Tamela. I'm told we'll be great friends."

"Oh, I believe we will."

She turned to Johnny and hooked her arm through his. "We should move along." Johnny only shook his head and led her past Lillian, Jack, and Chase. The light faded as quickly as it had appeared as they exited the shop. Tamela turned and, with a slight wave of her hand, the ivy stretched and grew until it reached the cobblestones, covering the door they had just exited from. Lillian gaped. She had expected potions and chants, not ... whatever Tamela had just done.

Jack and Chase chatted quietly while Johnny and Tamela walked in silence at the front. Lillian closed her gaping mouth and followed in step behind them.

"It's going to be so lovely having another woman aboard," Tamela said, falling back to where Lillian was. "These voyages get a bit drab when I am amongst only men. All they do is drink and play cards." She glanced at Lillian behind her, sizing her up. "You must be utterly bored with them by now."

Chase took Tamela's spot next to Johnny, and they laughed about something.

"I find them quite entertaining, actually." Lillian smiled softly, meeting Tamela's gaze before the woman turned away. "It's quite a change from my previous day-to-day. And I'm learning quite a lot from them."

"So I have heard. A lady learning to fight amongst pirates. Quite extraordinary," They walked down the cobblestone path toward the harbor city, now shimmering brightly in the afternoon sun.

"In truth, I am no lady. I was only a lady's maid," Lillian said plainly. This was the first time she'd said it aloud since that night with Kale, she realized. She assumed he had told Johnny and the rest. Judging by his lack of reaction, she was correct.

"Hmm," Tamela mused.

Johnny and Chase slowed as, just outside the harbor, new sounds drifted toward them. Gone were the murmurs and shuffling of feet, the moving of cargo. They'd been replaced by people running and shouting. Johnny exchanged a look with Chase, and they started walking faster. Tamela and Lillian hurried behind them, Lillian quite aware of the weapons in her pocket and thankful for Johnny's foresight.

Reaching the harbor, they picked up their pace. Others ran past them as they sprinted to the docks. Johnny cursed as the *Stardust* came into view, the source of the commotion. Another group of men had boarded, and the remaining crew were defending on deck. The sounds of clanging swords reached them as Chase broke into a full run.

From the looks of it, the battle had been raging for some time. The crew had the intruders bottlenecked on the bridge. The men didn't wear navy uniforms. They must be another band of pirates. Stevenson? She didn't see his bright red hair among them, but they were still a ways off. Johnny grabbed Lillian's hand, pulling her to a stop.

"What? What's the matter?" Lillian asked between breaths. She searched Johnny's face. He only held her eyes for a moment. "Johnny, we've got to hurry." She pulled her arm, but he held tight.

"Run, Lillian," he whispered. "Go. Go find somewhere here and make a life. Or find passage on another boat back to Aarilya. This isn't your fight."

"Johnny, this isn't the time." She pulled again.

"It's the perfect time. Lose yourself in the commotion and never look back. I don't want you to get hurt, Lillian," he pleaded. A couple ran passed them, the woman daring a glance back toward the fight. There wouldn't be much time before the authorities arrived. The navy. Maybe even Dall himself, though he tended to stick close to Aarilya.

"Johnny, you don't understand. This *is* my fight now. And you all—you're my family. My home." Tears filled her eyes.

He brushed a thumb over her cheek.

As screams filled the air, his hand fell away. The few remaining people in the harbor ran toward the city, toward those gleaming metal shops, searching for any still open. Lillian and Johnny turned toward the ship. Rick, Rich, and Eddie were pushing the other men toward the harbor with every sword slash as they took them down one by one.

Tamela's hands were in the air and her lips were moving, although they were too far away to hear what she was saying. The remaining attackers were hanging mid-air. They clawed at their throats as if there were an invisible hand closing around them. They made no sound, but their faces turned a deathly color, and their arms fell to their sides. They stopped moving. With a final wave of her hand, the four men were thrown into the sea.

Just as they hit the water, Tamela fell to her knees. Kale rushed forward and helped her up. They exchanged a few words, and Kale looked frantically across the harbor until his eyes found them. Johnny released Lillian's arm and stepped away, walking toward the ship as if he hadn't just been begging her to leave. Lillian stared after him for a heartbeat before following.

Chapter Twenty-Seven

Kale helped Tamela to her feet. Using such power on four men at once had drained her, though he was grateful for the help. The authorities were surely on their way by now. They needed to set sail.

"Where are the others?" He had seen Jack and Chase run past before Tamela had gotten there, but no sign of Johnny and Lillian.

"They were just behind me," she said, only slightly short of breath. "They'll be here soon. We should go now if we don't want to be arrested." He scanned the harbor for them. Mostly for her—Johnny could handle himself. There! Johnny held Lillian by the arm. Had she been hurt? Just as he spotted them, Johnny released her and headed for the ship, not waiting for her to follow. Within a few moments, they had crossed the now empty harbor to meet Kale and Tamela on the gangway.

"Everyone okay?" Johnny grunted.

Kale nodded. "Everything okay with you?"

Johnny pushed past them without responding. Kales eye's slid to Lillian, searching her face, then her body, for any unseen injuries.

"We're fine," she said, her eyes searching him as well. Blood coated his chest, but she relaxed when she realized it wasn't his own.

"What was that with Johnny?" he asked.

"Nothing."

"We've got to get moving, and fast," Tamela reminded them. Kale nodded, motioning for Lillian to board first. The crew were already readying the ship to sail.

"Weigh the anchor! Kidd, help Chase!" Kale commanded, then turned to Lillian. "Would you like to join me at the helm?" She was stunned for a moment. "It's the best spot to watch everyone doing what's needed."

She followed as he sprinted up the stairs, shouting commands to the crew. Just as they reached the top, and the ship began to pick up speed, Lillian sawa a group of navy men crowding onto the docks. A few civilians had returned with them, no doubt recounting what they had witnessed. Thankfully the *Stardust* was too far out for the authorities to do anything now.

"Who was it? That attacked?" Lillian asked as Kale took the helm.

"Stevenson."

"I didn't see him. He got away?" She shifted closer to him and leaned against the rail.

"He didn't honor us with his presence this time. Just sent some grunts to do his dirty work while we were shorthanded." He scoffed. "Coward. He must have been following us. There's no other way he would have known we'd be here. Or it was sheer dumb luck. But he'll know we have Tamela now. He'll double his efforts to find the treasure now that we're so close to the blood moon. We'll have to be swift and cautious as we travel to the isle." His frown deepened.

Tamela had slipped below deck to rest, and the rest of the crew tended to their injuries in the galley or kept watch on deck in case someone decided to chance following the ship. After a little while had passed, and Telayan was nothing but a shining and green mass of land behind them, Kale looked over toward Lillian. Her hair was braided to the side as usual, and in her makeshift uniform, she looked as if she belonged. Content.

"Did you enjoy your time ashore?" he asked. She turned toward him, a light in her dark blue eyes.

"I did. I'll be honest, I was surprised when Johnny said I was to go with them. But it was nice to feel useful. Even if all I did was tag along."

"And Tamela? What did you think of her?" He let the helm pull to the left a bit and kept it there.

"She wasn't what I was expecting." Lillian laughed, leaning against the side rail. "And I won't ever doubt her abilities again." She shivered, and he knew she had recalled how easily the witch had taken down those four men. Kale chuckled.

"She is one of a kind. Thank goodness she is a friend and not an enemy."

"Are there other ones out there? People with abilities like hers?" Lillian moved closer to where Kale stood at the helm.

"Some. Not many. Only one other as powerful as Tamela, and a handful of lesser magic. I haven't come across any in my lifetime." Lillian nodded, a loose hair slipping down over her face. Kale reached to tuck it behind her ear, then turned back to the helm. The ship creaked beneath them.

"Kale—" Lillian started.

"We've got a few days before the blood moon," he interrupted. "Would you like to resume your lessons with the crew?"

Her shoulders fell, but only for a moment. "I would love that. I fear I've become rusty in my complacency."

She moved to the rail next to him at the helm, their arms only an inch or so from touching. He could feel the warmth radiating from her.

"To be fair, you didn't learn all that much before your injury." He looked ahead once more.

"I had a good start." She crossed her arms indignantly, that small pout of hers starting to take form.

"Perhaps." He chuckled. "But it won't do much help if you needed to fight. This evening, after supper, we'll resume your training." Anything to give her an edge if they came to face Stevenson again. Or some other danger on the island. She was a quick learner, he'd noticed, and could pick up things that would be useful in a pinch. An admirable quality, one that would benefit her on the open sea ... or on land, where it was safer for her.

"And will you be my teacher this time?" She smirked.

"Aye. Along with others. I am sure Johnny would love the chance to continue his surprise attacks." Kale's smile faltered as he remembered their encounter at the docks. Something didn't sit right with him. The way they had been looking at each other. But he had been too far away to really read the situation.

"Is everything okay between the two of you?" he asked cautiously.

Lillian tensed. "Johnny is just ... Johnny." As if that was the only way to describe him. In fact, Kale was sure he had used the very same words. Johnny was Johnny, but he had been off the past few weeks, and Kale hadn't been able to wring the why out of him. He had been broody and sharp, not only with Kale but with the crew as well.

"He didn't hurt you, did he?" Kale's nostrils flared at the thought. Brother or no, he would throw him overboard if he'd laid a hand on her.

"No. Heavens, no. Johnny would never harm me." She waved the question away. "No one here would. I've never felt so safe in my life. So welcome." She smiled, setting a hand on his forearm. His skin burned where the heat from her palm seeped through his sleeve, right up to his chest. "Thank you for that."

"Of course." He cleared his throat. "It wasn't just my decision. The whole crew is glad you've chosen to stay aboard." He looked back out over the ocean, turning the helm back into position once more. Only a few more days until they'd reach the Isle of Kinslet. They now had the map, the blood, and Tamela. They just needed to avoid any more run-ins with Stevenson.

Later that evening, they all sat around the table finishing up supper. There was a sense of joy and excitement this evening, as though each battle they fought was a momentous occasion fit for celebration. Lillian smiled watching the raucousness she had come to enjoy. Tamela had chosen to take her meal in her cabin, claiming she'd had enough excitement for one day to endure a meal with loud, obnoxious men, although Lillian suspected she was still recovering from the events of the afternoon.

She caught Kale's eye as he made his way toward her.

"Are you ready for your lessons?" he said, so softly she could hardly make out his words over the noise.

She nodded and followed him out on deck, where the quiet was strange, almost overwhelming after the galley. The sun had begun to set, blasting its hues of orange and yellow and pink across the place where the sky met the sea. The ship groaned with each lap of the ocean against the hull.

"Are you here to learn something, or to watch night fall?" Kale teased, that playful gleam in his gray eyes.

"Just the two of us?" she asked, surprised.

"For now. Assume the stance you learned with Johnny." She did so, planting her feet firmly. "We aren't going to focus on your balance so much anymore, but you should resume practicing that on your own. Balance is key to everything in a fight, especially on a ship. It will help you defend as well as attack. Johnny was trying to toughen you up against taking an attack. We are going to focus more on dodging attacks, no matter what form they come in. It won't matter that you're weak if they can't get a hit in." She frowned at the mention of weakness. She didn't feel weak any longer. Not like she had when she first came aboard. Or helpless, like she had felt aboard the *Rossut*. She was ready to take on whatever being a pirate brought her.

Pirate.

She hadn't really considered the term for herself, but it felt right. Lillian the Pirate.

"Put your arms up, like Johnny showed you. Protect your face. Good girl, just like that." He grinned. "Now watch my moves. You need to anticipate your enemy's actions before they make them. That will give you ample time to dodge or defend yourself. If I swing my right hand, it will most likely land center, or to your left. Where should you move to avoid it?"

"To my right."

"Exactly. I'm going to move now, and I want you to"—he swung his right fist out, not at full speed but faster than she expected—"dodge!" She ducked down and to the right, only shifting her feet an inch or so, before coming back up to face him.

"Good. Never take your eyes off your enemy, that was good. Let's practice the same move some more. You want your body to get so used to the movement that it becomes instinct." He swung again, a little faster, and she shifted and ducked again. They continued the movement over and over again for the better part of a half hour. Then they switched to the other side. She sighed in relief as her muscles screamed. This time when he swung with his left, she shifted left. After moving right for so long, the new movement felt foreign. She tripped as she ducked down and nearly fell, but righted herself and continued to face him. Kale punched from his left again, and she shifted down and to her left. Punch, duck. Punch, duck. They continued until they were both breathless.

"I've got to hand it to you, you're very quick on your feet," Kale said between breaths as they sat on the deck for a moment's rest. He passed her a tin cup filled with water he had set aside. She drained the contents in a few grateful gulps. "Perhaps tomorrow we can start on counterattacks."

Night had finally fallen, and the evening air had turned brisk, though neither of them felt it through the heat of their skin from the training.

"Well, what have we here? You two look like you've been racin' round the ship." Eddie grinned as he exited the galley, the rest of the crew just behind him. He extended a tattooed hand to Lillian, who accepted it with a grin of her own. He pulled her to her feet and reached for Kale.

"Kale's just teaching me to dodge a punch, in case any of you scoundrels get any bright ideas."

"Who, us?" Eddie said, feigning shock. "We ain't scoundrels."

"Hooligans, perhaps," Kidd joked.

"Rakes for sure," Johnny said lazily.

Thomas shrugged. "But not scoundrels." They all laughed warmly.

Eddie clapped Lillian on the back. "Welcome to the crew, girl."

Kale watched as her eyes lit up at the mention of being one of them. The men circled around her, smiling and laughing as they traded banter. They'd give anything to protect her, just as he would. Perhaps everything.

He cleared his throat to get their attention. Once the laughs had settled to murmurs, he looked at each of them. "I'm glad you're all out here, actually. I think there's something we need to discuss, as a family." Everyone fell quiet. "We've all faced a lot of action these past few days. More than we've had in a while." Lillian laughed as the men cheered. "We've even lost one of our own," he continued solemnly. They quietly whispered Dave's name. "With Dall hunting us, now of all times, and Stevenson attacking at every port, I have to wonder if this bounty is worth the heartache. Perhaps this isn't the adventure for us."

"You're not serious!" Johnny exclaimed from the back of the group. "We've been planning this for years. *Years*, Kale." He pushed to the front.

"I know, Johnny, but is it worth it? Is it worth the lives we've lost? The lives we may yet lose?" Kale's eyes remained solemn. "At the end of the day, it's just gold." Kale and Johnny held each other's gaze, Kale's weary and sorrowful while Johnny's was dark and angry.

"We've been fine with the smaller bounties up to now. Staying out of the navy's path and tradin' ashore," Rich offered. The others muttered their agreement.

"Sure, finding a legendary treasure would be fun. But fun isn't worth the loss of life," Rick agreed.

"What of Kylah?" Johnny grasped.

"We got enough from the gem to tide them over for now. I can find more elsewhere."

"And the sword?" He still held Kale's eyes.

"What of it? Just another piece of loot."

Johnny's jaw clenched. "You'd let Stevenson take it, then? Become king of the pirates?"

Kale stood his ground. "Stevenson will never find the cave, not without the map. We can hide off the coast of Arbor until the blood moon has passed and then continue with our travels."

"I cannot believe you are considering this," Johnny said. "All of you. Does this mission mean nothing to you? The glory of being the one to find Captain Samuel's treasure, the sword? Presenting it to the Council of Pirates, after three hundred years?" His icy blue eyes were wild.

"I thought, Johnny, that you would be one of the first to agree with this. Seeing how hard you've tried to protect Lillian from the danger of this mission." Johnny's eyes flicked to Lillian, holding on her a moment before returning to Kale. His face hardened once more.

"We've put so much work and planning into this. We cannot just abandon everything we've worked toward," he said, deathly quiet. "Dave gave his life for this."

"Dave gave his life protecting one of our own from Dall's men," Kale said. "And if we continue, how many more will have to give theirs?"

Lillian moved to get between the two men. And say what? She wasn't sure. But Jack put a hand on her arm to stop her, shaking his head. She stepped back next to him. She'd never seen Johnny with such a wild expression.

"You always take the easy road, Kale," Johnny spat at him. "You back down from anything that has a decent payout. Only taking the small jobs. No risk, no reward Kale."

"Where do you draw the line, Johnny? What payout is acceptable for one of our friends' lives? What would you have us do?"

"I'd go after the damn sword!" He stepped to the side, and Kale matched him, keeping Johnny in front of him.

"And what are you going to do if we decide not to pursue the sword?" Kale asked calmly. Johnny growled.

"Shouldn't we stop them?" Lillian's voice wavered.

"This ain't our fight," Jack huffed. "They've gotta get it out of their system."

"I won't let you do this. *We* won't let you do this. We *have* to go after the sword, no matter the risk!" Johnny turned to the crew, making eye contact with each of them. Kale turned as well.

Jack sighed.

"What?" Lillian whispered.

"Mutiny."

"Well, what say you?" Kale said. For a moment, no one made a sound. The air was heavy. Kale waited, still as stone. The longer they stood there, the quicker Johnny's breaths became. Finally, each of the crew raised a hand. Slowly they turned it to a fist and pointed a thumb out. Lillian watched as each of them turned their thumb down.

Johnny let out a breath, his body sagging.

"The crew has spoken," Kale said softly. He and Johnny held each other's eyes a few heated moments more before Johnny turned away, his head held high as he walked across the deck and disappeared below. Kale followed.

"What just happened?" Lillian whispered.

"Johnny attempted a mutiny. And failed."

"And once a mutiny is begun," Rich continued, "the one voted against must either be put in the brig until we reach shore, where they can leave freely, or they duel to the death. Johnny chose the brig, at least. Must have broke poor Kale's heart." He shook his head sadly. Everyone stood there quietly until Kale returned on deck. He looked to Lillian first. She had yet to see such sadness in him. Any light he had let in over the past few days had gone just like that. Only darkness remained.

Her heart broke for him.

He looked over the crew. "Think on it tonight. We will discuss more in the morning." He left them to talk among themselves.

Chapter Twenty-Eight

Lillian's body ached as she slipped her shirt and trousers off, and put on her nightshirt. Sitting on the edge of her cot, she untied her braid and ran her brush through her soft chestnut curls. Kale had brought her the brush. He must have picked it up somewhere on shore. Such a small thing, but she had been grateful. She was just settling in and about to pull her covers up when she heard a thump in the room next door. She sat up, listening. Nothing for a few moments, then some soft scraping. Had she not been listening, she may have missed it. She roused from her cot and padded to her door. The hall was silent, and so she slipped out.

With no portholes to let the moonlight in, the hall was quite dark save for the soft light coming from beneath her door. And the door next to hers. She moved silently to the left, her feet cold on the bare wood. She listened against the door another moment. The soft scraping sounded again. She opened it slowly and was met with an exact replica of Tamela's shop back on Telayan. Tamela was placing small vials on shelves that had appeared out of nowhere.

"Well, good evening, Lady Lillian." Tamela set another vial on the shelf.

"Please, just Lillian. I am no lady," Lillian said. A small shrug was Tamela's only response. "I didn't realize this was the cabin they'd given you. I heard some noise and came to investigate."

"Couldn't sleep after the commotion on deck?" Tamela turned toward her, inviting her to sit in one of two chairs that hadn't been there before.

"You heard about that already?" Lillian asked.

"Heard. Saw."

"I didn't see you there."

"I wasn't," Tamela said. "Tea?"

"Please," Lillian said slowly. "Would you like me to fetch the water?"

"No need."

Lillian looked back down at the table to find a pot of steaming tea and two cups. The set was white china, with dark green vines snaking all around each base, dotted with the most delicate purple flowers. Lillian gasped. She ran a finger across the pot, then snatched it away from the heat.

"I see you have recovered well from this afternoon's ... events." Lillian took her in.

"Well enough." Her slender body bore no mark of the power she had used. Her face held no weariness, as it had earlier. Tamela poured the tea. The fragrance of a multitude of floral scents filled the room as the hot liquid filled each cup. A small purple flower popped up to float across the surface.

"Thank you." Lillian lifted a cup to her lips. It was just the right temperature, and the heavenly taste filled her mouth, caressing her taste buds. She moaned as she took another sip. "I hadn't realized how much I missed real tea."

"It's the small things that often are of comfort without us realizing it. A good cup of tea, with the right blend of herbs, can perform its own magic, from bringing comfort or warmth to healing injuries. I shall leave some with you when I depart." Tamela sipped her tea as well.

"That would be lovely." A yawn creeped up on her.

"There, now. You should sleep handsomely this evening." Tamela's smile was warm.

"Thank you, Tamela. I think you were right. It shall be quite nice to have another woman aboard."

Kale stood over his small table, the one that substituted for a desk when needed. The worn map was laid out in front of him, the two vials of blood next to it. He rubbed his face. How had he not seen this coming? He knew Johnny was restless, but enough to attempt mutiny? He shook his head, placing both hands on the table, and leaned over it. This wasn't right. They were family. Brothers. How could Johnny have turned on him? Maybe he should go down and check on him, talk to him. Find out what pushed him to this breaking point. Johnny had been strange the past few weeks. Kale had thought it was just having Lillian aboard, adding the stresses of the treasure hunt. But this went deeper. For Johnny to turn on him ... Something didn't sit right.

He heard the scrape of his door opening and closing just as quickly. He looked up to see Johnny standing there.

"How—" Kale started.

"We've been on this ship for eight years, give or take. You really think I don't know my way out of the brig?" Johnny raised an eyebrow. No smile, none of his usual wit in his words.

"Johnny. You knew the consequences."

"And what of your consequences, Kale? You promised that crew a lifetime of riches, only to rip it away right as it was actually attainable." He circled Kale.

"I ripped nothing away. I proposed a different path, that's all. That's something you've never grasped, even after all these years together. I don't make the decisions—we make them as a crew. As a family."

Kale's eyes narrowed as Johnny drew closer.

"You would have ripped them from me. Getting that sword meant everything to me!" Johnny glared at Kale, then at the table, moving closer.

"Obviously it meant more than your friends' lives." Kale stepped between Johnny and the desk.

Johnny's eyes flicked back to Kale's. "No risk, no reward Kale."

He lunged at Kale. Metal glinted as he pulled a blade from his vest. Kale sidestepped and pushed Johnny away. Johnny twisted and swung the knife deftly toward Kale's abdomen. Kale jumped back, the sharp edge narrowly missing him. Johnny lunged again. This time Kale grabbed hold of his knife hand. Johnny let out a groan as Kale twisted until he finally dropped it. Kale kicked it out of the way, forcing Johnny to his knees.

"Is this what you wanted Johnny? To lose a friend? To lose a brother?" Kale's voice caught on the last word. Johnny tried to pull away, but Kale twisted his arm further. Johnny growled. "Because that's what you risked for your reward." Kale let go of Johnny and stepped back, breathing hard. "Get out of here, Johnny. Take the rowboat and row yourself back to Telayan, or wherever the hell you want. I don't want to see your face again."

Kale turned his back on Johnny. He heard him stand but not move toward the door. What was he waiting for? To apologize?

"Never turn your back to your enemy, Kale." Kale turned, but before he could something hard smashed the side of his skull. He crumpled to ground, holding onto consciousness just long enough to see Johnny grab the map and the vials of blood from the table.

"Kale."

Someone was calling him, but the person was far away, as if they were down a long dark hallway beckoning him to follow.

"Ka-ale," the voice sang.

He could almost see the person at the end. If he could just get a little closer.

"Kale!" it said louder. Kale blinked as bright light burned his eyes. He blinked a few more times until he could focus on his surroundings. Jack, Rick, and Rich stood over him. He was lying on the floor. He tried to sit up but groaned as pain and dizziness hit the side of skull like a bag of stones.

"Easy there, fella," Jack said as Kale lay back down. "The ladies be on their way. Tamela's sure to got somethin' fer that head of yours." Kale groaned again. Rich handed him a wet rag, and he hissed in a breath as he pressed it to the wound.

"What happened?" Rick asked.

"Johnny," Kale grunted. "He took off with the map." He groaned once more. Black specks filled his vision.

"Guess we couldn't 'spect him to hold to the brig. Must'a taken the rowboat," Jack mused. There was a small knock at the door. Without waiting for anyone to answer, Tamela and Lillian pushed in. Tamela carried a few jars of herbs while Lillian held some fresh rags, already dampened. She gasped, her hand covering her lips as she saw his head. He could feel it caked with dry blood down the side, covering his ear. Her eyes finally met his after surveying the wound. She stayed close to the door as Tamela pushed through the small group congregated around him.

"Do you all have nothing better to do? Leave the medicine to the ladies." She clicked as the three men stepped back.

"Holler if ya need anythin'." Jack stepped out, leaving the door ajar.

"He got you good, did he?" Tamela muttered, spreading her jars across the table.

"A warning would have been nice," Kale hissed as he pressed the cloth to his head once more.

"You know I do not meddle. More trouble than it's worth," she said, not looking at him. She looked to Lillian and reached out a hand. Lillian gave her one of the rags. Tamela laid it out, sprinkling a few herbs from one jar then more from the other onto it. She folded the ends of the rag over the leaves and used her palm to crush them. Once she was satisfied, she opened the rag and pushed the now mushed leaves into one small mound.

Wrapping the rag around the mound, she twisted the ends around until it was tight, then handed the compress to Lillian. "Press this to the wound."

Lillian's eyes widened, but she took the rag and sat next to Kale. "This will most likely hurt."

"I trust you," Kale's attempt at a smile faded before it formed.

"I am going to go brew some tea. I'll be back shortly, Lady Lillian," Tamela said, stepping out. Lillian nodded, even though she'd already gone. She swallowed and took in the sight of the wound. She quickly, and gently as she could, pressed the rag to his temple.

He groaned as it pushed into the wound.

"I'm sorry. She didn't say how long to keep it here," Lillian said.

"It's all right." Kale breathed. "It's working." He relaxed a bit, still lying on the floor. After a moment, he opened his eyes and looked at Lillian. The worry etched on her face tugged at something in his chest.

"Hey." He settled his hand on hers. "I'll be okay. Tamela is a great nurse. She'll get it taken care of."

Lillian's shoulders sagged. "It's just ... He could have ... It could have gone so much worse." Her eyes shone with unshed tears.

He knew. He knew it could have been worse. If he had been asked the day before, he would never have thought Johnny could have attacked him. But when he did—the wild look in his eye as he swung that knife—Kale knew. And it broke his heart.

He pushed his own worry aside. "Would you have missed me?"

"You know I would have." She held his gaze. He cupped her cheek, running his thumb across the softness of her skin. She closed her eyes and leaned into his touch. That cautious, calculating part of him screamed at him to stop, not to give her hope. But something in his chest urged him on. He needed the comfort as much as she did.

"I'm right here, Lillian. I'm not going anywhere," he whispered.

The door swung open, and he pulled away. Lillian brushed the tears from her cheeks and adjusted the compress. Tamela was holding the teapot she had conjured the night before. Three teacups floated behind her in a line, like three little ducklings following their mother. She waved them to the table and started pouring.

"You'll need to sit up to drink, dear," she said over her shoulder. Lillian set the rag down , giving Kale room as he raised himself to a sitting position. His head throbbed at the movement, but it wasn't the stabbing pain he had felt earlier. Tamela's herbs were doing their job. Tamela handed Lillian a cup. She held it up to Kale's lips. It smelled fresh and citrusy. He took a healthy sip, sighing with relief as the pain ebbed almost immediately.

"I'm afraid, Tamela, that we're going to have to employ you full-time for your medical abilities." He savored another gulp.

"Nonsense." She waived her hand dismissively. "It is only herbs. I will teach Lillian. It is a necessary skill for the dangers you put yourselves through. I am surprised no one has attempted to learn it prior." Kale drained the last of it, and he leaned back against the wall. Lillian set the cup on the table.

"A minute more, and I shall feel well enough to stand."

"You are already well enough to stand. You are just acting a ninny." Tamela sipped her tea. Lillian chuckled. After a moment, he groaned and hefted himself up. He took the last damp rag from the table and wiped the remaining crusted blood from his ear and temple. The gash still shone, but it bled no more. Tamela conjured some gauze and made quick work of wrapping it around Kale's head. Oddly enough, his rogue hair still hung down over his forehead.

"All right, ladies," he said. "I believe we have a decision to make regarding our course. Let's gather the crew."

Chapter Twenty-Nine

Kale stood in front of the stairway that led to the helm, Tamela and Lillian next to him. The crew soon gathered around them.

"I hope everyone is well rested. I know I am." Laughter circled through the men. "But in seriousness, I hope everyone thought well and hard on our discussion last evening, for it is time we come to an agreement on which path we shall take."

"Aye. We're ready," Rick said, his arms crossed over his chest.

Kale moved up a step on the stairs and looked the crew over. "All right, then. All those for letting this one lie, and moving on to the next adventure?" He looked across the group and waited. A moment passed in silence, then another. When it became clear none would raise their voice, he moved on. "Those in favor of tracking down Captain Samuel's treasure?"

"Aye!" Every member of the crew said in unison. Kale smiled. "On we go, then! Now, who's serving breakfast this morning? I am starving."

"Eddie," Kidd groaned, earning himself a slap to the back of his head.

"You just ain't hungry enough. One day you'll be thankful for my cookin'." Eddie stared Kidd down.

Lillian followed Kale through the group and toward the galley. "Jack said Johnny took the map. And the blood. How are we going to find the treasure without them?"

"I've stared at that map so long I know every inch of it by heart. As for the blood, we'll just have to steal it back once we get there."

Lillian had spent the morning with Tamela going over the different herbs she used, and how to use them. It was an art form that would take Lillian more than a few days to master. Thankfully, Tamela had offered to let her borrow a few of her texts on the subject and renew her knowledge whenever they docked in Telayan. Lillian headed up on deck for some air, necessary after being cooped up below for the majority of the day. Kale appeared in the entryway just as she reached the top of the stairwell.

"Just the person I was looking for."

"Oh?"

"Thought you might like to continue your training."

Her face fell. "I thought we'd take a rest today, with your injury."

"What, this? Nothing but a scrape," he teased. "Besides, we only have a day until we reach the isle. The closer we get without running into Stevenson has me worried. I doubt he's given up, and there's bound to be a fight. I would feel better if you knew a little more of how to defend yourself." He ran his fingers down her forearm. Her skin prickled at the contact.

"I—I suppose you're right," she stuttered as a slight blush crept across her cheeks.

They made their way to the middle of the deck. Tony, Jack, Rich, and Thomas, who had all been hanging about, now moved closer toward them.

"Come on, Lillian! You can take him," Rich shouted.

She smiled as she readied her stance across from Kale.

"Here." He tossed an object toward her. She gasped and caught it before dropping it to the floor. It was a small wooden blade; she realized as she picked it up. "We're going to practice with a weapon, so you can get the feel of it. Whether it's a punch or a blade, the defensive maneuvers are the same. Keep that in your hand at the ready but continue to keep your face protected."

She took her stance once more, wielding the fake blade in one hand while keeping her other in a fist. Her body ached in protest.

He did the same, holding his own wooden blade. "Now, when I attack, I want you to dodge like we practiced but also use your free hand to push my weapon arm away. Show me." He swiped out with his blade hand slowly as he had done the day before. She dodged, groaning as her sore muscles screamed. As his arm came down she used her other hand to push it away from her body. "Good girl." He smiled. "Again."

They practiced the maneuver for the better part of an hour, switching sides as they went along. The four men cheered her on from the sides. By the end she was breathing heavily from the exercise. Rich handed her water and patted her on the back. She smiled as she took it, drinking it down.

"I think I should be offended that no one is in my corner," Kale teased. "Promise me, Lillian, that you won't go and start a mutiny. I doubt I would win." He grimaced.

They chuckled as Jack handed him some water as well. "How 'bout we raise the stakes some?" Lillian gasped as he pulled out a blade, the same one he had lent her the day before.

"You think you're ready for a real weapon?" Kale's eyes shone with a challenge.

"I think I can handle anything you throw at me." She took the blade from Jack and resumed her stance, returning his wicked smile. The men cheered on her boldness.

"In that case, let's have some fun. Let us spar, one on one. If you manage to draw blood, I'll let you act as captain for a day. After we retrieve the treasure, of course."

"I accept." She watched as he resumed his stance, still holding the wooden blade. Jack stood between them, meeting each of their eyes with a grin before raising a hand, palm out.

"Ten minutes. All ya have to do is draw blood, girlie. Set. Spar!" He stepped back as he shouted.

Kale circled. She followed his steps in the opposite direction. The blade was heavier than the practice sword. She was painfully aware of the metal gleaming in front of her. After practicing dodging all afternoon, it felt strange to go on the offensive. She kept her eyes on Kale's as he prowled around her, trying to back her into a corner. But she wouldn't allow it. Every move he made, she mirrored. When it became clear he was not going to be the one to make the first attack, she moved to strike. Before she could even raise her blade, he grabbed her empty hand and pulled her close to him, pinning her knife hand between them. His practice blade pushed into her side.

"You lose," he whispered into her ear, clearly enjoying this.

Her cheeks warmed and she pushed him away.

"Don't let him get into your head, Lilliana!" Tony yelled from the sidelines.

"He may be more experienced, but you are quick!" Thomas agreed.

"I'm not done yet." She began circling again, looking for any opening. His moves were slow, patient. If she didn't attack first, she had no advantage. She lunged again, and again he grabbed her.

She tried to maneuver away before he pinned her arm, but he was too strong.

"Same trick twice in a row." He clicked his tongue in disapproval, holding her against him. She huffed as she pulled herself free. Kale chuckled, resuming his stance. She watched his movements, calculating her options. This time she lunged to the other side of him. He grabbed her by the wrist and swung her past him, kicking her on the bottom hard enough that she lost her footing and fell to the ground, dropping her knife. Kale grabbed it before she had a chance to recover.

"Aw, Kale, that ain't fair," Rich called.

Lillian growled and slammed her hands on the deck.

"There's the girl I was looking for." Kale chuckled. "Gone is Lillian the Lady's Maid. Let us see Lillian the Pirate." His eyes danced as he held her blade out to her, butt first. She snatched it back and stood with a groan.

She was running out of time. Attacking first was getting her nowhere. She would have to trick him into attacking. The wooden practice knife was still in her pocket. She circled while a plan formed in her mind. Once she knew what she had to do, she looked into Kale's eyes and smiled. She was the predator now.

She stepped toward him as if to attack. He drew near to grab her, as he had before, but she spun out of his reach and faced away from him, for only a moment. He went on to attack while her back was turned, as she knew he would. Just as he moved close enough, she dropped to one knee and spun back to face him, bringing up her practice knife to parry his attack. He looked at the two weapons, stunned. She grinned wickedly as she reached up with her blade and knicked the top of his forearm, just enough to draw blood. He blinked at her. Then a wide grin formed.

Jack, Rich, Tony, and Thomas roared their congratulations. Pulling his wooden blade away, Kale offered her a hand. She took it graciously and stood.

"Welcome aboard ... pirate," Kale said. The men clapped Lillian on the back as they surrounded her. She held Kale's gaze, beaming. He nodded his approval, and she turned to the enthusiastic group.

"That was quite cunning," Kale said as Lillian finally stepped away from everyone.

Lillian crossed her arms. "It was the only thing I could think to do. You refused to attack."

He chuckled at her indignant pose, eyes still wild from the sparring match, her braid now mussed. She had some spirit in her. It was just a matter of drawing it out. She would make an excellent pirate, he realized. He had thought it before, but she'd still held on to that person she had thought she should be, the person everyone expected her to be. Now, though ... she was becoming her own person. And that new person was wholly pirate.

"Supper!" Kidd called, poking his head out of the galley.

Kale motioned for Lillian to go ahead. "Lady's maid's first."

"I thought I was a lady's maid no longer," she teased back.

"We'll see."

In the galley, Eddie spooned some stew into their waiting bowls. As they moved to sit, Kale gently took Lillian's elbow. She looked up at him questioningly, and he beckoned over the commotion of the room to follow him. He led her to the end of the table and motioned for her to sit. This was the first time since she'd come aboard that they had sat together at a meal. The men at the other end shouted when they realized she hadn't taken her usual place next to them.

"Hey! Lillian is ours during mealtimes," Chase yelled across the room.

"Her spot is down here with us," Landry added.

"If she's to be captain for a day, she ought to shadow the captain," Kale said.

"What's this about being captain?" Kidd asked.

"Lillian stabbed Kale durin' a sparrin' match." Rich gleamed.

Jack grunted his approval. "Girl done good."

Lillian smiled as she spooned a bite of her stew. They continued through their meal with the usual rowdy banter as the evening wore on.

After supper, Lillian and Kale had continued their defensive training, working her muscles until they were screaming as they had done the day before. They now sat together on the deck, panting from exhaustion. Lillian's braid was coming loose from all the activity of the day. She removed her tie and undid it, shaking her soft brown waves loose and running her fingers through them.

Kale lay back, tucking his arms beneath his head as he watched her. "Your hair looks nice down. You've kept it up since you've been here."

"The wind tangles it if I leave it down for long."

He caressed a few strands, tugging on the ends before letting go. She smiled down at him.

"When you talked about your family before, was it the De Sansols you spoke of?" he asked "Or your birth parents?"

"My birth parents," she said. "The De Sansols were kind enough, as best they knew how, anyway. But my parents, what little I remember ... They were the kindest people I'd known. I think they worked for another family. I remember a different house when I was younger. After they passed, no one wanted to take me in. Mrs. De Sansol was the only one who offered. There had to be kindness in that. Or perhaps she just wanted someone to keep Maria out of her hair." She laughed. "She always was a handful." Her eyes glistened at the memories of chasing Maria through the halls of the De Sansol mansion.

"What were your parents' names?"

She wiped a tear from her eyes before focusing on him. "My father was Theodore, and my mother was Maddy." She smiled at the thought of them. "I was fortunate enough my mother left her ring behind when they left. It's the only thing I have to remember them. I don't even have a picture. Sometimes it's difficult to recall their faces anymore."

She frowned as she absently twisted the small band around her finger. He ran his thumb gently across her forearm.

"May I?" he asked, motioning towards the ring. She nodded softly and pulled it off her finger. It felt naked without the weight of the band as she placed it in his palm. "Did you have to have it resized or did your mother wear the same ring-" he stopped abruptly as he fingered the small 'M' monogram inside.

"M for Maddie," she said softly.

"Marsh," he said under a breath.

"What?" She furrowed her brow. They were in the middle of the ocean, there were no marshes here.

"Not M for Maddie, M for Marsh," he said as he turned to her, his eyes still wide with realization as he took in her features as if it were the first time he was seeing her. She shook her head slightly.

"I don't understand. What's the meaning of Marsh?"

He dragged his gaze to hers. "Do you remember that night we talked about a family that had died at sea? A noble family, whom the other nobles erased any existence of?"

"Yes ..."

"Only it wasn't the family. It was only the parents. *Your* parents. Teddy and Maddy Marsh died at sea, leaving a child behind that went missing."

"No. No, that couldn't be," she said. "My parents worked for the Marsh family. They did die at sea but ... no. I would remember if we were nobles." But it was so long ago. She could remember small moments: playing in the grass as they picnicked, her father squeezing her tight before releasing her from a hug. But nothing substantial.

"At six years old? I don't think you would. You said yourself, you remember a different house when you were young. They made sure you forgot your family name so you could never claim it. But this," he held up the small band and pointed to the insignia of vines around the M, "this is the Marsh family crest. And if your parents only worked for the nobles, what were they doing at sea without you?"

"I—I can't remember. But they couldn't have been ..." She looked up at him. "How do you know their names?"

"Lillian, your parents ... They died trying to stand up for a pirate. Their story has been told, pirate to pirate, for twenty years. Nobles standing up for one of us? It was unheard of. The pirate was killed shortly after—after your parents. But others who were there that night made sure their story spread."

She stared at the deck.

He squeezed her hand. "Lillian. You *are* a noble. You are Lady Lillian Marsh."

They sat in silence a moment. A tear slipped down her cheek.

A noble. There was no way she could be a noble. She had worked for the De Sansols her whole life, been inside every home in Atwood, and not a single person looked at her as anything other than a maid. Apart from Mrs. De Sansol. She hadn't been exactly kind, but she had allowed her to study with Maria when she showed an interest, and to visit the harbor fair every year, which was more liberty than other maids in Atwood had. She'd always assumed it was because Mrs. De Sansol held some small glimmer of pity for the girl who had been orphaned.

But perhaps it was guilt.

How could they have hidden this from her? Taken the only piece of her left by her parents? It angered her, but it didn't surprise her. Every noble in Atwood was cruel, and the De Sansols were no different.

She might be noble, but she would never become like them.

A noble ... She felt it in her bones now, the truth of it. She was Lady Lillian Marsh. She had a home and a place in the world. But did she want it? She supposed it could give her a direction if she chose to leave the *Stardust*. She could return to Atwood, claim that empty home at the end of the lane, demand her inheritance. And spend her life surrounded by those cruel families who'd sneered at her for her entire life. She shook her head at the thought. She would never feel like Atwood was home—not after this. After meeting all these warm people. Even Tamela had been kind, accepting Lillian for who she was.

"Tamela." She gasped softly, looking toward the stairwell that led to their quarters.

"What about her?" he asked.

"She knew. She continued to call me Lady Lillian even after I told her I was only a maid."

Kale chuckled. "Ah. Well, Tamela has a way of knowing things normal people don't. I try not to think too hard on it. Although, this bit of information would have been helpful to know when Johnny took off with the blood."

She gasped again and laid a hand on his shoulder. "My blood!"

Her eyes were wide as they met his.

He grinned. "I guess we won't have to worry about stealing anything back from Johnny now, will we? Now we just hope we get there before him. And pray we don't run into Stevenson."

She grimaced. "Avoiding any altercation with Johnny would be best. I can't stand to watch the two of you fight."

He lay back, once more folding his arms beneath his head.

"Are you really okay with all this? The two of you being on different sides?"

"Johnny's always been on Johnny's side. Sometimes that aligns with what I am doing. Most times it doesn't. But it's never come to being separated like this. Never come to physical attacks."

He stared at the night sky. She lay down next to him.

"Sometimes it's hard not to feel lonely out here," he said. "On the open sea, nothing but stars in the sky to remind you there's anything else out there besides water."

They lay on the deck staring up at the stars. She could feel Kale glance at her. Her hair was spread out beneath her as she stared dreamily at the stars. She looked to him, and he smiled softly as he rolled over to face her.

"You ready for tomorrow?" she asked.

"Are you?" he countered.

"As ready as I'll ever be."

"If we had another few weeks of training ..." He frowned. "If there's a fight tomorrow, Lillian, I want you to run the other way. You are quick, and you are clever, but you aren't ready to face anyone if you don't have to."

She nodded slowly, contemplating what might happen when they reached the island.

"Swear it," he said firmly.

She held his gaze, finding only worry in the cloudy gray of his eyes. "I swear."

He stroked the pad of his thumb across her cheek. She set her hand atop his, holding the warmth to her face, her eyes closed as she breathed him in.

"Kale." She sighed as she opened her eyes.

Chase and Landry exited the galley, practically tripping over themselves as they stepped onto the deck.

Kale removed his hand and turned on his back once more. "You should get some rest. It's going to be a long day tomorrow."

Chapter Thirty

Kale lay out on deck, still staring at the stars after Lillian had departed to her quarters. He should rest as well, but he couldn't bring himself to just yet. His mind was reeling, calculating all the things that could go wrong tomorrow, trying to prepare for them. Truth was, there were too many of them, and no possible way to prepare for every scenario. If it were just him and the crew, it would be different. Even Tamela could handle herself. But Lillian ... She was an unknown variable. Even though she was picking up her lessons on defending quickly, she only had a few days' worth. Worse than that, worrying about her distracted him. And he couldn't afford to be distracted.

But what worried him most was Stevenson. They hadn't seen or heard of him, though they knew he was in the area. With the blood moon being tomorrow, Kale had thought Stevenson would be going wild trying to track them down and steal the map. Had planned for it, even. Stevenson was like a caged animal when he was backed into a corner, and the timeline of the blood moon was a corner with the highest stakes they had yet known. And yet ... nothing. He prayed Stevenson hadn't happened upon Johnny, wherever he had chosen to row. Telayan, most likely, as it was the closest landmass. If Stevenson had found Johnny, even without knowing he had the map and blood, there was no telling what the sadistic bastard would do to him. Kale shook his head at the thought.

He took a deep breath, the hardness of the wood beneath him pushing into his spine as he did. His chest was heavy with worry, with not knowing. He felt ... What had Lillian called it? His darkness creeping in. He chuckled. It was a good name for it. And she had asked to be the light that expelled it. One thought of her smiling face, her light laugh, and he indeed felt that darkness fade away. She had asked to stay. Perhaps, if they survived this, he would let her. Perhaps it wouldn't be such a terrible thing for them to have a relationship together. She had the makings of a pirate, after all. Even if she was noble.

Whatever was to come tomorrow, they would work through it. All of them.

As soon as she'd finished dressing the next morning, Lillian knocked on Tamela's door, which opened immediately. Tamela was already sorting some herbs for them to review and create compresses.

"Good morning, Lady Lillian," she said over her shoulder.

"About that." She fixed Tamela's back with a pointed stare. "If you were going to insist on calling me Lady Lillian, you could have told me why."

"You came to know, did you not?"

"I suppose so."

"This was the way of things. Just because one knows something does not mean one should meddle. It upsets the balance." She laid out the different herbs, pestle and mortar, and rags. "Your hair is down today."

Since she would spend the morning with Tamela indoors, Lillian had decided to leave it down, only pulling a small portion into a tie to keep it from her face. Tamela dipped her chin in a slight nod of approval.

"All right, let's begin. Do we need to go over the feverfew tea again?" Tamela asked.

"No, I've got that. Boil the flowers of the feverfew plant and use it as a tea. It is used for pain relief and to speed healing."

"Good. Now we are going to make the poultice for pain relief of scrapes and open wounds." Tamela laid out ingredients and instructed her on the process as well as the applications of each. Lillian wrote in a little notebook as she completed each step. She had expressed the wish for some way to take notes as they practiced, and Tamela had conjured it on the spot. Lillian knew once Tamela was gone, and she was in actual need of these remedies, she would not be able to recall their trainings. She jotted down the steps they completed and made small sketches of each of the plants they had used. After nearly a quarter hour had passed, she set her notes down and went to the pot, dipping her finger in to test it. She looked toward Tamela, who nodded her approval.

Lillian spooned the herbal mixture onto one of the rags they had set aside. Once she was happy with the amount, she twisted it as Tamela had done the day before, though not as cleanly, and dipped it into the remaining liquid. Once she pulled it out, Tamela sat forward and put her hand out. Lillian set the dripping poultice in her open palm. She squeezed it a bit, then brought it to her nose and sniffed deeply.

"This is decent. You need to work on your wrapping skills, but the temperature and mixture is good." Tamela closed her hand around the rag. When she opened it again the compress was gone, as were the herbs and pot Lillian had used to make it. "The last two important things you won't be able to make here, but I will leave some with you and you can restock whenever you are in Telayan. Write this down, dear."

Lillian sat down, making notes as Tamela continued speaking.

"For light burns, lavender is best. The oil, diluted with a carrier such as coconut or grapeseed oil and applied directly to the burned skin, will soothe and heal. Best lightly wrapped after with a clean, dry cloth." She waved her hand and small purple bottle appeared on the table. It had a simple brown paper label with a sketch of a lavender flower.

"And last, for infection. If you suspect a wound is becoming infected, you can use camphor. Do you remember what to look for when suspecting infection?" She raised her brow at Lillian.

"Um, redness around the wound, pus, and smell."

"And swelling. If the wound is swollen, it could indicate infection as well. You can either wash the wound multiple times a day in camphor, or you can soak bandages for a quarter hour in the solution and wrap the wound, re-dressing it three times a day." Lillian continued writing as a small sand-colored tub appeared next to the lavender oil, next to which appeared three medicinal herbology books.

"These will cover the basics, as well as some of the more common ailments," Tamela continued. "You can keep them. And once you are finished reading them, you can borrow more."

"Thank you, Tamela." Lillian smiled, placing a friendly hand on Tamela's arm. "It is nice to learn something useful."

"You are useful, Lillian, just being yourself. And I cannot wait to see you learn that and grow into yourself. We shall be good friends." Tamela returned her smile, and her friendly touch. "You best begin your training for the day, if you want to learn anything before we arrive."

Lillian nodded as she stood, pocketing the lavender oil and camphor.

"Chase, set that one up on top," Kale shouted as he hefted his own crate, placing it next to the stack they had constructed on deck. He turned to grab another when he saw Lillian at the top of the stairwell. She had left her hair mostly down, and her chestnut curls picked up with the breeze the minute she stepped out on deck. She tucked it behind her ear as she scanned the deck. When her eyes landed on him, she smiled. He pushed his hair out of his face, replacing his hat as she approached.

"What's all this?" she said, awestruck by the stacks of large crates spread across the deck.

"We'll be passing briefly through civilian territory with high naval activity. We put these out to disguise ourselves as a cargo ship so that no one reports us to the navy as suspicious."

"And this works?" She eyed the crates.

"Every time so far."

"What is that?" She motioned to the land mass off in the distance to the east.

"That's Laramose, a small island known for its exotic fruit trade."

"If the hidden island is less than a day's travel from Laramose, how has no one stumbled across it yet?"

"It is spelled, by the same witch who sealed the cavern. Only those who know of its existence will be able to see it. Others just pass by, none the wiser."

"I suppose we won't be doing any training this afternoon, then." She eyed the crates once more.

"Don't you worry. There's plenty of space on the top deck. It will be a good lesson in close quarters training." Kale grinned and motioned for her to follow him.

"Kidd!" he shouted as they ascended toward the helm. Kidd left the crate he had been pushing across the deck and followed them.

"I think it's time you sparred with someone else," Kale told her. "Kidd is quick, perhaps more so than yourself. It should be a good pairing." He tossed a wooden sparring blade to each of them.

As soon as Kidd caught the hilt of the training knife, he whirled around to face Lillian and advanced. Caught off guard, she stepped back and tripped, landing on her bottom. Kidd leaned down and stabbed her with the wooden knife, right in her abdomen.

"Now, wait a moment! I wasn't ready." She huffed as she stood.

"You won't always be ready in a fight. Ya gotta be a quick thinker." Kidd laughed as he stepped back a few paces. As soon as she stood, he advanced again. Where Kale's steps and movements had always been strategic and calculated, Kidd's were quick and erratic. She could hardly think before he was on her. She sidestepped swiftly, and he pivoted just as fast, backing her into a corner near the helm. She raised her blade, but his was already touching her abdomen once again.

Kale chuckled from his spot across the small deck where he was leaning against the rails with his arms crossed. Excitement danced in his gray eyes.

She shot him a look, earning another amused chuckle, before she followed Kidd back to the middle of the small deck. This time she advanced as soon as they were back in position. He sidestepped as she had before, and she pivoted to follow. Kidd ducked as she reached her blade out and pivoted himself behind her, pushing his wooden blade under her ribs.

"Ya gotta think quicker." Kidd grinned. She huffed as they returned to the middle. With Kale, she was able to think through his possible moves and her reactions. Kidd was too fast for her to form a rational thought. By the time she'd considered what she might do, he was already in her space. She had to quit thinking and start reacting on instinct. Or what little she had. She closed her eyes and took a breath as Kidd advanced again. She sidestepped and ducked as he pivoted to attack, moving behind him. He whirled around before she could reach out and advanced. She jumped back as he swung his blade toward her abdomen, narrowly missing her.

Kidd stepped forward again, pressing her back into the rails behind her. Kidd smiled, seeing she was distracted again. He stabbed his blade toward her as he moved forward. She ducked to the side and deflected his arm with her empty hand, just as she had practiced with Kale. Kidd dropped his knife, catching it with his opposite hand, and reached over, stabbing her under her ribs once more. She groaned as he stepped back.

"That was much better Lillian." Kidd beamed, his face and upper body covered in sweat. He wiped his brow with his sleeve as Kale handed him some water.

"I still didn't even get near landing a hit on you." She breathed as Kale handed her some water as well.

"Sometimes, Lillian, the fight is not about killing the opponent but rather keeping yourself alive," Kale remarked. Kidd nodded his agreement as he put the tin cup to his lips. "You need to hone your instincts before you worry about getting a hit in."

"Again?" Kidd grinned. Despite her frustration, Lillian smiled as she nodded. They returned their cups to Kale and resumed their spots. Just as she went to advance, something caught Kidd's eye in the distance. His arms went slack as he stared. Kale followed his gaze and went slack as well.

"Could that be ..." Kidd said. Lillian turned as she followed their gaze across the sea.

"I'd bet my ship it is. Go and fetch Tamela. Quickly!" Kidd took off running as Kale shouted the last word behind him.

"Who is it?" Lillian asked, spotting the ship in the distance.

"Dall."

Chapter Thirty-One

Kidd had sounded the alarm as he ran across the ship. All at once, everyone was scurrying about.

"Won't he think we are a cargo ship? With all the containers? I thought that was their purpose." Lillian followed as Kale ran to the helm.

"For other navy men, yes. Dall, on the other hand, knows my ship like his own. He may be too far out now, and the cargo will throw him for a minute, but if we don't hide quick, he'll make us." Kale spun the helm sharply. The ship groaned in protest.

"Hide where? There's nothing about?" She looked to the unending ocean surrounding them. Even Laramose was too far off to be of any help.

"Aye. But we may not need cover, only concealment." Kale smiled—the smile he always gave when he had something mischievous up his sleeve.

Kidd ran up the stairs, huffing from his hurried trek, with Tamela in tow.

"It's Dall. Can you do something?"

She looked out to where Dall's ship was. "How long until we reach the isle?"

"Four hours, perhaps five." His eyes held her dark, shimmering ones, awaiting her response.

"That should be enough time." She continued over to Kale, who stood to the side, relinquishing the helm but keeping one hand on a spindle to keep it steady. Tamela placed both hands on the thick wood and began chanting.

As she spoke, the air around Lillian prickled her skin. Within a minute or so, the edges of the ship began to shimmer. It climbed the railing and up past it into the air, all the way until it reached the top of the mast.

Tamela finished and the wall of shimmer around the ship solidified and turned clear. Lillian approached the edge of the railing. Standing this close, she could see a slight shimmer, bare remnants of what had been there before. She put her hand up, pausing just before the invisible barrier, then pushed her hand through. It set off a small ripple, nothing very noticeable if you weren't staring straight at it. She pulled her hand back in and turned it about, examining it. Off in the distance she could still see Dall's ship.

"Looks to be keepin his course east," Kidd whispered. They all watched, still anticipating a turn in direction. None came.

"Aye," Kale said. "We should be out of sight in less than an hour. Will it hold that long?" He looked to Tamela. She nodded. "Good. You both best get some rest. It's going to be a long night." He smiled softly. Tamela headed down with Kidd, but Lillian remained, watching him a moment.

Standing at the helm with the wind in his dark hair, the one stray hair hanging over his eye, he was quite handsome. Not that she hadn't noticed before. In fact, it had been difficult not to notice. But this may be the last time she had a chance to tell him. She reached up and swept the hair to the side. He took her hand and placed a kiss in the palm, holding his lips there. He had dropped small, light kisses on her forehead before, but this felt ... different. Here in the middle of the top deck, in broad daylight.

"For luck." He grinned as he released her.

"Kale—"

"Not yet." His eyes held hers as they stood there. "After ... after everything and we are safe once more. It's bad luck to say any goodbyes before."

The stubborn streak that he brought out in her contemplated continuing the words she had been holding in. She decided against it. "Why is Dall after you?"

"You mean other than because I'm a pirate? That's a story for another time. Let's just say we have some unresolved differences." He reached over and stroked her cheek. She leaned into his touch. "You should get some rest. Even an hour or two can make a differ-ence." He looked back out to the horizon, his hands steady on the helm. She nodded once more and proceeded down the stairs, only stopping briefly at the bottom to look up at him once more. The wind rustled his blue-black hair beneath his hat as he surveyed the seas surrounding them.

After. She would tell him after.

That evening they sat around the table, as they did every night. But this evening was different. The group was more joyous and even louder, if that were possible. But underneath it all, there was a tension so thick it was nearly physical. Lillian sat next to Kale once again. Tamela, who had finally decided to take a meal with them, sat on his left. She was quiet through the meal but smiled every now and again at the crew's shenanigans. Once everyone was finished and winding down, Kale stood. Everyone quieted at the movement. Expectant. He leaned his palms against the table and hung his head.

"Within the hour, we will arrive at the Isle of Kinslet. What awaits us there is the largest bounty we have ever gone after, with the highest risk. We have lost two brothers on this adventure, one in battle, the other to his own ego. I don't plan to lose any more. Though the payout is high, let us not risk our lives to retrieve it. If any part of this goes sideways, I say we retreat. What say you?"

"Aye!" everyone shouted in unison.

"I'm glad to hear it." Kale smiled finally. "We have been planning this for a good while. Everyone knows what to do. Thankfully there hasn't been a sign of Stevenson. If he hasn't shown his sorry face yet, he won't catch us before we hit the island. And if we run into Johnny, just stay out of his way. We don't want a fight if there isn't a need for one. He's only after the sword, anyhow. So raise your glasses." Kale raised his tankard and others followed suit. "To our health, our impending fortune, and our good looks." Kale grinned. "From stardust!"

"To stardust!" everyone yelled. Kale chuckled as he raised his drink to his lips. Everyone cheered before draining their tankards and slamming them on the table. Lillian sipped from hers and smiled as everyone continued the celebratory mood.

Chase picked up his guitar and played a lively jig. Tony and Kidd moved to the floor. They hopped and jumped to the rhythm of the music, lifting their knees as high as they could go, linking arms and switching sides often. She watched for a bit as they continued, and more men joined in. After a while, Lillian stood and joined in. Clumsy at first, she soon got the rhythm as she stepped along, laughing, and was passed from one man's arm to the next. Eventually even Tamela and Kale joined.

Lillian and Tamela stood with Kale at the helm as they approached the island. Or rather, as Kale said they approached the island. As far as they could see there was no landmass ahead, only the speck that was Laramose off in the distance behind them. Ahead of them was nothing but a light sea mist. Even in the dark, they should have been able to see something. Lillian's old fear crept back—the fear that they would find nothing, and the crew would be devastated after all the time they had put into this. Just as Lillian turned to bring her fears up to Kale, the hull of the ship groaned as if it were pushing against something. In a blink, the mist receded around the ship, and they floated through an invisible wall.

Ahead of them was a small island. That may be a strong word to describe what they saw—it was no more than a few small mountains. From the base of the hills to the edge of the water was lush and green. The grass beneath the trees looked soft and welcoming, beckoning them to come and lie down and enjoy the water on their toes. Lillian could see why Captain Samuel had enjoyed this spot.

Kale scanned the area as they approached. No sign of Johnny yet. The moon was high above them now, with the faintest tinge of pink around the edges. Perhaps three-quarters of an hour until it was in position. Lillian listened to the ocean slapping the sides of the hull as they pulled into shallower waters.

"Drop the anchor." Kale held the helm straight as they came parallel with the shore. Rick and Rich hefted the anchor over the side, and a few minutes later the ship lurched to a stop. It was eerily quiet within the walls of the spell. No other ship sounds, no sounds of the gulls flying above, or animals on shore. Just the ocean as it pulled in and out. They were silent as they loaded into the rowboat. This was the quietest the crew had been since Lillian had come aboard. She didn't know they'd had it in them to stay silent for so long.

"This place ... It has not been touched in three hundred years," Tamela whispered to Lillian. She nodded as she took in the now apparent overgrowth.

"It's going to make it difficult to find the entryway. And it's near to half an hour before the blood moon is fully risen. Everyone needs to be vigilant." Kale was at the oars, drawing them in as they neared the shoreline.

"You don't know where the entry is?" Lillian raised a brow.

"That portion of the map lacked detail." He grimaced. "If I had it here in front of me, I could find the way. But going off my memory ... Hopefully we can find it in time."

"Lucky for us, this place is small." Rich stepped out and held out a hand for Tamela, then Lillian. Kale surveyed the land before them.

"This way." He hurried west, watching the topography around him as he went. They walked down the shore a good ways before Kale paused, looking into the trees. "Here. Jack, cut down these shrubs heading southeast."

"How far?" Jack grunted.

"Until we reach a clearing." Jack took his sword out and hacked, Kale following close behind him and everyone else falling in line. Lillian huffed as they trudged uphill through the thicket. They pushed through silently across the island. No one dared make a sound as the silence of the island consumed them. They must be nearly to the opposite side by now, if it was as thin as it was long. As they crested the hill, Jack and Kale came to a stop. They looked at each other and ducked down behind one of the larger bushes, motioning for everyone to follow. They dropped to the ground at once, just as Lillian heard what had stopped them. Voices drifted up from below. She shifted quietly and slowly up to peer through the thicket. Not fifty meters ahead was Stevenson and his crew.

With Johnny standing next to him.

Lillians breath caught silently in her throat. Could Johnny have betrayed them? He wouldn't have turned his back on Kale, consorted with his sworn enemy, for treasure. Would he? Of course, she never would have thought he would have hit Kale over the head, and he did that. Her gut wrenched at the realization of the possibility.

Stevenson held the map and the vials of blood as one of his crewmen hacked at the shrubs at the base of the largest hill. After a few moments, a stone circle appeared beneath the greenery. It was flat and had markings upon it that they could not make out from their vantage point.

"Damn," Kale whispered. "I figured Johnny would show, but I never would have guessed he would have led Stevenson. The bastard." He swore again. It was clear, as Johnny stood, arms crossed, conversing casually with Stevenson, that he was there of his own free will. Lillian's heart dropped. Johnny, who had been a brother to Kale. Johnny, who had been nice to her in his own way, protective even. But perhaps this had been the plan all along, to lead Stevenson to the *Stardust*. Perhaps that's why he had been so protective of her in the end, practically begging her to stay ashore in Aarilya. What she couldn't figure out was *why*. Why risk the lives of the crew, his relationships with them? Just for the power the sword offered? Somehow that didn't seem enough to her.

They watched silently as the rest of Stevenson's crew disembarked one after another, lighting torches and placing them around the beach.

"He must have not had much luck replacing the members lost in our last battle." Kale smirked. There were only a handful of men aside from Stevenson himself.

"If we could whoop 'em when they was thirty, we could whoop 'em at six." Jack chuckled.

"Aye. The element of surprise is our best weapon right now. You three"—Kale motioned to Rick, Rich, and Thomas—"follow Jack to the east. The rest of you, follow me to the west. We'll attack at once and take them out quickly. Remember, this is time sensitive." He turned to Tamela and Lillian. "And you ladies, wait up here until it's clear."

"I realize I may not be of much help, but what of Tamela?" Lillian whispered.

"Tamela needs to conserve her magic for the entry spell."

"I'll say she does," a man's voice said from behind them.

Chapter Thirty-Two

They spun around to see five men surrounding them, guns cocked and aimed.

"Get yer hands away from yer weapons," he growled, reaching forward, and grabbing Tamela by the hair, yanking her back to him, "or the witch dies." He held the barrel of his gun to her temple.

"You won't kill her." Kale stood, his hands raised. "I'd wager you need her as much as we do."

The man bared his teeth toward Kale. "Test me and find out. The rest of ye, up! Conner, clear the way." He motioned and as they got to their feet, one of the other men pushed past. He cut the remaining shrubbery away so they had a clear path forward.

To Stevenson.

"Well, look what ye have here." Stevenson smiled wickedly as they approached, motioning for Johnny to join him. "Cutting it a bit close tonight, Kale. Could that be due to a visit from your old friend Dall?"

Kale had thought it odd that Dall was around these waters, but he had never thought ...

"You damned rat!" he shouted, taking a step toward Johnny. One of Stevenson's men placed a hand harshly on Kale's shoulder in warning. Kale shrugged it off and stepped back, fire burned in his eyes.

"You musta pissed him off somethin' bad." Stevenson stepped behind Johnny, putting one congratulatory hand on his shoulder, and holding up the worn map in the other. "Much as I hate to admit it, I never would'a found this place without yer rat's help." He chuckled as he tucked it back into his chest pocket.

Stevenson's positioning. The predatory gleam in his soulless eyes ...

Kale shot a glance to Johnny, shaking his head almost imperceptibly.

"O'course ... ye can't trust a mutineer. And this one's served his purpose."

Johnny understood Kale's warning, and he started to turn, but Stevenson's hand clasped harder on his shoulder. Johnny's eyes flicked to Lillian's, and he mouthed a single word as Stevenson's blade punctured through his abdomen: *Run.*

Lillian screamed as his shirt turned dark, the blood spreading across faster than she thought possible. His eyes still held hers as blood spilled from the corners of his mouth. She took a step back, and another, then turned to slip past as everyone was distracted, heeding his warning. But she wasn't quick enough. She'd only made it a few feet when one of the men grabbed her and yanked her back. She side-stepped and attempted to duck but he grabbed hold of her hair and yanked her harshly against him. His chest pushed into her back as he held her tightly. To her left, Kale was yelling. He tried to wrestle free of his guard, his eyes still on Johnny, but a second man was on him, and between the two of them, they pushed him to his knees. She could see tears spilling down his cheeks and her own filled her eyes.

Stevenson pulled his blade out of Johnny's back and tossed him to the side, as if he was nothing but an old shoe. Hot tears streaked down Lillian's face as his body crumpled, wholly lifeless. Despite everything he had done, he had been a friend. More than a friend, he'd been family. She shut her eyes tight against the rush of tears now freely spilling. He had tried to warn her, she realized, about what he was going to do. About his deal with Stevenson. That was why he had been so adamant she leave the ship. She still couldn't understand why he had turned his back on the crew, on Kale.

She looked to Kale then. Pure anger and fury shone from his eyes, the sheen of tears now drying. He focused that fury wholly on Stevenson.

"Now, Kale. I've taken yer friend, I'll take yer treasure, and then I'll take yer ship and leave ya stranded on this island, hidden away." He smiled his wicked smile. "Bring the witch forward!"

The men dragged Tamela to the stone circle, shoving her toward Stevenson. The moon was now directly above them and was larger than Lillian had ever seen it. The edges glowed a deep red that set an eerie tone over the island.

"Now, witch." He spat the last word as he popped open the first vial of blood, pouring it over the center of the markings, and then the second. The blood spread slowly across the ancient letters. He chucked the vials to the side and glowered at Tamela. "Do yer voodoo."

Tamela looked to Kale, who nodded, eyes still on Stevenson. A growl came from the red-bearded pirate at the obvious communication, and he shoved her closer. She stepped forward to the stone and took a breath, steadying herself as she read the incantation now covered in blood. It was an ancient language, one Lillian couldn't even guess at, but Tamela spoke it with an ease of someone who had done so since birth.

Tamela's eyes turned crimson and began to glow, as did the blood on the stone, which moved through the chiseled lettering, pushed by the magic along the proper course.

With each verse her voice grew louder, stronger.

She repeated the incantation twice more, her voice a shout as she finished. The blood sank into the markings and was absorbed. Tamela's eyes still glowed. Lillian gasped when she spoke—it was not her own voice that came out, but many.

We offer to you the blood of thine enemy
To appease the scorned.
Your anger, your heartbreak—be no more.
For we have completed the task given.
We offer to you the blood of thine enemy
To appease the scorned.
Now open thy doors, and give what is earned.

Everyone stood silent as Tamela finished the spell. Her arms dropped to her side, but her eyes still glowed red, shifting back and forth as if the magic was pushing back after being dormant for so long. Finally, Tamela's eyes returned to their shimmering dark color before rolling back as she fell to her knees. Two men picked her up by the shoulders and dragged her back as the stone circle cracked down the middle and slid to either side, revealing a small opening only large enough for one person to enter at a time.

Stevenson grabbed Kale by the collar and shoved him forward. "You first. Don't need to be getting meself caught in any traps." He pushed him until he met with the small entrance, then motioned for two of his own men to follow before entering himself. Coward. One by one, everyone else followed them down.

The ground was uneven as Lillian stepped in, one of Stevenson's men to her back. She almost lost her footing as it immediately slanted down. The man behind her shoved her and she tripped over herself. She shot a glare over her shoulder, earning another shove. They continued down. The further from the entrance they got, the darker it became, and soon it was nearly black. Then there was a soft glow that lined the cavern. Tamela must have conjured the light; it seemed to come from nowhere, but also emanate from the rock wall to their right. They continued down the steep walkway, sharp rocks jutting from the walls on all sides. After what felt a lifetime, but was probably no more than a quarter hour, they reached the bottom. Lillian was near breathless as they finally set foot on flat ground.

The tunnel opened up into a large cavern. Stalactites hung from the ceiling, looking as if any disturbance might loosen them enough to come crashing down on everyone. A soft dripping sound filled the cavern as water leaked from a good many of them. In the center of the open space was a mound of rock, topped with an circular stone identical to the one they had opened above. That had to open another door. There was no sign of the sword anywhere, and only a few piles of coin lay here and there. It was certainly not a lifetime of treasure.

Stevenson approached the rock mound, running his hands over the small pile of coin near the base of it. He looked around the cavern in search of similar piles of treasure and found only dark, dank walls of rock and dirt.

He swore before turning to Kale. "The hell is this?" he growled.

"What were you expecting? Three hundred years ago this would have been considered a fortune." He smirked as his gaze shifted to the coins Stevenson had ran his hand over, then back to Stevenson himself. "Is this not enough to cover the damage we caused to your ship last time?"

"I'd be more likely to find a larger sum aboard your ship!" Stevenson grabbed Kale by the collar.

"Aye, some days. Not this day, though."

Stevenson tossed him back toward his guard and paced, still eyeing every corner of the cavern as he walked.

"And the damned sword?" he shouted, his eyes darting wildly.

"I'd be willing to bet, sir, that it lies beneath the second seal." Tamela nodded to the stone circle atop the rock mound.

"Blast!" He growled as he went to back to the stone. "Another damned spell? Ye better have it in ya, girl."

"I don't believe this one is spelled, sir. It just needs blood. But you wasted *both* vials on the first seal."

"Gods blast it all!" he raged as he paced. His eyes shot around the cave wildly, as if he'd gone mad. Perhaps he had. Perhaps the loss of his expected fortune had snapped the last small thread his sanity had hung from. He whipped his eyes to Kale so forcefully Lillian flinched.

"You." He stepped toward Kale, his finger pointed toward his chest. "Ye would'na come if ye didn't have blood." He scanned the crew until his eyes found Lillian. A wicked grin spread across his face. "There she be."

"No!" Kale yelled as Stevenson approached Lillian. "She's no one. We planned to take the blood back from Johnny once we got here." He spouted the words quickly, trying to drag his attention from her. But Stevenson didn't so much as pause his advance. She stepped back quickly. The sharp, damp rock wall pressed into her back as if it offered her some form of safety.

"I'm only a maid, sir. My noble mistress perished in a shipwreck." She pushed herself flat against the wall. He drew closer. *Run.* Johnny had warned her. Kale had told her to run of things got bad as well. But there was nowhere to run down here. No way past Stevenson. She'd had her chance on the land above, and her shock at Johnny's death had frozen her. Just as the fear of the wicked pirate approaching her now had. Her head was buzzing and couldn't think past it, couldn't form a plan like Kale would have.

"No. I don't think so." He grabbed her arm, yanking her forward. She looked to Kale, her eyes frantic. Blind panic filled her. She couldn't think. She pulled against Stevenson's grip, but his rough hands only tightened more painfully.

She could see the utter helplessness in Kale's eyes as the panic consumed her. He struggled against his guard, a burly man nearly twice his size, but it did little. Stevenson pushed Lillian right up to the seal, forcing her to her knees. Her cries filled the small cavern as they scraped on the rough ground, coin spilling around her. She would no doubt have scrapes and bruises for weeks. If they made it out of here.

Stevenson leaned down so that his mouth was level with her ear. "Pity." His hot breath assaulted her ear, his words laced with venom. "Ye're a sweet lookin' one. I'd hoped to take ye back with me. And when I was done wi' ya"—his eyes flicked to the rest of his crew—"I woulda thrown ya to the wolves." She flinched as he planted a hard kiss to the corner of her eye.

"I'm not afraid of you," she hissed. She may be more frightened than she'd ever been, even when she had been beneath the sea with no air, but she would not let him see it.

"Ye should be." He chuckled as he drew his blade from the sheath strapped to his thigh. Kale growled in frustration, pulling against his captor's grip.

She gasped at the cold of the blade as Stevenson laid it against her throat. The man holding Kale clamped down harder on him as he fought. Kale kicked out, trying to get a decent enough purchase with his boots to topple him over. He groaned as the man kneed him in the back, dropping him to his knees. Lillian squeezed her eyes shut. She cried out as she the stinging metal tore her skin.

"No, wait. Wait!" She cried. "There could be another seal!"

"Pardon?" he drawled. The knife at her neck loosened the slightest bit. A sob escaped her.

"There could be a third seal, with more treasure. Don't waste the blood like you did on the first one," Lillian breathed. The cavern fell silent as Stevenson contemplated this.

Finally, he bobbed his head. "Aye. Better to be safe."

Lillian bit back another cry as Stevenson yanked her up by her hair. Tears coated her cheeks as Stevenson thrust her hand out over the seal. In one quick motion, he sliced her palm. She couldn't stop the gasp at the burning pain. He folded her fingers in and squeezed her hand so that the blood dripped down onto the markings below. He squeezed again, forcing more blood out, and another sob escaped her.

Dim, red light filled the center of the cavern as the markings glowed, just as the first had, and the blood began to move. It glowed brighter in the dark cavern and finally sank down into the etchings before disappearing. There was a loud crack as the seal split open, and it ran down the center of the mound. Stevenson looked up at the walls, his eyes alight and a smile spreading across his face.

"Ah ... There it is." He stepped toward the empty wall. Each of his men were mesmerized as well, moving slowly closer to the empty cavern wall. Tamela, Lillian realized as she took in the woman who stared at the empty wall as well. She was making them see something that wasn't there. Kale realized at the same time. He grabbed the knife from his guard's pocket and got to his feet, slitting the man's throat before he had a chance to make a sound.

Before the fear could return, Lillian followed his lead She pushed through the low thrumming in her head. Everything had been brought into stunning clarity once the knife had touched her throat. She couldn't afford to fear any longer. It would get her killed. It could get the crew killed. She couldn't allow that to happen, not because of her cowardice. She slammed her foot down on Stevenson's boot.

He yelped as he released her, but recovered and swung the blade out. Like second nature, her training these past few weeks kicked in, and she ducked and sidestepped just in time for Stevenson to stumble past. A spin on her feet brought her to face his back. She kicked out, pushing him right toward Kale.

Kale grabbed the pirate by his coat and kicked in the back of his knees, forcing him painfully down. He held the knife to his throat. Stevenson's men didn't dare move. The *Stardust*'s crew moved to circle behind Kale. He nodded to Tamela, who dropped the illusion.

Stevenson gasped. "My gold," he nearly sobbed.

"That," Kale growled, "was for my crew. And this? This is for Johnny." His voice cracked on his name. Lillian looked away as Kale plunged the knife through Stevenson's ear. Blood poured from the wound as Kale retracted the blade. Stevenson's eyes rolled back, and he slumped forward. Kale looked to Stevenson's men. "This is your only chance to leave here alive," he growled. Each of the men eyed Kale and the crew before the one that had held Kale nodded to the others, his eye on Tamela. They retreated toward the tunnel. One of them, a small young man with bright red hair sprouting from under his cap, stopped in front of Kale.

"Thank you," he said, before taking off up the tunnel as well.

Everyone cheered as the last of Stevenson's crew exited the chamber, patting Kale on the back. He looked to where Lillian still stood near the stone. His heart dropped at the trail of blood that had dripped down her neck from Stevenson's knife. He pushed past Rick and Rich to stand in front of her. With a shaky breath, he took her face in his palms, using his thumbs to gently wipe the tears from her cheeks. She had been so brave. He couldn't have been prouder of her than he was then.

"I'm sorry," he said. A tear slipped down his own cheek. "I am so very sorry."

Her lips quivered but she smiled softly. "We're okay." She set her hand on top of his, and he leaned his forehead against hers. "I'm okay."

He leaned down and took her lips in his own, each tasting the salt from the other's tears. There was no reservations this time, no guilt. He took her mouth freely and she responded in kind. It was passionate and frenzied, full of the life they had almost lost. He parted her lips with his tongue and delved deep inside. She gasped lightly in surprise but welcomed the warmth of him. He dumped all his worry and fear, relief, and happiness into kissing her, and she accepted it and gave the same. Finally, he pulled away, setting his forehead against hers once more, both breathing heavily, lips swollen.

"It's about damn time," Eddie said, crossing his arms. Laughter filled the cavern.

Kale pulled back to look into her eyes. "I told you they wouldn't stop me from kissing you. Now, let's get this sword out."

Chapter Thirty-Three

Jack and Eddie stood on either side of the rock mound, pulling broken pieces away and hefting them to the side. The rest of the crew stuffed the coin into cloth bags. Tamela grabbed a handful, studying it carefully as her dark, slender fingers hefted the weight, and tucked them into a hidden pocket before strolling over to where Kale and Lillian stood to the side. He held her hand tightly, refusing to leave her side since they had kissed.

"If you don't mind, Kale dear," Tamela said, "I'm going to find my own way home. I've had enough of … all this." She waved her hand dismissively.

"Do you have enough magic to get yourself back?"

"Plenty." She smiled softly as she approached Lillian. "And you'll make sure to bring this one to visit me again before too long, won't you?" Kale chuckled, and Lillian smiled as she took Tamela's hands in her own.

"I won't give him a choice."

Tamela patted Lillian's hands before dropping them. A bit of sadness settled in her eyes before she swept both hands in a wide circle and was gone.

"I thought you had no interest in the sword," Lillian remarked.

"I don't. Not in the sword itself. That was always … " He trailed off before he cleared his throat. "Always Johnny's goal." His voice broke as he spoke, and tears prickled behind her eyelids at the memory.

Johnny. She closed her eyes shut against the memory of the dark crimson color coating his abdomen. Then warm fingers were on her chin, pulling it up. She opened her eyes to see Kale's.

"We can't leave him here," she whispered. Kale only nodded before he turned back toward the crew as they hefted the rubble around.

"I'm not interested in the sword itself, but it can bring in a high price. Make up for the lack of coin here," he continued.

"You don't mind someone else becoming the pirate king?" She wiped her cheeks dry.

"It's only a title, and not one I ever wanted."

"Kale," Jack grunted. He started toward the men and pulled Lillian along with him. As they lifted the last piece of rock, the *Kingsword* came into view. It was long, nearly half her length, and the hilt was wrapped well with some kind of hide. Right where the base met the hilt was a marking with the initials *S.G.* etched in. Just above that was a round hole that looked like it may have once held a stone of some sort. Even in the dark of the cavern, the metal had a blue hue to it that nearly glowed.

"How do we know it's Captain Samuel's?" Lillian watched as Jack lifted the sword.

"Right here, girlie." He motioned to where the markings were. Upon closer examination she realized it was a crest. A sun on the horizon set behind a skull with two swords positioned as an *X* behind it. "When Samuel took to the life of a pirate, he created his own crest. 'Tis well known." He handed the sword to Thomas, who wrapped it in a piece of old cloth.

Kale ran his hands through his dark hair. "Let's get out of here."

They all boarded the boat, weary and tired. Removing the seal had removed the spell on the island, and with the mist gone, they could see the sun starting to peek above the horizon. Kale had mentioned they would take Johnny's body with them and give him a proper burial at sea, as he would have wanted. But when they had emerged from the cavern, it was nowhere to be found. Kale cursed Stevenson's crew for taking it and denying him that last bit of closure.

Lillian stretched lazily as she stepped onto the deck. She hadn't been able to rest earlier as Kale had suggested, and she was feeling it now. She started toward the stairwell leading to her cabin, but Kale pulled her back, right into his arms.

"Let's get those cuts wrapped up before you sleep." She nodded, and he pulled her to his cabin. It was quiet inside as Kale rummaged through his cabinet for bandages. "You can make one of Tamela's compresses later. This should do for now. Here, sit." He motioned to a chair, then sat in the other. "Let me see your hand." He held out his own. She winced as he spread her palm open. The gash was long and deep and had turned an angry red, still caked with dark blood.

"I should clean it first." She winced again as she tried to flex it.

"This should do the trick." He leaned over and kissed her. Softer this time, slowly. She closed her eyes as their lips met, then their tongues. Tentative at first, then deeper, and a little quicker. She could feel the rush of heat spread across her cheeks and then down her body. She jerked back and hissed as her hand stung. He smiled, holding the bottle of alcohol he had just poured across her wound.

"That burns!"

"That's what makes it a good antiseptic."

"A little warning would have been nice," she huffed as he wrapped the bandage around her palm.

"That's what the kiss was for. Now, show me your throat."

"You're not going to pour alcohol on that as well, are you?" She put a hand to the cut on her throat.

"No. You are." She looked up at him sharply. He took another piece of bandage and soaked it in the alcohol.

"Me?"

"Yes, you." He held out the rag for her to take. She stared at him , then sighed and took the cloth, hissing as she touched it gently to her cut. He reached up and pushed her hand a little firmer, causing her to hiss again.

"I am sorry." His face was sorrowful as he eyed her throat. "I should have found a way to stop him."

"You did."

"Not soon enough." His eyes were fiery as he looked up at her.

"I am fine. It's only a cut." She pulled the rag away, ignoring the splotches of red now coating it. He held her gaze a moment, then looked away.

"We will be returning to Aarilya to auction the sword. Some of that gold is yours, you know. Once we sell the sword, there will be enough for you to start a new life ashore ... if you want to." He ran his hands through his hair, his stray strand falling loose once more.

"Kale, I—"

"Think on it. Until after the auction. It is not a decision to take lightly." He stretched.

"I should let you rest." She gathered the rags from the table.

"I was thinking that perhaps you would like to rest in here tonight."

Her hand froze.

"Lillian ... I—I almost lost you. Before that moment, I hadn't quite grasped how much you mean to me. Stevenson had you, and I was powerless to do anything to stop it. The image of his knife to your throat, and the look ..." He closed his eyes against the memory. "The look of fear on your face when you turned to me. I will never forget my helplessness as I knelt on the ground beneath that guard. I could do nothing." He looked to her again and a tear slid down his cheek as he choked on his words. "All my training, all my experience at sea, and I could do nothing." He cupped her face, and her own tears began to fall once more, the sincerity in his voice as he finally opened up to her bringing them on.

"I almost lost you," he repeated. His eyes burned as he held her face in his palms. She could see the hurt there, the fear.

He was letting her in.

He closed his eyes, setting his forehead on hers, and she let her tears continue down her cheeks silently. Let the adrenaline and fear release with each tear. They stayed like that a moment before he pulled away, looking into her eyes as he leaned in and kissed her softly. He pulled back, a question in his eyes she barely registered before she stood on her toes and took his mouth with her own. The fluttering in her chest traveled straight down to her core as he met her emotion with his own, their lips and tongues probing and exploring and becoming more frenzied with each pass. Her hands were on his chest, if only to steady herself. His dropped to her waist, clutching her to him as if, were he to let go, she would fade away. He tilted his head, and she moaned softly as the angle allowed his tongue to explore deeper into her mouth. His answering groan had that flutter turning molten, building and swirling. He started backward, taking her with him—toward the bed.

His hands brushed her hips, and then her shirt was pulled from her trousers. He drew back from the kiss only long enough to lift the fabric overhead. Then his lips were on hers once more, warm and tender. The chill in the air nipped at her naked back, but his warm hands splayed across it. She slipped her own hands down his broad chest and tugged his belt loose. A groan escaped him. He stayed her hands, drawing back from their kiss, meeting her eyes with his.

His voice thick, he asked, "Are you sure?"

A grin crept across her lips as she tugged his shirt free.

"Yes," she whispered, and his mouth was on hers again, more intensely than before as his hands slid between them and helped her pull the rest of his shirt and vest free until his chest was bare beneath her fingers. She moaned and spread her fingertips along the hard muscles, then gasped as his lips left hers. He stared at her, all of her, a grin on his lips, and a blush crept across her cheeks. She felt embarrassed standing before him, naked from the waist up, her nipples pebbling from the chill in the air. She had never been naked in front of another person. Not like this.

"What is it?" she asked softly, trying to fight the instinct to cover herself.

Kale's eyes met hers, and his smile turned soft. "You are absolutely beautiful." He pulled at the band of her trousers until she stepped closer. Her blush deepened at the compliment, but her smile grew.

He divested her of the remainder of her clothing. She squealed as he scooped her up and deposited her on the bed, then stepped back. He kept his gaze on hers as he removed his pants, revealing his length. Her breath caught at the sight of him standing before her, utterly naked and all hard, tanned muscle.

"Come to me," she whispered.

His grin turned devilish and his eyes darkened. "No."

"No?" she raised a brow.

His hands shot out so quickly she hadn't seen them move. She hardly managed a gasp before he wrapped them around her ankles and dragged her to the edge of the bed. A graze of his knee sent shivers up her thigh as he placed it on the edge of the mattress next to hers. He leaned down so that his face was over hers.

"I'm the captain here. And right now, you're mine," he said before he took her mouth once more. Her body shivered at his words, and she instinctually lifted her hips toward him. She wanted to be closer to him, needed more of him near her. His hands were on her hips then, gripping them.

Then they were on her. She moaned deeply as his fingers brushed her gently. She angled her body to him, but he kept his fingers where they were, gently running the length of her most private area before finally parting her. He broke their kiss to watch her as he slipped one finger in. She gasped and let her head fall back, her eyes closed as she reveled in the intrusion. His answering groan reverberated through her as he drew his finger back only to push it in once more.

"Damn," he groaned as he slid another finger in. She was slick and welcoming. He continued his motions until she couldn't take it any longer. She needed more. She needed him. She needed to feel his skin pressing hers, his body close to hers. He'd almost lost her today, but she'd almost lost him too. They both needed a reminder that they were alive, and together.

"Kale," she moaned. His only response was a low, deep chuckle that had her quivering once more. But he removed his fingers and, finally, moved atop her. She gasped and her eyes flew open as she felt him push against her.

"Relax, love," he whispered before he pulled back and, adjusting his hips, pushed into her. He continued his slow rhythm, pushing a bit deeper with each thrust, until her hips rose to meet his. Their breaths grew short and quick until he leaned down and kissed her deeply. She opened her mouth to him and welcomed his tongue. Once she was fully focused on his all-consuming kiss, he pushed into her fully. She froze at the deep intrusion.

"Relax," he repeated. After a few breaths, she let her muscles loosen, and he moved within her again. He resumed their kiss, and the now familiar tingle from his touch turned into a blaze. He deepened the kiss as he quickened his movements, and she couldn't hold back any longer. Her moans grew louder with each thrust into her. Her arms wrapped around his shoulders and pulled him as close to her as she could, needing to feel every inch of him against her. He laid his forehead against hers as his quick breaths intertwined with her own. One last shiver ran through her body before she exploded, screaming his name as his thrusts grew erratic, and he groaned and stilled, then collapsed on his back next to her. Still panting, he drew her to him.

They lay there silently awhile. The only sound filling the cabin was their labored breaths. Finally, he placed a kiss atop her head.

"Stay with me tonight?" he asked, his voice low.

"I don't think I could move if I wanted to." She buried herself deeper into his chest. "You're stuck with me."

"Mmm," he murmured. "This won't happen again until you make your decision. Besides, I might still decide to leave you in Aarilya. Maybe you're more trouble than you're worth," he teased. "Now get some rest." A small, satisfied grin spread across her lips as she closed her eyes and sank into his arms.

The following afternoon they docked in Aarilya. Lillian stood on deck watching the bustle of the harbor. Kale and Jack had gone ashore to spread word of the auction. Kale had said it would take place in three weeks' time, on the little island where they'd stopped to celebrate Kidd's birthday.

It had only been a few weeks since she had left this same port with Maria and the De Sansols, a few days since they had left toward the Isle of Kinslet. She had been living a dream, and now she was finally awake. She still missed Maria dearly, even shed a tear or two for Mr. and Mrs. De Sansol every few nights. But she was a new person. Her own person. She had no obligation to serve others and could freely choose what she wanted to do without first considering if it would be best for someone else. Kale had given her that choice.

Lillian had thought a lot on Kale's offer over the last few days. If she had enough coin to start a new life, would she want to stay aboard the ship? It seemed the best option because she had nowhere else to go. But if it wasn't her only option, would she choose to stay? It had turned out to be a tougher decision than she thought. But the thought of leaving Kale, of leaving the crew, just when they were getting started? It broke her heart. No, she had made her decision. This was home now, the men were her family, and she would not abandon ship.

She waved as Kale and Jack walked back toward the ship. Kale smiled, returning her wave. The *Kingsword* hung from his belt, the hilt glistening in the morning sun. He had taken it with him as proof they had possession of it and to rally interest in the auction.

"Well, hello, Lady Lillian."

"I prefer Pirate Lillian, actually," she said. He grinned down at her and placed a palm on her cheek, stroking it gently with his thumb.

"I'll leave ya to it, then." Jack continued walking, a small smirk playing on his lips.

To her surprise, Kale leaned down and kissed her slowly, his lips soft against hers. His tongue probed her lips, then her mouth. He angled his mouth and probed deeper as his hand slipped behind her neck. Heat rose to her cheeks and spread down to her chest. She angled her body against his as her tongue rose to meet his. She almost gasped as he pulled away, grinning. His hand was still on the back of her neck, her chestnut curls tangled around his fingers, as he looked at her. Her cheeks were flushed and her breathing quick. She was surprised he had kissed her so openly. They had been intimate the day before, but they had just escaped near death. Her eyes flitted back and forth between his, questioning. His grin widened as he released her neck and stepped back, his eyes a bit hazy.

"I thought..." She cleared her throat. "I thought you weren't going to touch me."

"I didn't touch you, I kissed you. After nearly losing you yesterday, I feel like doing whatever the hell I want. And if there's even a slight chance I might leave you in Aarilya, I'm going to kiss you any chance I get." His gray eyes turned dark as pure fire filled them. "I'll see you at supper." He winked before walking away, the Kingsword swaying at his side.

In that moment she was glad she hadn't chosen to tell him she was staying.

Chapter Thirty-Four

Lillian and the crew were busy on deck, preparing to leave with the afternoon tide. They were to travel to each major port so Kale could get the word out about the auction. Lillian had just finished scrubbing the deck when Kidd approached her.

"Hey, Lillian." He stood over her as she sat back, wiping her brow.

"Hello, Kidd." She smiled.

"I have to go ashore and grab some last-minute supplies before we take off this afternoon. Ya wanna come along?" He grinned.

"Sure. That sounds lovely." She smiled, picking up her bucket.

"Ya wanna change?" He asked cautiously. She stopped. She hadn't thought of her yellow dress since she had altered her current outfit. It just wasn't practical aboard the *Stardust*. But to go ashore in Aarilya? She supposed she could put it on. Truth be told, a woman in a pirate's outfit would stand out like a sore thumb here.

"If you don't mind waiting." She faced Kidd now, her brows raised in question.

"Nope. I'll be right here." He leaned against the rail.

She hurried down to her cabin and dug through the pile of clothing she still had to mend to find the dress. She pulled it out from the bottom and held it up. A bit mussed, and the pale yellow flowers had paled even more from being in the ocean and not properly cleaned, but it would do better than the white top and trousers she wore. She stripped down and pulled on her under-things, then her dress, lacing it up as best she could. She ran her fingers down the soft fabric. Although she felt quite feminine, after wearing men's clothing the last few weeks, the laces were constricting.

She released her braid and ran her fingers through her soft waves. She didn't have time to properly style it, but she pulled it up into a soft bun and secured it with the tie. She looked at herself in the reflection of the porthole. The dress looked pale on her now that her skin had darkened with a nice tan, and her freckles were numerous, but she looked almost like a lady. And nothing like herself. Not the version of herself she had become, the wild and free one she had come to love.

Pirate Lillian.

As she stepped up on deck, Landry and Kale were talking and laughing with Kidd. All three of them stopped as she neared.

"Well, look what the cat dragged up." Landry whistled.

"Lookin' mighty nice, Lillian." Kidd smiled.

Kale kept an eye on her as she crossed the deck, his grin near predatory. "I thought you preferred Pirate Lillian."

"Well, I don't think Pirate Lillian would get the best reception at the local shops," she teased.

"Here, let me help." He motioned for her to turn around. Kidd and Landry busied themselves facing the opposite way as she complied, and Kale unlaced her dress, then slowly laced it back up, his fingers sending shivers up her back every time they brushed her bare skin. When he finally reached the top he stroked his thumb across from shoulder to shoulder. She shivered at the touch, eliciting a deep chuckle from him that brought back that fire in her core.

"Be safe in town. Aarilya is one of the safer ports, but there are still thugs and the navy to watch for. If anyone recognizes you, you really will be more trouble than you're worth."

"We will." Kidd grinned as he turned to face them once more. "You ready, Lillian?" She nodded, her eyes still on Kale's.

"I'll see you later." He leaned down and kissed her gently on the forehead. She smiled and turned to follow Kidd.

They had visited a few shops along the harbor and picked up the supplies they needed, as well as a few herbs Lillian had read about in one of Tamela's books, which would come in handy for stomach illnesses.

"Oh look!" Kidd grinned as he took up a morning paper from a young boy, handing him a coin. He opened it to reveal the main article on the front page. "They're gonna have a fair here in five days' time! Wonder if Kale'd let us come back for it."

"The harbor rair. They have it every year. It really is a lovely celebration. I've been twice." He handed her the paper. She skimmed the article.

Her heart dropped as she reached the the black and white picture at the end.

"Lillian? What's got ya spooked?" Kidd furrowed his brow as he watched her.

Maria.

The small caption read *Maria De Sansol—Survivor of the shipwrecked* Rossut. She looked up at Kidd, her eyes still wide. He watched her carefully, waiting for an explanation.

"I'm sorry ..." She shook her head, tears forming. "I—I have to go." She turned and hurried down the street, past the shops and up toward town. Kidd called after her, but she couldn't stop. *Survivor.* The word kept repeating in her head over and over again. Maria was alive. *Survivor.* She ran in a daze, quick as she could in the constricting dress.

Kale would understand. They all would. She had to see that Maria was alive for herself, and let Maria know that she was alive. She would make it back before high noon, then she could travel the seas with them with a clear conscience.

Survivor.

Kidd trudged up the gangway and straight to Kale, who still stood on deck, talking with Landry and Jack. His smile fell as he saw the look on Kidd's face.

"Where is she?" he asked flatly.

Kidd kept his head down, not meeting Kale's eyes. "She left."

"She just left?" He scanned the harbor, praying for some sign of her.

"She saw this, and she just ... left." Kidd handed Kale the second copy of the small paper he had purchased after Lillian had run off. "She said sorry." He shrugged sadly.

Kale scanned it.

Of course. There's no way she would stay with them knowing Maria lived. His heart shattered at the realization, the pieces falling somewhere deep within him, leaving his chest hollow. Dark. And empty. He crumpled the paper and tossed it to the ground.

"Fifteen minutes." He turned to walk away.

"Fifteen—Kale, we aren't meant to leave until midday!" Landry followed.

"What if Lillian comes back?" Kidd protested.

"She won't. She's back where she belongs now." Kale stalked off, feeling the darkness consume him as the *Kingsword* swung at his side.

Lillian thanked the man who had so kindly allowed her to hitch a ride on his carriage. They dropped her in front of the tall iron gates to Atwood. The place that she had once called home now felt foreign. She slipped inside and walked down the well-known path, the one lined on either side with mansions. The one that would lead to the empty house at the end that she now knew had belonged to her family. She paused as she considered continuing on to take a look at it, to see if any memories sparked now that she new the truth. But she shook her head. Time was limited, and she wanted to spend as much of it with Maria as possible. She turned up the small walk toward the De Sansol home.

Outside the wooden door, she hesitated. It was awkward, being there. Should she knock or just walk in? After listening as people scurried about on the other side, she decided to knock. The door opened immediately, revealing Curt, the steward.

"Lillian," he whispered. "Dear heavens, girl, come in. Come in." He stepped aside, allowing her to enter the grand hall.

"I saw, in the papers ... Maria. Is she here?" She looked toward the stairs.

"In her bedroom. Oh, she will be so pleased to see you." He led her up the stairs. Her heart pounded as they neared Maria's room.

Once they reached the door, Curt knocked once and waited. "It's Curt, Lady Maria. I have someone here who wishes to see you."

"Curt, you know I am not taking visitors just now. I am in mourning." She huffed, sounding so much like Maria, and oddly a bit like Mrs. De Sansol, that Lillian's tears threatened to spill.

"I understand, m'lady, but I really do suggest you take this visitor."

Maria groaned from within. Then there was a rustle of skirts and a chair scraping. Within a moment the door opened. Maria stood before her, the same tall pale red-haired young lady Lillian had missed so these past few weeks. Except a few new scrapes on her arm and collarbone. And she was a touch paler. Or perhaps that was just the pallor of her skin against the dark color of her mourning dress. They took each other in from head to toe. Lillian stepped forward, smiling, but Maria stepped back, meeting Lillian's gaze with a frown.

"Maria," Lillian started.

"Curt, you may remove this woman from my home." Maria turned away. Lillian blinked, as taken aback as if Maria had slapped her.

"Lady Maria, you cannot be serious." Curt stared in disbelief.

Lillian set her hand on his shoulder. "Maria." She followed her into her room.

"You are not welcome here," Maria snapped over her shoulder.

"Aren't you the least bit happy to see me? To know that I am alive?"

"No!" Maria whirled to face her. "You should have perished with ... with everyone else for what you did."

The anger in Maria's eyes was so hot Lillian took a step back. "What on earth did I do that you wish my death?"

"What did you do? Well, I suppose it is more what you did not do. Everyone wanted to stay below deck, but you forced us out. You did *not* stay with me during the storm." Maria advanced, forcing Lillian to retreat a step. "You did *not* make sure I was okay in the water." Another step. "And you did *not* come find me once you were safe." Maria huffed before whipping back around to plop on the nearest chair and fan herself.

Images from the nightmare that had plagued her in those first few days scrambled to the forefront of Lillian's mind.

You abandoned us.

No. Lillian shook her head at the thoughts. She knew better now. She had not abandoned them, she had tried to save them. It just hadn't been enough. Or perhaps it had, as Maria now stood before her, alive.

"Maria, I thought you were dead. I just learned you survived this morning."

"I have no doubt you did believe me dead. As I said, if you had stayed with me during the storm, you would have known I lived, and we could have survived together. But you did not." She stared out the veranda window as she spoke, still avoiding eye contact with Lillian.

In her mourning these past few weeks, Lillian had forgotten how incredibly selfish Maria could be. When she was nothing but a maid, she would have groveled and possibly pumped Maria's ego in a situation like this, just to avoid a meltdown and being stuck in Maria's room while she pouted for the day. But Lillian wasn't just a maid anymore. She was her own person.

She was Lillian Marsh.

She was Lillian the Pirate.

She walked toward the door before turning around one last time as she said, "Well, if that is how you want to view our situation, then I will leave you to it. I will stop by next time I am in Aarilya, and maybe then we can have a proper conversation." She waited just long enough to see Maria twist around violently in her chair, agape, before walking out. Lillian smiled to herself as she descended the stairs and walked out the door.

Lillian asked Rupert, one of the carriage drivers, for a lift back to the harbor. He was happy to oblige, as he was one of the few staff still employed that had been there before they had left. As they neared port, her stomach tightened. The closer they got, the more she realized her decision had been the right one. She looked forward to traveling the seas with Kale and the crew. She couldn't wait to feel the wind in her hair once more as she stood at the helm, looking out at the endless horizon. And for all the things she had yet to see. She smiled to herself as they approached the busy harbor. It was just as busy today as it had been that first day, but it felt so different. It felt like home.

It was still an hour until high noon as they came to a stop at the entrance to the port. Lillian thanked Rupert and wished him luck working for Maria, who seemed hellbent on filling her parents' tyrannical shoes. She headed into the crowd, weaving her way past all the market sellers and the people pushing, pulling, or carrying crates to their ships, until she was nearly to the docks.

As she came to the end of the busy crowd, she stopped short. Where the ship should have been was an empty dock. Lillian gasped softly, looking around frantically. Was she in the wrong spot? Had they redocked? There were only three other ships docked at that moment and none of them were hers. She looked out to the ocean. Maybe they had come under attack and had to leave. But there were no signs that there had been a fight, no sign of the ship out on the ocean, or the navy in the port. Which meant, if they were no longer in sight, they had to have left quite some time ago.

The waves lapped against the empty dock.

They were gone.

They had left her. *He* had left her. Her eyes filled with tears as she stood there, her heart breaking and the breeze whipping her hair about, sticking it to her now-wet cheeks. She was alone.

More trouble than you're worth.

Don't forget to leave a review!

Reviews help indie author's books get seen. Amazon and
Goodreads are the top sites seen by readers.
If you share something about From Stardust on your socials, feel
free to tag me! (unless you didn't enjoy the book. By all means post
your opinion but please don't tag me, it would only hurt my little
author heart)

Find more at meagankaye.com and join my newsletter to stay up
to date on book info and a FREE SHORT STORY featuring one
of the Stardust crew!

About the Author

Meagan lives in Arizona with her husband, kids, and a myriad of pets. When she isn't reading, writing or playing with her little ones she can usually be found curled up with a hot cup of tea and watching Grey's Anatomy.

Meagan enjoys writing because it is part of her soul, she has had a story in her mind since her earliest memories of her childhood, even before she found the outlet of putting pen to paper.